Crown of Emeralds

LOST FAE QUEEN TRILOGY

E. R. JENSEN

TRIGGER WARNINGS

Miscarriage
Imprisonment
Torture
Graphic fight scenes
Prejudice

OTHER BOOKS

The Lost Fae Queen Trilogy
Throne of Dusk
Heir of Blood
Crown of Emeralds

Twisted Talent Series
Hoodwinked in Hotlanta
Spellbound in Spud City

JADE WILD
COURT
LOCHAN SGÀILE
WHISP
EMBERGATE
WEST IRON
EMBER MOUNTAIN
COURT OF DUSK
COUR
GLASS OASIS

MOON
KET
EAST
SILVER
E SUN
EMERALD
MINES
EMERALD VALLEY
COURT OF DAWN
N
W
E
S

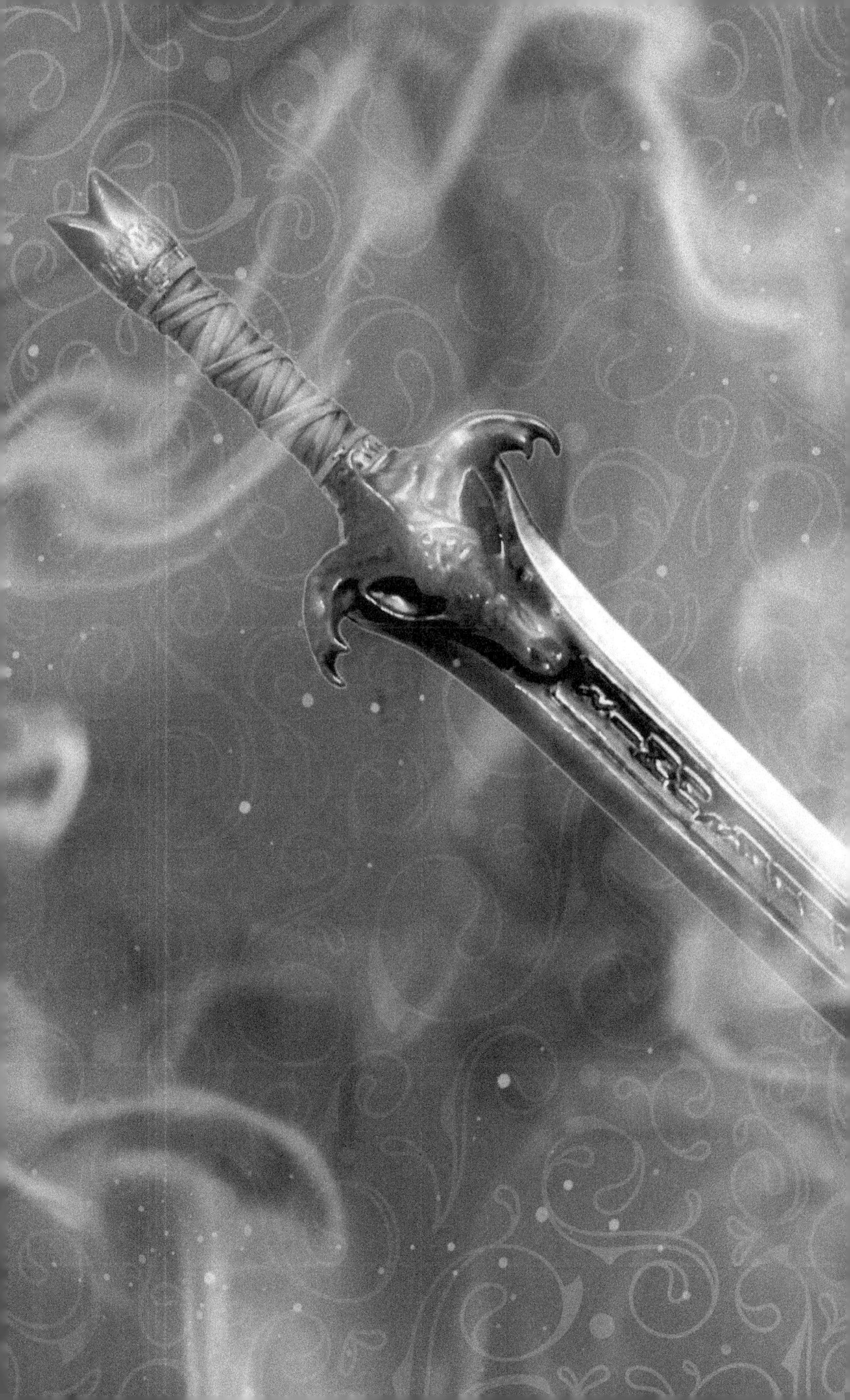

When tension rises and war with the humans has come, the Lost
Fae Queen will return.
First, she will prove her battle prowess.
Look closely or you might be blinded, for when the Fae Queen
returns,
Not all will know her, yet everyone will follow her.
Be warned, the Fae Queen must stay pure until the Great Cat
finds her and their souls unite.
With their souls bound, the heir will be found.
The Fae Queen's magic will return, and together they will defend
the Fae from the end of time.
Time is of the essence, or the Fae will fall to the darkness.
When Fleshrender, Dragonfang, and *Bloodsong Grimoire* are
united
The dome will shatter, and the end of time is near.
Fear not.
The wait is over, the blessing has come,
The heir of blood is found.
The compass will unite
Griffin, dragon, unicorn,
Fae, and human.
Together they will battle darkness.

Part One

One

The hard stone floor ground into my knees. I lifted my head to see that the top of the egg-shaped chamber had a shaft of dim sunlight flickering through it. With barely enough light to illuminate the room, only a few shadows danced on the obsidian walls. I could feel my magic just below the surface of my skin, though it was sluggish compared to how it had been when I touched the *Bloodsong Grimoire* on the pedestal and my magic spilled out of me.

I clutched my human grandfather, King Leonard, ruler of the South, to my chest as grief dug its talons deep. "I'm sorry we didn't have more time. I love you." I had known he was sick before he ordered me to retrieve the *Bloodsong Grimoire*, but I had believed we would have more time. No matter our differences, I would never have wished death by Dragonfang on my grandfather. *Or anyone.*

Memories from my captivity at Dorcha Palace—the seat of the Fae Court of Dusk—mixed with recent ones of my grandfather, threatening to overwhelm me. One thought was in the forefront of my mind: If I had sought the book earlier, my magic would have returned in time for me to prevent his death by barring

Prince Tanyth from the palace. Instead, he had been welcomed as a guest to my wedding and brought destruction in his wake.

My husband and soulmate, Tristan Gilvrye, a Fae snow leopard shapeshifter, rested his gray hand lightly on my shoulder to reassure me, yet I wasn't sure I wanted reassurance. My own failures had led us to this moment. *Do I deserve to be loved?*

A gray glow filled the room. *Tristan's magic.* I wasn't entirely sure I wanted to be able to see better. The empty stone pedestal and my grandfather's body were stark reminders of how I had failed. Failed to protect my grandfather and a magic artifact that had been in the Helias family for centuries, only known by the heir and current ruler. *Gone.* Forced to make a choice, I had accepted the trade, unaware of what the consequences of handing Prince Tanyth the *Bloodsong Grimoire* could be—Tanyth uniting the three magic artifacts, *Bloodsong Grimoire*, Dragonfang, and Fleshrender.

"It's not your fault," Tristan said softly. I sucked in a breath, realizing he could at least sense what I was going to say before I said it because of our soulmate bond. *Something else I must get used to.*

"I just handed it to him." My voice was shaky. "I should have known it wouldn't matter what I did. Tanyth would kill King Leonard anyway." Except in that precise moment, I had prayed Tanyth would go against his nature and prove that there was a smidge of light in him.

"We need to tell everyone," Tristan reminded me. He was being kind. Instead of throwing my failure in my face, Tristan was attempting to give me directions. *Maybe I want him to be angry with me. To say I was wrong to hand over the book, playing into Prince Tanyth's hand and giving him the third and final object he desperately sought to fulfill the prophecy.*

I pressed my lips together in a thin line. The last thing I wanted to do at that moment was face the nobles of my grandfather's court and their judgment of my decision that led to their king being murdered. But deep down, I knew Tristan was right. These were now my subjects, and I owed them the truth. The king's body was growing cold in my arms. Perhaps facing them would distract me from the reality of handing over *Bloodsong Grimoire.* "Okay, let's go."

Wrapping my arms around my grandfather's body, I slowly stood up, taking care not to drop him. I had to adjust my grip and get my arm under his robe lest I trip on it. I could feel the sticky blood on my forearm but tried to ignore it. *I can get clean later.* Taking a deep breath, I started our trek back up to the main level of the palace.

When we reached the end of the hallway and passed through the door with the bronze plate, I looked over my shoulder as Tristan ensured the door closed and would not open. *Not that it matters. The Bloodsong Grimoire no longer needs to be kept safe, since it's not here.*

My whole body was trembling when we reached the throne room. The guards took in my ashen, tear-streaked face and the body in my arms and opened the large oak double doors without question. Ignoring the astonished murmurs of the courtiers milling around, presumably waiting for my grandfather to give them audience for the day, I headed for the table at the side of the room and laid my grandfather's body there. Then, I went hunting for something to cover him with.

Hanging at even intervals were long gold-colored tapestries. Not seeing any alternatives, I walked over to the nearest one and tugged. It wouldn't budge. Closing my eyes, I sank deep into myself and found my magic. Vibrant green laced with gold, the ball was tiny, but I knew I just needed a smidge of magic. I opened my eyes and raised my hand, and a small flicker of green-and-gold magic appeared and floated to the top of the tapestry. Before the magic touched the fabric, it disappeared. I frowned and tried again, but I couldn't get even a spark to appear.

"Let me help you," Tristan said, walking over to me. A dark-gray ball of magic appeared in his hand and floated up to the top of the tapestry, then burned a line across it. The fabric fell in a heap at our feet.

Normally, I would have questioned Tristan, but at the moment I didn't care about why his magic worked and mine didn't. I merely wanted to cover my grandfather and make the formal announcement.

Tristan picked up the tapestry and solemnly draped it over King Leonard. I walked over to the throne and turned to face everyone who had assembled. More people than I expected. I had a fleeting thought about how terrible I must look—bloodstained pants and tunic, hastily donned in the middle of the night, and blood-smeared arms; I thought I might even feel some on my cheeks. As I gazed at these people, I could not find the words. I opened my mouth twice, but nothing came out.

Tristan took over, his voice rough. "This morning King Leonard, Lord of the South, was murdered by Prince Tanyth of the Court of Dusk." Blinking back tears, I watched the crowd. A few people started crying, while others sent Tristan accusing glares.

I belatedly realized that as far as everyone here was concerned, Tristan was scheduled to be executed this morning, and now he was standing with me as an equal next to a dead king. *No wonder they look angry.*

When it was clear that Tristan was not going to elaborate, I thought I might need to find my voice to calm my subjects.

Then, from the sidelines came a familiar voice: Thomas, my guard. "All hail Queen Serafina Helias, Lady of the South!"

Two

TRISTAN

My stomach pitted into tight coils as my anger raged—anger I had to keep in check, at least while I was standing in front of Serafina's subjects. *I should have known Tanyth had more parts to his plan when he spoke to me in the dungeon mere hours ago.* Standing woodenly beside Serafina in the large throne room lined with massive white stone columns and decorated in the cream-and-gold colors of the South, I refused to react to the nobles' anger. It was justified. The last thing they had been told was I had an appointment with the executioner this morning for the beheading of King Lionel, Serafina's great-grandfather, and for disguising myself as a human to win her hand during the marriage competition. Yet here I was, alive and informing them their king, not me, was dead. *These humans must think I am responsible for King Leonard's death.* Now was not the time or place for me to confront Serafina's subjects. At best they would believe me; at worst I'd give them fuel to start a civil war. *We might stand a chance against Tanyth, but not if everyone in the South is fighting among themselves too.*

"All hail Queen Serafina, Lady of the South!" I shouted with the others in the room. I wanted to shout different words, but it was not the right moment. Too many things had happened in a short period of time; I was not going to say anything aloud that had the possibility of pushing Serafina to a breaking point. Instead, I thought the words to myself: *All hail Serafina, the Lost Fae Queen.* The moment Serafina had set her hand on the *Bloodsong Grimoire*, I had known without a doubt that she was the Lost Fae Queen. There were too many coincidences with the prophecy for it to be anyone but her—*and me.*

If Serafina is the Lost Fae Queen, then I am the Great Cat. The prophecy left my role, aside from being her mate, unspecified. But I could not ignore that it was mentioned, which meant us being bonded was a critical component needed for Serafina when she faced the end of time. *Whatever that is.*

I assumed that with Serafina's mixed bloodline making her half-Fae and half-human, she was destined to not only lead the four Fae courts but also her human kingdom of the South.

As the cheers died down, my attention returned to the throne room. Lord John, King Leonard's steward—and now, I presumed, Serafina's steward—stepped forward. His usual calm confidence had clearly been shaken. His white hair was sticking straight up on his head, and his dark-brown jacket was buttoned incorrectly. He was even wearing one black shoe and one brown. I shot a glance at Serafina and noted how pale her skin was and the tremors running through her body. I hoped the steward would keep his speech short so I could get Serafina back to our rooms for some rest and a chance to process what exactly had happened over the past couple of hours.

"Guests of Queen Serafina, I know this turn of events comes as quite a shock to everyone. King Leonard was murdered by Prince Tanyth of the Court of Dusk. His actions, as you are aware, are a declaration of war," Lord John announced.

The last war the South had with Fae was against the Court of Dusk, which they lost when I beheaded their king. I wisely kept these thoughts to myself as gasps of shock rolled through the guests at the mention of war.

"As you can imagine, there is much for Queen Serafina to handle right now. I promise there will be a chance for you to speak to her about your concerns. For now, let us all retire, and prepare for war," Lord John ordered.

I was disconcerted that Lord John told everyone to prepare for war. Technically, it was Serafina's job to officially declare war and order preparations to begin, but I didn't think she was going to argue at this point. It was critical we presented a united front. Now was not the time to contradict anything the steward said.

When it was clear to the guests that Lord John was not going be forthcoming with additional information, they filed out of the throne room. I ushered Serafina over to a large tapestry at the back of the throne room depicting the gold mine. Thomas scooted past me and pulled the tapestry back, revealing a hidden door.

"Come on," Thomas said.

The door handle was cool under my hand. I gave it a twist, and the door swung outward into a silent hallway. Grateful we would avoid confronting any of the nobles, I gave Serafina's hand a light tug and together we stepped into the hallway. Oil lamps cast wavering light across the gray stone walls and floors. Ahead, I could see a few suits of armor; otherwise, the hallway was unremarkable.

Thomas was close on our heels, and my guard Nolan quickly caught up. Once we went around the first corner, I recognized the hallway this one teed into and relaxed a hair. My anger was ebbing away, but I was unable to shake the worry settling in my gut. War with Prince Tanyth might not be as simple as troops lining up and facing off. Nor were two guards going to be sufficient protection for the new queen. I tucked the thought away to tackle tomorrow.

We made it to our rooms; Thomas entered first and did a sweep before giving the all clear. I didn't want to break it to him that I could have done the same sweep with my magic in seconds.

Once inside, I cast a protective shield around the entire room. It was meant to alert me to any intruders, though it would only work while I was actively feeding magic into it, unlike a warding spell that you could set once and it would continue to function. Exhaling, I gazed around our home. The four of us were standing in the foyer with four white marble columns. Beyond the foyer was a dining room with a large dark mahogany table with seats for twelve. A semicircle of dark-blue couches faced the enormous fireplace made of gold-veined black granite. In another area, there was a massive mahogany desk, large enough for both of us to do business, with bookcases lining the walls. Then came the doors heading off to the bedrooms—the two that had been designated by King Leonard as bedrooms for our future young-lings, a large bedroom for Serafina and me, and then a separate bathroom for guests.

Of course, our bedroom also had a massive bathroom equal in size to the bedroom with a white marble tub *and* a shower large enough for four or five. The décor was a mix of dark wood—either mahogany or stained walnut—and cream-and-gold accents.

"I have a shield in place. You are dismissed," I said to Thomas and Nolan. Serafina was already drifting toward our bedroom.

"Very well. We will be in the hallway if you need us," Thomas responded neutrally. The guard was quite practical, and I was confident he could tell that Serafina was exhausted and needed a bath and rest.

I waited until Thomas and Nolan had departed, with the door securely locked behind them, then followed Serafina into the bedroom and shut the door behind me. *Just in case someone decides to check on us.* I wanted to discourage any attendants from barging in on Serafina's much-needed nap. I stifled a yawn. *Our nap.*

The large bed, heaped with too many cream-colored blankets for my taste, was centered on the back wall. The wood looked like spun honey, a stark contrast to the dark tones in the other rooms, though the cream-and-gold theme continued. The wardrobes were the same wood as the bed.

I spotted the discarded clothing trail leading into the bathroom and heard the telltale sound of the water running. Not sure if Serafina was going to want company, I opted to remove my boots and keep the rest of my clothing on.

To my surprise, Serafina was already sitting in the tub, even though the water was only an inch or two deep. I could see her shivering and decided to take matters into my own hands. A gray glow surrounded the tub, and then it was full of hot water.

Serafina gave me a half smile. "Thanks."

"Eventually, you will be able to do that yourself," I told her. I turned to leave.

"Where are you going?" Serafina demanded.

Pivoting, I chuckled. "I assumed you wanted time to yourself. The past few hours have been quite intense."

Serafina blew out a breath. "Yes, they have been. But that doesn't mean I don't want your company." She patted the water, making it ripple.

My lips parted as I gazed at her, her creamy skin glistening with water droplets and her perfect breasts rising and falling with each breath she took. Need wound through me. I dug my nails into my palms, trying to redirect my thoughts. *Company and sex are not the same thing.*

Shoving away the images creeping into my mind of what we could do in the tub, I undressed, starting with my dirt- and blood-stained gray shirt and black pants. Then came my undergarments. Regardless of what my mind wanted, my cock was erect and throbbing. Biting back a growl of annoyance, I slid the undergarment down and stepped out of it, then climbed into the tub, leaning against cool marble on the opposite end from Serafina.

Thankfully, her eyes were closed as she relaxed. *Unaware of my body's desires.* I fully intended to keep it that way. The last thing I wanted was for her to be worried about my needs before her own.

She cracked an eyelid and peered at me. "I can feel you through the bond," she said with a smirk.

Oops. A small detail I had forgotten about. With the dark spell that had blocked our bond gone, emotions flowed freely between us. Not wanting to make her feel as though I only climbed into the tub because I wanted to satisfy myself, I took a deep breath and let my eyelids slide shut. With one sense cut off, I listened to the others and what our mating bond was telling me. I could feel her desire, though she didn't seem inclined to act on it.

My cock twitched painfully, and my fingers drifted toward it in the water. I was tempted to satisfy my own needs instead of disturbing my wife.

"Are we going to fall asleep in the tub?" she teased through the bond.

"If that is where you'd like to take your nap," I replied intensely.

"Maybe after ..." she replied, and then sent an image of her riding my cock through the bond.

My eyes were still closed, but the sloshing water told me Serafina's most likely weren't. Curious about what she was going to do, I kept my eyes shut. A hiss escaped through my teeth as she wrapped her hand around my throbbing cock and began stroking. She ran her nails up my shaft, and I shuddered in response as pleasure washed through me.

Blood pounding, I opened my eyes and found Serafina's face was hovering just over mine. "My wicked queen, if you keep doing that, you're not going to have a chance to ride me," I rasped.

Serafina smirked, then straddled me; instead of letting go, she guided my cock into her channel before releasing her fingers. Her head dipped down for a kiss.

Three

SERAFINA

ot bathwater sloshed around us as I rode Tristan's cock in our gigantic white marble tub. I didn't care how noisy we were. I was desperate for something good to come out of today, to know that Tristan still loved me, still wanted me, despite everything that had happened between us and what was certain to be headed our way.

Each downward movement of mine, he met with an upward thrust. With the insanity of the past few hours, the last thing on my mind had been sex, but catching a glimpse of Tristan's mood through the bond sent hot desire rolling through me. *If this helps relieve even a tiny bit of our stress, why not?*

My body tightened, each stroke sending me closer to my climax. One more downward movement, and I wobbled, pleasure rolling through me. My body felt like a limp noodle.

Tristan chuckled. "Not yet, Sera," he said against my lips, then kissed me deeply. He rolled us over without having to withdraw and tucked my ankles over his shoulders.

"Is this comfortable?" he asked softly. I nodded as he gave an experimental thrust and almost sent me over the edge again. I bit the inside of my cheek, and Tristan took up a quick but steady rhythm of thrusts. My body responded as though he hadn't already wrung one orgasm out of me. My eyes locked with Tristan's, and he sent me exploding into another orgasm.

"Tristan!" I shouted. Tristan draped himself over the top of me but was careful to ensure I didn't take any of his weight. Not that it would have mattered much since we were in the tub.

"Ready for that nap?" Tristan teased as my eyelids began to droop.

"Perhaps," I said and kissed him. His cock was still between my legs, and I would've sworn I felt it stir slightly. *Even Fae need to rest between,* I reminded myself.

Blood thrummed in my veins as I regained my composure after the skirmish. Rhys was wearing a short-sleeved tunic and leather vest showing off his muscular arms, and his leather pants had me practically drooling. What I really wanted was to drag Rhys into a dark corner and rip his clothes off.

A smile curved my lips as Rhys bowed to me with a flourish, his rich voice wrapping around me. "The win is yours, my dear. Congratulations."

I blew him a kiss and reluctantly turned my attention to my grandfather, knowing if I kept him waiting much longer he would do something rash. With my gaze focused on my grandfather, we approached the dais, stopping when we were just below the step he was on. This close, I could see his jaw was clenched. His fists curled at his side, and his eyes blazed in anger. My eyes slid over to Prince Tanyth, who had a cocky smirk on his face, though he stayed silent.

"Guards!" King Leonard shouted.

I gasped as guards leaped forward, pushing me away from Rhys and then grabbing him, yanking his hands behind his back, and forcing him onto his knees.

Icy anger filled me. "What's the meaning of this!" I shouted, glaring at my grandfather. The guards would only be acting on his command.

"*Prince Tanyth shared with me the most appalling information. Rhys Mongan is not who he says he is at all,*" King Leonard replied sharply.

My heart skipped a beat. "*What?*" I gasped. Impossible. Rhys would never lie to me. *My heartbeat increased, fear mingled with anger. I refused to believe this nonsense that my grandfather was spewing.*

"*Remove the pendant,*" Prince Tanyth ordered.

I bit the inside of my cheek to prevent myself from telling Prince Tanyth he wasn't allowed to give orders here. The king would not appreciate my interference in front of guests. The guard waited for a subtle nod from King Leonard before yanking the pendant out from under Rhys's tunic and snapping the cord. I rocked backward as though slapped as my husband changed before my eyes. Gone was his dark-tan skin and his black hair and beard; in their place was a tall, gray-skinned, slate-haired Fae male.

My anger was no longer icy cold, but roaring hot. My face heated, and I backed up a few steps, wanting distance from him. "*You're Fae?*" *My voice was shaky.*

He nodded confirmation. I knew my question was ridiculous—his pointy ears, large stature, and unnatural skin color made it obvious he was Fae and not human. The worst part was I recognized him, though it escaped me where we'd met before.

King Leonard snarled, "*Tristan Gilvrye, you will be executed tomorrow for murdering King Lionel and deceiving us to participate in the competition for the princess's hand in marriage.*"

Thomas escorted me back into the palace. His hand didn't leave the hilt of his sword the entire time. A guard was stationed outside the door of my suite of rooms to ensure no one was going to try to tamper with them while they were empty. Thomas opened the door and beckoned for me to step inside.

I stepped through the door, but instead of it being the foyer of the residence I shared with Rhys, I was in a cell in the dungeon. I spun around in surprise, but the door I had come through was gone.

Shivers ran down my spine, and I peered around the cell. The door was locked with a giant padlock the size of my hand, and the stone walls were remarkably solid on the other three sides.

The sound of footsteps had me retreating until the wall hit my back, forcing me to stop. A large figure in a hooded cape stopped in front of the cell door, then threw back the hood. It was Tristan.

I stepped forward. "Help me, Tristan," I said.

Tristan shook his head. "I cannot. This is the price you must pay for lying about your miscarriage. The laws of the South will not allow me as your consort to change them in your favor."

"I didn't lie," I protested.

Tristan frowned. "But you did. You hid the truth."

"So did you, about your identity," I retorted. My anger was flaring again at how ridiculous this was. Since when was miscarriage a punishable offense that would lead to imprisonment in the palace dungeon?

"You forgave me," Tristan replied.

"Then forgive me for this. What happened to my body has nothing to do with the South," I responded, but my confidence was slipping. *Maybe he was right, and I deserved to be punished.*

I woke up with a start, my arms flailing. The bathwater rippled around me, and my cheeks were damp from tears. I cupped the water with my hands and splashed my face, hoping Tristan hadn't noticed I was crying. My throat constricted when I thought about the miscarriage. I if I didn't tell Tristan, it would drive a bigger wedge between us, but I didn't feel strong enough to handle his reaction; not yet. *I have time. It doesn't need to be now,* I decided.

My gaze flittered around the room, and I realized that Tristan was sitting in a chair, his blue eyes gazing at me intently. He was wearing a navy-blue tunic and black leather pants with knee-high black boots. I knew he likely had noticed the tears with his exceptional Fae eyesight, but I hoped that if I didn't bring it up he wouldn't pry. Tristan and I had yet to discuss how our mating bond worked. I was unclear on how much of my emotions reached him through it. For the most part, all I had received from Tristan was knowing when sex was on his mind.

"You've been asleep three hours," Tristan said, likely feeling the question through the bond before I could voice it.

My eyes widened in bewilderment. *Three hours?* The water was still as hot as it had been earlier, making it difficult to believe I had truly been asleep that long. Stifling a yawn with my hand, it dawned on me that I had been awakened in the middle of the night to attend my grandfather and his request to retrieve the *Bloodsong Grimoire*. Prior to that, I confronted Tristan about his deception as Rhys Mongan. Which meant this three-hour nap was likely the most consecutive sleep I'd gotten in over twenty-four hours.

I raised my arms, intending to wring the water out of my hair, when I noticed words scrolling across them. Lifting my right arm to my face, I studied it. The words were moving and had a faint glow. *Like dried blood.* I shuddered, wrinkling my nose in revulsion.

"Did you notice the words on my arm earlier?" I asked Tristan.

Tristan stood up to get a closer look. "No, but honestly, I was focused on other things." He ran his finger over my arm and the letters stopped moving but didn't disappear. "When did this start?"

I shook my head. "I think it was after we went to get the *Bloodsong Grimoire*," I responded absently, my thoughts churning.

Tristan tapped his mouth with his finger. "Didn't you say that prior to touching *Bloodsong Grimoire* the first time, the pages were blank, and then they had words when you removed your hand?"

I nodded. "Yes, that is what happened."

"I wonder if the words transferred to your skin when you touched the book a second time," Tristan said.

The idea surprised me and seemed rather far-fetched. *Why would the words from a magic object now be on my skin? If they're on my skin, are they also in the book?* We would likely never have the answer. Now that *Bloodsong Grimoire* was in Prince Tanyth's hands, the odds of ever seeing it again were slim to none.

A memory nagged at me. "Isn't there a story about the *Bloodsong Grimoire* in *Bedtime Tails*?"

Tristan nodded. "Yes, there is." He closed his eyes and recited:
"Become one with flesh
Summon the dragon with his fang
Bloodsong sang with glee
The one who can tame the three
Can maim all foes against thee.

"It's the prophecy that Tanyth has been pursuing for years. Now that he has all three objects, *if* the prophecy is to be believed, then he would have significantly more power than he did prior to uniting them," Tristan explained.

A shiver ran down my spine. *Power to do what?* With the return of the memories from my imprisonment at Dorcha Palace, likely nothing Tanyth intended to do with the three objects would be "good."

"Do you have any idea what Tanyth's plan is?" I asked, hoping Tristan's decades as lord commander of the Court of Dusk had given him insight into his intentions.

Tristan's eyes darkened, and he ran a hand over his face. "Based on the circumstances of the confrontation with him this morning, I would anticipate he wants to destroy you and then claim King Pharaan's throne for himself."

"Destroy me," I repeated, realizing that if Tanyth had merely wanted to kill me he had had the perfect chance, but instead he had killed my grandfather. An image of thousands of Fae forced into slavery under Tanyth's rule, whether to fight in his arena or serve him in any way he saw fit, rose in my mind's eye. Trying to erase those images, I dunked my head under the water and then lathered soap in my hair and over my body. There was more than one way to destroy a person. Going through the motions of getting clean, I recalled that at my parents' house Thomas and I had discovered my mother's book of *Bedtime Tails*, which had new prophecies in it. *I need to show it to Tristan.*

When I opened my mouth to speak, I yawned, and my jaw popped.

"I think it's time to take a nap in the real bed," Tristan informed me.

My arms felt as though they were filled with lead. I nodded tiredly in agreement. *My mother's book will be here when I wake up.* I promised myself I would bring it up then.

I climbed into bed, and Tristan tucked the covers around me. As tired as I was, I could not stop replaying memories from Dorcha Palace mingled with the dream of Tristan's betrayal revealed. Instead of the good memories—stolen moments with Tristan—I was reliving being forced to fight in the arena and the fear that Tanyth would kill me or force me to have sex with him. As I drifted to sleep, Tristan's body warm against my back, a small tendril of relief drifted around me as I realized that since my memories had been returned, I knew for certain that the only individual I had ever had sex with, and therefore the father of the miscarried child, was Tristan. While I might be facing the emotions of a miscarriage, at least it was not a pregnancy that was the result of rape.

Four

RETHYS

The dungeon at the bottom of Dorcha Palace in Ember Mountain was ripe with the smell of rotting meat and flesh. Even now, after a century as Prince Tanyth's captive, I had not gotten used to the stench. Instead, my nostrils burned constantly, a sharp reminder of how costly a small mistake could be. Taking a deep breath, I slowly unfurled my wings, stretching them into the corners of my cell, which was only half of their full span.

A tingling sensation along my spine was the only warning I got when the prince appeared in my cell. Tanyth's teal skin was almost black in the darkness of the dungeon and he was dressed in black leather, with that ridiculous antler crown perched on his head. I hissed and held my ground in the middle of the cage. I wanted to burn him but was biding my time, for it would come soon enough.

"Rethys, tell me again what you know of the magical artifacts," Tanyth ordered.

I stared blatantly into his dark green eyes with my gold ones. He held my gaze and then shifted his feet uncomfortably before looking away. I smiled at him, my muzzle inches away from his face, relishing the slight tremor in the prince's jaw, the bead of sweat forming along his forehead, and the subtle smell of fear.

Rocking back on my haunches, I continued to stare at him, and then I spoke into his mind. *"The* Bloodsong Grimoire *is a spellbook full of protection spells that even the simplest-minded and least-skilled Fae could use. Fleshrender is a sword of other-worldly magic that feeds from the death of the wielder's enemies and has the potential to transfer the magic of the enemy to the wielder when the enemy dies. Dragonfang is a dagger that was forged to obtain the ability to command me, and it is known to protect its wielder."*

While I recited the words I'd told him almost daily since he first captured me, the prince's anger was palpable. My plan had been to withhold the knowledge he truly sought for as long as possible. One of the few things I still had control over.

Dragonfang, with its dragonhead-shaped silver handle, emerald eyes, and silver-iron blade, appeared in Tanyth's hand, and he brandished the dagger between us. One thousand years ago, when Dragonfang was forged, a dark Fae of the Neriwraek family bound me to the dagger. The spell, though, had not worked quite as he had expected, and it gave me a link not only to Dragonfang but also to the other two magic artifacts of the prophecy, awarding me with the knowledge that when they were brought together, it would signal the end of time was near. Exhaling, I let smoke curl out of my mouth in warning.

"Rethys. You have been repeating the same drivel every time I come down here. Give me new information on the magic artifacts," Tanyth barked. The dagger glowed green, and I felt thousands of tiny pinpricks along my hide. If they had remained on my back I could have ignored them, but they spread to my underside and intensified until they were unbearable.

"United, Bloodsong Grimoire, *Fleshrender, and* Dragonfang *will make you the most powerful Fae to live,"* I replied, omitting the words Tanyth was looking for—the admission that the artifacts

would give the wielder godlike powers due to certain steps that had been taken at their creation.

Tanyth's lip curled. "Except I have all three and don't feel any different."

"Did you give the artifacts a blood offering?" I asked. It was the most common mistake I'd seen made by those seeking dark power, not realizing that blood was required.

"No," Tanyth responded. "Once I give them a blood offering, will their magic be connected to me indefinitely?"

My tail slapped the floor, making Tanyth jump. I chuckled in satisfaction at his response. *"Given I have never attempted to use them myself, I would not be able to answer your question."* Wanting to sow more seeds of doubt in his mind, I added, *"Nor do I know how many times the power can be summoned and will answer your call."*

Tanyth snarled and leaped forward. I swatted the dagger out of his hand with my claws. A jolt of Dragonfang's magic spread through me, and I fought to stay conscious. I hadn't expected its defensive mechanism to work so well against me. Falling forward, breathing heavily, hatred filled me. One day Tanyth would get what was coming to him.

"You are only alive because you amuse me," Tanyth said with what he must have thought was a wicked sneer. Instead, to me, he just looked like a weak Fae bully. Without another word, Tanyth used a star portal and vanished.

A century at Dorcha Palace had taught me one thing: Though I might "amuse" Tanyth, he was afraid to let me die and lose his only source of long-forgotten Fae history. Curling up with my tail draped over my muzzle, I fell into a light doze.

Five

TRISTAN

Heart hammering in my chest, I opened my eyes, nostrils flared. I could make out the end of the bed and the wardrobe on the wall. Serafina's back was warm against mine, a gentle reminder I was here in the South with my mate—my wife. The dragon tattoo on my lower back was throbbing. It had begun when the dragon Rethys entered my dream. An old memory of the arena battle when Travaran—Prince Tanyth's son and my close friend—and I had been pitted against Rethys for Tanyth's entertainment.

Sadness washed over me as I wondered if my life would have been different had I not been exiled from my home. *Would I have left anyhow to pursue life in one of the courts?* The Court of Dusk was the only Fae court known to hunt down shapeshifters. The Courts of Dawn, the Moon, and the Sun all treated shapeshifters as equals to Fae with different types of magic. I had seen a unicorn shifter at the Court of Dawn with my own eyes. My throat constricted. *I can't change the past,* I reminded myself.

Wide awake and afraid to disturb Serafina, knowing she needed as much rest as she could get, I lay as still as possible, tuned out the pain in my back, and let my mind drift to other matters. The first was concern at the glimmers of my wife's dream when she had been in the tub. Fear had radiated through the bond and hints that she had a secret. I refused to treat her like Tanyth would and pressure her into telling me until she was ready. My thoughts wandered to the matter of less than two days ago, when I had been masquerading as a human, Rhys Mongan. Many events had transpired since then. Looming war with the South's closest Fae neighbor, the Court of the Sun, had prompted King Leonard to ask Serafina to retrieve *Bloodsong Grimoire*. Even though I was confident the so-called proof Prince Tanyth had shared with King Leonard was fake, Serafina couldn't ignore the information until it was confirmed by a trusted source.

The few weeks I had spent in the palace and the city of Gaskal, I had learned that the number of humans who respected Serafina and would honorably serve her were few and far between. One particularly annoying noble couple came to mind: Duke Herman and Duchess Oriana. They were the perfect example of who not to trust as they were avidly anti-Fae.

I knew without a doubt that Serafina needed to establish her position as queen and solidify her views on Fae—and expectations for their treatment—quickly and publicly, thereby squashing any resistance before it became a major problem. Thomas and his faction of humans that had known Serafina's parents, Solana and Gareth, would likely need to take larger roles to help smooth things over. They were known within the city and, theoretically, should be able to encourage others to trust Serafina more readily.

Our greatest challenge would be time. *War is coming*. I anticipated Tanyth had begun preparations to attack the South before he had shown his face at the post-wedding luncheon. Which meant we were at a significant disadvantage. The South's history was unfamiliar to me. I didn't know when their knights had last been mobilized, if they were actively in training and prepared should war arise at any time, or if their skills had softened from lack of use.

My stomach was heavy as I remembered when the Court of Dusk had faced King Lionel, Serafina's great-grandfather, and how evenly matched both sides were. Doubt slithered into my thoughts. It had been my actions that turned the tide of the last war. *What if Prince Tanyth is expecting me to turn on Serafina's subjects? Or is going to manipulate me into doing so?* Chills iced my spine at the prospect of Tanyth orchestrating the events of the past few weeks and the betrayal of my wife. My years as lord commander of the Court of Dusk had shown me just how ruthless and power-hungry Tanyth was and that no cost was too high if it furthered his own agenda.

My skin rippled. Biting the inside of my cheek, I pushed back against my shapeshifting magic, hoping doing so wouldn't send too much down the mating bond and wake Serafina up. My years at the Court of Dusk had taught me to shield my emotions, which was proving useful with the mating bond, preventing Sera from being overwhelmed with the demons chasing me in addition to her own. Forcing myself to focus on something useful that would give me control to keep the snow leopard at bay, my thoughts turned to the knights Sera hoped to call upon. If King Leonard had been diligent with his knights, then her army should be one to be reckoned with. *I will have to find out.*

I knew I would have to push Serafina into defining *my role*, as well. With her memories restored, her anger at my deception posing as a human to win the competition to marry her had disappeared. Knowing her expectations would permit me to fulfill them and ensure the rest of her advisors respected the role too. *Does she want me to become essentially her lord commander? Or did she have something else in mind?* I also wanted to discuss the matter of my shapeshifting and if she intended to reveal that to anyone or not.

I reached out my fingers and lightly tucked a strand of her russet hair behind her ear. Serafina smiled and rolled toward me. "Good morning."

"Morning, my love," I said and kissed her. Serafina dazzled me when she deepened the kiss and with a featherlight touch ran her fingers along the length of my shaft. I sucked in my breath sharply and captured her hand with mine, stopping her.

"As much as I would love nothing more than to satisfy your needs, I think that we have a slew of important matters that require your attention," I said softly, ignoring my body's demand to bury myself inside her slick folds. We would have time tonight. If we weren't under the threat of war, making people wait on us wouldn't bother me. But this kingdom was now my wife's responsibility; I didn't want to be blamed and disliked more by the humans for distracting her.

Serafina nipped my lip. "I know. I was just hoping you'd decide to not be sensible this morning."

"Ah," I said and kissed her, then rolled out of her embrace and swung my legs off the bed. Serafina stretched like a cat, taunting me, before she also slid out of the bed. I closed my eyes for a moment and with my superior hearing recognized the sound of the door to our residence opening and Violet's footfalls as she entered the foyer, then the clink of plates and cutlery as she began to set out breakfast. I assumed she would soon be knocking on our door, though unless it was an emergency I doubted she would let herself in, respecting our privacy.

Unable to predict how our day would develop, I decided to broach the topic of my largest concern. "Sera, you need more guards."

Serafina gave me a startled look. "More guards?"

I nodded. "Yes. We're going to war. It is critical that you have the necessary protection. We cannot afford to underestimate Tanyth's desire to kill you."

She ran her fingers absently through her russet hair. My own twitched, and I clenched my fists. Now was not the time to get sidetracked. Serafina met my gaze. "Before you won the competition, I brought up the matter of palace security to my grandfather. He ignored me, and now ..." Her words disappeared, and I could see a hint of tears glinting in her eyes.

"Precisely why we need to solve the issue immediately," I replied.

"How do we know who to trust?" Serafina asked.

The weight in my stomach lifted. I was thrilled that she was as concerned as I was about the number of trustworthy people in the palace. "I expect the master of the guard would know who we could trust," I suggested.

"Maybe. Though I have a stronger relationship with Thomas. It could be worth asking him to hand-pick additional guards," Serafina said.

I had almost said she should ask Thomas but was worried about alienating Declan by asking one of his subordinates for advice. The master of the guard had to date not done anything indicating he did not deserve our trust.

Serafina spoke. "When I first met Violet McCormack, my lady-in-waiting, I offered to give her self-defense lessons. We never got around to it, but now I think it might be prudent to require my ladies-in-waiting to at the very least be able to defend themselves. If it is possible, they could double as another set of guards."

The thought piqued my interest. "I like the idea, but I have no idea where you'd find candidates. Perhaps that is a suitable question for Thomas, since he has likely witnessed much in his time as a palace guard."

A quick glance at Sera was a sharp reminder that neither one of us was dressed to see visitors. Hoping to steer us closer to readiness, I asked, "What would you like to wear today?" As she pondered, I used my magic to dress myself. It was one of the most convenient aspects of my shadow magic and a fairly common magic skill among Fae. I decided on navy-blue pants and a matching jacket with a gold leaf pattern on the cuffs, a black silk shirt, and black knee-high leather boots with daggers hidden in their tops, as well as daggers strapped to my forearms and at the small of my back.

Instead of answering, she sent an image to me through the bond. I smiled. She was catching on to how the magic of the soulmate bond worked. Threads of my gray magic wrapped around Serafina. When they vanished, she was wearing an elaborate outfit, more of a riding suit than anything. Her idea had been brilliant, allowing her to still be feminine yet practical.

A black satin shirt with billowy sleeves and gold details on the cuffs. A gold satin vest embroidered with black swirls. Tight black leather pants tucked into thigh-high black leather boots. A black satin overskirt with a panel missing in the front to allow her to move freely and a split in the back allowing for her to ride Dubhar if the day called for it.

I raised my hand to tackle her hair when she shook her head. "I will do my hair," Serafina said.

I was pleased that she wanted to try using her magic. "Imagine the hairstyle you want and apply your will to your magic."

Serafina nodded and pressed her lips together. I watched thin green tendrils of magic sprout from her shoulders and swirl around her head. Slowly her long russet hair changed from the messy tangles to smooth from being brushed, then the strands wove together. The finished result was Serafina's hair in two separate braids on each side of her face, which were then combined to go down her back. A thin gold crown sat atop her head, to remind everyone of who they were dealing with.

"You look lovely. How do you feel?" I asked. Yesterday when the *Bloodsong Grimoire* had unleashed her magic, it had sapped all her energy. We had yet to explore the depths of her magic, and I had no idea how quickly she could replenish her stores or how taxing doing her hair would be.

"Fine," Serafina replied.

Sucking in a breath through my teeth, I tempered my reaction to her tone. She sounded anything but fine. I wondered if she had gotten a sense of my dream, as I had with hers earlier, and was on edge because of that, or something else—like her grandfather's death.

"Would you like to talk about it?" I asked in what I hoped was an encouraging tone.

Sera declined. "It can wait. I'm sure there are matters more critical to the kingdom we must address this morning."

A lump settled in my stomach. I knew that waiting for her to reveal whatever was bothering her would likely weigh on me all day. Our bond was strengthening, as was our love for each other, but we had had quite a challenging start to our relationship, and I wanted to tread lightly. Shoving all my negative thoughts into a box in my mind and snapping the lid shut, I opened the door and walked out of the bedroom.

Six

SERAFINA

My response to Tristan was automatic. It was easier to say I was fine than to dive deeper into my real feelings. Just as it was easier—and more enjoyable—to ignore my emotions by giving in to the heightened sex drive I was experiencing with the mating bond firmly in place. Especially since we were about to have company. Using the magic was a distraction, and it was a relief when it cooperated and my hair braided itself.

At Jade Wilds, I had had lessons on history and battle while the Fae in training had learned about magic, which I was born without. Now, with magic thrust upon me, I had yet *another* thing to learn about. Except this change was not as simple as giving me information to absorb. Just like with any weapon, I would have to start with basics and then, over time and with training, would grow into mastery. However, my success or failure would influence the outcome of our war with the Court of Dusk. Small wins, like creating clothing and braiding hair, were the building blocks I needed to be able to fight in a battle. *Everyone must start somewhere*, I reminded myself. I could feel the magic coiling within me, ready to do my bidding. I wanted to test it. *Tonight,* I promised myself. I would ask either Tristan or Ghilanna to show me the basics.

I walked out of the bedroom toward the dining area where Violet was bustling around, setting out two places and arranging a couple of platters heaped with food. Tristan had followed me out and was cleaning his broadsword over by our desk. As I selected a chair near the food and sat down, I noticed how tense Violet was. Her hands shook as she poured juice into the cups.

"What's wrong, Violet?" I asked with concern. I knew if I wanted Violet to fit the vision I had for the lady-in-waiting position, I had to take steps to strengthen our friendship.

Violet's caramel-colored eyes met mine for the briefest of moments, then she lowered her gaze. "It's not my place to say," she replied haltingly.

Sighing, I placed my hands on the table, willing Violet to meet my gaze. "We're friends, or at least that's how I feel about you. I promise you can say anything, and I won't hold it against you."

Violet's neck drew taut, and her gaze flitted to mine, then fixed on the table. "You shouldn't trust him. He betrayed you," Violet said shakily.

My eyes widened as I realized Violet was talking about Tristan. Caught off guard and not wanting to turn this into a confrontation, I replied calmly, "I understand that there have been many major changes in a short period of time, but I trust Tristan with my life. My history with him is complicated. What I need you to accept that that he is not just my husband, he is my soulmate, which is a magical bond that pairs of Fae can share. I hope you will trust me and our friendship. However, if you would like, you can have the day off to think things over and then decide if you still wish to serve me. The choice is completely up to you, and I will not hold it against you if you feel that being my lady-in-waiting is no longer the correct fit for you."

Originally, I had hoped to broach the subject of teaching her to use weapons like Tristan and I had just discussed, but I sensed this was not the right time and would likely drive Violet away.

Violet took time digesting what I had told her, her brow furrowing as she likely ran the words over and over in her mind. Eventually, Violet replied, though she would still not meet my gaze. "I thought he had enspelled you."

My mouth twitched at Violet's words. In some ways she was right, except it had been the mating bond, magic beyond our control, that had entwined Tristan and me together. As new as the mating bond was to me, I wasn't comfortable diving into an explanation with Violet over how it might work.

"I appreciate your concern, but I promise I am not under a spell and can act freely of my own accord," I replied, giving her what I hoped was an encouraging smile.

Violet curtseyed deeply, finally meeting my eyes. "I have a few personal chores to attend to this morning and will use that time to consider all that you have said." Curtseying again, Violet departed.

As she stepped out the door, another set of footsteps entered. Thomas gave me a bright smile. "Sorry to intrude on your morning. But there are a lot of matters we need to discuss, and every moment counts."

I shrugged and waved at him to come all the way into our residence. Tristan put his sword back into the weapons cabinet and then headed over to the table and pulled out a chair for himself near me.

When Thomas reached the table, he selected his own seat facing us. He announced, "I'm going to talk while you eat."

"Okay," I replied agreeably as my stomach rumbled loud enough for Thomas and Tristan to hear. I blushed and focused on my plate. I could feel Tristan's laughter through the bond.

Thomas cleared his throat. "There are several tasks that need to be addressed tomorrow at the latest. The first is deciding on a date for your coronation. While you are technically queen already, the people of the South will respect you more if you hold the official coronation."

I paused with my fork raised to my lips, then lowered it, frowning. "Do we have time for that?"

Thomas opened his mouth to speak when Tristan chimed in. "Thomas is right. You are the symbol of the South. They need to see you."

I snorted at the ridiculous notion that I, a half-Fae with magic, was now the symbol of the South. "We can't fit the entire population of the South in the throne room or wait long enough for everyone to travel here."

"We know that," Tristan said patiently. "It's more about the symbolism of the coronation. Word will spread. Trust me, it is important."

It was a challenge to wrap my mind around people throughout the kingdom accepting me as queen, especially when I'd had barely two weeks to reacquaint myself with the culture of my subjects. The nobles had been cordial at the wedding but were not singing my praises. *No one expected King Leonard would be dead so soon.* I sighed, deciding to rely upon their wisdom in this matter. "Fine. What else is on the list?" After the wedding, King Leonard had shared very little with me. We had gone through the rituals with the *Bloodsong Grimoire* and the gold mine, but he had wanted to wait to go into details about what it would take to run a kingdom. *Now he's dead, and I'm going into this blind.*

Thomas continued, "The second matter is creating a war council. Historically, the Lord of the South has formed one if there is a major threat. Usually, it comprises nobles and a general or two. Typically, the members of the war council also include the ruler's most trusted advisors."

Perhaps I'm not as blind as I thought if I have people I trust, like Thomas, guiding me.

"I don't have any advisors," I replied through a mouthful of sausage.

"Yes, I am aware you don't formally have advisors," Thomas agreed. "Traditionally, the new ruler's advisors are chosen after the coronation; however, I think with war already looming, you might be better off to do it the other way around. It will also be a good opportunity for you to express your thoughts on the matter of Fae in the South and what their roles will be. Including, I might add, the role Tristan will have."

I swallowed my sausage and took a swig of cranberry juice, considering my response. "If I place Tristan in an official role as an advisor, won't people balk?"

Thomas tipped his hand from side to side in a maybe motion. "It's possible it will cause problems. However, it could also be an easy way to push him into a formal role with the justification being his lengthy experience as lord commander at the Court of Dusk and knowledge of how the Court of Dusk could wage war. We won't have to rely on hearsay. He has firsthand accounts. It's hard to argue that he shouldn't be part of the war council with the amount of knowledge he can bring to the table. No one else can claim that. Not about matters of battling with Fae."

Tristan interjected, "That's not entirely true. Callyn also has a significant amount of battle experience, and she was part of the Court of Dusk longer than I was."

Thomas took a sip of water before responding. "Including Callyn on the war council would be a decision for Serafina. I would be careful with how many Fae you put on the council though. I don't think it will go over well with the nobles if Fae outnumbered humans. Even a fifty-fifty split could cause problems. Though your argument there could be simply that you're half of each."

The biggest problem I had with needing fifty percent of the war council to be humans was I didn't know many that I trusted. *Do I need to trust them?* I mused.

To my consternation, Tristan, clearly reading my thoughts through the bond, replied, *"You must be able to trust that they won't give the information they learn in the war council to the enemy. But it may not be a bad thing to have varying opinions. You might learn something useful."*

He had a valid point; the individuals on the war council did not need to share my same likes and dislikes. They just needed to be loyal to me as Lady of the South.

"When do you need the list of the war council members?" I asked, mulling over a list of possible names.

"Ideally in a few hours," Thomas said.

Not long to think about it. "Do I need to ask them?" I inquired.

Tristan replied, "It is your right as queen to require them to agree to serve on your council, but your request will likely be received better if you meet with them before publicly announcing your decision. That way they could refuse without losing face."

I nibbled on my lip. *Tristan is right.* "I will add that to my agenda for the day," I finally responded with a nagging feeling that I was going to have a lengthy task list when this conversation ended and not enough hours to complete it in.

"Good," replied Thomas. "Do you have any matters you wanted to discuss with me?"

"You can tell him," I said through the bond to Tristan as I put another bite of food in my mouth, hoping that since Thomas respected Tristan's experience as lord commander, it would come across better from Tristan.

Tristan gave me the barest of nods. "There is one matter. Choosing a larger contingent of guards. While we both greatly appreciate you and Nolan, two guards are hardly enough to provide adequate protection. Not if we're likely facing covert attacks. Serafina also had the idea of using the ladies-in-waiting as an additional source of protection."

Thomas's face took on a thoughtful expression as he considered the request. "There are a few more guards I know personally who would be trustworthy and do not have anti-Fae tendencies.

However, the matter of using ladies-in-waiting as guards will be a challenge. None of the noblewomen who are worthy of an invitation to serve their queen would be willing to pick up a weapon."

His response, though expected, was unfortunate. I washed down the mouthful of food with more cranberry juice, then replied, "What about women who are not of noble birth? Or those from the families that welcomed Solana?"

Thomas tapped his fingers lightly on the table. "Valerie can use a sword. She might know others who can as well. But it's not going to be easy to convince them to serve you as ladies-in-waiting. Nobles might think the position offers prestige and an ear with the queen. City-goers are too busy with their own lives to care about shining royal boots. The other matter is that training willing women would take time we don't have."

The idea of having ladies-in-waiting doubling as guards was fizzling out before I'd even had the chance to conduct the experiment. Sifting through ideas, one wild possibility came to me, but I knew it would buck many of the South's traditions. *If I don't ask, I won't ever know the answer,* I reminded myself and blurted out, "What if my ladies-in-waiting were Fae?"

The guard's brown eyes widened in shock, then softened. "An intriguing idea."

"They are trained," Tristan supplied.

My concern wasn't with them having the training. It was whether being Fae would cause more tension within the palace. Thomas had already pointed out that I needed to be careful that my war council was not more than fifty percent Fae. *Does the same rule apply to ladies-in-waiting?*

"Honestly, I don't know how it would be viewed if your ladies-in-waiting were Fae. It might depend on if they are dressed like warriors, full armor and bristling with weapons, or if they blend in," Thomas responded.

"The purpose of having Fae as ladies-in-waiting would be for them to blend in. To be an extra layer of protection, but not drawing unwanted attention to themselves. Even if it was just Ghilanna to start with, that would help, right?" I asked Tristan.

He looked as though he wanted to protest. *Likely suggest I should have Callyn too.* But I was worried Callyn would be needed to do other tasks. As a lady, when I was appearing in public, her movements would be restricted to staying near me.

Thomas resolved the issue by replying, "Ghilanna is a good place to start. I would recommend discussing the matter with her today, and then we can decide how to proceed based on her response. Now, when you're done eating, Lord John has some matters he'd like to discuss as well."

Before I could stifle it, a groan escaped my lips. Tristan patted my hand comfortingly, his blue eyes bright. "I'll make it up to you later." He sent an image of his face buried between my thighs down the bond.

I shivered in anticipation, wishing I could drag him to the bedroom now. *"Promise?"* I squeaked down the bond.

Tristan just grinned and squeezed my hand. Focusing on the food was a challenge after that. But I had to try. It wasn't going to go over well with the people I had to work with if I was too focused on satisfying my rampaging desire to have sex with Tristan every waking moment. *It would aid in producing an heir,* a traitorous part of my mind informed me. The problem was the cultural differences between humans and Fae. Fae accepted the fact that sex was an important aspect of life and encouraged it. Humans felt as though it should be kept behind closed doors, a secret, even though it was expected that married couples would have sex.

With the impending war, I didn't think the excuse of fulfilling King Leonard's dying wish for me to produce an heir as soon as possible would be well accepted, especially if I wasn't mentally ready to be pregnant again. The first step would be to tell Tristan tonight about the miscarriage. I forced myself to keep eating, knowing with the long day ahead of us, I would regret not having a hearty breakfast while I had the chance.

I was setting down my fork, plate polished clean, when Thomas opened the entry door and admitted Lord John. Unlike the last time I saw him, his white hair was neatly combed and he was wearing a brown-and-cream jacquard jacket with brown pants. I stood up, not wanting to have a second meeting at the dining room table. "How about we sit at the desk?" I suggested.

Lord John nodded and the three of us arranged ourselves around the imposing mahogany desk. I sat in the large, throne-like chair behind the desk with Tristan off to my side and Lord John opposite. He had a sheaf of papers in his hands, which he laid in a neat stack on the desk.

"I hope you got enough sleep last night?" Lord John asked, keeping his expression neutral.

"Yes, I am well rested and ready for whatever you need to discuss," I replied resolutely. An entire kingdom was relying on me to lead them. Giving up now meant abandoning them in their time of greatest need. Even though I felt underprepared for the role, I didn't want to let the South down; I was born here in Gaskal, as was my father. A stack of fresh paper and a quill were to my left. I was tempted to start writing my list for the war council but didn't want to be rude to the steward. *I need him on my side.*

"Good. I know Thomas discussed the creation of a war council. I am here to talk about other matters. Specifically, regarding Tristan and Fae. You are aware that Tristan was slated to be executed yesterday morning for murdering King Lionel. Your grandfather might have granted you power to free him, but that does not change the fact that your subjects saw you marry a human, and now your husband is Fae," Lord John explained. His voice was brittle and emotionless. I couldn't get a read on him.

Tristan opened his mouth, and Lord John shook his head. "Let me continue, please." Tristan nodded once, and the steward plowed onward. "In this situation, I believe the best thing to do is to share some of the truth, but not all of it. We are going to war with Prince Tanyth. We now know he was responsible for your illness. It would simplify things to lay *all* the blame on his shoulders. He forced Tristan to wear the pendant and cast magic on you, Serafina. I believe this is the best way for your subjects to swallow the news. If they have a villain, then they can still be angry, but it will be directed elsewhere."

I lightly tapped my fingers on the desk. It was a reasonable plan that would solve a number of issues I faced and would go well with my decision to tell at least those in our inner circle about the mating bond and shapeshifting. "I agree with your recommendation of blaming Prince Tanyth."

Lord John sighed deeply, relief written on his face.

"The other most pressing matter is scheduling the coronation. The best scenario would be for it to take place in three days. That gives us two days to prepare and to get invitations out," Lord John said.

I sucked in a breath. *What is it with everything being so tightly scheduled?* The competition and wedding events had all been two to three days apart. I responded, "Three days from now is acceptable. Now, if you don't have anything else for me, I would like a chance to discuss matters with Tristan before I go hunting for the people I want to ask about the war council."

The faintest of smiles flitted over Lord John's lips and then disappeared. "That was it. I will start preparations for the coronation. You will, of course, get to review the invitations before they go out as well as meet with the seamstress to sort out your outfit."

"Thank you," I replied, not wanting to encourage him to linger to discuss the details of those matters. I assumed there was some sort of standard invitation. I didn't think it was important to weigh in on that. I did, however, want a say in what I was going to be wearing, even though I knew some of it was likely to be traditional for the position, just as it had been for the wedding.

Lord John stood. His chair scraped loudly on the floor, and I cringed imagining the deep gouge likely visible in the wood floor. "Good day, Your Majesty," the steward said with a bow and then departed.

I exhaled when the door shut behind him. "Wow. Talk about a lot to do!"

Tristan shrugged. "What did you expect?"

"I don't know," I admitted. "Maybe just time to get used to the title of queen before being thrust into my obligations."

"War means you don't have time," Tristan said softly.

I sat in silence for a few minutes, massaging my temples and trying to gather my thoughts. *I could tell him now,* my mind suggested. I ignored it, though the muscles in my chest tightened at the prospect of that discussion. "The war council."

Seven

TRISTAN

I gazed at Serafina sitting regally in the high-backed chair behind the mahogany desk and wondered again what at the forefront of her mind was causing her to be so tense, but she would not discuss it. We had time. *I could press her*, I mused, then quickly dismissed the idea. *It's not like I have bared all my deepest darkest secrets to her, and she's not begging me to do so. I can respect her decision to wait till she's ready*, I told myself. The mahogany desk was a beautiful piece of furniture, and I wanted nothing more than to drape her over it and make love to her. I shoved my thoughts into a box and snapped it shut. I needed to focus on what Serafina clearly wanted my thoughts on—the war council.

"Do you have any concrete ideas yet?" I asked. As soon as the words left my mouth, I could see her whole list through the bond. Images of each individual flashed into my thoughts.

Serafina smiled. "I do. My first pick is you."

I gasped, feigning surprise, and she smacked me in the arm. "Ow!"

Serafina rolled her eyes. "Stop it." I blew her a kiss, and she smacked me again. "Be serious, Tristan. Do you want to be on my war council?"

"I'm perplexed that you felt the need to ask," I replied.

Serafina swatted me again. My blood heated when my chin dipped down, and my eyes settled on the peaks of her breasts just visible at the top of her vest. Unable to resist, I caught her hand and tugged her halfway out of the seat toward me. I captured her lips with mine, demanding. She melted into my arms and scooted off her chair and onto my lap, straddling me. I gently teased her lips with my tongue, and when she parted them, I deepened the kiss.

"We need to work," Serafina said in my thoughts, but her words were not very convincing, and neither were her actions as she began to grind against my cock, sending pulses of desire straight to my core.

"If you want to work, *then you should stop what you're doing immediately,"* I replied.

She giggled against my lips, and instead of moving off my lap, kept kissing me. I felt my pants warming up, and I pulled back, concerned. Our legs were glowing with her green-and-gold-laced magic, and our pants were gone. Not needing any more encouragement, I grasped her hips and adjusted her position, lowering her slowly onto my cock. She was drenched, and I glided in smoothly.

With Serafina straddling me and the confines of the chair arms, it was difficult for me to find leverage to thrust. Not to be deterred, I lifted and lowered her using the strength of my arms to create the rhythm we needed. I could feel her body tightening around me as her pleasure heightened. I was pleased this position was giving her what she needed, but it left me wanting more. I lifted Serafina up and stood, sliding her onto the edge of the desk.

"You should lay back," I suggested. Serafina did, and I fell to my knees in front of her, unable to resist her glistening folds and making good on the promise from earlier. Her thighs squeezed

my face as I pushed her to her climax. Her body spasmed, and I slowly rose to standing.

Positioning my throbbing cock between her legs, I eased inside. Serafina gasped, and I felt her tighten. Her legs were against my chest. I tipped her hips up, changing the angle and intensifying her pleasure and mine as I thrust. Desperate for my own release now that Serafina had gotten hers, I drove myself into her, harder and faster.

The only thing Serafina did was whisper, "More."

One, two, on the third thrust I exploded into my orgasm, taking Serafina with me. "I love you," I gasped as spasms rolled through me.

"I love you," she replied and slid her legs down to dangle over the edge of the table so she could wrap her arms around me.

Satiated for the moment, my whole body tingled with the magic from the mating bond, which was proving the bond's demand for frequent physical contact was indeed a factor, not just hearsay. I used my magic to put our pants back on and to straighten out our clothing and Serafina's hair.

Taking a deep breath, I sat in the chair I had vacated and schooled my face into a serious expression. Sera was sitting on the edge of the desk. "You only mentioned one name for the war council," I said to Serafina.

She stuck her tongue out at me. "Well, I got distracted. But you're right. We need to focus. No more distractions."

"The good thing is I already know your list," I informed her.

Serafina's eyebrows shot straight up. "You do?"

I nodded. "Yes. The mating bond let me sense your list when you were initially thinking about it."

Tucking a wayward strand of hair behind her ear, Sera considered my words. "Can you 'sense' other things?"

Deciding the truth was my best solution, I responded, "Sort of. I know you had a bad dream while you were in the tub. You deliberately shared an image of what you wanted to wear this morning, and of course just now." I chuckled. "It's definitely boosting our sex drive."

"Hmmm," she mused. "Why are you getting things from me through the bond and it's not going the other way?"

"I learned how to wall myself off before I ever left Glass Oasis. I suspect I am going to have to consciously work on letting the barrier down for you to get more from me through the bond," I explained.

Then, she asked the question I expected. "How do I build my own wall, to keep private thoughts private?"

Counting to five, I released my breath, reminding myself that we were in this together. "I learned it as a self-defense mechanism. I thought we had agreed to not keep secrets from each other."

Serafina looked away, her shoulders slumped. "We did agree to that. But ... now is not the right time. I have tasks to attend to."

"Or it's the perfect time. Get everything out in the open now so that it won't color our interactions with others throughout the day," I cajoled.

Serafina barked a harsh laugh. "I promise I will tell you later tonight, but for now be grateful that it is not your burden to bear too." She took a deep breath. "To confirm we are indeed on the same page, my list of war council members is you, Lord McCormack, Thomas, Josiah, Valerie, and Ghilanna."

Even though I had known the names, now that Sera had spoken to them, I allowed myself to consider each person or Fae in depth. Lord McCormack was an obvious choice, given she was already acquainted with him and as far as I knew liked the aging noble. He was a close confidant of King Leonard's, which made him valuable to her. I wasn't sure Thomas was the best choice given his young age and as far as I knew minimal experience with war. As a palace guard not much older than Serafina, I did not think he had much worldly experience. Though the next names, Valerie and Josiah, reminded me that Thomas was also part of the faction of humans with direct ties to Solana. Both could be very useful given their interest in establishing a deeper relationship with the Fae.

Ghilanna was also easy to understand since she was one of Serafina's closest friends who was also a Fae. However, reviewing the list, I was not sure there was enough battle experience among the group to expect us to do the South justice. *We need at least two more people, or to replace two with individuals who have been in a battle.*

"What about Declan Green?" Serafina said at the same time I suggested, "How about Callyn?"

We smiled at each other. Sera's eyes lit up and I could visibly see her relaxing. Serafina spoke, her voice more confident than before. "Do you think adding two more would be too much? That puts us at eight. I would make nine."

I shook my head, declining to answer because Sera needed to learn to trust herself. Keeping my tone warm, I replied, "That's not a decision I can make. How many differing opinions do you want to have to wade through? Do you think all eight of those individuals need to be on the *war* council? If the answer is no but you still want to give them important roles, then perhaps making them official advisors is the best option. There's also the matter of your ladies-in-waiting. Both Ghilanna and Valerie came up during that discussion. As your ladies-in-waiting, you could still consult with them, but when it comes to the actual battle strategy, you won't have too many sides to sort through."

"Who would I remove from the list?" Serafina asked as she twisted her fingers together uncertainly.

"Are you truly asking for my opinion, or is that a rhetorical question?" I replied.

Serafina flicked my arm. "Yes, I want your opinion."

From her reaction, I knew that what we were communicating through the mating bond was still largely one-sided, Sera to me. I untied my hair and retied it to capture the loose strands my magic had missed. It was a delaying tactic, and both of us knew it, but I wanted to find the words to tactfully explain my thoughts. "Thomas, Valerie, Josiah, and Ghilanna have minimal battle experience," I started.

Serafina's face flushed. "Ghilanna has just as much as I do."

"Yes, I know that. But you asked for my opinion on who to remove from the list, so I am explaining it," I told her, keeping my tone neutral. When it was clear she was not going to interrupt again, I said, "It can be helpful to have a war council consist of people who will assess a battle situation quickly and provide viable action plans. My concern is not with their involvement with the initial planning. It is that once we are attacking Tanyth and adjusting on the fly, they could slow us down because we will have to take the time to explain things."

Serafina did not seem thrilled. She responded, "Won't you have to explain those very same things to me? Will I slow you down too?"

"Yes and no. The advantage you have over Thomas, Valerie, Josiah, and Ghilanna is I can pass on my knowledge to you through the mating bond. You will be able to understand far quicker than them because you can see how I analyze things," I replied. To my amazement, her emotions were not seeping through the bond, making it impossible for me to gauge if she was going to chop those four off her list or not.

"Lord McCormack, Declan, you, and Callyn," Serafina responded, mulling over the words. The list would put us at five. One could argue it's not enough, but I figured it was a good place to start.

"I will talk to each of them and Valerie, Josiah, Thomas, and Ghilanna. If I can find everyone. I might as well talk to them about advisory roles even if they will not be on the war council," Serafina said.

"You will have your work cut out for you today," I commented, half wishing I could accompany her. I knew that she needed to meet with these potential advisors on her own.

Serafina shrugged. "It is what it is. What are *you* going to be doing while I'm running around?"

Wanting to keep myself busy, I devised a plan and replied, "With your permission, I am going to meet up with Callyn."

Serafina sighed. "You don't need my permission to go see your friend. I am not your captor, Tristan. You are free to come and go as you please."

Before I could stop myself, I replied with the first words that came to mind. "Even as a snow leopard?" There had been fewer than five years in my life that I had been able to freely shapeshift without fear of discovery, and it weighed on me. The need to let that side of myself free once and for all. To be accepted for all of me, not just half.

Serafina's eyes widened, and I could see the muscles in her jaw twitch. "If you feel that is what you need to do, then yes. I love you. I, your wife, not your captor. I want to rule the South with you at my side, but I refuse to force you to be here if this is not where you feel you belong. However, I would recommend proceeding with caution if you are going to start wandering around as a snow leopard. None of the humans know you can shapeshift, and I would hate to see you wrongfully hunted down."

My chest tingled as I digested Sera's words. I reached out and snagged Sera's hand with mine, raising her knuckles to my lips and kissing them. "I want to be right here with you," I said firmly. "As for the shapeshifting, we could start by introducing me as a snow leopard during each of your meetings," I suggested.

Serafina laughed. "I thought the point of the meetings was for me to convince them to be on the war council, not terrify them."

I bristled at her laughter, then realized she was right. Neither one of us wanted to use scare tactics to get them to agree to be on her war council, which is precisely why I wasn't going with her in the first place. "What if we show them when we all meet? That way we can prepare them for it."

"Sure. Now, I really must get going if I have any hope of talking to three people in two hours," Serafina said, tugging her hand out of mine.

I stood and planted a quick kiss on her lips, then backed up, giving her space to get past me and over to the door.

Once Sera left, I considered what I would need to take with me to meet up with Callyn. Meeting with her outside of the Gaskal wall would put me far enough away that I would be out from underfoot of Sera and her informal meetings with the potential war council members, but not too far. Nolan and a pair of additional guards were waiting for me in the hallway. Except I didn't want a guard shadowing me today. Ensuring my safety in the palace or when I was around Serafina publicly was one thing, but it was difficult to be stealthy with a human guard, and I refused to tell the whole city every move I made.

I slowly opened the balcony doors that were double my height and almost entirely glass to prevent them from squeaking. When the gap was large enough, I slid through and used a small pick set to lock the door, thus ensuring no one would suspect where I had gone too quickly.

The balcony railing was pale gray stone, like the rest of the exterior of the palace. The rungs were simple flat slats with no ornamentation. The top of the railing was wider than my hand with a slight convex curve to it. Using my arms, I pulled myself onto the railing and then leaped to the ground below, my cloak flaring around me as my feet impacted the grass. Our rooms were on the third level of the palace, giving us a nice view over the top of the wall and making it challenging to reach us should someone be foolish enough to attack Serafina in her quarters. *Unless they used a long-range weapon.*

Drawing on my shadow magic to obscure me from view, I made my way along the edge of the building, hopped a low railing meant to deter people from loitering on this side of the palace, and then slipped through the open side gate. The guard watching the gate had stepped a few feet away and his back was turned, making it easy to slip past him. *I'll have to have a word with Declan. If I can get through, then Prince Tanyth could send an assassin, and we would be clueless.* It was one of the few times I wished I had learned how to make warding spells. Though Tanyth had not liked using them, relying instead on fear tactics to discourage intruders, I knew other Fae courts used them at the very least as intruder detection.

Ice gripped my spine as I realized that likely any assassination orders would fall squarely on Bane's shoulders. Friends for almost as long as I had known Callyn, Bane and I met while training at Embergate, and later he served as my second-in-command at Dorcha Palace. While I worked to hide my aversion to some of Tanyth's orders, Bane embraced them. Had I not been hiding my true self all those years, I wasn't sure if Bane and I would have stayed friends or become enemies. It would be foolish to assume that Bane would flip on Tanyth. He worshiped the prince, and since Travaran's death, there had been times where it had seemed as though Tanyth was grooming Bane to be his heir.

Very few among those living at Dorcha Palace would openly support Serafina. They were too afraid of Tanyth. After Callyn rescued me, I had had no way of keeping tabs on what was occurring beneath Ember Mountain, which meant it was impossible to determine if Fallon, Verrona, and the others were alive. *How many Fae did he kill in his anger after I "died"?* I pondered. *Unless he turned all of them to his side, like he did with Fiera.*

My throat tightened as I considered Fiera, Sera's fiery red-haired friend who had risked everything to save Serafina, despite the warning I had given her when we'd crossed paths in Lochlan Sgàile. I doubted Tanyth considered Fiera as little more than a prisoner, even if there really was a mating bond shared between them. What concerned me was whether Tanyth had woven a spell around her or had corrupted the bond between them to make her believe his story. I struggled to swallow the idea that Fiera—at least the Fiera Sera had spoken of—would have readily embraced Tanyth and his dark ways.

No matter which way I spun it, Fiera stood squarely in the middle of the conflict between Serafina and Tanyth. What would Serafina do if she was forced to fight or kill Fiera? Would she do what was necessary, or would years of friendship stay her hand and potentially cost her her life? The last thing I wanted to do was put my beloved mate in that position, but I knew all too well how unpredictable war could be and what it meant to be willing to go to any length despite the cost to oneself.

Sticking to the shadows, I made my way toward Wayside Inn, ducking into alleys to avoid being seen and weaving through the city streets past white and pastel-colored storefronts, staying off Helias Way, the main thoroughfare. When I was half a block away, I could sense Callyn through her magic in the room at the inn. Wayside Inn was a large building made out of a mix of wood and light-gray brick, which took up the better part of a block near the city gates. Not wanting to risk being recognized by anyone inside, I lightly tapped on the outside of her window with a tiny thread of magic. Confident she had gotten the message, I fell in behind a large wagon on its way out of the city. Guards stood at the massive gray stone city gates topped with large gold spheres, lazily giving each person or wagon a brief inspection and then letting them pass. For the most part, they didn't move from the post by the gate, which meant they could miss a lot of things, including that their queen's husband was leaving Gaskal. Once I was far enough past the gate that I was certain the guards were focused on the next wagon, I ditched my position at the back of the spice wagon and walked into the forest, then shifted into a snow leopard.

Prowling through the forest, the scent of pine mingling with the sweet scent of maple sap, I worked my way toward the meeting spot Callyn and I had used several times since our arrival in Gaskal. It was deep within the forest, making it less likely any of the humans from the city would venture out here. I leaped onto the large boulder and lay down, settling in to wait.

It didn't take long before I saw Callyn making her way on the deer trail. Her white hair was in two braids that bounced on her chest as she moved. In the shadowy forest light, her pale skin took on a grayish hue, a striking contrast to her purple eyes. She wore a tight-fitting black leather corset with an assortment of straps I couldn't figure out the purpose of. Her pants and boots were also black leather. A scabbard was belted around her waist with a sword and dagger.

"I got your message," Callyn said.

I shifted to Fae form and shrugged. "I knew you were in your room."

Callyn climbed onto the rock and sat down next to me. "Rumors have been flying around the city. Care to fill me in?"

"Sure. We think the Court of the Sun is preparing to attack the South, and King Leonard sent Serafina to get the *Bloodsong Grimoire*. It's supposed to help if we're fighting against Fae," I said. Callyn gave me a quizzical look. "Serafina wasn't told anything useful about what the book does. But that doesn't matter. When we were in the book's chamber, Tanyth showed up and wanted to exchange the book for King Leonard. Serafina agreed and handed over the book, then Tanyth killed the king and vanished."

Callyn's eyes widened. "I knew the king was dead, but there are two stories I keep hearing. One is that you killed the king, and the other is that he died in his sleep. Obviously, neither of those is correct."

I took a deep breath. "No, they're not. The one thing they did get right, though, is Serafina is now the Lady of the South."

"I felt tremors, though I am not sure if they were physical or magical. Did you feel those?" Callyn asked.

I shook my head. "No. However, it's likely what you felt was when Serafina touched the *Bloodsong Grimoire*. Her magic was unleashed, and the binding Tanyth put on her memories was destroyed."

Callyn eyes were wide. "The prophecy is true."

I rubbed my sweaty hands on my thighs. Saying these things out loud to Callyn made them all the more real. "I think so." *Does believing the prophecy is true help us?* The prophecy only said the Lost Fae Queen would face the end of time. It did not foretell what the outcome would be. Over the years, I found the only thing I could rely on was myself. *Be the best version of me.*

"Does she acknowledge that?" Callyn asked softly.

"I'm not sure. Honestly, I don't know if it is important that she acknowledges it right now. What is critical, though, is that we are taking the necessary steps to prepare the South for war. I have yet to determine if Prince Rhangil is a viable threat. What I do know for certain is Prince Tanyth most definitely is, and he has successfully acquired Dragonfang, Fleshrender, and the *Bloodsong Grimoire*."

Callyn shuddered. "Then we're doomed."

I swallowed, not expecting Callyn to utter those words and for me to have to be the one to encourage her to keep hope alive. "There must be a reason this is happening now. Her magic appears, and then Tanyth gets his hands on the third object. The end of time is not here yet. We still exist."

"You wanted to talk to me. Is there anything else?" Callyn asked, her voice shaky. I half expected her to leave without hearing my answer.

"Yes. I wanted to give you a heads-up that Serafina is going to ask you to be on her war council," I said.

Callyn laughed harshly. "Is that because you don't want to be the only Fae on the council? Or because she actually wants me on it?"

I rolled my eyes. "We are going to war with Tanyth. You and I are her best resources for what his strategies will be. Besides, I thought you were helping me get Serafina back because you also believe she can be the bridge between humans and Fae."

"I might have prayed that Serafina is the Lost Fae Queen, but until now I didn't believe the power Tanyth sought with the three objects was real. As much as it pains me to admit it, I don't think we are strong enough to face him, not with the power he holds with Fleshrender, Dragonfang, and the *Bloodsong Grimoire* united," she replied, her voice rough with emotion.

"I understand this is a lot to process, but please go to the palace and meet with Serafina. No matter what you believe the outcome will be, we need your help," I pleaded. I had never seen Callyn like this; she had always been my rock. *Now I'm going to have to be hers.* "Serafina has magic now too." *Untrained and untried, a risk to her allies as well as an unknown threat to our enemies.* I kept the darker thoughts to myself. They were the last thing Callyn needed to hear, not with her own doubts already casting long shadows over her.

"Fine, I will talk to Serafina, but I need some time to think. *Alone*," Callyn said firmly.

To respect her wishes, I shifted back to snow leopard and bounded away into the shadowy forest.

Eight

RETHYS

The distinctive footfall of leather boots on the dungeon stairs told me Fallon Leoydark Daralei was coming. Like many of the Fae employed by Prince Tanyth, Fallon had signed a blood contract to become an advisor in the Court of Dusk and had instead found himself as little more than a well-dressed slave.

Since Tristan Gilvrye's escape and Prince Tanyth's clear distraction, Fallon had resumed his daily visits that had ceased upon Serafina Wyantha Helias's arrival. He was different than most of the inhabitants of Dorcha Palace, caring and compassionate. *Much like his birth mother,* I mused. I found myself looking forward to his visits, much as I had enjoyed Meriel Leoydark's when she had sought sanctuary with me. They were two among a very small number of Fae I'd encountered throughout my life who treated me as an equal, not as a barbaric animal.

I chuckled to myself, running my tongue over my sharp teeth. There were times when behaving barbarically was entertaining, when a Fae or human deserved it. But unlike my brethren, I preferred to study and live in peace in my cave with my treasure hoard of books, gold, and jewels. *Perhaps that is why I am alive, and they are dead.*

Fallon, a brown-haired Fae with dark-tan skin, rounded the corner. He wore a dark-gray cloak with a hood drawn over his face, though I could see his features perfectly fine. The dim light in the dungeon could not hide anything from me.

"Good evening," Fallon said with a bow.

I blinked at him, not sure I was up to a candid discussion tonight.

"The prince grows restless," Fallon said, stepping close to the bars and staring into my bright gold eyes.

"He has been restless since Tristan escaped," I replied dismissively.

Fallon shook his head and the hood slid off. "This is different."

I considered his words and recent events. Tanyth had united the magic artifacts—*Bloodsong Grimoire*, Dragonfang, and Fleshrender—but had not yet used them. *This is the distraction I need.* I tucked the information away and considered my response. Telling Fallon too much could influence how the Lost Fae Queen prophecy was fulfilled, a risk I was unwilling to take.

I took a deep breath and exhaled, filling the cell with smoke. Fallon began coughing. I ignored his annoyed stare. It wasn't my problem he couldn't handle a little dragon smoke. *"Unlock the door."*

"What?" gasped Fallon, eyes watering and voice brittle.

I stepped forward, curling my tail around my feet, and gave him a toothy grin. *"Unlock the door."* This time I threaded magic into the order.

Eyes wide, Fallon lifted the key ring off his belt and unlocked the door to my cell, staring blankly at me.

I barreled past him, and Fallon's back slammed into the bars. *"Now lock the cell and go back upstairs. The illusion will work for three days."*

Confident Fallon would follow my instructions, I continued down the hallway. I paused at the stone with a faded image of a dragon head in the corner. With my right claw on it, I gathered my magic. *"Be ready,"* I warned Fallon, and then released the magic and vanished.

Nine

SERAFINA

Taking a deep breath, I rose from my seat in front of Declan Green's black-painted desk. Declan, the master of the guard, rose immediately, sending his bright-red cape swinging against his plate armor. As we stood next to each other, the top of Declan's cropped straw-colored hair was at the height of my chin.

"I appreciate your candor this morning, and I look forward to meeting with you and the war council later today," Declan said and then dropped into a deep bow.

"I will see you then," I replied, reminding myself to act like a queen. Shoulders and back straight and chin tipped up, I swept out of the office.

Thomas was waiting for me with a contingent of six guards. Two more than we'd had earlier. *I guess he took Tristan's request to heart,* I mused.

"Lord McCormack is busy presently. I thought it would be a good opportunity to explore the small armory that's just down the hall from Declan's office," Thomas said.

We halted in front of the armory. The heavy wooden door was open, but a locked, barred metal door prevented entry. Thomas removed a key from his belt and inserted it in the lock.

"Shouldn't I have my own set of keys?" I asked.

"Yes, and as far as I know, that's something on Lord John's list. Along with an extended tour so you know what the keys will unlock," Thomas explained.

A shiver of excitement went through me at the prospect of getting my own set of keys. *I can go anywhere I want.* It was a strange feeling to finally be free of the restrictions that had filled the past twelve years. Sure, my time in Jade Wilds was far better than what I had spent in Dorcha Palace as a prisoner, or even the past few weeks here in Gaskal, but until now I had had someone dictating what I could and couldn't do. Now, I was my own woman.

The tips of my fingers felt warm. I lifted them to my face and realized that my magic was spilling out of them. I buried my hands in the hidden pockets in my overskirt, hoping no one would notice. The last thing I needed was to scare my guards or cause mayhem inside the armory because I couldn't control my magic.

With a groan, the heavy metal gate swung inward and clanged into the gray stone wall. Thomas led me inside, and the rest of the guards stood watch in the corridor. The darkness closed in the farther we moved from the door. Decisively I pulled my hands out of my pockets and held them in front of me. Strands of green-and-gold magic swirled around them. I closed my eyes, imagining the room washed in Fae light. Thomas's gasp indicated that my magic had done *something*. I opened my eyes and was met with blinding white Fae light. My eyes watered from how bright it was. Warmth spread through me that I had believed in my own abilities and tried something new—and it worked.

"Can you...dim the light?" Thomas asked, his voice cracking.

I nodded, then realized he couldn't see my head moving. I focused on dimming it, and the Fae light slowly reduced intensity until it was bearable. "Better?" I asked.

"Absolutely," Thomas replied. "You know, there *are* lamps down here. I already had the flint out and everything."

I shrugged. "I wanted to experiment, and I figured you wouldn't mind."

Thomas ran his hand over his face. "I don't. As long as you're aware that I don't know anything about magic and cannot help you or stop you if you lose control."

My throat tightened because he was worried that I might lose control. *Is that something that could happen?* I'd have to ask Tristan. Thomas's cheeks were flushed and I realized he was waiting for an answer. My tongue felt like sandpaper in my mouth. Hoping my voice sounded normal, I replied, "Yes, I am aware."

Looking around the armory, I studied the wood-paneled wall in front of me. It contained a rack full of over one hundred identical silver-iron longswords. The hilts were wrapped with functional brown leather but otherwise unadorned. Above the longswords, displayed horizontally, were a double-headed axe and a halberd. The next wall had utilitarian brown leather scabbards and chain mail tunics on hangers strong enough to withstand the weight. There was a stack of silver-iron breastplates and a box of helmets. A whole set of shelves was dedicated to whetstones and tools to clean and take care of the various weapons and armor in the room.

The last wall held a few axes and different styles of swords, and empty brackets. It was obvious that the silver-iron longswords were what King Leonard had preferred his guards to have. Not that I could fault him for that decision. They were practical and, as far as swords went, easy to wield. They were perfect for people with varying skill sets—and expensive. The forge process for silver-iron was more complex than normal iron, and it required two types of ore.

I removed one of the silver-iron longswords and tested the edge with the pad of my thumb, confirming it was sharp. A tiny droplet of blood rolled down the sword's blade as it cut easily into my skin. Ignoring the blood, I gave the sword an experimental swing to check its balance. Satisfied with the result, I returned it to the rack.

"Everything seems to be in order in here," I said to Thomas.

Thomas smiled and agreed. "The master of the guard is good at his job. He conducts monthly inspections of the gear in here himself and twice a year, I believe, of the larger armory downstairs."

"Let's go meet up with Lord McCormack," I said. I would have loved nothing more than to try out one of the silver-iron swords in a sparring match or against a training dummy, but if I had, I would've run out of time to conduct my meetings to create the war council.

After exploring the armory and meeting with Lord McCormack, I desperately needed to pee and wanted a few moments to myself to digest what I had learned. The simplest location that would accommodate both needs was my residence.

"Thomas, I would like to return to my rooms for a break, then we can continue with the meetings," I informed him as we walked down the hallway. I noticed the floor changing from stone back to polished wood as we moved toward the residence and away from more public areas. Occasionally, we would pass a painting—not the formal portraits that were downstairs, but scenes from the royal family's everyday lives over the centuries the Helias family ruled the South. I was certain we were on the opposite side of where my residence was, though it was difficult to tell since the stone-walled palace halls were nearly identical. Aside from the paintings, they looked much the same, making me realize that I needed to spend time getting to know my way around better. Then I wouldn't have to rely on others when I wanted to find something.

We reached the residence and Thomas, along with two of the six guards, did a quick sweep of the rooms before motioning for me to enter. I sighed when I realized this was going to be my new normal, especially after Tristan had shared his thoughts on how dismal the security had been until now. The only solace I had was that if it became truly unbearable to have that many guards as queen, I had the authority to order them to leave. *It would anger Tristan,* I reminded myself and vowed to only use it as a last resort.

I walked into the entryway and past the tall columns. With each step, I relaxed more as the weight of the meetings and my responsibilities momentarily lifted. Thomas stationed himself inside the front door and ordered the rest of the guards to wait in the hallway. My bladder clenched painfully, and I sprinted for the bathroom, petrified of peeing on myself. Relief coursed through me as I sat on the toilet and relieved myself.

Washing my hands, I froze when I heard a slight creak. "Thomas?" I called softly, my imagination running wild. Keeping my movements slow, I bent over and unstrapped the dagger from around my ankle, then crept to the bathroom door and peered around the edge. Through the wide-open windows, I could see a brown-cloaked intruder nimbly climbing over the balcony railing, unaware I had heard them. Magic tingled at my fingertips, but I ignored it. The dagger was firmly in my grip, a weapon I knew how to use. Sneaking into the shadowy corner at the head of the bed, I watched and waited. I wanted to know who was breaking into my room and why. If I attacked before they were in the room, then they would likely escape the way they came, and all I would know is that the guards on the palace wall and gate were failing me.

Muscles taut, I quieted my thoughts and focused on the task: catching them off guard. With the hood tugged down an excessive amount, it was impossible to tell who it was, though based on stature alone I had a nagging suspicion it was a Fae.

The intruder's back was turned, their focus on quietly closing the windows and positioning the drapes. Sprinting toward them, I lunged forward, slamming them into the glass windows.

The sound was muffled by the heavy curtains, reducing the odds that Thomas would hear anything going on. The intruder thrust their elbow back, and it caught me on the lower part of my ribs. I winced but kept my hold on the other arm, yanking it between us. I knew from experience the position was uncomfortable. Gripping the dagger, I held it to the intruder's throat.

"Who are you?" I shouted.

A rush of booted feet was all the warning I got before the bedroom door slammed against the wall and someone flipped a switch, turning the oil lamps along the wall up to their highest setting. Blinking in the sudden brightness, I kept my grip firm. The intruder shifted under my hands, but I refused to allow the guards to distract me. Thomas and two other guards advanced on us. When I was confident the intruder was under the guards' control, I released my grip and stepped back.

Exhaling the breath I had forgotten I was holding, I backed up till my legs bumped against the bed, and I instinctively sat down. Thomas maneuvered the intruder around so they were facing me, then forced them onto their knees. Another guard yanked the hood and mask off.

I felt the color drain from my face as I gazed in shock. "Fiera?"

Her beautiful red hair had been roughly chopped to chin length; a dark-purple bruise surrounded her right eye and upper cheek. She also had bruises around her throat, as though someone had tried to choke her. Fiera's green eyes were dull, and her mouth was drawn. Sadness welled up in me as I realized that my friend was not here as an assassin, but likely to escape whatever hell Tanyth had subjected her to.

A shudder rippled through me as I recalled fighting in the arena, starving and without a weapon. The last time I'd seen

Fiera was at the banquet the day after my wedding. My friend had claimed to be happily married *and* mated to Tanyth.

"Are you all right?" asked Tristan through the bond.

Pressing my lips together, I averted my eyes from Fiera. *"I discovered Fiera breaking into our bedroom."*

"What?" snarled Tristan. His reaction felt so real I would've sworn he was here in the room with me. I half expected him to use a star portal and appear.

"I'm fine. Thomas and I have it under control," I replied in what I hoped was a reassuring tone and that it came through his end as vividly as his snarl had. *"There's no reason for you to come back. Enjoy your time with Callyn, and I'll see you later."* Not wanting to give Tristan an opening to argue, I returned my attention to Thomas and ignored the frustration Tristan was sending my way through the bond.

"I couldn't take it anymore. I had to get away from Tanyth," Fiera said, her voice breaking as tears trickled down her cheek.

Taking in Fiera's appearance and her tone, I wanted to believe what she was saying, but it was a struggle to do so. Less than a week ago, she was here with Tanyth, happy and not showing any indicator of distress.

"Why did you come here of all places? You could have gone to Jade Wilds. Commander Meriel would have willingly offered you protection."

Lower lip quivering, Fiera peered up at me. "Because I thought if anyone would understand, it would be you. You were his prisoner too, Serafina."

Fists clenched, I willed away the memories that rose to the surface. Fiera was right. I did understand, at least to some extent, why she had come here. I was one of the only prisoners who had ever escaped the Court of Dusk and lived to tell the tale. Unlike Tristan and Callyn, who had been originally hired by Tanyth to work for him, Fiera and I had both been captured against our will.

I needed time to think about Fiera and determine what I was going to do. "Thomas, please escort Fiera to a secure room where we can hold her. Make sure she has food and water. I want four guards with her at all times."

Thomas bowed. "Yes, Your Majesty." He motioned for the guards to gather Fiera and led the way out of my bedroom. I knew Thomas would return shortly and was confident guards were posted in the hallway for my protection.

Hands shaking, I walked into the living area and sat down on the blue velvet couch facing the dark fireplace. I desperately wanted to believe that Fiera had come here on the run from Tanyth, but if my time in the Court of Dusk and here in the South had taught me anything, it was that not everything was as it seemed. I was also acutely aware that Tanyth could have found a way to destroy the mating bond between him and Fiera or even put her under his dark magic.

"Your Majesty, are you all right?" called Violet's voice. I heard the door click softly shut and realized the guards must have let her in.

I patted the sofa cushion next to me. "Not really. Come join me," I replied with a forced smile.

Concern plain on her face, Violet settled herself on the couch. "Was that Prince Tanyth's wife I just saw being escorted in the hallway?" she asked.

I nodded, and she took my hand in hers and gave it a comforting squeeze. "Do you need me to get Tristan?"

I shook my head. "Thank you for the offer, but he knows. I told you this morning about our mating bond. Well, it allows us to communicate mind-to-mind, and he was the first person I informed that she was here."

"I see. Have you had lunch? You look pale and in need of nourishment," Violet replied.

I giggled, and my stomach gurgled. "I haven't, and you're right. I'm famished. Maybe we can go see Cookie?"

Violet smiled warmly. "That would be wonderful."

We headed down to the kitchen for a quick midday lunch, accompanied by several guards.

Francis Cookie, the head cook, greeted us with a broad smile. "I've been expecting you, Your Majesty and Lady Violet."

I raised my eyebrows, wondering how Cookie had known, unless Violet had sent a message ahead of us.

She waved her hand, beckoning us into her domain and a seat at the small table. Sure enough, there were two place settings, each with a cup of water and a steaming bowl of stew waiting for us. "No one sent word to prepare your food and send it somewhere in particular. Since it's well after lunchtime and you usually don't miss a meal ... As for having enough for two, well, it's easy enough to find someone who is hungry around here."

I smiled. Cookie was right. My habits were predictable, and there were enough people living within the palace compound that nothing ever went to waste. Sliding into the seat, I murmured, "Thank you."

Violet sat across from me, and we both dug into the meal. I took a spoonful of stew. Small bite-sized pieces of venison, carrots, potatoes, onions, and some other vegetables I couldn't name were in a thick, savory broth. It was delicious.

Cookie brought a basket of rolls over, and I eagerly helped myself to one, alternating bites of stew with bites of the fresh roll. The bowl was half empty, and I set down my spoon.

"Are you already full?" Cookie asked, eyeing the bowl and then my face.

I shook my head. "No, I'm going to eat more. I just wanted to slow down. Have you started preparations for the coronation meal?"

Cookie's nose twitched. "From my discussions with Lord John, there isn't supposed to be a meal."

"I thought that was one of the things we weren't able to skip?" I replied.

Cookie shrugged. "You'll have to take that up with Lord John. Unless you want to make your own choice and host a banquet regardless of what your steward recommends."

The cook had a valid point; as queen, I could do as I pleased. However, I was confused that the banquet that historically accompanied a coronation was not on the agenda. "Is there a less formal meal instead?" I asked aloud.

Cookie pursed her lips and sorted through a stack of papers on the table that I believed was her desk, filled primarily with recipe books. "Yes, here it is," she said, waving a small piece of paper in the air. "'Passed hors d'oeuvres after coronation,'" Cookie read from the paper.

I sighed in relief. The formal meal was being replaced with a greater opportunity to mingle with the guests instead of arranging us at a large table, making it difficult to talk to anyone other than the two or three people seated next to me. "Good. I will keep the steward's plan in place."

I dug into the rest of the stew, not wanting to let it get cold, as Violet mopped up the last of her broth. As I took the last bite, Cookie approached me again. "Is there any special dish that you would like me to make for you?"

"Now?" I asked, wondering why she wanted to make me more food after I was full.

Cookie shook her head. "No. It does not need to be right now. I know you spent years with the Fae. I wasn't sure if they had anything you missed eating. Or even if your husband had a request. I'd be happy to learn how to make something new or adapt one of my existing recipes to meet your needs."

Her request caught me off guard. I hadn't spent much time thinking about food, beyond ensuring I consumed enough to meet my body's needs. "I will have to think about it and get back to you."

"Very well," Cookie said and bustled off again.

I sat back against the seat and raised my arms above me, stretching. This morning, when I had last seen Violet, she was taking space to think things over. I couldn't decide if I should ask her or if I should wait until she broached the subject herself.

Violet carefully wiped off her fingers and dabbed at her lips with her napkin, then set it down. "I will continue to be your lady-in-waiting and will accept that means I need to learn how to fight to defend myself—and you—from any danger. With Fiera's appearance, it is clear that you need me, and I don't want to let you down by not being there again."

I stretched my hand across the table, and Violet set hers in mine. I squeezed gently. "Thank you. I have much to learn from you as well. I am still figuring out how to navigate being queen, and your experience and insight as a noblewoman would be welcome."

Thomas arrived at that moment, snagging our attention. "I received a message that Ghilanna is waiting for you in your residence. I know she was on your list of people to meet with today."

"Thank you," I replied. Meeting with Ghilanna could serve multiple purposes now. I was hoping she could interview Fiera to gather more information. Returning my attention to the cook, I said, "Cookie, thank you so much for your time and the delicious food."

Violet and I stood up in unison. Cookie gave me an encouraging smile and then disappeared into the depths of the kitchen.

With Violet at my side and the three guards at my back, we followed Thomas to meet Ghilanna at my residence. The purpose of the meeting had morphed as the day progressed. She had ignored my grandfather's orders and followed me to the South and the city of Gaskal. I was confident that Ghilanna would agree to my ideas. If anything had become clear since my arrival at the palace, it was that Ghilanna had my back, no matter what anyone else said. Two of the roles, advisor and lady-in-waiting, would require her to have her own set of rooms in the palace.

I found solace in the thought of having my best friend nearby, especially if Tristan and I had to be in different places to tackle matters of the kingdom. Either role would also allow Ghilanna to freely come and go in the palace as she pleased. *Is King Leonard going to roll in his grave knowing that Fae are serving as royal advisors and living in the palace?*

The guards held open the doors and Violet and I strolled inside. A Fae female with dark-brown skin awaited me on the dark-blue sofa by the fireplace, her black hair braided back from her face and ending in a mass of tight curls around her shoulders. Her head turned, and her coffee-colored eyes met mine.

"Good afternoon, Your Majesty and Lady Violet," Ghilanna said.

I rolled my eyes at her use of my title. "Are we being formal now?" I teased.

Ghilanna shrugged. "I'm just following the human customs. Besides, Lady Violet is with you, as are your guards."

Violet blushed in what I assumed was embarrassment. I patted her arm reassuringly, then replied, "When I'm here in my own quarters with friends, I prefer to be informal. Which is what I have asked Violet, Thomas, and a few others to do." Moving over to the couch and sitting on it, I hugged Ghilanna. "I'm glad you're here. There is a lot I want to discuss."

Ghilanna smiled. "I expected that was the case. Where do you want to begin?"

Violet was hovering just behind the couch. I waved her over. When she was seated across from us in a dark-blue chair that matched the couch, I said solemnly, "Fiera was captured sneaking into my bedroom."

"What?" gasped Ghilanna, "Did she attack you?"

I lifted my hands between us. "I'm fine. I promise. Fiera is claiming that she has escaped from Tanyth, and he destroyed their mating bond."

"Is she telling the truth?" Ghilanna inquired.

Brows narrowing, I replied, "I have no idea. I *want* to believe her. Tanyth is absolutely capable of what she is claiming. I have lived through it myself. But I don't know how to sense a mating bond. I also think I am too close to it. Having been Tanyth's prisoner, I can sympathize with Fiera, and I'm worried that is going to cloud my judgment. Would you be willing to talk to her for me? Find out what she wants?"

"I would be happy to question Fiera," Ghilanna said, though her tone said otherwise. Fiera had been Ghilanna's friend for years before I'd shown up at Jade Wilds; I could only imagine how difficult it would be to interrogate your best friend.

I sighed in relief. The dark part of me had doubted Ghilanna would agree. "Good, that's settled then. Later, Thomas can show you where Fiera is being held," I said. Taking a deep breath, I moved on to the next topic. "I have decided that to help improve safety measures, having ladies-in-waiting who are skilled fighters would be prudent. I know you are not interested in waiting on me or doing many of the traditional duties. However, when I go out in public or to meetings outside of these rooms, I would like to have more protection. If you're willing, you will be a critical part of that. My plan is that you will look the part and then be there to protect me if the need arises. Violet has agreed to start training to learn how to defend herself."

"Yes, I am happy to be your lady-in-waiting or any other position you feel I would be able to aid you. My only desire is to help you navigate your new role as Lady of the South," Ghilanna explained.

I smiled as warmth spread through me. It felt good to have Ghilanna's unwavering support. "I'll take that to mean you would also serve as one of my advisors?"

Ghilanna chuckled. "Of course I will serve as an advisor."

I blew out my breath in relief and cast a glance at Violet. *There is no reason to ask Violet to leave. She will be privy to this information soon enough.* Plunging onward, I said, "Excellent. A few days ago, Thomas and I went back to my parents' house looking for more answers, and we came across Solana's copy of *Bedtime Tails*. Except hers contains what I believe are new prophecies." My mother's house was also where I met Valerie and Josiah, the two city-goers whose families had been taught skills ranging from self-defense to healing by Solana. The two of them led a group of humans, who recently started calling themselves the Copper Wolves, who felt that Fae and humans should coexist peacefully as they once had centuries ago.

A worn brown leather satchel sat on the table between us and Violet. I reached into it and pulled out the book, and the strange crown came out with it. I placed the crown on the table and offered the book to Ghilanna.

Violet inspected the crown as Ghilanna skimmed through the book. Out of the corner of my eye, I noticed when her finger stopped moving on the story about the dragon. I recited the story in my head as Ghilanna's finger ran over the words and then hovered over the illustration.

My eyes widened as I made the connection that had been right in front of me all along.

"Rethys is real, and he's alive and in Dorcha Palace," I said, my voice soft.

Face blanching, Violet yanked her hand back from where she was tracing the dragon on the crown. Ghilanna cast me a confused look and said, "Rethys is real?"

I tugged on my earlobe as I considered my response, then replied, "Yes. I saw him fight in the arena. I believe Tristan had an arena battle against Rethys too."

Ghilanna tipped the book so I could see the illustration depicting the dark-green dragon with black belly scales standing over a treasure hoard of gold and jewels. A shiver crept down my spine as I remembered Tristan's description of his fight in the arena, the sand clinging to his sweat-dampened skin as he faced Rethys with Travaran at his side.

Ghilanna's voice drew me out of my thoughts, and she read the story aloud.

"The treasure of Rethys is hunted far and wide by seekers of fame and fortune. Hundreds have perished in their quest, intent only on their personal gain.

"One day, a Fae accidentally stumbled upon Rethys's cave, seeking shelter from the storm. He saw the sleeping dragon and could feel the warmth radiating off the creature. The Fae curled up in a ball against Rethys's side and fell asleep.

"When he awoke, the first thing he noticed was a mark on his arm. The light in the cave was dim, so he stepped outside to inspect it. In the sunlight, the mark became clear. It was a tattoo of a dragon.

"'You are the first to come here, not to steal, but because you needed shelter. If you are ever in need, you can summon me through the mark. If your heirs are worthy, they too will be able to summon me through the mark, if they can earn it,' Rethys spoke into the Fae's mind.

"'Thank you,' the Fae said."

Moments ticked by. The silence grew between the three of us. A quick glance at Violet told me she was at a loss for words, not that I could blame her—the humans didn't have prophecies, and as far as I knew, most didn't believe that magical creatures like dragons were real. I was struggling to keep my thoughts away from the memories of the battles in Tanyth's arena.

"Have you seen the tattoo on Tristan's back?" Ghilanna finally asked.

"Tristan doesn't have a tattoo," I replied quickly, trying to think through the various times I'd seen him naked. I blushed, realizing I had no idea if he had one. Those times I had been far too focused on other body parts.

Ghilanna flicked me on the leg. "I'm pretty sure he does, on his lower back. I heard the guards who escorted him to the dungeon gossiping after his arrest."

"Does it matter if he has one? Tattoos are common enough among humans and Fae," I responded, leaning heavily against the back of the sofa.

Ghilanna replied, "This story talks about a Fae being marked by a dragon tattoo. I was just wondering if it's referring to Tristan."

Violet snorted in disbelief. "I thought these were just stories that had been made up about Fae. How do you expect anyone to believe that the story about Rethys, the dragon you're both claiming is real, is tied to Tristan because of something his ancestor did centuries ago?"

Amusement filled me that Violet's reaction was like my own. Though I knew Rethys was real, the part about there being a connection between Tristan and Rethys was ridiculous. However, Ghilanna's expression was serious, and I wanted to make sure I explored matters she felt were important, even if I didn't understand them. "I will ask Tristan about his tattoo when I see him again."

Satisfied with my answer, Ghilanna turned to the next page. "This is also Solana's handwriting," Ghilanna pointed out. I peered over her shoulder, recognizing the writing and the words on the page. I followed along as Ghilanna read the lines aloud, presumably for Violet's benefit.

"TRUTH IS IN THE BLOOD
BEFORE THE WINTER FLOOD
TWO SPELLS WILL BIND
FIGHT THE END OF TIME."

Ghilanna stared at the page for a while. I was about to prompt her to speak when she did so on her own. "Given that this is Solana's writing and most of what she shared with Josiah and Valerie had to do with Serafina, I am going to go out on a limb and assume this poem or prophecy is the same. Remember how you told me that the two most important things you learned as an heir had to do with being an heir of blood?"

Violet leaped out of her seat excitedly. When Ghilanna and I both focused on her, she blushed and sat back down in her chair. "Sorry," she mumbled.

I smiled. "I can tell you have something to add. I would love to hear your thoughts on these matters. You likely know far more about the human culture and traditions of the South than we do."

"Okay," Violet said hesitantly. "There have been a few times over the years where my father has made vague references to the two rituals that an heir of the South is required to do. I remember what he said because I always thought it sounded gross. My father spoke of both rituals requiring the heir of the South to make an offering of their blood. That a pinprick wasn't sufficient. It had to be a whole dagger slice across the hand. When I first heard him say it, I didn't believe him, but then I met King Leonard and saw the scar across the palm of his left hand."

Ghilanna's fingers twitched on the book, and I could feel her body tense. "With your information as support, I believe we're on the right track, and that the reference to 'truth is in the blood' and 'two spells will bind' refers specifically to Serafina as the heir of blood and the two rituals—which we now know were binding spells—fully tying you to the South," Ghilanna explained.

Violet nodded excitedly, lightening my mood slightly. "Since I met you, Serafina, I have been trying to learn more about Fae. I even found a copy of *Bedtime Tails* and have been reading it. There's a story that mentions the end of time." Violet paused, tapping her thigh with her fingers in thought. Suddenly, she snapped her fingers. "I remember. It was the Lost Fae Queen story."

"You have an aptitude for this," Ghilanna told Violet kindly. Warmth spread through me that Ghilanna was going out of her way to make Violet feel a part of our group. It was needed, especially if we were going to trust one another if there was another attempt on my life.

"What does all of this mean?" I pressed.

Ghilanna absently twirled one of her curls around her finger as she replied, "If we're right, then Solana's words support the theory that you are the one destined to fight the end of time."

My back stiffened, and a heaviness settled in my stomach as dread filled me. Why was everyone so quick to assume that I was the Lost Fae Queen? "I'm only half-Fae. Shouldn't that disqualify me?" I muttered under my breath. If Ghilanna heard me, she showed no indication. *How am I supposed to fight whatever the end of time is if I can't even use my magic properly?*

The raspy sound of pages flipping filled the room as Ghilanna continued to look through the book. The turning pages paused, and she read aloud:

"Table awash in gold
The blood rises within
Building the bridge
Following the compass
The blessing will come
Thwarting the mess
The courts will be renewed."

Peering over her shoulder, I saw a rough sketch in colored pencil of a yellow rectangle and a circle on top.

"Oh!" I gasped. "The crown appeared when I was doing the gold mine ritual." Violet snagged it off the table and offered it to Ghilanna. The crown had a wide gold base with four points, like a compass. Three of the points had detailed depictions of Fae creatures: a unicorn, a griffin, and a dragon. The fourth had a massive square emerald set with two smaller emeralds framing it.

Ghilanna set the book down and took the crown Violet was offering, running her fingers over each piece. "This crown is exquisite," she murmured.

"Why did it show up during the gold mine ritual? I also don't understand why a crown that clearly is of Fae origin would have anything to do with a human gold mine," I said, hoping Ghilanna would have answers. Violet looked just as confused as I did. *Commander Meriel would know.* I could send her a message, though I wasn't sure it was something the commander would respond to through a letter.

"I don't know why it showed up now or how it's tied to the gold mine. But this is something we should share with Josiah and Valerie. It's possible Solana told them something that is not written in this book or anywhere else," Ghilanna said.

"I can meet with them tonight," I said.

Ghilanna frowned. "I would highly recommend *not* going yourself. Serafina, you are now a queen. Traipsing around the city for meetings alone with the Copper Wolves is dangerous."

I snorted. "Now you say it's dangerous, but a few days ago it was fine?"

Ghilanna rolled her eyes and huffed. "Circumstances have changed. We weren't at war, and Tanyth hadn't murdered a king. The semantics of you going into the city versus summoning someone for a meeting are quite different. Your subjects could also take it wrong if they see you conducting a personal visit with a few people in the city and not doing the same for everyone else."

Violet chimed in. "Ghilanna is right. It's not safe for you or for them."

I sighed. They had valid points. I was certain Thomas would agree too if I asked his opinion. "Will Josiah and Valerie be willing to meet in the palace?" *When I asked previously, they wouldn't.*

"I will ask and see what they say," Ghilanna replied.

I ran my fingers over the smooth leather of my pants. I still needed to meet with Callyn today *and* give Lord John my list of advisors on the war council. Which meant I didn't have much time to spend with Ghilanna. *I must start somewhere*, I reminded myself. Taking a deep breath, I took Ghilanna's hands in mine, meeting her gaze. "Before you leave, will you teach me how to use my magic?"

"Of course. I thought you'd never ask," Ghilanna replied eagerly.

Violet rose from her seat and smiled. "This is my cue to retire for the afternoon. I'll leave the two of you to the magic lesson." When she got to the end of the couch, she turned back toward us. "Thank you for including me, Serafina. It means a lot."

"You're very welcome," I replied.

I heard a knock on the door. I hastily extinguished the ball of green-and-gold magic hovering in the air, then realized that I had no reason to hide my magic. *Everyone in the palace knows I have magic now.* It was going to take time to get used to it being common knowledge.

Ghilanna stood up and opened the door, then called to me, "I will see you later, Serafina."

"See you!" I responded, wondering who had shown up that Ghilanna felt like she had to leave. Technically, as one of my ladies-in-waiting, she had every right to stay. *Maybe Tristan can continue my magic lessons tonight.*

Lord John passed by Ghilanna as she departed. I couldn't blame her for not wanting to stick around. He walked over till he was standing in front of the couch where I sat. "Violet told me you had asked Ghilanna to give you magic lessons this afternoon. I am glad to see you are learning to use your magic."

I swallowed, not sure I could believe that he was *glad* about anything related to magic.

"There are matters we must attend to, and there is only so much time in each day," he continued. "Thomas updated me on the progress you've made in creating the war council. I was hoping to take you to King Leonard's chambers before you attend your last meeting. I want you to see some of his possessions, as well as become familiar with how to find the room in case you wish to access it on your own. He assigned your residence with the full intention that this would be where you live. Of course, as queen, the choice is yours."

I gave him an amused glance, wondering what my grandfather's chambers were like that the steward was implying I would not want to live in them. *It's not like I have too many memories of him that grief would prevent me from living in his rooms.* Another thought came to me: Lord John expected me to meet with Callyn, yet here he was taking me to do *another* task and, therefore, eliminating the time I could be using for the meeting.

Lord John stood up as though we were leaving immediately. I frowned. This was exactly a situation where I wanted Violet and Ghilanna with me, not only for extra protection, but also because they were females I trusted to keep things to themselves should I come across anything of a sensitive nature within King Leonard's chambers.

"Excuse me," I said, earning me a dismayed stare from the steward. "Ghilanna and Violet need to come too."

Eyes narrowed, the steward looked at me, then sighed. "As you wish."

I strolled over to the door and tugged it open, sticking my head into the hallway. Thomas was there; apparently Lord John had given him a heads-up that we'd be going somewhere. "I know Ghilanna just left, and Violet is in her rooms. Can you send for them?"

Thomas nodded and gave orders to two of the guards in the hallway. They dashed off in opposite directions to deliver my message. Faster than I expected, the guards returned with Violet and Ghilanna in tow.

Ghilanna gave me an amused look when she stepped back into the residence. "Ready for another lesson already?" she teased.

I shook my head. "Sorry, this is a different matter. We are going to King Leonard's chambers, and I thought it would be a prime opportunity for the two of you to come along and offer extra protection and discretion."

Violet nodded. "Of course I will accompany you." Though she hadn't had any training yet, I was pleased at her response.

"I will come if you wish it, or I could use the time to interview Fiera. Your choice," Ghilanna replied. She had a valid point, and with Thomas and Violet in the king's chambers with me and guards stationed outside, adding one more to our party would not have much of an impact.

"Why don't you interview Fiera, and then we can catch up after I finish at the king's chambers," I said.

"Okay, I'll see you in a bit," Ghilanna said, and let herself back out.

Lord John led the way to King Leonard's chambers, his gait slow but purposeful. They were on the third floor, just like mine, except they were on the south side and mine were in the east. The steward paused at a door. It looked like any other door we'd passed in the hallway. He removed a ring of keys from his belt and inserted a large gold key into the door. The lock clicked, and the door swung open. Once Thomas and the other guards did a quick sweep of the room, Lord John gestured for us to go inside. Violet was right on my heels, and Thomas took a post inside the room next to the door with the rest of the guards remaining in the hallway.

"Now that you're here, there are several things I want to bring to your attention. The first is your grandfather's private weapon collection." Lord John pointed to one of the walls, which was covered in an assortment of weapons, primarily swords. "Since these rooms are now yours to do with as you wish, you can decide to keep anything in here or move it wherever you would like. If you do not personally want his weapons, I would recommend returning them to the armory. That way, should you change your mind, they will be readily available," Lord John explained.

"Okay," I said. Deciding what to do with my grandfather's weapons was not high on my list for the foreseeable future. While Ghilanna might have had ideas about the weapons, I knew it was out of Violet's expertise.

"The next thing is to show you where the genealogies are. Given the nature of the books, they are kept here in the king's chambers to ensure they are preserved for all future rulers," Lord John said.

My interest piqued when he said genealogy. One of the questions I hadn't found the answer to despite searching the entire royal library was whether the Helias bloodline had ties to the other human kingdoms. I had learned at one of the prewedding banquets that my grandmother, Queen Glenora, was the daughter of King Hanover, Lord of the West. Which made me a great-granddaughter and theoretically in line for the West's throne, though I knew King Hanover had far more living relatives than I did. The chances were higher that I would perish and King Hanover would take over the South, not the other way around.

Lord John pointed to a bookcase that had over twenty matching burgundy books. I inspected them. Volume numbers were stamped on the spines in gold. "I'm assuming volume twenty is the most current," I said.

"Yes," Lord John confirmed. "Now, before you start examining the genealogies, I have one more matter to discuss. The *Bloodsong Grimoire*. It is your responsibility to keep it safe."

I gulped, guilt rising. "It was stolen by Prince Tanyth." Nervously, I studied the steward's face to gauge his reaction.

Concern lined his face, though the anger I had expected was not visible.

"That's unfortunate. The *Bloodsong Grimoire* is reported to hold the secret of how to defeat even the most powerful of Fae. Without it, we will be at a significant disadvantage when facing the Court of Dusk," Lord John replied.

I debated revealing that the words from the book were visible on my body. I doubted it would help matters at that moment and decided to keep that information to myself. *It will only cause more problems.*

Lord John clears this throat, and I met his gaze. "I will let you take whatever time you need to explore these rooms. There is far more here than the few items I mentioned."

"Thank you," I replied, wondering if his words were a warning that I didn't have much time to explore or merely pointing out that I now had access to a wealth of information that I had only to take the time to see.

When the steward departed, Violet relaxed and wandered around the room, exploring it more. "Where do you want to start?" she asked.

A benefit of bringing her along that I hadn't considered was she could help me browse the books for anything useful. "I'm going to look at the most recent genealogy. I don't know how familiar you are with the South's royal family tree."

Violet shrugged. "Not terribly familiar. Is there anything in particular you're looking for?"

"At the wedding festivities, I learned that Queen Glenora was the daughter of the Lord of the West. I am curious how frequently the bloodlines of the other three human kingdoms mingled in my family or if it was just the one instance," I replied.

"Hmm," Violet murmured. "Honestly, I never paid much attention to where men and women who married into the royal family came from when I was studying the history of the South. But I'm sure it would be notated somewhere in the books."

"My thoughts precisely. I'm going to start with the most recent one—volume twenty. Do you want to start with nineteen?" I inquired.

"Sure, and I can make a list if we find any, that way we won't have to remember the details," Violet offered.

I smiled at her thoughtfulness, and I removed volumes nineteen and twenty from the bookshelf. Handing Violet volume nineteen, I peered around the room until my gaze settled on a pair of chairs against the wall. I chose one and settled into it, quickly absorbed into the task as I flipped through the pages and found a list of names that included dates of birth and death, as well as a list of spouses, the location they came from, and any children produced. Starting at the back, I flipped past the blank pages until I found the most recent entries. My name was the last entered. On the page before mine, there were entries for my cousins, who would have been younger than me had they still been alive.

I reached the page that had King Leonard Helias and his spouse, Queen Glenora. Sure enough, there was a note about a princess of the West. Now that I knew what I was hunting for, I skimmed the pages more quickly. I was at the very front of the book when I came across a similar note. "Princess of the North." I counted the number of generations between me and the bloodline tying us to the Lord of the North: eight. There was a lot of dilution in the bloodline that ran through my veins. *Does it matter?* I had no idea, or if it even meant anything that I had confirmed I was a descendant of not just one but three of the human kingdoms. I wanted to look at the other books and see just how many times the kingdoms had mingled, but I was all too aware of how limited my time was. I still needed to talk to Callyn, and I also was supposed to be writing down my findings. Glancing over at Violet, I saw her piece of paper was blank, and she was engrossed in studying the pages of volume nineteen.

I replaced volume twenty in its designated spot on the bookcase, and my eyes traveled to the desk, then back along the
bookcase, reading the titles on the book spines. *He has a copy of*
Bedtime Tails? Disconcertment coursed through me. I tugged
the book off the shelf and flipped through it, almost dropping
it when I realized it also held my mother's writing. *Just like the*
copy from my parents' house. A strange thing for a Fae-hating king to
possess. Another question to ask Josiah and Valerie when I see them.
Not wanting to waste more time thinking about a book that was
already familiar to me, I shoved it back on the shelf and turned
my attention to the desk.

Violet seemed content with the genealogy book, and Thomas
was alert at his post by the door. I eyed the large, comfort-
able-looking mahogany chair with worn brown leather, behind
a desk that was very similar to the one in my suite of rooms. I
approached it and noticed what I assumed was a journal sitting
on the desk. In fact, several similar books were stacked in a neat
pile on one end. *My grandfather is dead. There is no reason not to*
read his journals, I told myself.

I sat in the chair and opened the journal to the page the red
ribbon bookmark was on. It was dated the day of his death.
Curiosity piqued, I lightly gripped the journal with my left hand
to keep it from shutting. Green-tinged-with-gold magic flowed
from my hands into the journal and swirled around me.

I blinked rapidly, trying to make sense of what was happening. I glanced down at my lap and noticed legs sticking out. *Not*
my legs. I let go of the journal and stood up. My hands were
transparent. Stepping away from the desk, I realized my grandfather was sitting in the chair and Thomas and Violet had vanished. Focusing on my grandfather, I noted how much younger
he looked; his hair and beard were still mostly red with just a few
traces of white, and his eyes were bright with emotion.

"Gareth cannot marry a Fae!" King Leonard growled. My eyes
widened in shock. *This was over thirty years ago!*

A man in his prime with vibrant red hair, blazing blue eyes, and a thin gold crown on his head frowned. "Father, I have tried to reason with him. But he's in love with Solana. I even took him on a month-long hunting trip. If anything, that made him fall deeper in love with her."

The king slapped his hand on the book on the desk. I thought it was a journal, but it wasn't. It was a book with a Fae title. I recognized the language, but from the angle I was at, I could not make out the words. *How odd.* "I was warned this could happen and to do everything in my power to prevent it."

The prince—who I suspected was Prince Lawrence, heir of the South and eldest son of King Leonard—responded, "You could kill her."

King Leonard and I gasped in consternation at the same time. I covered my mouth with my hand, but they did not seem aware I was even there. King Leonard glared at his son. "Even if I was that heartless, you're a fool for suggesting it. Killing the daughter of the King of Fae would be a declaration of war, a war we have no hope of winning. We barely survived against the Court of Dusk."

Prince Lawrence opened his mouth to speak again, but King Leonard held up his hand, cutting him off. "You're dismissed." He stood up and turned his back to the prince, not giving him a chance to protest.

I watched Prince Lawrence's face turn red with anger. His hand gripped his sword as though he might attack the king before he thought better of it and departed. When I heard the door close, I returned my attention to my grandfather. I was half expecting the magic to throw me out of this memory—or whatever it was I was experiencing.

King Leonard heaved a deep sigh and moved back over to his desk, absently running his fingers over the cover of the Fae book. He looked up, his gaze meeting mine, as though somehow he knew I was there—*which is impossible.* His forehead wrinkled in thought, and he walked through me to the shelves behind me. There was a decanter of brandy and a set of glasses. He poured a glass and returned to his chair at the desk.

Settled and sipping the brandy, King Leonard deliberately turned to a page toward the middle of the book. His lips moved as he read the words to himself. I could not see them though. Every time I tried, the words blurred themselves out.

"She will be the doom of the South," he whispered.

The room swirled with my magic and then extinguished. I slumped forward onto the desk and passed out.

My arm was vibrating. I took a deep breath and opened my eyes. Thomas was shaking my arm with a worried frown. "Are you okay?" Violet gazed at me with concern from the other side of the desk.

I lifted my head. I had a steady throbbing headache in my temples, but I didn't feel like I was going to pass out again. "Yeah, I'm fine."

"Is the illness coming back?" Thomas inquired.

I shook my head. "No." I debated how much to tell them, then decided of all the people working for me, Thomas knew the most and was least likely to balk at my use of magic. Violet was becoming more comfortable with the idea that magic was commonplace with Fae—*and now me.* "I touched the journal, and it activated my magic. I believe I saw a meeting between King Leonard and Prince Lawrence in this room. It was when my father decided he wanted to marry my mother."

Thomas sucked in a sharp breath. "I've heard stories about that time. The tension between Prince Gareth and his family."

"You saw Prince Lawrence?" Violet questioned with awe in her voice.

I nodded. "Yes."

"Father said that King Leonard changed after your parents married. That at times he seemed like an entirely different person, not my father's best friend from childhood," Violet responded.

I blinked at this revelation, musing that the king had not always hated Fae, but that whatever he had known during this vision could have been significant enough to drive him to change so dramatically. Then I remembered the book with the Fae title that had been on the desk and caused King Leonard so much concern. I had come across *Bedtime Tails* in my perusal of the bookshelves, but not this other book.

I considered my options. Scouring the shelves could take hours, even if I asked Thomas to help me. Thin threads of green magic began sprouting from my hands. "I suppose I can try," I said more to myself than my companions, earning me quizzical looks. I closed my eyes and took a deep breath, recalling the book to my mind. It had had a faded blue cloth cover with the Fae words stamped in gold. Casting my magic around the room, I focused my will. *Find the book.*

I opened my eyes and was unsettled to see swirls of my magic darting around the room, as though my magic was literally searching for it. Thomas glanced at me but kept his thoughts to himself. Violet on the other hand was shifting back and forth on her feet nervously, making me wonder if they could see and feel the magic too. The threads of green gathered in front of the shelf that held the decanter of brandy. I stood and walked over to it. Unlike most of the other shelves, this one only held the decanter and two glasses; there was nothing else. Not sure what to think, I lifted the decanter and placed it on the desk with the glasses.

"Did you cast a spell?" Thomas asked, his tone wary.

"Yes, to find a book that I saw in the vision. But there isn't a book on that shelf," I said and walked back over to it. I ran my hand over the smooth wood. I was at a loss for what to do.

"May I?" Thomas asked.

I nodded, not sure what he would be able to do that I couldn't. Thomas grabbed both edges of the shelf and then pulled downward, as though it was a latch. To my astonishment, the shelf folded down. There was a grinding sound, and the wall moved, swinging into the office. When it stopped, I stared open-mouthed at a narrow stone corridor and wondered what could be at the end.

"Just as I expected," Thomas said with a satisfied smile.

I raised my eyebrows. "You find hidden passageways on a regular basis?"

Thomas shrugged. "No, but Declan has shown me a few. Since you decided to keep me as your personal guard, he thought it crucial for me to know about potential escape routes should the palace come under attack. This door, however, was not one I was aware of. I'm not sure Declan knows about it either. Do you have enough magic to light the way for us?"

I wasn't sure I should say yes, but I was embarrassed to admit I had no idea how to tell when I had reached my limit. Holding my hand up, I focused on creating a ball of light. Quicker than I expected, a green globe filled my hand. I sent it forward ahead of Thomas. His sword was in his hand, ready to vanquish any hidden foes.

"I'll wait here," Violet said in a shaky voice.

I gave her what I hoped was a reassuring smile and waited for Thomas to inspect the room. He motioned for me to enter. The Fae light floated above us, adequately illuminating the entire space. It was not much larger than a broom closet. There was a small table covered in a thick layer of dust. In the center of the table was the book with the Fae words. I recognized it immediately. Fingers wrapped around my arm, tugging me to a halt before I could grab the book.

"Given that you have now had two incidents with books and magic, how about I pick up the book first?" suggested Thomas.

Reluctantly, I let my hand fall to my side, acknowledging the wisdom of his words. Thomas stepped around me and picked up the book from the table. He wiped off the cover on his pant leg before offering me the book. When nothing magical occurred, I took it. The book was not very thick, and if it had not been for the Fae words stamped in gold, I likely would not have paid much attention to it.

"*Fàisneachd.*" I read the title aloud. My voice echoed in the small room.

"You can read Fae?" Thomas asked.

"I know some words. *Fàisneachd* means 'prophecy,'" I explained, raising many questions. I cast a glance around the room. There wasn't anything else remarkable that caught my attention.

"I'd prefer to read this in the other room, if you don't mind," I informed Thomas.

"Good idea," Thomas replied. Without waiting for my say-so, he led the way back into the other room. Thomas shut the door and replaced the brandy decanter and the glasses. Thankfully, the floor in here was stone, and there was no obvious mark or other indicator that the secret door had been opened.

Opting for a more comfortable seat, I selected one of the overstuffed chairs by the cold fireplace that I had sat in earlier, plopping into it and putting my feet up on the table. I cracked open the book, coughing as a cloud of dust sprayed off the cover into my face. When the dust settled, I peered at the first page.

Violet poured three glasses of water and set them on the table. I recognized the elegant script covering the first page as Commander Meriel Leoydark's, dragging my attention back to the book and reminding me that not only was Meriel leader of the Jade Wilds training camp where I'd spent twelve years, she was also a seer. According to Ghilanna and Fiera, quite a few of the prophecies in *Bedtime Tails* had been forseen by Meriel. The first page was written in Fae, and I could not understand any of it. The second page was written in the common tongue.

When the bloodline of South mixes
with the Court of Dawn, the end of time draws near.
Three is one, and one is three.

I suspected King Leonard's comment about us being doomed had to do with the line about mixing bloodlines and the end of time drawing near. I found it interesting that even so long ago, King Leonard had put some weight on Fae prophecies. *Almost as if his intolerance toward them was a way of pretending—as though if he didn't like them, the prophecy wouldn't be able to come true.* I had no idea what the last line referred to.

The book continued with each alternating page in Fae followed by what I assumed was the common tongue translation. I found it fascinating that Meriel would have translated a book of Fae prophecies and given it to King Leonard. Or perhaps this was another heirloom passed down through the generations of kings.

I paused my skimming when I reached a page that caught my attention.

> *In dawn's silver light*
> *Iron shackles the dragon*
> *Copper hides the moon*
> *Golden sunlight hails a griffin*
> *From dusk an emerald emerges*

Then, penciled into the corner as though it was an afterthought:

> Metal alloys are impenetrable and tough
> Friendship is the foundation of trust

"What is an alloy?" I asked. It wasn't a term I had come across before in this context.

Violet shook her head, and Thomas shrugged, responding, "I have no idea. Maybe the author is merely scribbling or it's spelled improperly."

"Perhaps," I conceded, thinking, *Allies is sort of close.*

I read it again, substituting the word *allies* for *alloys*. I wasn't entirely sure that was the correct substitution, but it made more sense that the scribble was about making allies with the other three kingdoms, which were represented by the metals.

"Is Meriel suggesting that I seek out the other kings? I thought that the South already had solid alliances," I said.

Thomas snorted. "Where did you get the idea that we're allies with the other human kingdoms?"

Violet burst out laughing, then covered her face with her hands as her cheeks heated in embarrassment.

I frowned. Some of the ideas I had about how to handle going to war with Tanyth hinged on us forming alliances with the human kingdoms. "They were cordial at the wedding."

"Exactly, they were cordial. We may not be openly at war with them, but I would say the amount of tension between each human kingdom is only marginally better than with the Fae courts," Thomas responded.

I ran my hand over my face. I hadn't expected to discover that the human kings were not my allies. *Are we really going to battle Prince Tanyth alone?* "Do you think they'll come if I call on them for aid against Tanyth?"

"It's questionable. I would not hinge any plans on them showing up. King Hanover ignored King Lionel's plea for help the last time we fought the Court of Dusk," Thomas explained.

I took a deep breath, debating if I wanted to look at the book more or call it quits for now. The book had been hidden, leading me to question if I should leave it here in hiding or take it with me, assuming no one knows it exists.

My stomach rumbled with hunger, making my mind up for me. "Let's go back to my suites so I can take a break and eat dinner. I'll explore King Leonard's chambers more another time. It's been quite fruitful. We've already found two books." I put the Fae book underneath the journal. Lord John had given me the key in a manner leading me to believe this was the only key to the chambers. *It should be safe enough to leave the book in here for now.*

Ten

RETHYS

ind whistled over my wings as I soared through the air, high above the clouds. It had taken me years to collect the trickle of magic that worked its way through the dark spells Tanyth had on Dorcha Palace and amass enough power to be able to leave. Down below me, not more than a tiny speck, was the cave with my hoard. I could feel it calling to me and slowly began the downward spiral to return.

Landing in the cave mouth, I gazed upon the piles of jewels and gold lovingly. Collected over the ages, each jewel had a history, which I had carefully documented in my book collection. Picking up a large emerald in my claws, I moved over to the far wall of the cave covered in thousands and thousands of books. The lightest touch of magic reached me, and I knew Serafina had found *Fàisneachd*. Setting the emerald on my work table, I summoned my copy of *Fàisneachd* with my magic.

Immediately after I set the book on the table, the emerald glowed, and the book opened of its own accord and flipped through the pages until it stopped on one toward the end.

If the humans will not accept the Lost Fae Queen and change their ways, then the world is doomed. Division between the Fae courts has grown stronger as the Court of Dusk's power has increased with the acquisition of Fleshrender and its corruption. Communities that once lived in harmony now fear for their lives and have gone into hiding or have been hunted till near extinction.

The faded words I had written two hundred years ago. At the time, there had been two other living dragons and herds of unicorns throughout the lands of the Courts of Dawn and the Moon. Between secret poaching expeditions conducted by humans and Tanyth's determination to eliminate or capture any magical creature or Fae shifter he could get his hands on, many lives had been lost.

The emerald continued to glow brightly even after I finished reading the page. I reached with my talon to pick it up, when the pages of the book started flipping again. I let my talon lay lightly on the table and waited, curiosity piqued, for where the book would stop.

It opened on a page near the middle, though I was certain the page had not been in the book previously. The edges were blackened as though it had been too near a fire. I ran a claw over it; the paper was extremely brittle.

Thalanil Neriwraek Journal #1-25
To make magic objects that will give the wielder godlike pow-
ers when united:
Three Fae-made magic artifacts
A pure-hearted Fae
A shapeshifter Fae
Unicorn horn & blood

Snarling, I shot backward, then twisted and sprinted for the door, wings flapping. I was in the air before I had room to fly and almost slammed into the ceiling of the cave in my haste. Rage boiled the blood in my veins. I had suspected what had happened to create *Bloodsong Grimoire*, Fleshrender, and Dragonfang. I flew mindlessly, relishing the burning in my wings as I sapped my energy and with it, my anger.

The Neriwraek family had had dark tendencies from the very beginning, starting with Thalanil. Oddly enough, it appeared to coincide with the color of their skin. Though Fae could be any color, the Neriwraek family consistently produced individuals with teal skin and an affinity for cruelty. It was rare for them to produce a youngling with skin ranging in the warm colors such as tan or brown, and when those children did appear, they were rumored to have diminished magic abilities.

It was no coincidence that Thalanil had transformed simple Fae magic artifacts into darker relics with a strong affinity for evil and that his great-great-great-grandson had desired those artifacts for himself. Or that Tanyth had sucessfully found them. Over my lifetime, I had collected Fae-crafted objects, and on occasion the creators sought me out to trade or steal the objects. Fae families frequently passed down stories of these objects, and often the objects had an unnatural desire to be reuinted with their makers.

As the sun disappeared, blanketing the sky in darkness, my anger was entirely gone, and I headed back to my cave.

Eleven

TRISTAN

Letting the snow leopard's instincts take over, I lost track of how long I wandered in the forest, concern over the appearance of Fiera and images of my past haunting me and doubts clouding my mind. That I don't deserve what I have with Serafina. I betrayed her trust, and she had forgiven me. *What if I betray her again? What if Tanyth also did something terrible to me, and even now I'm under his spell, preparing to do something even more unforgivable than before?* Spooking at even the slightest shadow that crossed my path, a few times I would have sworn I'd caught a glimpse of Travaran tracking me. But no matter how hard I looked, there was no one there. *Just my imagination.*

I chased down a rabbit, relishing the distraction the hunt provided. It was small and barely more than a snack, but the act of hunting allowed me to drive away the dark thoughts and become aware through my mating bond that Sera was making dinner preparations. The renewed awareness of the bond was driving my need for contact or close proximity with her to an extent that was almost impossible to ignore. A need that, now that the binding spell that had blocked our bond no longer existed, I could satisfy. When the dark magic had been at work, even touching had not helped; only sex. I huffed out a breath. Everything I'd heard over the years about what a mating bond would do to a couple was right, including the increased sex drive—not just to satiate the physical needs. It was far more than that. A union of our bodies and souls.

Mind made up, I sprinted through the forest, dead leaves swirling around me as I no longer tried to mask my presence. I ran to where I had originally shapeshifted and returned to my Fae form. My slate-colored hair fell over my shoulders, mostly obscuring my pointed ears, though I knew that since I was not trying to hide that I was Fae, here in a human kingdom, I would be noticed immediately. I strolled boldly through the city gates, earning me a few wide-eyed gasps as the gate guards in their navy uniforms with gold embellishments recognized me. The whispers I heard confirmed they had been aware I was not in the palace and would send word ahead of me to notify Nolan I had returned.

Nolan was waiting for me at the wrought iron palace gate with two other guards. This gate was about half the size of the city gates to restrict entrance to the palace, though it also had large gold spheres on the stone columns supporting the gate. Nolan's chain mailed arms crossed over the cream-and-gold tunic on his chest, a brooding look on his face. "I can't protect you if you don't tell me where you're going." The other two guards, dressed the same as Nolan, stayed out of our interaction.

I forced my jaw to unclench so I could reply. "I didn't need your protection for what I was doing. Besides, I am not going to be very effective at the duties Serafina wants me to perform if you insist on gluing yourself to me."

"Of course, I'm not going to be in your bedroom," Nolan said stiffly, his face flushing.

Eyes narrowing, I growled, "Those are not the duties I was referring to. Meeting with Fae who do not hold humans in high regard is not going to be possible with you following me. I'm sure you can join Serafina's squad if I cannot use your services."

Nolan shifted unhappily on his feet. Ultimately, we both knew it would be Serafina's decision, not ours, if I would be permitted to come and go from the palace without a guard. Given how she felt about her own guards, I doubted she would have an issue with me ditching mine. But the conversation with Nolan brought up a good point. We were going to have to tell more than just the war council that I could shapeshift. To be honest, Nolan and Thomas should be at the top of our list, given they were most likely to encounter me as a snow leopard.

We walked in tense silence to my residence. I paused in front of the door, putting my hand on the doorknob. "I will talk to Serafina." I stepped into the residence and shut the door firmly behind me.

The usually bright room was lit by flickering Fae light, mimicking candles. I cast my gaze around, wondering what this was about. A shadow darted past, and then I stumbled forward as something tried to sweep my feet out from underneath me. Regaining my balance, I spun, fists raised. I was pretty certain the shadow I kept seeing was Serafina. The shield in the room had not alerted me to the presence of an intruder, so it couldn't be anyone else.

A fist struck my lower back. I thrust my elbow back and felt it connect. I smirked. *Two can play this game.* I moved away from the door, wanting more space to maneuver. Serafina leapt through the air, trying a high kick. I ducked and grabbed her bare leg with my hands, pulling her close. Instead of struggling, I felt her relax. I cautiously loosened my hold on her. She wrapped her arms around me and then pulled my face down for an intense kiss.

I put my hand on her back and realized that she was not wearing any clothes. *"My wicked little queen,"* I said to her through the bond, running my hand down her back and cupping her buttocks.

"I could hear your thoughts when you were running around the forest. What did you expect me to do?" she asked, and her hand brushed against the front of my pants. My cock responded to even the barest of her touches.

Instead of answering her, I deepened the kiss, thrusting my tongue into her mouth, wishing it was my cock instead. But I wasn't going to get greedy. This was Serafina's plan, and I was not going to ruin her fun by making any suggestions.

"I want you to sit in the chair," Serafina said, surprising me when she switched to speaking aloud instead of through the bond.

"Which chair?" I asked.

She released my face and sashayed away. Sure enough, there was a chair in the middle of the space between the four white columns. I raised my eyebrow, surprised by her choice.

Casting a glance over her shoulder, she teased, "Are you coming?"

I didn't need to be asked twice. Vanishing my clothes with my magic, I stalked over to the chair and sat in it. It had a straight back and no sides. Serafina straddled the chair but took her time lowering herself onto me. I was taut with burning-hot desire, desperate to bury my cock inside of my soulmate.

Serafina's russet hair curtained around my face as she met my lips for a scorching kiss, then guided my cock inside of her drenched folds. I moaned in pleasure against her lips as she began a steady up-and-down rhythm, driving me deeper and deeper into her core. Unlike this morning, the chair Sera had chosen allowed her to have full control. It was refreshing to be able to surrender mind, body, and soul to the female I had waited decades for.

Serafina increased her speed, heightening our pleasure, and I shuddered as my muscles spasmed, my release rolling through my body. Serafina sagged onto my chest, her muscles twitching. I smiled. "I love you."

"I love you too, Tristan," hummed Serafina with satisfaction.

I lost track of time as I slumped on the chair in the center of our residence, entwined with Serafina. I should have cared that someone might walk in on us, but I didn't. This was our time, for a little while, to pretend that there was nothing more important than the two of us.

Eventually, Serafina unwrapped herself from around me and stood up. The lights in the room brightened, and I sighed as she used magic to dress herself, donning a dark-green tunic and tan pants with her hair in a loose braid draped over her shoulder. I followed suit, opting to wear the navy tunic with gold leaves. The need that had driven me here was sated, which left me wondering about the discussion we'd had earlier and Sera's promise to tell me whatever it was she had been holding back.

Capturing her hand in mine, I brushed my lips over her knuckles. "I love you."

She gave me a bright smile. "I love you too."

Encouraged, I plowed onward. "You said this morning there was something you wanted to talk about. Well, we are alone, and it is later. Will you tell me now?"

The smile fell from her face and her eyes dimmed. "I suppose now is fine," she mumbled.

My eyebrows rose, and I locked gazes with my wife. "You can tell me anything."

She crossed her arms and rubbed her hands over them as though warming herself up. I could even see goosebumps on her arms as a shiver rippled through her.

"I had a miscarriage." Sera's voice was soft, barely more than a whisper.

I swallowed hard, trying to understand what she was saying. "You're pregnant?"

She shook her head. "No. It was … it was before." Her lip quivered, and I fought the desire to shake the words out of her. My whole body was drawn tight in anticipation and dread, wondering what her explanation would mean and how it would change our relationship.

"It happened during the tournament," she managed to squeak.

My throat constricted and blackness clouded my vision at the thought of anyone else having sex with her. The timing would have been about right for it to be Tanyth. I still had no idea about everything that had happened to her while she was his prisoner, especially at the end when she was drugged and I had been collared and locked in a cage in the dungeon with the other beasts.

"Tanyth?" I said, choking on the words.

Cringing, she took a step back, as though she was afraid I was going to hurt her. "No. I have my memories back and know for sure that you're the only one I've ever had sex with."

The knots in my stomach released a tad bit. She was still exclusively *mine*. Except that didn't resolve the fact that Sera had been pregnant and chose not to tell me. I ran my hand over my face and started pacing. Tears welled in my eyes and threatened to spill over as comprehension filled me. *We could have had a youngling, and now that has been ripped away.* I paused when I reached the far end of the room, keeping my back to her, and let my eyes slide closed. Emotions rolled through me. Anger at her for not telling me sooner and at Tanyth for putting her in a high-stress situation that had likely led to the miscarriage. Fear that she would blame me, since it had taken both of us to create a pregnancy. The final emotion that swept over me was overwhelming love for my wife and soulmate, who had had to go through a miscarriage alone in a tumultuous time in our lives, and yet here she was, still fulfilling her responsibilities as Lady of the South.

Spinning around, I rushed back over to Sera, gathering her in my arms. "I love you and am here for you, no matter what. I only wish you would have told me sooner so that I could have done more. This is our burden to bear together."

Sera melted into my arms, her body shaking as she sobbed against me. I held her, cooing nonsense words and waiting for her to calm down enough to speak.

In time, her sobs lessened, eventually turning into sniffles, and she spoke softly. "The miscarriage happened when I had no memory of being intimate with anyone. The whole situation turned into a nightmare. Put yourself in my shoes. I was being touted by King Leonard as a virgin, and then I had my monthlies, only to find out it was not a normal cycle, but a miscarriage. I still haven't entirely wrapped my mind around it. Beyond the fact that we did conceive and I was not able to carry to full term. What if ... what if I'm not capable of having a child?"

"Oh, Sera!" I gasped, hugging her tighter. "If you are willing to try again, then I will be with you, every step of the way."

We heard a tap on the door. Sera startled in my arms. I loosened my hold on her and stepped back, brushing the tears off her face with my thumbs. "I guess we ran out of time to ourselves," I said mournfully.

Sera's expression was drawn. She extracted herself entirely from my arms and walked over to the door tensely as it swung open.

"Dinner, Your Majesty," called Thomas. I recalled that dinner had been one of the reasons I had returned to the palace.

A maid pushed a cart inside and proceeded to arrange various trays on the dining table. I wondered if Serafina had invited someone else for dinner when the plates kept coming. *Far more than what the two of us would eat.* When the cart was empty, the servant bowed and departed.

Serafina giggled. "I have no idea why they brought this much food. I will have to talk to Cookie about it. This seems wasteful if it's just the two of us." There was an entire goose, two platters of vegetables, a pot of soup, and two baskets of fresh bread.

Trying to keep the mood light, I decided to skirt around the difficult subject of the miscarriage and pregnancy. "How was your day?" I asked, filling a plate of food while I waited for her response.

Serafina replied as she filled her own plate. "I have three of the four war council members figured out, both Violet and Ghilanna agreed to be ladies-in-waiting, and Ghilanna taught me some basics of magic too."

"Wonderful," I replied between bites. "I know Fiera also showed up. Did anyone besides you question her?"

Serafina's eyes met mine. "Ghilanna did, but I have not been able to check back in with her. Hopefully, she'll come by when we're done eating. I'd also like you to talk to Fiera. I *want* to believe her, but I'm afraid of what will happen if I do and she's lying. I also went to my grandfather's chambers." I waited for her to continue, sensing there was much she wanted to share. "Remember how we were looking for genealogy books a while ago? Well, I found them, and ... I am related to West and North. I could not confirm if I have ties to East or not."

The news was surprising. If Serafina had the blood of three, possibly four, human royalty lines running through her veins, she might be able to control all four metal mines. I did not know enough about how the mine magic worked and what that would gain us, other than leverage against the other kings. Whether or not it would help in the war remained to be seen.

"Did you find anything other than the genealogies?" I prompted.

Serafina nodded. "Yes. There was a journal on his desk, one that had an entry as recent as the day he died. But when I touched it, my magic reacted, and I ended up within a memory from when Gareth and Solana wanted to be married."

I stopped chewing my food and swallowed, immediately regretting it as the food lodged in my throat uncomfortably. *Is Serafina a seer like her mother?* It seemed strange that the journal of a human who disliked Fae would have had its own magic. I suspected Serafina's magic was causing things to happen on their own.

She continued, "In the vision was a Fae book. I decided to search for it and found the book in a secret room. It's a book of prophecies that Commander Meriel translated."

I rocked back in my chair. What an odd turn of events. *Did King Leonard fool everyone into believing he hated Fae while he secretly supported the ties between the South and the Court of Dawn? Or is this prophecy book entirely unrelated?* I had more questions than answers, though I was not convinced any of them would aid us in the war against the Court of Dusk.

"Perhaps we should set up a meeting with Commander Meriel," I suggested, though I was itching to get a look at the book myself. Taking it to the very Fae who had translated it would likely provide us with more insight than just my translations would.

"Precisely my thoughts," Serafina replied, then returned her attention to devouring her dinner. Realizing that I should do the same, I forced myself to eat.

Full, I set my fork down, wondering if Serafina would be open to being dessert, when there was a light tap on the door.

"Come in!" Serafina called.

I sensed Callyn's presence as soon as her hand was on our door.

"Good evening," Callyn said as she entered, hovering a short distance from the dining table. A cloak of woven browns and grays hung around her shoulders and her longsword was tucked into a brown leather scabbard at her waist.

Serafina smiled at her. "Come sit and eat if you're hungry."

Callyn chose a chair between us and sat. "I ate already, thanks. Tristan told me that you had a matter you wished to discuss."

"Yes, I do. I would like you to serve on my war council," Serafina replied.

I held my breath. Even though I had warned Callyn about this earlier, I still wasn't sure how my friend was going to answer, especially with how she had reacted in the forest.

Callyn nodded. "I accept."

"Excellent," replied Serafina.

"Marek wants to meet tonight," Callyn said.

"He might have some valuable information," I chimed in.

I turned toward Serafina to watch her expression as she responded excitedly, "Maybe he knows if what my grandfather said is true, that the Court of the Sun is marching on our border."

Callyn shrugged. "I'm not privy to the information he intends to discuss, but I agree it is likely, since he can fly on Asteria and scout without having to risk drawing Prince Rhangil's attention."

I knew we did not have a report yet on whether Prince Rhangil's troops were massing on our border or if that had just been a ploy by Prince Tanyth to gain access to the *Bloodsong Grimoire*. As Prince Rhangil's son, Marek could have information that would tell us if Tanyth had lied or if Prince Rhangil was also preparing to attack the South.

Serafina was fiddling with her cup of water, likely weighing her next words. Finally, Serafina met Callyn's gaze. "I would like to meet with him. I know that last time it was necessary to keep the meeting secretive due to my standing within my grandfather's court and Marek's relationship with his father. Is that still necessary now that I am queen? I would like Ghilanna to come, and I will have to have at least Thomas as well ... unless Marek wishes to come to the palace."

Callyn shrugged. "Marek has no issue with Ghilanna and Thomas coming. He would rather not be parted from Asteria, though, and I'm not sure how your subjects would react to a griffin flying overhead, so it would be best if you went to him."

"Then it's settled," Serafina said firmly.

I coughed. "What about the rest of your guards? We cannot throw caution to the wind."

"Thomas will be sufficient," Serafina replied.

I pressed my lips together in a thin line and didn't respond.

"Are you no longer confident that between all of us, I won't have more than enough protection? I'm not defenseless," Serafina said through the bond. I could feel her grumpy tone.

"As queen, you must also keep up appearances. One guard is not going to go over well with Declan," I pointed out.

I could hear Serafina's huff through the bond. *"Fine. One squad, but they must wait a suitable distance away when we meet. I don't want to offend Marek."*

There was a double tap on the doors, then they opened, admitting Ghilanna, who was surprisingly dressed almost identically to Callyn. *Impeccable timing*, I mused. Though I had to admit the clothing was likely a coincidence since it was fairly standard hunting attire.

"Ah, you're all here!" Ghilanna exclaimed. "I was hoping I could talk to Serafina about what Fiera said, but having all three of you here is even better."

I waited impatiently for Ghilanna to divulge the information. Callyn cast me a questioning glance, but I ignored her, knowing that in a few moments we would all be privy to the answer.

"What did you find out?" asked Sera.

Ghilanna pulled up a chair and sat at the table across from us. "I'm almost certain that Fiera is telling the truth. She said that Tanyth used Fleshrender and severed their mating bond, even described the sensation of the severing. She recounted the experience with too many details for it to be a false tale."

I exchanged a look with Callyn, then decided she was owed a better explanation. "Fiera was caught this morning breaking into our bedroom after I had left. She claims to have run away from the Court of Dusk."

"Ah, I see," replied Callyn dryly. I couldn't blame her for being skeptical; I felt the same. Personally, I would have liked to see Fiera interrogated in the dungeon instead of being given a comfy room and politely interviewed, but alas, I was not the ruler of the South, and Sera had given the orders herself. "I would like to take a run at her too."

I smirked. The way Callyn said it made me think she was going to fight Fiera, not ask her questions. With how Fiera had treated Sera the last time we'd seen her, I had a few choice things I wanted to say to her as well. "Perhaps we can talk to her together after the meeting with Marek?" I suggested.

Callyn snorted. "There's no point. The less time we waste on Fiera, the better off we'll be. We have far more important matters to attend to. Honestly, it would be prudent to just toss her in the dungeon and leave her there."

Sera gasped at Callyn's comment. "You may not like Fiera, but she was my friend who got captured by Tanyth because she was trying to save me a second time. She killed Travaran so I could get away. I am going to give her the benefit of the doubt, and I expect you to do the same."

Callyn clamped her mouth shut, pressing her lips together into a thin white line. Heavy silence swept through the room until Callyn blurted out, "Are you ready to depart?"

"Yes," Serafina, Ghilanna, and I replied at the same time.

We made our way to the stables. I knew Serafina would have liked to spend more time grooming Dubhar, but we didn't want to make Marek wait too long. To me, the unicorn still looked like a black stallion. I wondered when he would feel comfortable revealing his true form to the humans within the palace. *He's in the same situation as me. Is a human settlement a safe place for Fae like us?* I wasn't sure. I doubted very many humans believed unicorns were real. Like most Fae creatures, they were characters in stories, just a figment of the imagination.

I grudgingly accepted the reins of a black mare. Thankfully, she did not seem to care that I smelled like a snow leopard, which was a relief. The last thing I needed was to make a fool of myself in front of Marek and the guards by demonstrating how much horses disliked me.

Our entourage was larger than I expected. I suspected Declan was informed of where Serafina was going and had ordered more than one squad of guards to accompany us. Not that I could blame him. News of more slander painted on walls in the city had trickled up to the palace, and I doubted it would stop anytime soon. The question was not if it would escalate, but when.

Callyn gave the guard captain our destination, and the first squad led the way out of the side gates and into the meadow. Once we were out the gate, the two squads arranged themselves in a square around us. I could feel the shield Ghilanna had around Serafina, though I wasn't sure if Serafina knew it was there. Her attention was focused on the far side of the meadow, the path into the forest.

Twelve

SERAFINA

nlike my prior meeting with Marek, this one was in the old forest—a mix of rowan, spruce, and beech trees on the far side of the meadow. I hoped he would forgive me for bringing the guards. Declan's note that had come with the guard captain had been quite firm. I knew if I wanted Declan to trust me, I would have to be willing to give up the privacy I wanted for this meeting. He was merely doing his job—keeping me safe, which would be impossible if I wouldn't allow his guards to protect me.

Immediately after his hooves sank into the soft grass of the meadow, Dubhar surged forward into a canter. I felt a pulse of magic from him, and a gap opened between the guards ahead of us, their dark-brown cloaks fanning out over their horses' rumps. Riding through the gap, we quickly overcame the first guard and pulled ahead of the group.

"Are you trying to get me in trouble with the guards?" I murmured, running my hand along Dubhar's velvety neck.

Dubhar cast a glance at me, his stride never faltering, then sped up even more. I sat deeper in the saddle and relished the feel of his muscles bunching underneath me, galloping effortlessly across the field. I could sense through the bond that Tristan was hot on our heels. I wondered how the little mare was keeping up. The others were strung out behind us.

I saw a glint of something in the air ahead of us, and I thought I was able to make out the shape of Marek riding his griffin Asteria, skimming the top of the trees in the forest. Dubhar slowed to a flowing trot when we reached the dirt forest path, but he didn't hesitate. I wondered if he could talk mind-to-mind with Asteria or Marek or if he somehow just knew where we were going.

The path split in a Y and Dubhar halted. I peered over my shoulder; Tristan grinned at me, his dark-gray hair a tangled mess from the wind. I could see Callyn and Ghilanna not too far behind him. I hoped they would be as amused as Tristan was. I doubted Thomas was going to feel that way. At least I had an excuse: The unicorn did it. I giggled, wondering what Declan would think if I told him that. Almost as bad as saying the dog ate my paperwork.

When the guards were close enough to see which way we turned at the fork, Dubhar continued onward. We veered to the left, deeper into the forest. I wasn't even sure if it was a real path. Then, the beech trees opened into a clearing. Dubhar walked straight to the middle, then halted. Asteria—a bronze-feathered griffin with an eagle head, piercing gold eyes, hooked beak, and leon lower legs and paws—landed directly in front of us, and Marek dismounted. Then, the griffin took off again. I presumed she was patrolling to ensure there would be no aerial attack. Given we were dealing with a Fae enemy, it was wise. I didn't think the humans had the resources to launch an aerial attack without us having a lot of time to prepare.

I slid out of the saddle and walked over to Marek. He was average height for a Fae—slightly shorter than Tristan—with bronze skin a shade lighter than Asteria's feathers. His eyes were brown with flecks of gold, and his hair was reddish-brown with sun-touched highlights. A large sword was strapped on his back, the hilt visible over his shoulder. Thick black leather pants and a vest, both covered in small metal plates, served as his armor.

"Good evening, Marek," I said, loud enough that my voice would carry to those in the clearing with us. The guards were still filing in, and Tristan was giving them orders to stand around the perimeter.

"Good evening, Serafina," Marek replied calmly.

When the guards were situated, Tristan, Callyn, Ghilanna, Thomas, and Dubhar approached us. Callyn raised her hand, and white magic laced with purple swirled around her. Chairs appeared in front of each of us with a gap between two of them, large enough for Dubhar to stand and be part of the group.

"Thank you, Callyn, for providing the chairs," Marek said. "Are the guards with you trustworthy?"

Thomas nodded. "Yes. I personally selected them."

"Good. Now let's sit. I felt it was critical to meet. Things are rapidly changing in the South, and it is vital that you have as much information as possible to guide your own decisions," Marek explained. "I am aware that Prince Tanyth told King Leonard that my father was preparing to attack. Asteria and I have flown to the border and confirmed this is not true. For the moment at least, the Court of the Sun is not mobilizing."

I sighed in relief. Marek's presence and role in aiding Tristan to win the competition supported his claim of being on my side. Being Prince Rhangil's son did not mean he would follow in his father's footsteps and ally himself with Prince Tanyth.

He is one Fae with one griffin. His support may not mean much if I'm not able to secure alliances with more than individual Fae or humans. A handful of us was not going to be enough to defeat Tanyth. I *must* form an alliance with a Fae court or human kingdom.

"I would not recommend approaching the Court of the Sun or the Court of the Moon individually when seeking their alliance. Instead, reach out to King Pharaan. The other three courts answer to him, and he should be able to require them to ally with you against Prince Tanyth," Marek said.

"Won't that make them angry? To not have a say in the matter, to just follow King Pharaan's orders?" I asked.

"They owe fealty to King Pharaan. Answering his call to arms is part of that. You went to Emerald Valley. This would be the same," Marek explained.

I wasn't sure he was right. The number one difference being the battle at Emerald Valley was facing humans, and this call to arms would be going against Fae. *Not rogue Fae, either, but a court.*

"You are short on time. I am trying to simplify matters so that you won't have to travel to three courts versus one. Especially when you might have to send representatives to the North, East, and West too," Marek said.

The main thing his words drove home was that I was running out of time. From my month as a prisoner at the Court of Dusk, I knew Prince Tanyth was always ready to attack or defend. He didn't need time to muster his Fae. They were merely waiting for the orders designating when and where. Whereas I still did not know the status of my knights.

"Should I postpone the coronation and go to the Court of Dawn immediately?" I asked.

Marek shook his head. "No. The alliances you seek will be better received if you have the official coronation. Then, there will be no doubt in their minds that you are the Lady of the South."

I leaned heavily against Tristan as the guards led us back to our rooms. My eyelids were determined to slide closed, and it was a miracle I made it without having to be carried. Ghilanna and I had agreed we would sort out her lady-in-waiting duties tomorrow and could discuss clothing with the seamstress when she came for my coronation fitting.

I climbed into bed, then realized I had not gotten undressed. "Can you …" I wiggled my fingers at Tristan.

He gave me a tired smile. "Of course." A blurry gray glow encased his hands, and then my clothes were replaced by a loose-fitting nightshirt. I slid under the covers and fell asleep.

A tall, teal-skinned Fae with black hair in hundreds of tiny braids and a towering crown of antlers stood before me. Prince Tanyth. *We were in a barren desert. I shivered as icy wind blasted by us and noticed I was naked save for the heavy crown on my head. Reaching up, I felt the four points and immediately knew it was the crown the gold mine had gifted me.*

Tanyth stared coldly at me. "You are no match for me. Surrender before I kill your loved ones."

Throwing my shoulders back, I met his gaze. "You cannot intimidate me."

Tanyth smirked and raised his hand. Teal magic laced with black swirled around him, expanding to engulf me.

When the magic disappeared, I was sitting on a throne placed high on the edge of the light stone arena at Dorcha Palace. My feet dangled into the air below me. I shuddered and tried to look away but found I could not. Tanyth's magic locked me in place.

I watched with apprehension as Ghilanna, dressed in a long undyed cotton tunic, stumbled through the gate and into the arena. She hovered by the edge and then abruptly was propelled forward. She tripped, falling onto her face in the sand. Ghilanna slowly pushed herself back up to standing, spitting to clear the sand from her mouth.

My friend peered around, immediately spotting me. Her gaze fixed on mine. I wanted to call out and warn her of what was to come, but no words would emerge from my mouth. The crowd, however, was humming with excitement. Ghilanna crept toward one of the walls. Halfway there, a high-pitched whistle sounded, followed by a loud clang. A square began to form in the middle of the arena near where she had been standing. First, a head of dark pewter-gray hair became visible. Not Tristan, *my mind begged. What Ghilanna was wearing and Tristan's entrance were achingly familiar. I shivered, praying I was wrong. The platform raised higher and higher, revealing Tristan in his glory as lord commander of the Court of Dusk. In one hand he had a plain sword, and in the other, a dagger. He wore black leather pants with metal plates sewn into them, but his torso was bare.*

A cheer went up as Tristan raised his sword, saluting them.

Then a hush fell over the crowd, and Tanyth's voice echoed around the arena. "My dear guests! Tonight, we shall watch Lord Commander Tristan Gilvrye, warrior elite, face trespasser Ghilanna Qira." The position of my throne over the edge made it impossible to see where Tanyth was.

Then, another whistle sounded, drawing me out of my thoughts. Clenching my fists tightly, I watched as the walls began to move. Ghilanna leaped forward to avoid encountering the wall. When the walls ceased moving, the arena had shrunk to less than a quarter of its full capacity, roughly the size of an ordinary practice ring. Ghilanna and Tristan were only a few paces from each other; both had calculating expressions, as though they were sizing each other up.

A horn blew, startling me. If magic hadn't held me in place, I would have likely just toppled into the arena. Tristan launched himself, slashing with his sword and dagger. Ghilanna ducked and rolled to the side. His sword whizzed over her back. She rose in a crouch, fists ready. Tristan was faster. He spun, positioning himself behind Ghilanna. My friend could not block the slice he made with the dagger across her arm. Blood trickled from the wound onto the sand. Ghilanna acted as though it was nothing more than a small scratch. Dodging Tristan's next two strikes and maneuvering herself slightly behind him, Ghilanna leaped into the air and landed a kick on Tristan's low back, hitting him squarely on his dragon tattoo. He grunted and stumbled forward. Regaining his balance, he bellowed in fury, and his sword and dagger became a blur of motion as he went through combination after combination. Slice after slice peppered Ghilanna's skin. From where I was, I couldn't tell how deep they all were, but the sheer number was immense. Unless Ghilanna could figure out how to get one of Tristan's weapons, I knew she was doomed.

Ghilanna cast a pleading glance at me before ducking under Tristan's next strike and trying to trip him. Instead, Ghilanna missed and fell forward onto her hands and knees. Tristan halted in front of her, sword ready. In one fluid motion, Ghilanna stood up and flung the handful of sand in his face.

"Argh!" he shouted, squeezing his eyes tight and dropping his dagger to wipe the sand away. Ghilanna scooped the dagger up and staggered toward him, slicing at his lower legs. The dagger connected with his hamstring, but even distracted and unable to see, Tristan reacted. Thrusting his sword, he slammed it into Ghilanna's stomach.

"No!" I screamed as Ghilanna collapsed to the ground, her blood soaking the sand.

I slept restlessly, plagued with dreams of Tanyth and his horrible arena. When I woke up, I flung my arm over to where Tristan should have been only to find his side of the bed cold. Frowning, I got up and threw on a gold silk robe, then headed out of the bedroom in search of him. Thankfully, Tristan hadn't gone far. He was in the entryway. *Where I set the chair.* I shivered as thoughts of what we did on that chair came unbidden.

Tristan was running sword drills. He had a pair of cutoff tan pants on, and his torso was bare. As he moved I caught glimpses of the dragon tattoo on his lower back just as Ghilanna had said.

"Good morning," I said. I wanted to join him, but I couldn't remember where I had put my father's sword.

"Morning," Tristan replied, not missing a step in his drill, though his gaze lingered on my face.

"If you have a spare sword, I can join you," I said, walking forward so I was standing next to one of the columns.

"What happened to your sword?" Tristan asked, lowering his and turning to face me completely.

"The original sword I arrived in Gaskal with went missing. My father's sword ... I brought it back from my parents' house, but I am not entirely sure where it went after I returned," I explained.

"Perhaps Thomas or Violet knows where it went. I can't imagine someone would have gotten rid of it," Tristan said.

I frowned. It seemed like once again it was not going to be a simple matter of having my own weapon. I was going to have to search for it. I marched over to the door and yanked it open, sharper than I intended. George and Thomas were just outside and cast me worried glances when I poked my head out. "Do either of you know what happened to my father's sword?"

Thomas nodded. "Yes. I put it in the weapons case."

"Where is that?" I asked, chin jutting out.

"Inside. I can show you," Thomas said. I scooted away from the door to give him room to enter. I followed Thomas curiously as he walked to a cabinet on the far side of the room near the windows. He opened it, and inside was my father's sword, as well as a set of armor, an axe, and two daggers.

I sighed in relief. "I thought it had been taken."

Thomas chuckled. "Definitely not. I thought you had explored everything in here; otherwise, I would have shown you sooner. I apologize."

I waved my hand at him, blushing. "Don't be sorry. I assumed it was just another wardrobe. I'm glad to know there is a specific place to store my weapons and armor. It will make it easier to keep track of them."

"I know you are going to practice with Tristan, but before I depart I thought I would let you know the agenda for the day. The seamstress is coming this morning after you eat breakfast. Once you've met with her, then you have a lunch meeting with the war council," Thomas explained.

"Thank you for the heads-up," I said.

Thomas bowed and returned to his post in the hallway. I removed the sword from the case and headed over to Tristan.

After changing out of the robe and into a white tunic and black pants, I joined Tristan, my father's sword held loosely in my right hand. The tension in my muscles from the bad dreams had started to drain away, and the sword work would hopefully do the rest.

I worked through my warmup, and Tristan asked, "What did Ghilanna teach you in your magic lesson yesterday?"

I shrugged. "Nothing terribly exciting. We went over making a ball of magic to create light and as a weapon. I was able to make three at once but couldn't get all three to go where I wanted. Even with one, it would get about ten feet from me and then fizzle out."

"Did she go over shielding?" Tristan asked.

I shook my head. "No. We didn't have a lot of time, and she thought it would be better if I got comfortable with one or two things instead of trying to learn too many at once."

Tristan gave me a thoughtful look. "I'd like to introduce you to shielding."

"Okay," I agreed.

"Come here," he said and crooked his finger at me. I stepped forward and he sheathed his sword and placed his hands lightly on my shoulders. "Remember how I said I could give you my knowledge of battle strategy quickly through the bond? Well, we're going to try it right now for shielding."

"Okay," I said again. I could feel tingling along the bond and under his hands from the magic.

Immediately, images and thoughts passed through the bond. Tristan pictured the sword being shielded from strikes in his mind, and then the sword was encased in a shimmering shield of gray magic. Because of how Tristan was transferring his knowledge, I could also feel the precise amount of will he was putting behind his magic to ensure the shield would accomplish its goal.

Tristan removed his hands from my shoulders, and I smiled at him. "I'm pretty sure I can make a shield now."

"Let's try it," Tristan encouraged.

I stared at my sword, green-and-gold magic swirling out of my hands and down the length of the blade. Slowly, the whole blade was encased in a green-gold shield.

"Now what?" I asked.

"The trickier part is to see if the shield is strong enough to withstand a hit and if you can hold it while also practicing," he replied.

My eyes widened, and I set my jaw resolutely. "Let's find out."

Tristan dropped the shield on his sword—or at least I could no longer see it—and then lightly crossed his sword with mine. "Remember, you must focus your mind on holding the shield, while also doing strikes and blocks. Eventually, you will be able to keep a shield up with merely a thought. Let's begin. One, two, three!"

He took a step back and initiated a high strike. I raised my sword in a high block, and I grinned when there was no clang as Tristan's blade hit mine. The shield was holding. We worked our way through high, low, and middle strikes and blocks. My shield never wavered, though sweat beaded on my neck and forehead as the exertion took its toll.

Taking a deep breath, Tristan lowered his sword and suggested, "You can let go of the shield now."

I sagged in relief and lowered my sword, allowing the shield to dissolve. "I was about to ask to stop. I'm exhausted."

Tristan smiled. "You did brilliantly."

"Thanks. Should we clean up before the seamstress comes?" I asked, casting a glance at his chest glistening with sweat while I put my sword in the weapons cabinet.

He gave me a knowing look. "I think we have time for a quick shower."

I swatted Tristan playfully. "Not too quick I hope." Giggling, I sprinted toward the bathroom.

Tristan claimed to be overheating when I turned the temperature even hotter on the water, and he ducked out, leaving me blissfully alone. Letting the water cascade over the top of my head, I forced my mind to be completely blank.

A quiet knock on the door drew my attention. Wondering if Tristan had changed his mind and was returning for round two, I called out, "Come in!"

Facing the door, I was surprised when Ghilanna stepped through. Her black hair was in two tight braids, and her hands were barely visible under the towel she held out in front of her as though it were an offering. Giving her a slight smile, I turned off the water, then took the towel and wrapped it around myself. A smile flitted over my lips. "Good morning. I wasn't expecting you."

Ghilanna humphed. "You offered me the position of lady-in-waiting. I figured I should get used to performing some of those duties."

"I am capable of getting my own towels. Besides, you said yourself that you were going to be a lady only in name and not fulfill any of those duties outside of the protection detail," I said, sticking my tongue out at her.

Ghilanna ignored me and switched topics. "Are you going to choose an outfit out of the wardrobe, or are you going to try using your magic?"

I'm going to have to get used to the idea that I can magic my own clothing. I used the towel to roughly dry my hair and then hung it up. My skin was slightly damp, and I could feel a trail of water trickling down my back from my still-wet hair. "I would like to try using my magic."

"Good. Bring an image to your mind of what you want to wear. If it's simpler, you can do each piece of clothing individually instead of all at once. Then, when you have the image in your mind, draw on your magic and will the clothing into existence *on you*," Ghilanna explained.

I nodded and concentrated on what I wanted to wear. Full dark-green satin pants that gave the illusion of being a skirt. A gold blouse with billowing sleeves and a ribless corset out of the same material as the pants with a delicate swirl pattern in gold thread. I topped it off with a green leather belt and matching scabbard. Following the steps Ghilanna had given me, I felt my body tingling as I worked the magic. I could see small tendrils of my green-and-gold magic weaving around me too.

Ghilanna tugged me over to the bathroom mirror. I gazed at myself and was pleased to see that I was wearing exactly what I had envisioned. My father's sword was even in the scabbard at my waist. I ran my fingers over the fabric, half expecting it to disappear.

"Excellent job. I like that you did not go with a simple pants and tunic but chose an outfit like those in your wardrobe to challenge yourself," Ghilanna said warmly.

I blushed at the praise. "Thanks."

"The more you use your magic, the more naturally it will come to you. I know getting dressed seems like a simple task, but it's a good one for you to practice," Ghilanna responded.

"I suppose I should practice shielding like Tristan taught me?" I asked. Ghilanna's point about practicing was valid, and if I told her what I was learning, she would help me remember to work on it too.

Ghilanna chuckled. "You're forgetting your hair."

"Oops," I said and ran my hand through it. Knowing I couldn't have rumors being spread of how un-queenly I was, running around the palace with wet hair, I drew on my magic again and willed my hair to be dry and braided in a simple plait down my back.

"Now you're ready. I will escort you to the breakfast room. The guards are already waiting for us in the hallway. For practice, you should shield starting now until we reach the meeting room. I will ensure you're shielded once we're inside," Ghilanna said.

I pressed my lips together, not wanting to protest. I had no idea how long it took to learn how to properly hold a shield around oneself while focusing on other tasks. Or how draining it could be to hold a shield long-term. As much as I hated having to rely on Ghilanna or Tristan to shield me, I would have to be patient until I became more proficient in shielding.

"Very well," I said with a nod.

With Ghilanna in the lead and the cream-and-gold-uniformed guards falling into place around us, we made our way to the room chosen for the breakfast meeting. We went down the wide stone staircase with leaves carved into the railing to the main level of the palace. Then we turned left and passed through an oak door with a rose carved on it I hadn't opened before. Inside was a room oozing warmth and coziness. The walls were covered in linen fabric with roses in soft pastel pinks, yellows, and purples and hung with paintings of children frolicking in the meadow with butterflies and wildflowers. In the center of the room was a square table with four overstuffed chairs covered in rose-pink velvet.

"Valerie and Josiah will be arriving momentarily. Food is on its way now and will be set up buffet style," Thomas explained.

I moved over to the side to inspect one of the paintings. That would allow me to keep an eye on the door too. Servants came in and were followed immediately by Valerie and Josiah. Valerie looked uncomfortable in a formfitting cobalt-blue satin dress with a copper brooch of a howling wolf's head pinned to a white scarf around her throat. Josiah wore a black jacquard jacket with a piece of cobalt-blue fabric pinned at his left breast and the same copper howling wolf pin.

"Hi!" I said, waving to them, absently realizing my greeting was more casual than expected of a queen, but I didn't care.

"Your Majesty," Josiah and Valerie said at the same time, bowing deeply.

I waved them off and stepped forward to embrace Josiah. "It's good to see you again."

"You look well," Valerie said conversationally.

"The food is here. Why don't you help yourselves and then we can talk," I said, not sure how to respond to Valerie's comment. I might look well, but I didn't always feel that way, though it was a relief to finally have spoken to Tristan about the miscarriage. I was not ready to confide something that personal with Valerie. Though we had met a few times before I fled from the South with my mother, it was Josiah with whom I had spent hours every day.

Josiah bobbed his head in acknowledgment and led the way to the buffet. When all three of us had loaded our plates, we sat at the table. Ghilanna poured us each a cup of water and juice. Apparently, my friend had decided to insert herself into the breakfast. *Because she doesn't trust them? Or because she just wants a firsthand account of the meeting?* I mulled over the idea and took a few bites of my food, then launched into the discussion.

"It is my intention to have the South open its borders to Fae, welcoming them to live peacefully with us, if they so choose. Which means I am going to need help from you and the rest of the Copper Wolves. I know you said previously that there are many within the city of Gaskal who feel comfortable with Fae thanks to my mother's work. What are your suggestions for spreading those feelings? Aside from a declaration that we are open to more than simple trade agreements between the South and Fae courts."

Valerie stopped chewing her food, then hastily swallowed it. "Publicly declaring your stance toward Fae will go a long way toward encouraging others. Of course, you cannot force your subjects to change their minds. The opposition will always be there. It is critical you are firm about the repercussions of violence against Fae."

Josiah chimed in. "Going to war with the Court of Dusk is going to heighten tension, but we also want the South to learn that not all Fae are bad. It is critical that you start this effort as soon as possible. If the number of Fae in the South increases from potential alliances with the other three courts, it could create an uprising if you haven't addressed matters first."

I nodded and took a sip of juice, pondering their words. My current plan was to publicly address my standpoint on Fae and humans immediately after the coronation. When I consulted with Lord John, he thought it would be awkward if I handled it prior to the coronation but that it was common for new rulers to address their subjects and bring to light any significant, immediate changes they were implementing.

"Excellent advice. I will make the announcement during the reception following the coronation." I paused before shifting to the next topic. "There have been several situations in the past few weeks, one as recent as yesterday morning, that have led to increasing concern about my safety within the palace. To address the issue, I have decided to have a total of four ladies-in-waiting serving me. Their primary purpose would be to provide extra protection, as Ghilanna is providing for me this morning." Ghilanna cast me a sharp look but stayed silent at my revelation. I gave myself a mental shrug. I wasn't going to earn Valerie's trust by omitting information, and what Ghilanna was doing was a good example of the type of tasks Valerie could expect to have.

Valerie gasped in surprise and choked on her food. Josiah pounded on her back, and finally the coughing ceased. Valerie took a long drink of water to soothe her throat, then spoke. "I doubt you're going to find any noblewomen who are capable or willing to defend you. I doubt most of them would defend themselves if they were put in such a situation."

"Yes," I replied. "That is precisely why my new ladies-in-waiting will already be trained and comfortable using a weapon. I don't have time to force noblewomen to accept training and become skilled at defense. I was hoping that you, Valerie, would be willing to fill one of the spots."

Josiah burst out laughing. "Val? A lady-in-waiting? Are you mad?"

Valerie punched him hard in the shoulder, and Josiah immediately sobered up. "I'll do it," she said, glaring a challenge at Josiah.

I smiled to myself. I had expected Valerie to decline. "Wonderful. Ghilanna has agreed to formally train Violet. Perhaps you can help with that as well."

"Where is Violet? Your plan is to have extra security, yet you're at this meeting with only Ghilanna?" Valerie demanded.

Point to Valerie for the question, I thought, but I didn't want to say it aloud. "Ghilanna is a Fae warrior, and I am trained in the same manner."

"I see," Valerie said softly.

"Josiah, I would like to ask you to be one of my advisors. Though you will not be on the war council, you will be called upon at times or have access to me that is not granted to others should time-sensitive matters arise. It is my desire that your familiarity with my subjects in Gaskal will help me gain a better understanding of them. Valerie will be visibly in my inner circle, but I would prefer to keep your role more hidden in the hopes that those living in the city will continue to have an open dialogue with you," I explained.

"A spymaster?" asked Josiah, his voice higher than normal.

I shrugged. "Is that what you want to be?" I knew I probably needed one, and Josiah was right. All the reasons I listed for why I wanted him as an advisor would make him a good spymaster. He was well liked throughout the city and could use that to expand his foothold throughout the kingdom too.

"Whatever you need me to do, I will do my best. I also understand that there is a lot happening very fast. Valerie and I will do everything in our power to assist you, as will the other Copper Wolves. Queen Serafina, you represent a dream many of us wanted but hadn't dared to voice aloud until we met your mother. A world where Fae and human can walk side by side without fear," Josiah said somberly.

I swallowed hard, feeling as though the weight of the world, not just this kingdom, was now resting on my shoulders. But he was right. I had had the same dream as long as I could remember. To be accepted for who I was instead of being judged for it. "Thank you," I said in a shaky voice, my emotions getting the better of me.

Lowering my gaze, I focused on eating my breakfast as I collected myself. Josiah and Valerie did the same, for which I was grateful. My plate clean, I felt like I had mastered my feelings and could get back to business. "All of my ladies-in-waiting will have rooms within a reasonable distance of mine so that you are readily available for any protection detail that I will need. If there are no other matters to discuss at this time, then I can show you to the room."

Valerie fidgeted with her napkin for a few moments before she briefly met my gaze, her voice tight. "Am I required to reside in the palace?"

"No, though it would be preferable, since your role is to guard me. The room you're assigned will be available for your use however you see fit," I responded, trying to prevent my tone from coming across as an order.

Valerie frowned. "I am not sure my husband would appreciate me living in the palace full time when he cannot afford to be away from the forge for long periods. It's his livelihood."

"I understand. Perhaps we can work out a schedule for the next few days so you can know ahead of time when you'll be needed in the palace," I explained.

Ghilanna chimed in, "Once you know where your room is, you will be able to get to it without a guide or special permission."

"Okay, then let's go check out my new room," Valerie said with a forced smile.

Together, we headed down the hallway toward my residence.

Thirteen

TRISTAN

I sprawled on the blue couch facing the fireplace, a round pillow digging uncomfortably into my back. As I tried to determine what to do while waiting for Sera and Ghilanna to return, a memory surfaced. Tanyth had sent me with a squad to investigate a group of humans in Lochlan Sgàile and to eliminate them. I had chosen to scout alone, taking the rare opportunity to shapeshift. Except someone had seen me.

A branch snapped behind me, and I spun, claws out. A red-haired Fae female glared at me, sword raised. Cursing my stupidity, I kept my eyes on her as she took a half step forward and I shifted back to Fae form, broadsword out.

"I don't want to fight," she said. I raised my eyebrow. Her sword and actions told a different tale. "I'm Fiera. I know you came from the Court of Dusk."

"What do you want?" I asked, keeping my voice low.

"Your prince captured my friend Serafina, and I want to know where she's being held," Fiera said.

Surprised by Fiera's boldness, I answered, "Dorcha Palace. It's impenetrable."

"I'll find a way in," she said confidently.

Yet she had failed. Bane, my second-in-command, had captured her and brought his prize to Tanyth. Deep down, I knew that the bold red-haired female who had been willing to walk into the darkest of shadows for her best friend still existed. I prayed that we could get through whatever Tanyth had done to Fiera for everyone's sakes. Fiera and Ghilanna were the first trainees who were willing to set aside the cultural barriers between Fae and humans and befriend Sera for herself, seeing past her human-like appearance and lack of magic.

A cough drew me out of my thoughts. I straightened on the couch, knowing what task I would tackle while Sera and Ghilanna were busy.

Nolan had a neutral expression while he waited for me to focus on him, then he spoke. "Thomas mentioned that a decision had been made regarding what we're doing with Fiera. I was wondering if you were going to tell Fiera or if I should send someone to do it."

"Yes, I will tell her. Would you let Violet know I would like her to accompany me? I think the conversation will be less intimidating if I have a female with me, especially given everything Fiera has gone through recently," I responded, rising to my feet.

Making my way over to the weapons cabinet, I withdrew my scabbard and longsword. The broadsword would have been overkill for a meeting like this. I slid my feet into knee-high boots and buckled the scabbard around my waist.

Violet—hair in a neat bun, hands clasped lightly in front of her, burgundy dress immaculate—was waiting beside Nolan when I was ready to go. "Forgive me, m'lord Tristan, but what is it you want me to do?"

I frowned, then sighed, deciding that it would be better if I explained myself. Violet didn't know much about Fae—or me, for that matter. The more I could share with her, the better she'd handle herself. "Through several interviews, it has been determined that Fiera is not a threat and not under any dark magic.

You have witnessed how Sera has handled getting her memories back from the time she was a prisoner at the Court of Dusk. Fiera has gone through similar experiences. Who knows what twisted things Tanyth told her about me? I've done unspeakable things for him, so he had lots to draw on. I thought your presence would help, since you are a female. She doesn't know you and you can serve as a friendly face to her. Until we have gotten to know her better, she needs to be supervised at all times, but I don't want to make her uncomfortable."

Violet nodded in understanding. "I am happy to help." She patted the basket on her arm. "I've got fresh clothing and towels for Fiera to bathe and change."

"Excellent. Let's go," I replied. My voice sounded more cheerful than I'd intended.

I sat backward in a chair, elbows resting on the back, watching the seamstress measure everyone—Sera, Ghilanna, Violet, and Valerie. Though magic could create clothing, it was far easier to call up a garment that already existed. Especially with an intricate dress like the coronation gown, where it was possible to miss a critical piece from lack of knowledge. With the ladies-in-waiting, since Violet and Valerie were not Fae, they needed actual garments; it would be quite silly if they couldn't get dressed unless one of the Fae or Sera were around.

I knew I had to be measured as well but was glad to let the ladies go first. The plan was for the seamstress to make the coronation gown as well as design what the ladies-in-waiting would be wearing for the coronation and other outings and a few new outfits for Sera. Now that she was queen, Serafina had the final say on what she would wear. I could tell by the glint in her eye when she glanced over at me that she was thoroughly enjoying directing the seamstress to make things that were quite different from what King Leonard had previously ordered.

Eventually, the seamstress called for me. She was quick and efficient in her measurements, taking notes in precise handwriting in a tiny notebook. The measurements also included sizing for armor and boots, not just the clothing I was to wear as the queen's husband. Before I knew it, the seamstress was dismissing me.

Sera was going through stacks of fabric samples but looked up when I drew near. "Done?" she asked.

"Yes," I replied, and she set down the fabrics and stepped into my arms. I hugged her tightly, then let go. Sera smoothed her hand down her dress. "Time for the war council meeting," she said, loud enough for the others to hear her.

Declan, Lord McCormack, and Callyn had all agreed to be on the war council. The question was what would happen once we were all in the same room together, *and*, I reminded myself, how they would react when I revealed I was a snow leopard shapeshifter. Callyn knew already, but Declan and Lord McCormack certainly did not. With the decision to include the three ladies-in-waiting in the war council room, that added two more who were not privy to my secret as well. I was prepared for any reaction. I had to be, given my life was at stake.

A shiver rippled through me, and I felt the faintest hint of fur start to grow on my arms. Clamping down hard on my emotions, I forced myself to think of a glassy lake. Thankfully, no one seemed to notice.

Sera linked her arm in mine, and we walked at a stately pace through the door and into the hallway with Violet, Ghilanna, and Valerie at our backs. They would stay in the shadows during the meeting as extra protection. Lord John led the way, talking about tasks he had been working on.

"I have a sample invitation for your approval." He passed Sera an invitation, and she inspected it, then handed it to me, shrugging. It was simple but elegant cream-colored paper with gold writing:

We request your attendance at the coronation of Her Royal Majesty, Queen Serafina Wyantha Helias, Lady of the South.

I handed it back to Lord John. Not only was this not a matter I was interested in, it wasn't my kingdom. Sera needed to be the one to decide what the invitations should look like.

"The invitation looks fine. I give my approval to have them made and distributed," Sera responded.

Lord John halted in front of a room on the opposite side of the palace, on the same floor as our residence. Sera seemed to know roughly where we were. The guards opened the set of double doors, and Lord John ushered us inside.

The walls of the room were walnut tongue and groove, with a chair rail painted in gold. At the center was a round table of walnut inlaid with pale maple leaves. Five high-backed walnut chairs were spaced evenly around it, and at the far end of the room was another table with a map and a few odds and ends sitting on top of it. Four tall but narrow windows provided some natural light over the table with the map, where Declan and Lord McCormack were having a quiet conversation. Callyn had not yet arrived. *Maybe that was on purpose.* I couldn't blame her for wanting to wait as long as possible to enter the room. Regardless of what the master of the guard and Lord McCormack had said about being tolerant of Fae, words were just words. We would have to see by their actions if they had been truthful.

Sera circled the room once, inspecting it and greeting Declan and Lord McCormack. I waited near the door. A few minutes later, Callyn appeared. A slight twitch of her lips and the tightness in the way she held her arms led me to believe something had happened. But now was not the time to ask.

Smiling, Sera came over to Callyn and took Callyn's pale hands in her own tan ones. "Did you have any trouble finding us?"

Callyn pressed her lips together, but Sera met her gaze. Callyn lowered her purple eyes and replied, "The guards at the gate did not want to let me in. One of the stable hands recognized me and was able to talk the guards down, but they were saying they might throw me in the dungeon just for being Fae."

Sera's blue-green eyes hardened. "Did you get their names?"

"Leo and Paul," Callyn replied.

Thomas was still in the room and came over when Sera motioned for him. "Your Majesty," he said with a bow.

"Please send the guard captain to relieve Leo and Paul of their duty at the palace gate. I want them to go to the dungeon. I will talk to Declan about it after this meeting," Sera said.

My heart swelled with pride that she was taking matters into her own hands and firmly assuming control of the situation. If her kingdom was going to be tolerant of Fae, then it must start at the palace.

"As you wish, Your Majesty," Thomas said with a bow and departed to give the guard captain his orders.

Lord John cleared his throat. "Your Majesty, I will leave you with your war council. Lunch will arrive in an hour."

Sera nodded and Lord John bowed, then departed, pulling the doors firmly shut behind him.

"War council members, please join me at the table," Sera said, sweeping her arms forward.

No one moved. I bit the inside of my lip and decided I would set the example for the others. I chose a chair and sat down. Callyn sat at the opposite end of the table from me. I was intrigued when Serafina sat beside Callyn, leaving the two vacant seats for Lord McCormack and Declan, forcing them, I realized, to sit next to me and Callyn. I was aware of Violet, Ghilanna, and Valerie at their posts around the room but needed to keep my focus on the war council members. How this meeting went would set the tone for our interactions in the future, including whether Declan would respect me and Callyn.

Serafina smiled. "First, I want to thank the four of your for agreeing to be on my war council. As you know, Prince Tanyth has declared war on the South. The good news is that last night I received confirmation that at this time we are *not* facing war on two fronts. The information King Leonard was given about the Court of the Sun massing on our border was incorrect."

Lord McCormack and Declan visibly relaxed at the news. I tensed, waiting for the demand that Sera reveal the source of the information, but it never came. A stark reminder of how different humans were to the Fae in the Court of Dusk.

"The purpose of the meeting today is to come up with a plan. I am new to the South and have not been privy to much information. I'm hoping we will resolve that today. The first question is, what is the status of my knights? Are they battle-ready or have they been allowed to forget their training and pursue other activities?" Serafina inquired.

Declan's face was difficult to read. *I'm sure mine is too.*

Declan replied in a level voice, "There are one thousand knights in a fort a half-day's ride south of Gaskal at Fort Salmon. The residents of Fort Salmon have been training for one to two years, so they are green with no battle experience, but they are fit and should be battle-ready as soon as tomorrow. However, the other two thousand knights that are scattered among the nobles' castles may not be battle-ready. There are about fifty at Red Rock as well."

"What about infantry?" I asked, wondering why Declan had started with the knights.

Declan frowned. "Historically, other than the palace guards and personal guards that serve the nobles, the South does not use infantry."

My eyebrows shot upward. *No infantry?* I had thought the South had infantry at the Court of Dusk's battle against King Lionel, but now I wondered if they trained their knights to ride as well as fight from the ground and just had one battle-ready class instead of two.

Lord McCormack chimed in before I could respond. "Ages ago, the Lord of the South had a massive horse-breeding operation and supplied the horses for all the knights. Over the centuries, the royal family has distanced themselves from the hands-on aspect. That is why the South only has knights."

"While I would love to have an in-depth history lesson to fill the gaps in my knowledge and introduce Tristan and Callyn to our kingdom," Sera said with a smile, "I think we're getting off track. We have one thousand knights who are green but ready, and two thousand veterans, status unknown. It is of utmost importance that we determine the status of the two thousand as soon as possible. It will determine whether we hold a chance at standing against Prince Tanyth alone or if our only hope of survival is with an alliance."

Lord McCormack tapped his fingers on the table. "The problem with standing alone, even if we have all three thousand knights, is who will be left to keep the kingdom together if we win? Perhaps if you and Tristan stayed here at the palace, we could manage."

"No," Sera said firmly. "You will not lock me here in the palace for safekeeping. If we're going to war, then I will be there fighting with my subjects."

Lord McCormack bowed his head and stayed silent. I had expected nothing less than Sera's response. She was not one to sit by and let others fight for her.

"Who should we send to determine the status of the knights?" I asked.

Declan shared a look with Lord McCormack, then met my gaze squarely. "Lord McCormack and you."

"Me?" I choked on the word.

Callyn smirked at me, and Sera nodded in agreement. "Yes. That is a good plan. The nobles know Lord McCormack, but Tristan, as my husband, you can represent me and give them a chance to meet you. It'll also allow us to see how they are going to respond to dealing with Fae."

The edges of my vision darkened as the room closed in on me. I sucked in a breath and found my airway was blocked. My panic rose.

Travaran handed me a scroll, and I opened it, recognizing Tanyth's handwriting immediately.

"I have been notified of an intruder in the southern part of the territory. Take a squad and eliminate the problem," I read aloud.

Smirking, Travaran yanked the note out of my hand and shredded it. "No reason to take a full squad. It'll just be the two of us."

I heard muffled words but couldn't make them out—the memory's hold on me was too strong.

Elimination was a harsh punishment for trespassing. I hoped I would be able to question the trespasser and clear up the misunderstanding. Surely there was no reason to kill if it was indeed a mistake.

I sniffed the air and caught a whiff of smoke and an unfamiliar animal.

Travaran's eyes lit up in recognition as he caught the scent as well. Usually, we planned our attack, then split up. I unsheathed my sword, but Travaran made me uneasy when he didn't follow suit. Instead, his magic swirled around his fingers.

Smoke burned my eyes and the back of my throat. On the other side of the firepit was a brown bear. There was a sharp snap from where Travaran should have been, and the bear's head shot upward.

Bears didn't make fires. Which meant it had to be a bear shifter. Icy fear rolled through me. With Travaran there, I wasn't in a position to save the bear shifter.

There was a sizzle and the smell of burning flesh as turquoise magic hurtled through the air, pelting the bear shifter. In the moments it took me to reach them, Travaran had killed the shifter.

Travaran inspected the bear shifter, who had turned back into her Fae form upon death. Suddenly, he tipped his head up, staring at me with anger on his face. "Betrayer!"

Limbs flailing, I thrashed against whoever was gripping my arm. The chair I had been sitting in flipped over backward, but the hands holding my arms kept me from falling. I kicked out for a moment, then got my feet under me, wobbling on shaky legs. Once I was standing, Declan and Lord McCormack let go of me and backed away cautiously.

Sera's face was pale, and she looked worried but stayed close to the table. I wasn't sure if it was because she was afraid of me or afraid Declan or Lord McCormack was going to do something stupid.

Callyn marched right up to me and gripped my shoulders firmly. "Memories are a bitch."

I exhaled, and the tension started to drain away. "Yes, they are."

"You know, this is not the Court of Dusk. Serafina is not going to allow anyone to give you orders to execute a human or Fae without cause," Callyn said softly.

Lifting my arms, I broke her hold on me and ran my hand over my face, then lowered it. "I know. But everyone has a past, and it's not always easy to forget."

Fourteen

SERAFINA

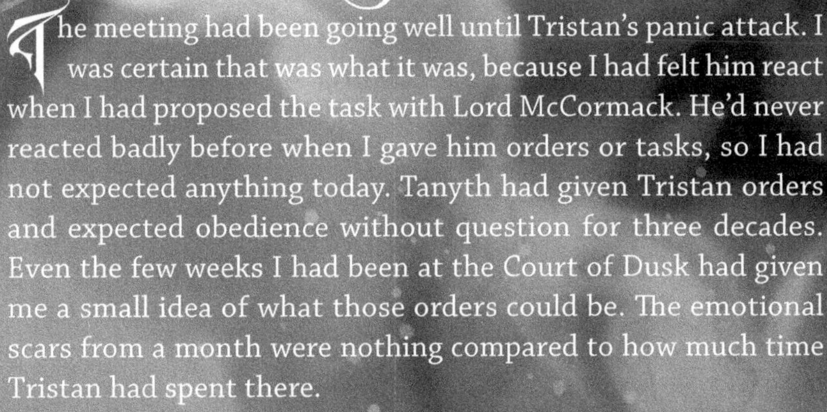

The meeting had been going well until Tristan's panic attack. I was certain that was what it was, because I had felt him react when I had proposed the task with Lord McCormack. He'd never reacted badly before when I gave him orders or tasks, so I had not expected anything today. Tanyth had given Tristan orders and expected obedience without question for three decades. Even the few weeks I had been at the Court of Dusk had given me a small idea of what those orders could be. The emotional scars from a month were nothing compared to how much time Tristan had spent there.

Thankfully, Callyn had reacted faster than I did, and now Tristan's panic attack was over.

Declan smacked his hands on the table, trying to get everyone's attention. "Is Tristan capable of doing this task?" Declan demanded.

Bristling, Callyn returned to her spot at the table. "Yes, he is able to do this task of finding the knights with Lord McCormack."

Annoyed at Declan, I snapped, "If it had been me, would you voice your doubts to the council?"

Declan abruptly sat down in his chair, eyes lowered. "No, Your Majesty."

"Then you owe my husband the same respect," I ordered. Declan mumbled something incoherent that I hoped was an agreement or apology.

I cleared my throat, and all eyes fell on me. "I am aware there have been some tensions here in the palace and in Gaskal between the humans and Fae. I want to be clear that ultimately, I hope to establish alliances with the Fae courts, not just mere trade agreements. Our ancestors were once able to live in harmony, and I fully intend to set things in motion so once again that will be the case. I understand I will meet with resistance, but I wanted to start with the members of my war council. I expect each of you to lead by example, treat each other with respect, and encourage others to do the same."

I briefly closed my eyes, then reopened them. "There are two matters that I need to bring to your attention. The first is that I want to formally give Tristan the title of general." No one seemed startled at this announcement, so I plunged onward. "The second is to inform you that some Fae are shapeshifters. Which means they can turn into animals or magical creatures. My *husband*, Tristan, is a snow leopard shapeshifter. There will be times in the near future where he will need to be a snow leopard. Tristan, if you would please show them." I gestured to the table with my hand.

His eyes widened slightly, and then he obliged. In one smooth motion, Tristan shifted into a snow leopard, landing on the table as the shift completed. Declan shot backward in his chair, toppling it over. Lord McCormack froze, his knuckles white on the armrests. Though he looked uncertain, he was not afraid of Tristan. I couldn't blame either of them for reacting. Tristan jumping onto the table was quite intimidating. Tristan leaped from the table to the floor and sat in front of Lord McCormack. He came halfway up the man's chest.

Declan was shaking, though trying to control it. Gazing at Tristan, he said, "Is he planning on venturing around the palace like this?"

I shrugged. "Possibly. Though if it's any consolation, very few Fae can shapeshift into a snow leopard. So if you see one around the palace or in Gaskal, you'll know it's Tristan."

Callyn, who had been quiet, decided to join the conversation. "Most humans would attack a snow leopard on sight. Is it wise to traipse around as a snow leopard for no reason?"

I pressed my lips together. She had a valid point, and honestly I wasn't sure what Tristan's plan was, other than he wanted to make sure the war council knew he could shapeshift.

Saving me from responding, Tristan shifted back to his Fae form and replied, "If I did choose to shift, there would be a reason. But the other purpose of this demonstration is to introduce you to the idea that there are Fae shapeshifters and Fae who are bonded with griffins. Everyone in here needs to be willing to be open-minded about who might decide to ally with us."

Declan laughed harshly. "Griffins don't exist, so it would be impossible for us to ally with a Fae who rides one."

I bristled at his tone and ignored Callyn's warning glance. "They *do* exist, and it just so happens we already have alliances with them. Marek Fenmyar is the heir of the Court of the Sun and is a bonded griffin rider. He has sworn fealty to me, along with a unicorn named Dubhar."

Declan clamped his mouth shut, muscles tense. I shifted my gaze to Lord McCormack, wondering if he had equally strong opinions about who or what might choose to ally with me.

"Is this unicorn perhaps disguised as your beloved stallion, Dubhar?" Lord McCormack asked.

I was surprised he had paid enough attention to know what horse I was riding, let alone how close our relationship was. "Yes, the black stallion I have been riding is a unicorn."

Lord McCormack steepled his dark fingers together. "Intriguing."

"You might be right, Declan. Marek and Dubhar could end up being our only nontraditional allies. But they *are* our allies, and you will respect them as your equals. They wish—as do all of us in this room—for the South to be successful in defeating Prince Tanyth," I said. It was a struggle to keep my voice firm. I knew if I did not believe we could defeat Tanyth, then no one in this room would. As it stood, the odds were stacked against us. *I have time to change that.*

Coughing, Callyn drew everyone's attention to her. "Now that we have a plan to determine the status of the knights, shouldn't we end this meeting so that Lord McCormack and Tristan can get on their way?"

At that precise moment, the door opened, and servants brought in five covered plates, a tray of glasses, and a full pitcher of water.

"After lunch?" I suggested. I was met with murmurs of agreement. When the servants departed, we dug into our meal in silence. I presumed everyone was too absorbed in processing everything we'd discussed to bother with small talk, which suited me fine.

When the war council meeting adjourned, Tristan left with Lord McCormack to work out the details of their trip. Declan departed to meet with the four guard captains to discuss the treatment of Fae, which left me alone with Callyn. I knew there were likely things I needed to attend to, but I got the sense that Callyn wanted to talk. Knowing Callyn would speak more freely in private, I sent Valerie home, asked Violet to check on Dubhar, and instructed Ghilanna to consult with Thomas to see if any messages had arrived.

From the unbound memories of my imprisonment at Dorcha Palace, I knew she had helped me as much as she could while I was Tanyth's prisoner, but I wasn't entirely sure we were friends. Maybe in time. Callyn's purple eyes met mine. "You should tell him."

I knew instantly the *him* was Tristan. "Tell him what?"

"Everyone has dark secrets, Serafina," Callyn replied.

I swallowed and swore I could hear my heart pounding in my chest, it was so loud. "I don't have any secrets from Tristan, not anymore. Besides, how would you know what I've gone through?"

Callyn's expression darkened. "You were a prisoner for weeks. I served Tanyth for over fifty years. You have no way of comprehending what I had to do, the sacrifices I made, just to survive. Or even the cost of getting Tristan out … for you."

I fumed at her words and her assumption that because she had been at the Court of Dusk longer, what she had gone through was worse than what I had experienced throughout my life. "You didn't save him for me. You saved him for yourself, so you wouldn't feel guilty about abandoning your best friend, your fuck buddy." As soon as the words left my mouth, I realized my mistake, but it was too late.

Callyn growled low in her throat. "You will never understand. All your life things have been handed to you on a silver platter. Even the challenges were not as hard as they should have been. Even now, all you do is whine about how things affect you, with no regard for anyone else. You're a selfish bitch, and I'm done." Callyn shoved past me and collided with Ghilanna, who was stepping through the doorway and had clearly heard the tail end of Callyn's tirade.

I walked to the back of the room, wanting space. Callyn's words cut deep. *Just as mine hurt her*. My hands trembled, and I shoved them in the hidden pockets of my skirt, trying to breathe. *Do all Fae think of me as Callyn does, that my life was easy and I'm not worthy of their help?*

I heard Ghilanna's soft footfalls behind me. Of all my attendants and advisors, she was the only one who had ever really known me. Her dark-brown arms wrapped around me from behind, and I leaned into her, letting the tears trickle down my cheeks. "I shouldn't have said what I said."

"Hush," whispered Ghilanna. "What was said, was said."

Ghilanna's arms tightened around me. "There has been something weighing on you since the competition started."

This time, I pulled away and turned around to face Ghilanna. "If I tell you, will you promise to not tell anyone else? It is a private matter between myself and Tristan."

Ghilanna nodded. "Of course. I will keep your secret, Sera. No matter what it is."

Taking a step closer, I spoke in a soft voice that only Ghilanna could hear. "I had a miscarriage."

Ghilanna gasped, dumbfounded. Clearly, that was not the secret she thought I was keeping. I realized that there were many details of my relationship with Tristan I had not had time to share with Ghilanna.

"Who was the father?" she asked, keeping her voice equally quiet.

"Tristan," I said, my voice breaking. Ghilanna pulled me into her arms and rocked me as I cried.

"You haven't been married long enough ..." Ghilanna started.

Wiping my eyes, I sighed and leaned back into her embrace. "I suppose now is as good a time as any to have that talk we have not made time for." We sat in two chairs near the map table, and I dove into the short version of my experiences at Dorcha Palace. "I hated Tristan when I first met him," I explained, earning a chuckle from Ghilanna. "Though I must admit even when I hated him, I was attracted to him. He was assigned to train me. Over time, our feelings for each other changed. Tanyth forbade Tristan from touching me, but he found a way to sneak around the rules. Or so we thought. Every moment, I lived in fear of discovery. The soulmate bond formed, and then our relationship was exposed. Even though Tanyth threatened to force me to sleep with him, it never went that far," I said, in answer to Ghilanna's silent question.

"I know conceiving can be difficult for Fae, and now that I have failed to carry a child to term, I am afraid it won't be possible. Besides, how can I fathom bringing a child into a world that is about to be ripped apart by war?" I asked, not expecting Ghilanna to have an answer.

"I'm sorry you went through this alone, Sera, but Tristan loves you," Ghilanna said.

"I know he does, and he responded better than I expected to the news," I replied quietly.

Ghilanna gave me a quick hug, then sat straighter in her chair. "Commander Meriel wants to see you," Ghilanna informed me. "We were busy earlier, and I didn't want you to be distracted from the war council meeting."

"When?" Though Tristan and I had talked about possibly discussing a few things with Commander Meriel, I hadn't figured out the best way to go about setting up a meeting.

"An hour from now. I'm to take you to Jade Wilds using a star portal," Ghilanna replied.

I squashed the disappointment that Meriel was not coming here to the palace but instead had sent for me. *Like I'm a trainee.* I shook off the negative thoughts. Likely it had more to do with the risk of coming here as a Fae than the inconvenience of traveling. I was known at Jade Wilds. My stomach churned. The last time I was there, Meriel had sent me away to become King Leonard's heir.

"Fine, I will go. We should take Fiera with us too. The timing should work well with when Tristan is departing to find the knights."

"Yes, that's the plan. To give you a chance to say goodbye before he leaves." Ghilanna gave my hand a squeeze.

"Very well. Let's plan on going to the stables in an hour," I said decisively.

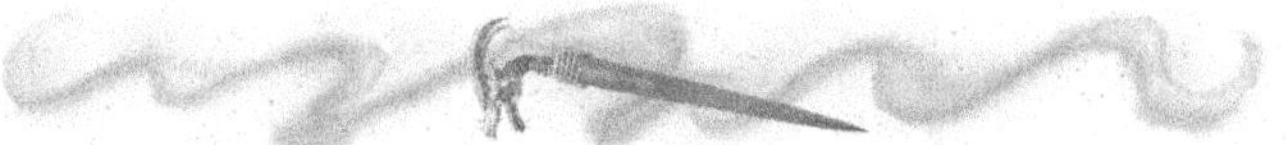

The door to my home suites shut behind me with an audible click. Violet was hanging out with Valerie, and Ghilanna was going to talk to Fiera about coming with us to Jade Wilds. I sighed in relief, ready for a short period of time with Tristan to myself. His trip wasn't going to take too long. We both had to be back in time for the coronation, but I dreaded our separation. *I'm going to have to get used to it,* I told myself.

"Sera?" Tristan called from the bedroom.

"It's me!" I replied, deciding I would tell him I'd had a fight with Callyn. I didn't want him to end up stuck in the middle.

I stepped through the doorway, and Tristan pulled me into his arms, lips on mine. I melted against him, desire uncoiling in my stomach. "Do we have time?" I mumbled against his mouth.

Instead of answering, Tristan deepened the kiss. His cock was pressing against the apex of my thighs. I tugged on the edge of his tunic, too busy kissing him to wrap my mind around the process of undressing with or without magic. Thankfully, Tristan took the hint and our clothing disappeared. With his cock pressing against my entrance, I felt my body respond and was soon soaked and more than ready. I tugged on his hips, wanting to feel his cock inside of me.

Tristan chuckled against my lips. "I promise, you'll get what you want. But we have time. There is no reason to rush."

Tristan led me over to the bed and gently pushed me onto it. My legs were draped over the edge. Instead of asking me to scoot farther back, Tristan dropped to his knees in front of me and gently spread my legs wider. He began trailing light kisses along the inside of my thighs, lightly brushing his tongue over my clit before moving back to my thigh. My core was throbbing, and he was driving me wild while not giving me the satisfaction

I desperately wanted. Slowly rising to standing, a satisfied smirk on his lips moist with my fluids, he nudged my legs farther open and then guided his cock inside of me. Finding his rhythm, Tristan lifted my legs around his waist and bent over me, changing the angle and heightening my pleasure tenfold. I started shaking as tension built within me. Lightly pinching my nipples between his thumbs and forefingers, Tristan sped up his thrusts.

I almost blacked out as wave after wave of intense pleasure cascaded through me. I felt Tristan's body spasm as he got his release, but to my awe, though his rhythm slowed, he did not stop.

"What are you doing?" I whispered. As the words left my lips, I was shocked to feel my body responding again.

Tristan chuckled and leaned over, his in-and-out rhythm slow and steady. He took my right breast into his mouth and gently sucked. A shiver ran through me. Tristan took my left breast into his mouth, swirling his tongue around the nipple, lightly grazing it with his teeth. I gasped as tension built in me again. His velvet lips met mine, eager and demanding. I lost myself in them, momentarily forgetting everything but the feel of our bodies together.

Fifteen

TRISTAN

The slower rhythm allowed me to give Sera a chance for her body to adjust. I had been serious when I told her I intended to make the most of our time together and not rush. Her muscles were tightening, and I felt myself on the brink of my release. *Not yet.* I drew myself almost all the way out before quickly thrusting back in, bumping her back wall. I moaned in pleasure, and my control frayed even more. I slid my finger in alongside my shaft and flicked her clit. Sera's response was immediate and intense. Her whole body clenched, and then spasms rolled through her. I lost control, and the orgasm exploded within me. I draped myself across her, thoroughly spent, but careful not to let her take my full weight.

I lost track of time as we lay there, Sera wrapped protectively in my arms. I could feel the soulmate bond, a strong thread of magic between us. *Perhaps it is the bond that increases our stamina to be intimate.* The thought led me to wonder if that was because the purpose of the bond was to allow Fae to reproduce, or if it was just how the bond worked—another aspect of a culture that believed strongly in intimacy between individuals as an important part of who we were.

Gradually, I was able to convince myself that we needed to clean up so I could leave. Sera wrapped her arms around my waist, trying to hold me in place as I started to push off the bed. "I need to go."

Sera wrinkled her nose. "I wish you didn't."

I kissed her lightly. "Remember, the plan is to not just determine the status of the knights but to gauge the response to Fae."

"I know, I know. It would be nice to have a day or two where we could just be together without anyone else," Sera replied.

Running my fingers through her hair, I savored this moment we had. "As queen, you could make that decision." We both knew she wouldn't, not with war imminent.

"When this is all over, I will make sure we can have our two days, uninterrupted," Sera said with a smile that didn't reach her eyes. The odds of us both surviving a war on the scale I expected it to become were also low. I knew she would fight tooth and nail against any request that she stay safe and off the battlefield, the same as I would. *Except she named me general. It would not go over well with the knights if their general was forced to sit on the sidelines.* I shoved the thoughts away and stood up.

The choice to stay in the bed had meant there was no time for a shower or bath. At the moment, it was very obvious from our appearance that we had had sex. Among Fae warriors it might not matter, but here in the palace, neither one of us could afford to leave the privacy of our bedroom in such a state. Taking a deep breath, I used my magic to clean the fluids off my skin, brush and re-braid my hair, and get dressed. Wanting to give Sera the opportunity to experiment with her own magic, I opted not to do the same for her.

I was dressed in a black jacket with gold trim, a gold medal denoting me as general dangling on the shoulders; a white tunic with a gold vest with the emblem of the South embroidered on the chest; and black pants tucked into knee-high black boots. A longsword in a scabbard was belted at my waist.

While I was busy taking care of my own preparations, Sera had decided to take care of hers. When I turned around, she was dressed. An assessment of her attire had me assuming it wasn't for a meeting within the palace. Sera's russet hair was in a tight braid that hung down her back past her hips. She wore a gold-and-cream tunic over black pants, belted at the waist with a double looped belt bearing her father's longsword in a sheath. A black cloak settled over her shoulders with a gold clasp in the shape of the South's emblem, the only adornment visible on her.

"Commander Meriel requested a meeting," Sera said, her blue-green eyes locking with mine.

I shrugged. "We wanted to meet with her. It is a good task for you while I'm gone. Perhaps she will have some insight to talking to King Pharaan about an alliance. You're taking that book, right?"

She nodded, closed the gap between us, and kissed me, then pulled back. "Don't be late for the coronation."

"I won't be late, I promise," I replied, kissing her swiftly, then stepping an arm's length away to resist the temptation to take her back to bed. The blood thrummed in my veins at the thought.

"Be safe," Sera said and turned on her heel—a smart decision before I picked her up and had my way with her again.

I waited in the bedroom until I heard Ghilanna, Fiera, and Sera talking. Grabbing my discarded pack off the floor, I swung it over my shoulder and headed out of the room.

Including Lord McCormack's two personal guards and Nolan, our party totaled fifteen. Another difference between Fae courts and I assumed all human kingdoms was that women were not encouraged or allowed to be guards or knights. Fae welcomed males and females to earn the rank of warrior. The only thing a female couldn't do was officially rule a Fae court, though over the centuries there had been several times where an exception was made and a queen had ruled the Court of Dawn.

Courtesy of the mating bond, I was aware the moment Sera stepped through the star portal and traveled to Jade Wilds. Though the bond was muted with the distance and I doubted she could hear me if I were to speak through it, its presence reassured me. With time not on our side, I had not taken the opportunity to smooth things over with Callyn before I departed. Sera might have felt it was irreparable, but I knew that was unlikely. Tension was running high between all of us as we navigated new territory—the dynamics of our own relationships and sharing information that was highly personal, such as my ability to shapeshift.

Clenching and releasing the grip on my reins, I surveyed the area around the road with scattered rocks and a few sparse bushes here and there. I was riding alongside Lord McCormack with the guards fanned out around us. "How many nobles are we hoping to meet with?"

Though I knew the South was smaller than the Fae courts, it was not a small kingdom to cover. Beyond my few glances at the map in the war council room, I had not taken time to learn where the knights could be stationed. Our task was threefold: investigate the status of the veteran knights, ensure word was spread throughout the kingdom about Sera's impending coronation, and feel out the nobles' attitudes toward Fae.

"Ideally, we will be able to go to all ten castles. Travel time between them will be tight. It could be impossible depending on how long we stay at each stop," Lord McCormack said conversationally.

"Who do the knights answer to?" I asked, trying to determine a plan if we met resistance.

"Ultimately, they answer to Serafina, and therefore your orders would supersede anything given by the lord housing them. However, there will be individuals who don't want to take an order from a Fae, no matter the title. Given how much time we have and the impending war, if we are certain they will not turn on us, I don't think it is critical if there are some who refuse the call to arms," Lord McCormack said.

I frowned but realized he did have a point. Punishing people for refusing orders would take time we didn't have. The best option would be to write down a list of names and deal with their disobedience later.

Our first stop was Hunter's Hollow. A narrow, well-used dirt path veered off the wide main road and into what looked to me like a small village. Our group was silent save for the jingle of the horses' tack and our armor as we rode in a double column into the middle of the village. Benches surrounded a large fire circle in what appeared to be the central square, which was where Lord McCormack directed the guards to halt.

I peered around, wondering where the veteran knights who lived here were. I counted about thirty small wooden houses arranged in neat rows on three of the four sides. The fourth side had a large blacksmith shop with a thatch roof. From what I could tell, no one was around.

"I thought you said there are veteran knights here?" I asked.

Lord McCormack's gaze flicked to mine, then back to watching the dirt road leading into the spruce forest. "There are. Some of them live in these houses. Others live up at the pond."

My horse pawed the ground impatiently. I kept my expression neutral. "I don't understand."

"Sorry, I'm not used to traveling with someone who isn't familiar with where we're going. The Hunter family has a large estate up on the hill with the pond, and there are training yards and barracks up there. When they think they're going to have visitors, everyone goes to the pond until they can determine who has come calling. Be patient. Lord Hunter will appear momentarily," Lord McCormack explained.

Just as Lord McCormack had predicted, within a few minutes, we could hear hoofbeats on packed dirt. A man in chain mail with a helm on his head, making it difficult to see his appearance, rode on a white horse that had patches of mud on its coat. I grimaced, wondering why this lord had not taken the time to at least have his horse groomed before showing his face.

"Greetings, Lord Hunter. We met before. I am Lord Theo McCormack, and this is General Tristan Gilvrye."

I gave the lord the slightest of bows from my saddle. His eyes roved over me before focusing his attention on Lord McCormack.

"To what do I owe the honor of a visit from the esteemed Lord McCormack?" drawled Lord Hunter, laying it on thick.

I bit the inside of my cheek to prevent myself from saying anything I'd regret. I immediately disliked the man. Then, I recalled that I had been acquainted with another individual from Hunter's Hollow during my competition for Serafina's hand in marriage—Frederick Hunter. *How different things would be now if I had lost the last joust run.* Running my hand over my face and brushing strands of hair behind my ears, I reminded myself to be patient and let Lord McCormack handle this.

Lord McCormack replied, "We are here to determine the status of the veteran knights residing at Hunter's Hollow and to extend an invitation to Queen Serafina's coronation."

Lord Hunter's hands twitched on the reins, the only reaction that I could discern. "Most of the knights train daily. Why is their status important now?"

Lord McCormack shifted in his saddle. "Queen Serafina is issuing a call to arms for all knights in the South. General Gilvrye is here to conduct an assessment and report his findings to the queen."

There was a flurry of movement on the path Lord Hunter had traveled down. A muted hum of booted feet could be heard, and then they appeared: a double column of knights. There were around eighty of them wearing plate armor that had seen better days with clear spots of rust and dents that had never been repaired. Watching them move together as a unit, I was pleased to see that Lord Hunter was correct. These knights did train on a regular basis. *Eighty is a start.*

The knights halted about twenty feet away from us. I dismounted and moved over toward them. One of them stepped forward and removed his helmet, placing it under his arm. He had light-gray eyes, a trimmed salt-and-pepper beard, and dark-brown hair with streaks of gray.

"I'm General Tristan Gilvrye. To whom do I have the pleasure of speaking?" I asked formally.

The knight bowed and then straightened, his arms relaxed at his side. "Captain Hershel Green. I keep this motley crew in line."

A few chuckles behind Captain Green had me wondering what he did to keep them in line. It didn't matter. He had approached me and replied to my question without hesitation, clearly not intimidated by the fact that I am Fae.

"I need you to report to the palace in Gaskal the day after the coronation. We are at war with the Court of Dusk, and it is critical we prepare as quickly as possible," I explained.

Captain Green fisted his hand and placed it over his heart. "I will serve the Lady of the South in whatever capacity she requires. As will my men. We will be in Gaskal the day after the coronation as you have requested."

"Very good," I replied and started to turn away.

Captain Green coughed. "Pardon the question, General, sir. But is it true? That our queen can fight with a sword?"

I turned back to Captain Green and nodded. "Yes, that is true. She spent twelve years training with the Fae and achieved the warrior title after participating in the battle at Emerald Valley."

Whispers rose up behind Captain Green, and he raised his hand to shush them. "Will she stand with us in this war against a Fae?"

"Yes, that is her plan," I confirmed.

"Good. It is about time the kingdoms change their mind about women fighting and leading. I ... *we* would be honored to serve Queen Serafina," Captain Green replied with a genuine smile.

"I will relay your words to her upon our return. I am thrilled to have men such as you and your regiment at our side in this war," I replied. Warmth filled me that there were decent humans in this kingdom after all. Loyal to their kingdom, but not as close-minded as King Leonard had been.

"Now, if you'll excuse us, we have more places to visit and are short on time," I said.

The lines of Captain Green's throat tightened, then he spoke. "The knights at Castle Piore have gone soft. Some of them can't even ride a horse for more than ten minutes without getting sore. There are others, though, who have kept up with training as King Leonard wished. Many of them don't live within the compounds of the nobles. If it would help, I can spread the word."

Surprised but pleased by Captain Green's honesty and willingness to aid us, I offered him a warm smile. "Thank you. Please notify as many knights as you can and have them gather the day after the coronation in Gaskal." I reached out and gave Captain Green's forearm a squeeze, then returned to my horse.

"I'm ready to move on when you are," I said to Lord McCormack.

Lord Hunter was talking in a low voice to one of our guards and not paying attention to us. Lord McCormack sighed. "Yes, I am ready."

I whistled, signaling our guards to come to attention. When their eyes were on me, I commanded, "Move out." I dug my heels into the sides of my horse and shot forward down the path. Not having a chance to second-guess the order, the guards fell in around us.

"How did it go with Captain Green?" Lord McCormack asked.

"Well, he was pleased about Serafina knowing how to use a sword and offered to pass on the word to the scattered knights that we will not easily come in contact with," I responded.

"Great. Captain Green is a good man. I was hoping he would help us. Time changes folks, though. I didn't want to prematurely get your hopes up," Lord McCormack replied.

I couldn't blame him for being cautious. Eighty knights was a start, and hopefully we would meet others like Captain Green loyal to the South and less concerned about the particulars of who was ruling the kingdom or the reason for the call to arms.

Though the primary purpose of traveling with Lord McCormack was to inspect the knights and deliver coronation invitations, it also gave me the opportunity to become more familiar with the kingdom of the South. The rocky hills were prohibitive to many crops, though we had passed a few areas where the land flattened out enough to permit growing some grains and hay. There was even an area where beef cattle were grazing. The forests, on the other hand, were lush—a mix of spruce, rowan, beech, alder, and the rare oak—and created many opportunities for the South. Hunting game such as caribou, southern gray fox, and badgers provided meat and furs, and the wood could be harvested to turn into weapons, furniture, and even parchment paper.

The castles and homesteads we visited varied as much as the land did, though I had learned the differences were directly influenced by what was necessary in that part of the kingdom. The nobles who had frequent dealings with bandits had more guards and often thick stone walls. There had even been a village surrounded by a black stone wall with two tall watchtowers.

Our final destination for the day was Castle Piore. The road had inclined steadily for the past few miles and was getting steeper. Just when I was going to suggest walking to give the horses a rest, the road leveled out and revealed Castle Piore, with its black stone walls nestled against the mountains. I shuddered as an image of Dorcha Palace, built into Ember Mountain, momentarily replaced that of Castle Piore. I shook my head, willing the image away. *I am in the South. This is not Dorcha Palace.*

We halted outside the massive iron gate. A guard peered at us from behind it. I dismounted and strode side by side with Lord McCormack up to the gate.

"We are here to see Duke Piore," Lord McCormack said sternly.

Captain Green's warning was in the forefront of my mind. A fine layer of dirt coated everyone in our party. I wished I had thought of using magic to freshen us up before we approached the gate—to make a better impression—but it was too late now.

"I will inform the duke you are here," the guard replied and hastily retreated.

I sighed. The other nobles had allowed us to come within their gates instead of requiring us to remain outside. *Hopefully this is not setting the precedent for the rest of the visit.*

Faster than I expected, the guard reappeared, and the chain rattled as the pulley system slowly cranked the gate open. The gate clanged loudly when it reached the top. The guard beckoned us forward into the large courtyard and a swarm of what looked like villagers surrounded us as we dismounted. The villagers took our horses, and the guard led us up the stairs into the imposing black castle. The stone was formed from what I thought was black granite. There were high towers on each corner of the castle, though the building itself was narrow. The area behind the wall was significant and would allow for many guests—*or protection from raiders*, I thought.

The hall we entered was gloomy. Small arched windows high in the walls at set intervals provided the only source of light.

Even Dorcha Palace had more light than this, I mused. I heard the click of shoes on the polished stone floor before anyone else did; the slight difference in steps, as though the person had suffered an injury recently.

I kept my stance relaxed. Duke Piore came into view. He was a middle-aged human, likely forty or so, with dark-blond hair going gray at the temples, a clean-shaven face, and brooding blue-gray eyes. The duke was wearing a black velvet jacket with puffy shoulders and tight-fitting sleeves. A row of gold buttons held the jacket closed. His pants were rusty orange and gathered at the ankles, reminding me of iron left outside during a rainstorm. The duke had a thin sword belted at his side with a filigree guard, more for show than use. My own broadsword would easily slice it in two.

"Lord McCormack, General Gilvrye, what a pleasant surprise," Duke Piore said in a clipped voice. Word must have traveled ahead of us as we made our way here. Serafina had not sent messengers to warn anyone of our visit.

Lord McCormack took the duke's offered hand and gave it a firm shake. "Good to see you, Duke Piore," he said.

"Likewise," replied Duke Piore, though his tone indicated otherwise.

I assumed he would shake my hand too. Instead, when Lord McCormack released his grip, the duke's arm fell stiffly to his side. I pressed my lips together, ignoring the intended slight.

"If you don't mind, we would like to stay the night as your guests," Lord McCormack said. "It is safe within your walls, unlike camping at the base of the mountain would be."

Schooling my face into neutrality, I was amazed that Lord McCormack was concerned for our safety if we slept outside of the castle. I was not aware there were currently raiders within our proximity and was confident that I could easily dispatch anything that sought to cause us harm.

Duke Piore put on a show of coughing, taking his time making a decision. I was about to prompt him to respond when the duke spoke. "Yes, you are welcome to stay as my guests. You and the general can stay in the castle guest rooms. The guards, however, will need to spend the night in the stables. I do not have space for them anywhere else."

I bit the inside of my cheek, drawing blood. The duke was lying to our faces, and we all knew it. Per my discussion with Lord McCormack earlier, we could not refuse any offer of housing, regardless of it falling far below the appropriate care the duke should be presenting us with. Disputing his offer would greatly increase the chance of him refusing any request we might make going forward, including denying us access to the knights who were under his command.

Sixteen

SERAFINA

I took a deep breath, inhaling the sweet smell of hay and horses. Dubhar had called me into the barn and I'd told Ghilanna and Fiera to meet me there, deciding we could just as easily take the star portal from there. Thomas was vehement about coming with us and accompanied me to the stable.

Ghilanna and Fiera stood in the middle of the barn aisle. The hardpacked dirt was swept clean of hay and grain. White magic was forming around Ghilanna's hands as she readied herself to make the star portal.

"We'll go through first and make sure it's safe. Come quickly once you've spoken with Dubhar," Ghilanna said.

The portal appeared, and Ghilanna stepped through so she could hold it open for us on the other side. Thomas went through with Fiera. Dubhar's voice entered my mind.

"I'm coming too," he announced.

My eyebrows raised in amusement. *Who am I to argue with a unicorn?* "Okay," I replied agreeably.

"Get on me, then we will go through together. Your friend is not expecting an extra body so she might not keep the portal open long enough for both of us," Dubhar said, though it was almost an order.

154

I had assumed Dubhar was a normal unicorn—a sentient being, but still an animal. Now I found myself wondering if there was more to Dubhar than he had let on. It had been convenient to ride him to the meeting with Marek, but Marek had made room for the unicorn in the circle. If Ghilanna hadn't made this meeting feel rushed, I would have taken the time to investigate my ideas. For now the best option was to keep my thoughts to myself and wait for a better time to broach the subject.

I opened the door to Dubhar's stall, and he gazed at me with his silver eyes, his iridescent black horn shimmering in the sunlight streaming through the windows. A bale of hay appeared in the corner and I took the hint and used it climb onto his back. Shooting a glance around the barn hoping no one was witnessing this, Dubhar and I walked through the star portal.

Magic slid over us, and then we were stepping into the training yard at Jade Wilds. Ghilanna's mouth opened wide in awe as Dubhar stepped through the star portal with me on his back. The majestic black unicorn was a sight to behold. Meriel's arm was draped around Fiera's shoulders, and she had a slight smile on her face, as though she had expected Dubhar to come with us. Not a surprise given she was also a seer and often was privy to tidbits of what the future would hold.

"Welcome, Dubhar," Meriel said with a formal bow.

Dubhar tipped forward, bending his knees and almost sending me careening from his back as he bowed to Meriel as well. *Intriguing.*

Feeling awkward perched atop Dubhar, I slid off his back to stand on my own two feet. "Ghilanna said there was a matter you wanted to discuss. I'm sure you know that I am busy with preparations for the coronation in two days. I found *Fàisneachd*," I said and patted my pocket where the book was. I hoped Meriel would tell me what I needed to know quickly, so I could return and handle my other tasks.

Meriel stepped away from Fiera, her expression drawn and hands clasped in front of her. Her voice was grave. "It has been a long time since I translated *Fàisneachd*." Straightening her shoulders, Meriel beckoned to us. "Come, let's have some tea and talk."

We all filed into the tent, even Dubhar. I was nonplussed once inside to see that the unicorn easily fit. I would have sworn the last time I was here there was no way a unicorn of his size would have managed to even get through the tent flap. The table was set for four with room for Dubhar to stand close, not excluded. Thomas stayed by the entrance, and I wondered if Meriel had given him instructions before I'd come through the portal. The silver tea set and blue velvet chairs were just as I remembered.

Those times felt so far away now, even though it had been only a few short months ago that I had been in this very camp preparing for the battle at Emerald Valley. *Now look where I am, Lady of the South!* Meriel poured steaming tea into the four cups and set the pot down. She then gazed at the three of us.

"Originally, I invited you here, Serafina, because I wanted to recommend that you ask King Pharaan for an alliance. He can issue a call to arms requiring Prince Almar and Prince Rhangil to send support in your war against Prince Tanyth. *Fàisneachd* changes things," Meriel explained.

"Changes them how?" I demanded, then blushed, feeling ashamed. Meriel hadn't even had time to speak, yet here I was behaving like I was twelve again. "Sorry," I mumbled. Fiera giggled, and I blushed even more. *Just like old times.*

Meriel chuckled, then her expression sobered. "Events are in motion now that we could not stop even if we wanted to. Now that Tanyth has killed King Leonard and taken possession of the *Bloodsong Grimoire*, the end of time is drawing near. It is critical that you are ready, Serafina. You cannot fight your fate."

"What fate? I don't understand. I never wanted to be a princess or a queen, or to have magic," I replied, struggling to keep my voice calm.

"Over a thousand years ago, it was foretold that there would be a female who would lead the Fae and the humans in the final battle with the end of time. As years passed, small details have come to light. When examined separately, they could refer to many different females. Yet together as a whole, there is only one alive today who meets the criteria," Meriel said in a serene voice.

"You are mistaken. I am not going to lead Fae and humans to battle the end of time," I protested.

"Isn't that the very thing you are proposing to do? Unify humans and Fae against Prince Tanyth?" Meriel countered.

"Yes, but—"

She cut me off. "Then you are already taking the necessary steps."

"Tanyth is the end of time?" I asked in bewilderment, my heartbeat racing at the prospect.

Meriel's jaw tightened before she replied. "I don't know. That is the one thing that has always been unclear—who or what the end of time is." She took a sip of tea, casting a glance at Dubhar, who appeared to be napping, then continued. "You should not waste time worrying about what you will face on the battlefield. Instead, focus on securing alliances within your kingdom and with your neighbors. Your position is unique among the humans, Serafina. Yes, you are a woman, unheard of as a ruler, but you also have the blood of all four kingdoms coursing through your veins."

My pulse quickened at Meriel's revelation. *The only human with royal bloodlines from all four kingdoms.* "Can I control all four mines?" I asked shakily.

Pretense of a nap gone, Dubhar's silver eyes opened, and he dipped his head. *"When you master control of your own magic, yes, you will be able to draw on the four mines."*

Ghilanna gasped. I assumed she had heard Dubhar's words as well. "Will I need to go through the same ritual that I did with the gold mine?"

Dubhar snorted. *"No. They are all connected. Silly humans have never understood what was within their grasp."*

"Hush," Meriel reprimanded Dubhar. The unicorn gave her a side-eye stare but stayed silent.

"If Serafina can control the magic of all four mines, why would she need to forge alliances with the human kings?" Fiera asked. Her question was a good one, and I wished I'd thought of it.

Dubhar smacked his lips together and tossed his head, narrowly missing knocking the teapot off the table. Meriel looked as though she wanted to slap the unicorn. Dubhar spoke. *"The threat of war with Tanyth is very real. Showing up with a handful of Fae and humans will not be sufficient. Even if Serafina can master her magic."*

Sipping my tea, I considered this new information—that fate had decided over one thousand years ago that I was to be the female who would face the end of time with a mix of Fae and humans at my side. None of this made sense. *It doesn't change my current course of action,* I reminded myself. Regardless of a Fae prophecy saying I was supposed to fight the end of time, the Court of Dusk had declared war on me, and I couldn't afford to sit idly by and let Tanyth destroy the South. From my own experiences as his prisoner, I knew he would not stop with destroying one human kingdom. He was power hungry and would destroy all of them.

"You mentioned learning to control my magic. I have had a lesson from Ghilanna on making balls of magic, and Tristan started to teach me how to shield and do simple daily tasks such as getting dressed. There is only a finite amount of time available each day. Even if I had a week to dedicate solely to magic lessons, I doubt I could learn everything in such a short time," I responded.

"This is another reason why you must go to Uaine Palace and talk to King Pharaan. He knows of techniques that could be beneficial in this circumstance for you to learn magic quickly. They're similar to how Tristan taught you to shield," Meriel said.

"I will consider it," I replied, deciding a neutral response would be better than nothing.

"There are words on her arms," Dubhar said, once again addressing all four of us.

"Words?" Fiera blurted out.

Sighing and wishing Dubhar would keep things to himself, I pushed up the sleeves of my tunic. The words were faintly glowing as they scrolled across my skin. "They appeared after I touched the *Bloodsong Grimoire* the second time, when it released my magic and removed the binding on my memories."

Meriel gently took my hand in hers and examined the words on my arms. "Strange," she said softly.

"What do the words mean?" I asked. Meriel always had answers.

Meriel shook her head. "Unfortunately, Serafina, I am not all-knowing. No existing prophecy mentions words appearing on someone's skin after touching the *Bloodsong Grimoire*. My best recommendation is to ignore them. Eventually, their purpose will come to light. If they are not doing any damage to you, there is no reason to attempt to remove them, if such a thing is even possible."

Meriel's response was not comforting, but there was nothing I could do about it. My magical knowledge was limited, and Meriel clearly was not able to help me. Trying to redirect the conversation, I said, "You invited me here to discuss something. What is it?"

Instead of responding, Meriel drank her tea. Only when her cup was empty did she set it down and fold her hands in front of her, ready to talk. "It was a trivial matter." She lifted her hand and a thin box appeared in her palm. She offered it to me. "Solana asked me to give this to you before your coronation."

Twirling the end of my braid between my fingers, I studied the box, debating if I wanted to open it. Finally, I reached out and took the box from Meriel, cautiously lifting the lid. Inside was an ornate key with three emeralds set on it in an arc. I was expecting jewelry, not a key.

"What does this go to?" I asked.

A ghost of a smile crossed Ghilanna's face. "I believe I know."

"Oh?" I asked, my voice sharper than I had intended. *Secrets and more secrets.* Frustration bubbled up that no one, not even my mother, could be straightforward about a matter.

"Do you remember the case that was in the blacksmith's in Gaskal?" Ghilanna asked.

I shut my eyes, trying to remember the blacksmith shop. I had only been there once—it was the first or second day after my arrival in Gaskal.

I stood in the well-lit smithy and weapons store. The room was uncomfortably warm due to the forge being in the back, not outside. On one of the walls was an intricately carved mahogany case with a massive lock and glass doors. I distinctly remembered the carved wood being warm to the touch, and hidden within the carvings of decorative flowers and vines were unicorns, dragons, and griffins. In fact, the case was much like the crown that had appeared at the gold mine.

Taking a deep breath, I returned to the memory. The weapons in the case. *The first weapon was a longsword with a dark-brown leather-wrapped grip and a plain pommel, but the hilt had a row of emeralds across it. The next weapon was even larger, a greatsword with pearlescent sheen to the metal. The third weapon that was easy to see was a dagger with a handle encrusted in an assortment of gems, though over half of them were emeralds. The blade on the dagger was thin, as though it were meant to be an ornament instead of functional.*

"Does this key go to the case?" I asked.

Ghilanna nodded. "Yes, I believe so. It would make the most sense. Valerie and Josiah said after you and Solana went on the run from the assassins, the key disappeared. The case and its contents have been in their care for safekeeping, but without the key, it would be impossible to remove anything from the case. The magic on it is far too powerful."

Moistening my lips with my tongue, I gave Meriel's hands a gentle squeeze. "Thank you for giving me this." I pulled the blue book out of my pocket and set it on the table. "What can you tell me about the book?"

Dubhar snorted, spraying all of us with tiny droplets of unicorn spit. Disgusted, I glared at him. "What that necessary?"

"*I had an itch,*" Dubhar replied. I rolled my eyes at his response.

"*The book you brought doesn't matter anymore. King Leonard was given the book after his father died to try to encourage him to pursue friendly relations with the Fae. It was successful until your parents met,*" Dubhar explained.

I accidentally bumped the base of the table with my foot, making the whole top shake. Dubhar's explanation made sense—except for the part of how he would know these things. This whole time in the tent it had been clear that while Meriel and Dubhar might be acquainted, they definitely did not have access to the same information.

Stealing a glance at Ghilanna, who gave me an encouraging nod, I said, "Dubhar, how do you know these things? You speak as though you were there or given a firsthand account at some point."

Meriel half rose in her seat, but Dubhar tossed his head. "*She deserves to know,*" he said, then, putting the full weight of his gaze on me, began speaking. "*I am a unicorn, but I am also Fae. Unlike a shapeshifter such as Tristan, whose base form is Fae, my base form is a unicorn. I can also create an illusion or shapeshift to become a horse since they're cousins of unicorns. Thousands of years ago, it was agreed that my family would be charged with observing humans and Fae, particularly those in positions of power, to ensure that there was balance. I'm one of the only Watchers still alive and continuing to fulfill the role. Your question of how I know what was going on with King Leonard is that I was there. At the time, I was used as his personal war horse."*

The explanation was shocking. Dubhar had spied on my human family. Voice shaky with emotion, I replied, "When you revealed yourself to me as a unicorn you said that you had been waiting, just like Marek. Does that mean your role now is more than only as a Watcher?"

Dubhar chuckled. *"Yes. I will fight by your side."*

Fiera set her teacup down hard and tea sloshed over the edges. "Since when has anyone been waiting for Serafina for anything?" she demanded.

Meriel reached over and patted Fiera's hand. "It has to do with the prophecies. I'm sure Ghilanna will catch you up soon enough. I'm so glad to see you are free of Tanyth."

Fiera's lower lip quivered, and tears trickled down her cheeks. "What would you know about Tanyth?"

Meriel withdrew her hand and sighed. "More than you think. I was in love with Tanyth once, until he almost killed me and I realized how naïve I'd been."

Blinking, I recalled Meriel's journals that I had snuck into her tent to read when I'd been in training here. She had warned me then what kind of a Fae he was, and yet I'd still ended up at the Court of Dusk. *But if I'd never been captured by Travaran and subsequently by Tanyth, would I have ever met Tristan?*

Footsteps approached us. I twisted in my seat and saw Thomas. "Sorry to intrude, but we have important matters to attend back at the palace, including sending letters to the North, East, and West if we are requesting their aid."

Meriel's gray eyes met mine. "You are a good queen, Serafina. Just believe in yourself. I will see you soon."

I finished the last sip of my tea, then stood up. "Till next time," I said and saluted her, then walked out of the tent with Ghilanna, Fiera, and Thomas on my heels.

I turned around, expecting Dubhar to follow us, and was disappointed when the unicorn remained in the tent.

"I will return when I'm done here," Dubhar said into my mind.

"Dubhar is staying here," I informed the others.

Ghilanna nodded and opened the star portal. Thomas and Fiera went through first. Then, I grabbed Ghilanna's hand, and we stepped through.

Seventeen

RETHYS

𝔓iles of rubies, amethysts, and diamonds surrounded me in my cave. To distract myself and delay my inevitable visit to Jade Wilds, I decided to count and sort the gems within my hoard. Oddly, the number of emeralds had grown in my hundred-year absence, which shouldn't have been possible. I had been locked away in Dorcha Palace, unable to add to my collection. It was yet another sign that the end of time was rapidly approaching.

Selecting the smallest of the emeralds, I placed them in a black velvet pouch and then vanished it for safekeeping. With one last look around my cave, I departed, leaping into the air and letting the thermals carry me effortlessly into the clouds. Using the magic of Jade Wilds as a beacon, I flew toward the Fae training camp. As I approached, I wrapped myself in magic to hide my appearance, which would serve a dual purpose—hiding me from sight and from the warding spells that protected the Fae training camp from intruders. The last thing I could afford was for a Fae to mistake me for an enemy and attack.

A familiar black unicorn with a silver mane and tail and an iridescent horn and a white-robed Fae female stood at the edge of the forest under a large oak tree. Preparing to land, I revealed myself to them, and their conversation halted.

"Why are you here?" demanded Dubhar.

I gave him a smile, revealing rows of razor-sharp teeth. *"Likely the same reason you are."*

Meriel looked between the two of us, uncertainty in her gaze. "You two know each other?"

Dubhar stomped his foot and tossed his head. *"Of course."*

The temptation to banter with Dubhar was high, but with limited time, I reminded myself I had come to talk to Meriel. Summoning the pouch of emeralds into my talons, I offered it to Meriel. *"For you."*

Giving me a quizzical look, she took it and dumped the contents into her hand. Gray eyes wide, she met my gaze. "Another sign," she said, voice soft, as though she was trying to digest the message.

"Yes. But that is not entirely why I'm here. Your son …" I started.

Meriel dropped the emeralds in shock. "What did you say?"

"Your son is at Dorcha Palace," I said firmly.

"Impossible. He was fostered by Prince Almar and then got a position in Prince Rhangil's court," Meriel replied shakily.

Shifting back and forth on my feet, I debated how to proceed. Facts were facts. *"Fallon Leoydark Daralei has served under a blood contract to the Court of Dusk for ninety years. I know this because I was captive in the very same palace for one hundred years."*

"No. It's impossible," Meriel said.

"If it's any reassurance, neither one of them knows," I said, hoping that tidbit would calm her.

Instead, it had the opposite effect. She barked a laugh at me, face flushing. "Except for the fact that my son has been living in hell for ninety years, and I've done nothing."

I closed my eyes, considering my options. To Meriel, I was merely an ancient magical creature; one that, as a seer, she had spoken of in prophecies, but until now, our paths had never crossed. She had no reason to trust me, and I had no reason to give her anything. *"If Tanyth dies, Fallon would become prince. He is the rightful heir to the Court of Dusk."*

Dubhar whinnied in surprise and half-reared, his gaze drifting between me and Meriel. Meriel's pain was clear on her face and tears freely streamed down her cheeks. "There are others in the Court of Dusk who would gladly kill Fallon before he'd take the throne. You have no way of guaranteeing his safety. Especially when my carefully laid plans still landed him in the very place I desperately wanted to keep him away from."

"You're right. I cannot promise he will be safe. But Fallon is smart and resourceful. Have faith in your son as you have had faith in the Lost Fae Queen all these years." I paused, trying to decide how much more to say. Unlike Dubhar, I was not related to Fae in any way, and sometimes their way of seeing the world was far more confusing than mine. *"I realize that my appearance here has caught you off guard, but I wanted you to know that I am as invested as you, Dubhar, and King Pharaan in seeing the Lost Fae Queen prophecy is fulfilled and in ensuring Serafina faces the end of time as prepared as possible,"* I said. *"I made a vow long ago, and I intend to fulfill it."*

Dubhar whispered, *"The compass will unite dragon, unicorn, griffin."*

Meriel wiped the tears off her face with the edge of her sleeve, then replied, "When I gave the original prophecy, I believed that those were metaphors for each of the Fae courts. It is clear now that I was wrong." She whispered under her breath, likely hoping we wouldn't hear, "What else was I wrong about?"

Voices and footsteps in the distance indicated we would have company in a few minutes. The last thing I wanted was to explain my presence to more Fae or for word to get back to Tanyth that I was doing what he would call *interfering*. Especially when it would put Fallon in a precarious position.

"Consider going to the Lady of the South's coronation. A show of your support would go a long way to proving Fae and humans should

live in harmony," I said and spread my wings, slowly beating them and lifting off the ground.

When I was hovering with my talons near Meriel's face, she put up her hand as though she could stop me. "What do you know?" she demanded.

Giving her a toothy smile, I shook my head, refusing to answer. I visualized my cave in my mind and my magic uncoiled within me, and in an instant, I had left Jade Wilds and was walking into my cave.

Eighteen

SERAFINA

Ghilanna let go of my hand while we were traveling through the star portal. Something about the star portal felt off—more like walking through a tunnel than stepping through a door like it had in the past. She exited a full minute before I did but clearly hadn't noticed anything strange; she was walking down the aisleway and hadn't realized I wasn't right behind her. I could see Fiera and Thomas as they slipped out the barn doors at the end of the aisle. Inhaling deeply, the sweet smell of hay hit my nose, and I opened my mouth to call out for them to wait for me, but my words were cut off as firm hands wrapped around my neck and the sharp point of a blade pressed into the base of my throat. I swallowed and felt the blade nick my skin.

"Not so brave now, are you, half-blood slut." The man's voice was familiar, but I couldn't place it. Mind whirling, I considered my options. With the dagger at my throat, I would not be able to use my sword quickly enough to prevent whoever this was from slicing my neck open, which left relying on Ghilanna noticing and saving me or figuring out an alternative solution.

168

Not sure I had enough control of my magic to launch an effective attack on someone I couldn't see, I recalled the shielding lesson with Tristan. *I can shield my head and neck.*

"Who are you?" I asked.

Instead of answering, he pressed the dagger harder into my throat, and I could feel blood dripping from the wound. *Focus.* My eyes slid shut, and I ordered my mind to focus on the green-and-gold magic swirling around my core. I imagined a barrier forming over my head and neck, preventing the dagger from doing more damage. The magic tingled over my skin as the shield formed.

"Bitch!" he said, a little too loud.

Ghilanna whirled, and white balls of her magic shot through the air. The grip on my neck loosened, and bright blue magic collided with Ghilanna's. I drove my elbow into the mystery man's stomach, and his hold released. I lifted my leg and kicked backward. My foot connected with his knee with a satisfying pop. I shot forward to Ghilanna's side, not wanting to give him a chance to grab me again, then turned.

A tall blond-haired Fae male with gray eyes stared coldly at me. He wore black leather armor with silver-iron spikes on the back of the arms and side of the legs. *Bane.* Behind him, I could see a star portal form, and Bane hastily backed into it, then vanished.

I let out my breath, tipping forward with my hands on my thighs and panting to catch my breath as the adrenaline rolled through me.

"Who was that?" Ghilanna asked as she threw a shield around us like a bubble.

"That was Bane. He was Tristan's second-in-command at Dorcha Palace. I imagine now he's taken over as lord commander of the Court of Dusk in Tristan's absence," I replied.

"It must be a message that Tanyth can get to you whenever he wants. My concern is that he was waiting in the stables for us. How did he know when we would be here?"

"It wasn't a secret that we were traveling to Jade Wilds through a star portal," I said.

"Yes, I know that, but Bane would have had to acquire the information. We don't have your schedule posted where anyone can see it. I believe there is a spy in the palace," Ghilanna said.

I gasped. *A spy?* I had never considered how my grandfather acquired his information. Now I realized it was likely from his own network of spies. This was a subject I knew nothing about. *How do you prevent spies within your ranks?*

Ghilanna broke through my thoughts. "We need to get inside, and you should have your master of the guard come at once to discuss this matter."

I nodded. Ghilanna's idea was solid. "Okay."

As soon as the master of the guard had left, I summoned my ladies-in-waiting and Fiera. The squeak of a door on its hinges startled me. I had been staring into the fire thinking about the conversation with Declan and his ideas to enhance security around the palace. They were all valid ideas, but I was uncertain that merely posting additional guards would prevent Bane from getting into the palace again. I wasn't skilled enough with my own magic to be part of any magical defense that we could put together.

Scrubbing my hands over my face, I turned toward the door where the four of them were standing.

Violet rushed forward. "Serafina, are you okay?"

I sighed, wondering how bad I looked that it would cause Violet concern. "I'm fine. There's an important matter I need to discuss with the four of you, and it can't wait until tomorrow. Please come sit." I motioned for them to join me on the couch or in the chairs near the fire.

Ghilanna had always been perceptive, and it was evident by her response. "Not a fan of Declan's heightened security plan?"

I yawned and shook my head. "No. He proposed what we've already done, increasing the number of guards. If that is our only solution, soon we'll be wading through a throng of guards anytime we leave a room while we're in the palace."

"Then what would you suggest?" asked Violet.

Ghilanna and Fiera were watching me as though they had a good idea of what I would say. I responded, "The original plan for you as my ladies-in-waiting was for the purpose of security. It is clear now that we need to be more proactive in our approach. Ghilanna and Fiera are well-trained in the use of their magic. From now on, we will shield. I will shield myself, and Ghilanna or Fiera—you can work it out among yourselves—will provide a magic shield for all five of us."

"Five of us?" Valerie said in concern. "It would be four—you, me, Violet, and Ghilanna."

"Fiera will be the fourth lady-in-waiting," I replied. Valerie opened her mouth to protest, but I raised my hand, and she clamped her mouth shut. "I did say we need to be more proactive. Fiera has magic training. I am just learning how to use my magic. She is an invaluable resource, and there is no reason to exclude her. Besides, I trust her with my life and with yours.

"The next matter is training. We need to get comfortable fighting together, and Violet needs to be taught the basics."

"I will see that everything is arranged for us to have practice space available tomorrow," Violet responded.

I shook my head and stood up. "I appreciate the help, but this can't wait until tomorrow. Training starts right now."

Their reactions were mixed. Ghilanna had anticipated where the conversation was going, and Fiera, having trained with me at Jade Wilds, did not seem overly concerned about the odd time to be training. Violet and Valerie, on the other hand, were unhappy.

Ghilanna approached the two of them. "Look, I know this is unusual, but what happened today with Bane cannot happen again. We need to be on our toes, which means we have to train."

Fiera moved over to the space between the four columns. "Can we practice here?"

I smiled; she had assessed the space the same way I had. "Absolutely." I yawned again. The day was starting to catch up to me, but this had been my idea, and I couldn't excuse myself or they would never respect my plan. "Ghilanna, will you lead? Let's start with a hand-to-hand drill."

Fiera helped Violet and Valerie space themselves out enough and then we all faced Ghilanna.

Ghilanna explained the drill and did a few slow-motion examples. Violet experimented, and Ghilanna adjusted her stance and fist position, then took her spot at the head of the group and led the drill. "Strikes first! High! Low! Middle!" Three sets of strikes were followed by three sets of blocks.

Settling into the rhythm, my thoughts drifted to another practice session in the palace as my body did the work.

Dark-tan skin, thick black beard, and shoulder-length wavy black hair, Rhys was sexy—and as a competitor, off-limits for anything other than friendly conversation or sparring. I blinked, and Rhys transformed into Tristan. Tristan lunged forward with a series of six right-left jabs at my stomach. Smirking, I ducked and rolled, popping up behind him, leading with a left hook, then a right jab at his bare low back where the dragon tattoo was. Tristan whirled and to my dismay covered my fist with his hand, preventing me from completing the move. I jerked my arm backward, and he released my fist. I stumbled a few steps, then regained my balance, lunging low with a right-left, then an uppercut, then pivoted and thrust back with my elbow, jabbing him in the gut. I skipped to the side as Rhys's fist sailed past my jaw.

Blinking, I swayed before regaining my balance and speeding up my punches and blocks, hoping no one had noticed that I was daydreaming.

Sprinting toward Tristan, I attacked right hook, left hook, jab, jab, right hook, dropped to the floor, and rolled behind him. Doing a backflip to my feet, I pulled my left leg in toward me and spun with a kick. Moments before my kick would have connected with the edge of his rib cage, he caught my foot in one hand and twisted his wrist, pulling me off balance, then let go, and I staggered away.

Before I could regain my balance, Tristan charged, scooped me up over his shoulder, and spun, making me dizzy as my stomach roiled. Thankfully, Tristan dumped me on the floor before I threw up. I had mere moments to recover and opted for a scissor-kick. To my astonishment, it worked; Tristan landed with a thud on his back beside me. I twisted and rolled on top of him.

A fist sailed toward my face. I ducked and reacted with a right-left jab aiming for Ghilanna's stomach. She blocked it and stepped back with an amused smile. "I guess you are paying attention. We were beginning to wonder since your speed has been varying so much."

My face heated in embarrassment. "I was thinking about sparring with Tristan," I muttered.

"No one is doubting your skills in hand-to-hand combat. I was thinking about having us pair up. It would be easier if you sit out. One, I'm not sure Violet would be willing to hit you, but we're not ready to try two on one, so someone has to be on the sidelines," said Ghilanna.

She had a valid point, and the objective was to get Violet comfortable. Pitting the two of us against each other was likely to have the opposite effect on her. I retrieved a chair from the dining room table and positioned it just outside the columns so I could watch. Fiera paired with Valerie, and Ghilanna with Violet.

Violet surprised me with the speed that she had picked up the hand-to-hand combat strikes and blocks. Though she was not sparring very fast, her positioning was correct. As I watched, my eyelids kept sliding shut. Unable to stay awake any longer, I let sleep take me.

Bracing myself against the warm shower tile, hot water cascading over my head, I moaned as tension built within me. I could feel every thrust of Tristan's cock as he glided in and out of my canal. His fingers massaged my breasts, sending me closer to the edge.

"I love you," he whispered into my ear, then took my earlobe into his mouth, gently sucking.

Suddenly, Tristan was gone. I spun in surprise, my blood running cold when I faced Tanyth in the shower. He was naked, and unable to prevent myself, my eyes drifted downward to his shaft, which was at attention. Tearing my gaze away, I stared at Tanyth, fear coiling in my belly.

"Ride my cock, Serafina. I want to hear you scream my name," Tanyth ordered, his voice wrapping around me.

"No," I said, though my voice came out as an embarrassing squeak.

A dagger caressed my neck, just as it had earlier in the stables. "I await your command," Bane growled harshly.

Tanyth gave me an evil grin, his sharp canines flashing in the light. "You have two choices. You can either fuck me, or I will make Tristan watch while I carve you to pieces before starting on him."

I woke with a start, thrashing blindly, and fell out of the chair onto the hardwood floor. I lunged to my feet and sprinted for the bathroom. Retching, I made it just in time for the contents of my stomach to make it into the toilet.

Tears dripped down my cheeks as my stomach heaved. I stood there, braced against the toilet, until the heaving subsided. Shakily, I washed my face. Fiera appeared in the mirror. I had to look over my shoulder to confirm she was indeed standing behind me.

"Dreaming about Tanyth?" Fiera guessed with a shudder.

I nodded. "Are you still practicing? How long was I asleep for?" I could see dark circles under Fiera's eyes and wondered if she was plagued by nightmares about Tanyth also.

"We stopped a few hours ago, but no one wanted to wake you up. I volunteered to stay. C'mon, let's get you in bed so you can be rested in the morning," Fiera said and gently took my hand in hers. I let her lead me into the bedroom and was quiet when she handed me a nightshirt. Turning away from her, I undressed and pulled on the nightshirt, then climbed into bed.

Fiera tucked the covers around me. "Sweet dreams, my friend," she whispered.

"Stay with me," I pleaded, hoping Fiera's presence would keep the nightmares at bay.

Fiera nodded and slid under the covers next to me. I rolled over, my back pressed against hers, closed my eyes, and fell asleep.

In the training yard near the center of Jade Wilds, Commander Meriel was waiting for us. Fiera was wearing a dark-blue tunic under her leather breastplate, her pale skin a stark contrast to her fiery red hair in two braids down her back. Ghilanna had a bright-purple tunic under her armor, making her an easier target if this had been a real battle and not training.

Commander Meriel, a hood pulled over her white hair, rested her hands on her sword held loosely in front of her. "Are you ready for our last training session?"

The words caught me off guard. "How can you be so sure it will be our last?"

Commander Meriel shrugged and the hood fell back, revealing that it wasn't Commander Meriel at all, but Bane.

Bane lunged at Fiera, blocking her strike with his armored forearm and punching her hard in the stomach. Gasping, Fiera doubled over, and Bane twisted her sword out of her hand and threw it on the ground, then yanked Fiera's arms behind her back and forced her to her knees.

My grip tightened on my sword. I looked to Ghilanna and discovered she was no longer there with me. In fact, we were no longer in Jade Wilds. Instead, we were in the throne room at the Court of Dusk, and Prince Tanyth was sitting on his throne. He wore his large antlered crown, as well as that cape with gray paws on the shoulders. Just like when he captured me.

"My dearest Serafina. How do you like your wedding present?" the prince inquired with a wicked smile.

I glanced at him in confusion. Wedding present?

Bane kicked Fiera in the back and sent her sprawling onto her face in front of me. "Happy wedding," Bane growled.

My body was frozen with fear. Fiera glared defiantly at Bane as she pulled herself back onto her knees. Her face was covered in dirt, and her bright-red hair was disheveled, but she otherwise seemed unharmed. Suddenly, arms wrapped around me and forced me to move backward, away from Fiera. I struggled, but the iron grip refused to let up. A strangled sob escaped my lips as I fought.

"No!" I screamed, startling myself. I sat up in bed, breathing heavily. Fiera quickly created a Fae light. It glinted off the dagger in her hand, which she tucked under the pillow when she saw I noticed it.

"Another nightmare?" Fiera asked calmly.

"Unfortunately, yes, though this was about you, not Tanyth," I replied.

Fiera gave me a wide-eyed stare, then stood up and slid the curtains back to peek out the window. She swept the curtains open, revealing the pearly gray fingers of dawn creeping up over the mine.

Blowing out my breath, I agreed with Fiera that it wasn't worth going back to sleep, not when we had a long day ahead. "I'm going to take a bath," I informed her.

Fiera nodded. "I will do the same but in my own rooms. I'll make sure that Thomas knows you're awake, and I'll send Violet to help with anything you need."

"Thank you," I replied gratefully, then ducked into the bathroom and filled the tub.

The bath was soothing, and it helped to wash away the bad dream. Lord McCormack and Tristan were supposed to return tonight, and the coronation was tomorrow. There was no indication through the bond that I had to worry about anything going on with Tristan. He felt healthy and focused on his task. The last thing I wanted was to distract him, so I opted not to try communicating with him through the bond, simply thankful that I knew he was there.

Reluctantly, I stood up in the tub, water cascading off me. I reached for a towel without looking and was surprised when it was pressed into my hand. Taking it, I wrapped it around myself, then peered at the person. It was Violet, just as Fiera had promised. A smile flitted over my lips. "Good morning, Violet."

"Good morning to you too. Lord John requested I tell you that the West replied to your letter about forming an alliance against the Court of Dusk."

"And?" I prompted.

Violet shook her head. "Sorry, but he didn't tell me what they said, and I wasn't sure if you wanted me to read your correspondence."

"I'll read it after I get dressed," I replied, realizing the wisdom of Violet's words. There were times where the letters could contain something a lady-in-waiting shouldn't know.

Relying on my magic, it only took a few minutes before I was ready to eat breakfast and face the tasks of the day. Violet and I exited the bedroom together. Valerie was waiting for us at the breakfast table.

"Good morning," I greeted her.

She gave me a tired wave. "Good morning. Sleep well?"

"More bad dreams," I responded, spotting the letter on the table. I grabbed it and removed the paper from the small tube. We had sent the messages via pigeon, hoping for the quickest nonmagical method of obtaining a reply. I unrolled the small piece of paper, then sighed as I read it.

Your Majesty, I regret to inform you that my knights are on an extended training mission in the mountains and are unreachable until they return in two months. I wish you the best in your efforts against Prince Tanyth.

Sincerely,
King Hanover Atwood, Lord of the West

"Did he agree to help?" asked Valerie eagerly.

I shook my head and offered her the piece of paper. "No, he gave us a lame excuse. Though it is a valid one. I expect it's his way of not burning bridges should our situations ever be reversed."

"We still have the East and the North," Valerie said.

I admired her confidence that the other kings would agree to help us. After the war council had squashed my hopes of an alliance, I was more inclined to believe we would get similar responses from the two remaining kings, perhaps even from the Fae as well. Meriel and Marek both felt that King Pharaan *would* lend his support, but they knew him better than I did. I hardly counted less than a handful of meetings with the King of Fae as a guarantee he would support the South.

I took a plate out of the stack and heaped it with eggs, sausage, and an assortment of autumn squash. Valerie and Violet followed suit. When we had all settled at the table, I looked at both of them. "Tristan and Lord McCormack will be back today. What time they arrive might affect our agenda. Currently, after breakfast we will have a short training session in here, then there is a run-through of the coronation, the final fitting with the seamstress, and a review of the palace guard with Declan. Assuming we have time tonight, we'll do another practice session. I promise we won't stay up as late as last night. Tomorrow is going to be a long day for all of us."

Valerie shrugged. "You want us here to protect you. Whether the day is long or short is irrelevant. Your safety is what matters."

"Thank you. I appreciate the time you're taking, Valerie. I know this is a lot different than what you're used to in Gaskal," I replied.

A star portal appeared between the columns. I was up with a sword in my hand before Violet and Valerie even knew anything was going on. Ghilanna and Fiera stepped through the portal.

"I'm so sorry," Ghilanna said. "I shouldn't have used the star portal to come directly in here."

I lowered my sword and returned to the table, leaning the weapon against the wall before sitting down. "How about you tell me why you used a star portal and didn't walk through the door like normal?"

"Marek sent word, and you were taking a bath, so I took Fiera with me. I figured you wouldn't mind having her meet Marek given she is now essentially one of your advisors too," Ghilanna explained.

She was right. We had vetted Fiera, and it almost felt as though neither one of us had ever been at Dorcha Palace. *Except for the nightmares,* I reminded myself.

"Who is Marek?" questioned Valerie.

I glanced at her and then at Ghilanna. Since we had reached a point where there were no secrets between me and my ladies-in-waiting, I responded, "Marek Fenmyar is a Fae male who is the heir to the Court of the Sun and one of my allies."

Valerie's eyes widened at my words. "If you already have an ally tied to another Fae court, why can't this Marek fellow command those Fae warriors to fight with us against Prince Tanyth?"

Fiera decided to respond for me, for which I was grateful. "Heirs do not have the power to give orders to warriors of a Fae court. That ability lies solely with the prince. Marek and his father, Prince Rhangil, have been at odds with each other for quite a few years. It is unlikely that they will resolve their issues simply because Serafina wishes an alliance."

"I see," murmured Valerie, then busied herself with eating her food.

There was a lump in my pocket. I shoved my fingers into it, wondering what I'd forgotten about. My hand wrapped around the key I'd gotten from Meriel. I tugged it out and set it on the table in front of me. The emeralds flashed in the light.

"May I?" Valerie asked, her hand hovering over the key.

"Of course," I said and gestured for her to pick it up. She did and ran her fingers over it, inspecting every inch of the key, even raising it up to eye level, as though she was looking for something.

"I have confirmed this is the key that will open the weapons case in the blacksmith shop on the main road," Valerie said, reverently sliding the key across the table. "The Copper Wolves have been guarding that case for you for the past twelve years. Now that you have the key, we have instructions to give you the case. The sword with emeralds is for you. I will send word to Josiah and make arrangements to transport it to the palace."

Sweat beaded on my forehead and chin, and I could feel it trickling down the small of my back. I fought the urge to wipe my face, knowing if I did, I would give Valerie and Fiera the advantage. Each of us had a sword, Fiera and I were both shielding ourselves, and Ghilanna had a shield over Valerie to prevent us from doing any real damage to each other. Throughout the morning, Valerie had proven she wasn't afraid to spar with me. Fiera had suggested doing a match that could also serve as a demonstration to Violet for what a sword fight with uneven sides might look like.

Neither side had the advantage, though I suspected Fiera was holding back to ensure Valerie had enough opportunities to feel as though she was a valuable part of their team. *And she is, especially in a fight against humans.* A group of Fae warriors would be an entirely different matter, but I couldn't dwell on that.

Valerie thrust her sword toward my stomach. I dodged to the left and did a backhand swing as I pivoted, connecting with her back. Thanks to the shield, the sword thumped into her back but didn't cut through the skin.

"I yield," Valerie said loudly.

I lowered my sword and swiped the sweat just as it dripped into my eyes. "Finally," I muttered.

Fiera heard my comment and chuckled. "You're out of practice."

"I do practice," I protested.

"Uh-huh, and how often do those practices end in hot sex with Tristan?" Fiera teased.

Blushing, I looked away, but not before catching Violet's shocked expression.

"Shouldn't we clean up before we report to the throne room to do the coronation rehearsal?" Violet asked, eyeing all of us distastefully.

I giggled at her expression, aware that she didn't realize she wasn't in a much better state than we were. "We have time to shower," I replied.

Fiera huffed. I shot her a look, and she wagged her fingers at me, red magic swirling around them. "Magic is a nice tool. We can get presentable again without needing to take the time to shower. Besides, I think we spent far longer than you think practicing, which means Lord John is due any moment to collect us."

Sure enough, there was a loud knock on the door. Exhaling, I gathered an image of what I wished to wear and my appearance to be like—clean, with no indication of the recent physical exertion. When I was done, I stood in front of the ladies wearing a deep-green satin dress with a gold beaded belt and long sleeves. Ghilanna, Fiera, Valerie, and Violet were dressed in black silk wide-leg pants that could pass as a skirt with white jacquard bodices and billowing sleeves, perfect hiding places for an assortment of daggers. Violet was the only one who looked uncomfortable, but whether it was from having magic worked on her or what she was wearing, I wasn't certain.

"Come in!" I called, knowing we'd just made the steward wait while we magically cleaned up. It was worth it though. I doubted he would have any kind words to say to us with how we looked moments ago.

Lord John entered the room, his stride purposeful. "Excellent, you are all here and ready for the rehearsal. The high priest is waiting for us. Let's go."

Josiah caught up to me on our way out of the throne room when the rehearsal ended. "A word, Your Majesty?" he asked. His face was flushed as though he'd been running.

Curiosity piqued, I nodded and indicated we should go into the room directly in front of us. Thomas went in first, confirming it was safe, and then I led the way. It was a small, windowless room with burgundy fabric covering the walls and a small white desk shoved to one side. With Fiera, Ghilanna, Violet, Valerie, Josiah, Thomas, and myself, it was quite crowded.

Thomas cleared his throat. "Your Majesty, if I may?" he said formally. I inclined my head, indicating he should continue. "Perhaps the conversation would be more comfortable if we wait for you in the hallway. There is no threat here."

I immediately summoned a shield around myself, belatedly remembering the incident with Bane yesterday. If Josiah was indeed fulfilling his role as my spymaster, having this many witnesses to our discussion would not give us much secrecy. "Valerie may stay. The rest of you, please wait in the hallway."

Ghilanna raised her eyebrows at me in an unspoken question. I shook my head. Valerie was also a member of the Copper

Wolves, and I doubted she and Josiah had many secrets from one another.

When the room had cleared, Josiah clasped his hands together in front of him. His eyes were bright, and the edge of his collar was damp from sweat. "Your Majesty. The city is getting increasingly restless. They have progressed beyond painting words on walls today. A store was broken into and then lit on fire because there was a rumor it was one you have been patronizing. Some citizens believe you're rallying the knights not to fight against Fae, but to slaughter anyone who disagrees with your sentiments toward Fae."

My jaw tightened at his words, but there was nothing I could do at that moment. "I am giving a speech after the coronation, and everyone is free to attend. Hopefully that will help resolve the problems, and it will not require me to have a show of force."

Josiah nodded. "The timing of the speech should work. Though I must warn you, any later than after the coronation and there will likely be rioting."

I swallowed, my throat suddenly dry. I was at a loss for how to reply. *What does a queen do to stop rioting?*

Valerie jumped into the conversation. "Don't worry, it won't come to that. Your speech is straightforward and will give your subjects a chance to really know who you are."

It was hard to be as confident as Valerie sounded, but I knew I had to rely on her wisdom. She had lived in Gaskal her entire life. If anyone knew how to predict the outcome, it would be Valerie and Josiah.

It was late evening when I finally had a chance to be alone in my home. The ladies had agreed to give me time to myself, for which I was grateful. Tristan had not returned yet. Not a reason for alarm, but I would have liked to have him back all the same. The high priest had demanded perfection in the coronation rehearsal, leading to many do-overs. At the beginning, the mistakes had been because I hadn't understood what was required of me, but then they progressed into tripping over my own feet or changing one word so that it was wrong. The longer we spent practicing, the more my nerves had unraveled. It reminded me too much of being a prisoner at Dorcha Palace, where every move was documented and could be used against me.

I closed my eyes, trying to forget one comment the high priest had said. It was directed at Lord John and not meant for my ears, but I had heard it all the same. "Fae and humans are not biologically compatible with each other. How does the queen expect to bear an heir when her husband's seed will never be what she needs?"

A sob hitched in my throat. I opened my eyes and squared my shoulders. *I will not let the high priest, a human who has no medical experience whatsoever, dictate what may or may not be possible. I already know I can get pregnant.*

Moving into the center of the four columns, the area Tristan and I had been using to spar, I withdrew my father's sword from the green leather scabbard and swung it through the air experimentally. Taking a deep breath, I created a shield around my sword and then eased into a slow warm-up routine, wishing Tristan was here and hoping he was having success finding the veteran knights and convincing them to gather in Gaskal the day after tomorrow.

The steady rhythm of the sword work allowed me to relax and focus on something other than the horrible priest. Tension ebbed out of me over the hour I spent practicing. When I completed combination fifteen, I drew to a halt, lowered my sword, and released my hold on the magic shield. My heart thrummed in my chest with the exertion, and my whole body was relaxed. The worries of the day had drained away, exactly as I had hoped.

Placing the sword in the weapons cabinet, I took a quick shower and then slid into bed.

Heavy metal bars pressed into my back. A rough brown wool blanket covered my shoulders. As my vision cleared, I realized I was in a cage that was too small to stand or stretch out fully without hitting my head on the bars. My hands were shaking as they gripped the blanket. I peered around in the dim light, and I was able to determine that I was near the back of a large hall. The other side was blocked by a throne on a raised platform. I shuddered in revulsion as recognition flooded me. Not again. It was impossible to forget this cage, the one I had been kept in when I first arrived at Dorcha Palace. Tightening my grip on my fear and anger, I inhaled slowly through my nose, trying to identify anything useful. The scents of smoke and burnt meat came to me.

A sharp cramp in my stomach followed by intense pain and the feeling of wetness between my legs had me peeking under the blanket. Blood smeared my thighs, and I could see clots. Scooting away from the mess toward the door of the cage, I wondered if perhaps they had forgotten to lock it.

I froze when I heard booted feet heading my way. The blanket slid from me, and I screamed in pain as a contraction swept through me. There was a sucking sound, followed by a plop.

A sharp breath above me drew my attention away from my internal problems to whoever was standing outside the cage.

"Tristan?" I said in bewilderment. He was towering over me, his gray skin and dark slate hair blending into the shadows, but I would recognize my bonded anywhere.

"Murderer," he snarled.

I recoiled in shock at the accusation. "I didn't murder anyone."

"Yes, you did, two individuals in fact. My best friend Travaran and my unborn child." His voice was sharp and full of rage.

My jaw fell open. How dare he blame me for the miscarriage? "Fiera killed Travaran, not me," I ground out.

"I might have forgiven you for Travaran, but our unborn child? I cannot forgive that. You deserve everything Tanyth wants to do to you." Tristan either didn't hear me or didn't care about who had actually killed Travaran. He turned on his heel and disappeared.

Covering my face in my hands, I broke down, sobbing.

I woke up with a start. My face was damp, and snot dripped from my nose down my chin. I sat up, trying to process. *It was just a dream. A bad dream. Tristan doesn't blame me for Travaran's death or the miscarriage.* My hands shook as I gripped the sheets, willing myself to calm down. After a few minutes, I gave up and headed into the white marble bathroom. Washing my face with cool water, I finally was able to shove the horrible dream out of my thoughts by focusing on the words I would be required to say at the coronation.

With no idea of what time it was, I decided that I should at least try to get more rest. It was going to be a long day with the coronation in the late afternoon followed by the reception. Even another hour or two would make a difference.

Lying in bed, I shut my eyes, but my thoughts were still whirling around. I took a deep breath and counted backward from ten, hoping the meditation technique would help ease me back into sleep.

Light tapping on the door woke me up. Rubbing the sleep from my eyes, I was amazed I had fallen back asleep—*without dreams.* I felt far more rested than I had yesterday. *A good start to coronation day.*

"Serafina," called Violet's voice through the crack she had opened in the door.

"Hmm?" I mumbled, trying to wake myself all the way up.

I heard Violet's footsteps as she moved around the room and the sound of her tugging the curtains on the windows, followed by a rush of bright light. Thankfully, the wardrobe was positioned in such a way that it blocked a good portion of the light. My eyes quickly adjusted, and I sat up in bed, lifting my arms over my head and stretching.

"The maid is setting up breakfast now. Ghilanna thought you might want to spar with us before you have to go through your final preparations for the coronation," Violet said.

My stomach rumbled. I flung the covers the rest of the way off and scooted off the bed. I looked around the room for the robe I'd worn the other morning. Violet must have anticipated my need, and she came over holding it out.

I smiled gratefully and slid the robe on. "Thank you."

"My pleasure," replied Violet.

I followed her out of the bedroom to the dining area. Just as she had said, the maid had arranged a platter of fruit, eggs, and sausage. Ghilanna, Valerie, and Fiera were waiting for us too.

"Good morning," I greeted them.

"Good morning. Happy coronation day," Ghilanna said cheerily.

I grimaced at the reminder that I would be once again participating in a ceremony and then during the reception giving my speech about how I wanted Fae and humans to coexist in peace. *Maybe we could just spar all day and accidentally forget to go to the coronation.* Exhaling, I reminded myself, *Except then I wouldn't be able to give my post-coronation speech, and there would likely be rioting in the city—not an ideal outcome.*

After filling a plate with an assortment of melon, scrambled eggs, and two kinds of sausage, I sat down and eagerly ate my food, deciding it was easier to focus on that instead of contemplating the events awaiting me this afternoon.

Violet nibbled at the food on her plate. I noticed her gaze kept drifting to Valerie and then back to me. Tired of waiting for her to say what was on her mind, I asked, "Is there something you'd like to share with us, Violet?"

Violet fiddled with her fork, then set it down. "I was wondering if I could learn how to use a staff. Thomas and I were talking about weapons yesterday, and he thought it would be easier because there are more staff-like objects that I could repurpose as weapons. I have been working on the basic drills—high, middle, and low strikes and blocks for the hand-to-hand combat—when I have free time between chores and attending to you."

"Sure, we can work with staves when we're done eating," I replied and eagerly dug into the rest of my sausage, then chased it down with a cup of tea. One thing that I had discovered that worked even better than meditation to settle my mind was training. Teaching Violet how to use a staff would be the perfect way to start the day and not dwell on the fact that Tristan and Lord McCormack had not yet returned and what implications that would have on the impending war.

Soft harp music filled the air as I made my final preparations before entering the throne room for the coronation ceremony. I smoothed my hand over the gold brocade of my dress. Using the seamstress's knowledge of clothing appropriate for a queen, I had designed an outfit that would allow me to easily alter what I was wearing after the ceremony for the reception without having to go through the entire process of undressing and redressing. The gold brocade was more like an overlayer, a false corset with a thin skirt that draped elegantly over the heavy golden silk underneath. Part of the ceremony involved putting on a fur-lined robe as well as placing the crown on my head.

Lord John poked his head in the room. "Are you ready?"

"Yes," I said, though I didn't feel ready. *It will be just like the wedding,* I reminded myself. Except for the small matter of

Tristan still not being here. We waited as long as we could, but it was not possible to postpone the coronation any longer.

Throwing my shoulders back, I willed a skintight shield around my body and then strode toward the door. "Let's go."

Per the high priest's instructions, this was the only part of the ceremony where the only protection I would have nearby was myself. Even if Tristan had been here, he would not be permitted to walk with me down the aisle.

Across the hallway, the guards, dressed in their ceremonial cream uniforms with gold buttons, yanked open the doors to the throne room, and a blast of horns erupted inside the hall. Seats creaked as the guests rose.

Head held high, I walked toward the dais with measured steps. The throne had been removed for this ceremony. The high priest, whom after yesterday I detested greatly, was waiting for me. He wore a plain white robe with a gold cord tied around his waist, and his chain of office—a gold feather—dangled on his chest.

Halfway down the aisle my shoes began to pinch my toes. Clenching my jaw tight, I forced myself to continue. *It wouldn't do to stop and adjust my shoes in the middle of this.* Then, I realized I had a solution: *magic.* Slowing my steps and earning myself a glare from the priest, I focused on making the shoes fit looser. My relief was instantaneous.

I halted directly in front of the high priest, catching a glimpse of Fiera in the shadows behind him. She gave me an encouraging smile that I couldn't return. I kneeled on the hard stone in front of the priest, as I had rehearsed.

The high priest's voice rang out across the hall:

"By the grace and love of our gods and people, we are gathered today to celebrate the life of our kingdom, the South, and to pray for Serafina, our queen; to recognize and give thanks for her service to our kingdom; and to witness with joy, her crowning. Let us dedicate ourselves in body, mind, and spirit to renewed faith, a joyful hope, and a commitment to serve one another in love."

The high priest paused, and the guests and I all took a collective breath. Then, he continued.

"Today I present unto you, Queen Serafina Wyantha Helias." The high priest gazed upon me. "Your Majesty, the kingdom of the South, established by law, whose settlement you will swear to maintain, seeks to foster an environment in which individuals of all cultures and beliefs may live freely. The Coronation Oath has stood for centuries and is enshrined in law. Are you willing to take the oath?"

Projecting my voice so all could hear, I responded, "I am willing."

Lord John brought forth the robe, a garment of the finest cloth of gold, edged in white ermine fur. The high priest draped the robe over his arms, extending them to me. I reached my left hand out to set it lightly on the robe, doing my best to not flinch when the scratchy material rubbed against my skin.

The high priest spoke. "Will you solemnly promise and swear to govern the people of the South according to their respective laws and customs?"

I replied, "I solemnly promise."

"Will you use your power to cause law and justice, in mercy, in your judgment?"

Firmly, I replied, "I will."

The high priest dipped his head in acknowledgment and then unfolded the robe, presenting it to me. "Receive this robe, a symbol of honor and courage. May you be a brave advocate for those in need."

"I accept," I replied and then stood and turned to face the audience.

The high priest placed the robe around my shoulders, and I reached up and secured the heavy gold clasp. The added weight of the robe was stifling. Pivoting one hundred and eighty degrees, I took the step up the dais and turned to face the priest. This way, the guests could now see part of my face, instead of having to stare at my back.

Next, Lord John stepped forward, bearing the sword with the emeralds from the locked case. Traditionally, it would have been my grandfather's sword, but the high priest had surprisingly agreed to allow me to swap weapons. The steward placed the sword hilt in my right hand. I gripped the leather lightly, trying not to betray my nerves. I knew if I started shaking, the guests would surely see the sword's movement.

The high priest spoke. "Receive this queenly sword. May it be to you, and all those who witness these things, a sign and symbol, not of judgment, but of justice; not of might, but of mercy. With this sword do justice, stop the growth of iniquity, protect the people of the South, help and defend widows and orphans, restore the things that are gone to decay, maintain the things that are restored, punish and reform what is amiss, and confirm what is in good order. That doing these things you may be glorious in all virtue and so faithfully serve our people of the South."

Lord John stepped forward again and slipped the sword out of my hand, placing it on a stand a few paces away. I felt naked without it in my hand. Swallowing hard, I pushed away the desire to hold it. *I can finish this ceremony without a sword. I am the queen.* I returned my focus to the high priest, reminding myself the ceremony was almost over.

Lord John brought forth the crown. There had been a heated debate over the crown. Unlike the sword, the high priest had been rigid in his beliefs that we mustn't change the crown, citing it had been the same one used in the coronation ceremony for centuries. My argument was that the gold mine, the lifeblood of the South, had given me a different crown, and it would be unwise not to use it in this ceremony.

Reluctantly, the high priest took the four-pointed crown into his hands. There were gasps from the crowd as they presumably noticed the change.

He began reciting the blessing of the crown. "Queen of queens and lady of ladies, bless, we beseech thee, this crown …"

My gaze drifted to the guests, tuning out the high priest's long speech. There was movement along the walls. My heart quickened as I thought Tristan had finally arrived, except there were too many people weaving in the shadows. Tristan would not have done anything that would take away from my moment. Palace guards in cream and gold were stationed at specific intervals around the room, but it wasn't the guards who were moving. These were others. The cloaks they were wrapped in let them blend with the shadows. Hairs on the back of my arm rose as a feeling of foreboding crashed into me.

The priest's words droned on. "She may be crowned with the gods' gracious favor …"

"Tristan!" I called along the bond. Something was wrong, but I didn't know what. I jumped at least a foot into the air when the priest set the crown on my head. The movement startled him, and he fell over backward. A touch of magic was the only thing that kept the crown from toppling off my head onto the floor. *What a terrible omen that would be!* Embarrassed for startling the priest, I reached down to help him to his feet when I heard the soft twang of arrows being released.

Instinct took hold. I lunged for the sword just out of reach on the stand and tripped over my robe, hissing as my knees hit the hard stone floor. Throwing my hands out to catch myself, I accidentally hit the stand the sword was on, sending it toppling over and skidding out of reach. Screams of terror filled the hall. My hands shook as I crawled along the floor, desperate to reach the sword. Fiera was positioned closest to me, with Ghilanna near the entrance to the throne room, and Violet and Valerie were sitting on the benches with the guests and blending in. Thomas was there stationed with the palace guards. *Where are they?* While there were rules about who could be on the dais with me, we had taken as many precautions as possible to increase my safety and that of the guests for the coronation. We should not be under attack. *Yet we are.*

I closed my eyes and exhaled, reminding myself, *I am a trained Fae warrior. I survived imprisonment at Dorcha Palace. I am not going to let today be the day I stop fighting.* Gritting my teeth, I lunged for the sword and used my magic to vanish the robe that was hindering me. Fingers clenched around the sword hilt, the added weight and warmth of the robe gone, I lurched to my feet. A sword clanged into the stone where I had been moments before, sending a spray of sparks toward me.

My sword raised, I twisted, blocking the next strike and parrying. The attacker was wearing a dark-gray hooded robe, making it difficult to distinguish any features that would indicate who it was. A few blocks and parries showed me that it was a human, not a Fae. I couldn't decide if that was better or worse, knowing that humans had turned against me too.

I felt magic flowing through the air to my right. A quick glance, before diving with a low strike at my attacker's feet and rolling behind him, told me it was a star portal. *Please be Tristan,* I prayed. To my shock, it was my grandfather King Pharaan, bright green magic swirling around him. Hot on his heels was Onvyr, followed by Meriel *riding* Dubhar. The portal shut with a pop. Swirls of blue, green, white, and iridescent black magic wove between them. Though it wasn't Tristan, the combined experience between the four of them far surpassed anyone in this room.

My distraction had cost me a sting on my arm, from where my attacker had gotten a lucky slice. It wasn't a deep wound, but I had made a novice mistake, and it was a harsh reminder that I had let my shield slip. Magic filled the air as the newcomers swept down the dais and into the fray. With renewed hope that we could overcome this, I sped up my attacks, feinting low, then thrusting straight at my attacker's stomach. He fell for the feint, leaving his guard wide open. My sword slid with a sickly slurp into his stomach, and he slumped forward. I backed up, giving my sword a deft yank, peering around as I tried to figure out my next course of action. I was afraid to wade into the middle of it, distracting those who couldn't afford to be distracted. I spied Ghilanna and Valerie, fighting back-to-back in a corner against a group of five. Violet was sneaking up behind the man who appeared to be the leader, for he was barking orders. I watched with pride as Violet slipped a small knife out of her sleeve and stabbed the man three times in the lower back before dashing away.

My heart soared as I saw my grandfather and the others in his group cut a wide swath through the cloaked attackers. *We're going to win.* I took a half step forward, mouth opening to say something, when I felt the air move. A low whoosh was the only warning I had. I barely brought my sword up in time to block the sword strike. The hood slid back, revealing Leo, one of the guards who had caused problems with Callyn two days ago. *He must have let the attackers in.* I stumbled backward, trying to get my footing.

"What are you doing?" I demanded, desperate for answers.

"Killing you while your guards are distracted," Leo snapped.

My eyes widened in shock, and I took another step backward, bumping into a bench. "Why?"

Leo spoke harshly. "A lot of people want you dead. Take your pick. Today was the perfect opportunity."

I blocked his strike, trying to come up with a way to end this peacefully. I wanted answers. Killing Leo would not help me get them.

"You swore your fealty—" I started. A shimmering at the corner of my eye caught my attention. Shifting my feet, I watched in apprehension as another star portal opened. I shuddered as Bane leapt through and charged straight for Meriel, whose back was to me.

Leo swung high, aiming for my collar bone. I ducked and came up behind him, sword pressed to his neck. The last thing

I wanted to do was kill him, but if that's what it came to, then I would.

A big boom at the doors to the throne room sent me careening forward, and my sword plunged into the base of his neck before I knew what was happening. Sorrow filled me; my intention had not been to kill Leo. I pushed it away and turned toward the clouds of dust obscuring the throne room doors.

Nineteen

TRISTAN

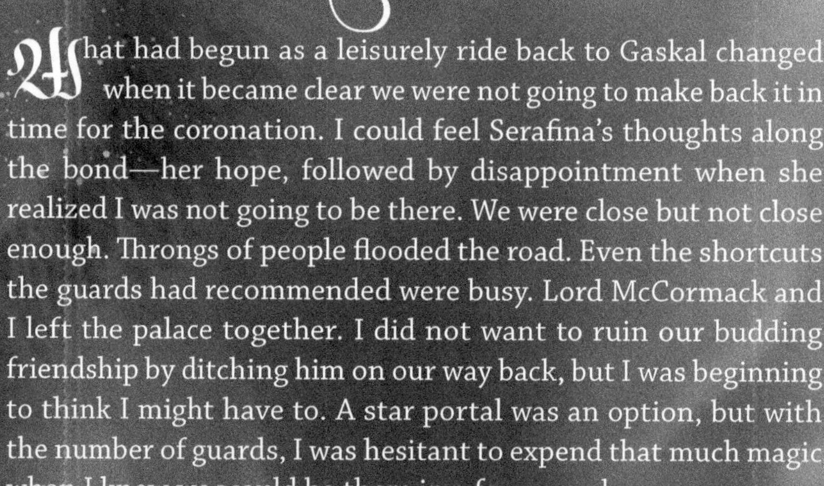

What had begun as a leisurely ride back to Gaskal changed when it became clear we were not going to make back it in time for the coronation. I could feel Serafina's thoughts along the bond—her hope, followed by disappointment when she realized I was not going to be there. We were close but not close enough. Throngs of people flooded the road. Even the shortcuts the guards had recommended were busy. Lord McCormack and I left the palace together. I did not want to ruin our budding friendship by ditching him on our way back, but I was beginning to think I might have to. A star portal was an option, but with the number of guards, I was hesitant to expend that much magic when I knew we would be there in a few more hours.

The desperate *"Tristan!"* through the bond made the decision for me. I reined my horse over to the side of the road, indicating the guards should cluster around us.

"Serafina! What is going on?" I called, trying to keep the fear out of my voice, but there was no response. Just the continued feeling of fear and needing me there. "Something is wrong at the palace. I *must* go now," I said tightly to the guards.

Lord McCormack was alarmed. "What's happening?"

"I don't know. Serafina called me through the mating bond, and now I can feel fear through it. I think they're under attack. She isn't responding to anything I'm trying to say to her."

The guard captain raised his hand. I nodded at him to speak. "Can you do the ... magic travel thingy?"

I chuckled at his explanation of a star portal, but he did have a point. If the palace was under attack, they would need all the help they could get, which meant the whole squad I had with me could turn the tables and put the odds in our favor. "Yes. I can take all of us through, but not the horses," I added as an afterthought. Fifteen people would be enough of a strain.

"There is a merchant not far behind us. We can give him the task of getting the horses into Gaskal," Lord McCormack said.

"Is he trustworthy?" I asked.

Lord McCormack nodded. "Yes. He brings all sorts of supplies into Gaskal for the palace. His caravan can handle the horses easily."

"Good. Arrange that," I said, then addressed the guard captain. "Have your men start dismounting. No need for us all to wait to handle the horses."

The whole group dismounted and the guards quickly checked their weapons, preparing for whatever awaited us at the palace.

"I am going to open the star portal, and you will pass through in pairs. I will go through last. Using a star portal is much like walking through a door. On this side, we're here. The other side will be within my personal suite of rooms. Since the only thing I know with certainty is that the queen is in the throne room, I think starting at my suites will be safe. Otherwise, I could be dumping you in the middle of enemies," I explained.

The guards murmured their acknowledgment. Thankfully, they were all taking this turn of events in stride, more concerned for the safety of those at the palace than about stepping through a Fae star portal. Closing my eyes, I dropped into my core of magic and drew on its power, willing a star portal to appear.

Feeling the gentle tug of magic as it flowed out of me and into the portal, I opened my eyes.

"Ready?" I asked. I didn't want to hold the portal open any longer than necessary due to the energy drain. "Go in pairs."

Five minutes later, when there were only two guards left and the horses, Lord McCormack returned with six gangly youths. Each took charge of two or three horses apiece.

"Are you ready?" I asked tensely

"Yes, let's go," Lord McCormack said.

Lord McCormack grabbed the backs of the shirts of the last two guards and practically shoved them through.

"I'll see you in a moment," I told Lord McCormack, and he strode through. Now, it was my turn. Exhaling, nostrils fluttering, I stepped through the portal and pulled it shut as soon as my feet hit the familiar wood floor in the foyer of my home.

The residence and hallway were silent. Lord McCormack took one guard with him and was going to look for help while I led the rest of the squad to investigate the throne room. The closer we got to our destination, the more pronounced the screams were. I hastened my steps, almost running down the hall, sword in my hand, ready to take on whatever foe awaited us. Rounding the corner, we came face to face with Prince Tanyth. I skidded to a halt and unsheathed my broadsword.

Prince Tanyth's dismay at my arrival quickly morphed into a malicious smile. "How fitting. You come to the rescue at the last moment and right into my open arms."

My heart skipped a beat as I examined Tanyth. His cloak with snow leopard paws on the shoulders swirled around his legs, a dark leather breastplate with the Court of Dusk emblem covered his chest, and his right hand held Fleshrender. I could feel its malevolent power even from where I stood. Tucked into his belt was Dragonfang with its dragon-head hilt and vibrant emerald eyes. Gripped in his left hand, so tightly his teal knuckles were almost white, was the *Bloodsong Grimoire*.

Dread flooded me; my vision darkened. *No!* I shouted at myself, refusing to let another panic attack take hold—not now, when everyone's life hinged on what I did next. With the three objects united, Tanyth had unfathomable amounts of magic at his disposal.

"Fight me yourself, Tanyth, or do you not have the balls anymore?" I taunted.

Tanyth burst out laughing. "You should hear how pathetic you sound, Tristan. How far you've fallen. You were glorious once. Alas, that time is long gone."

Before I could respond, Tanyth raised Fleshrender. I felt a pulse a second before a blast of teal magic erupted from the sword. I threw up a shield across the entire hallway, deciding protecting the whole squad was the best option.

Tanyth howled in anger when his magic fizzled out as it came in contact with the shield. He sent blast after blast at me, but the result was the same. My curiosity grew the greater Tanyth's frustration became.

"I thought you were going to kill me!" I shouted.

That earned me a snarl that reverberated through the entire hallway, and Tanyth raised the sword again and sent another bolt of teal magic. "Work, damn you," he shouted, brandishing the book in the air.

Work? Like the magic artifacts aren't working? A wild idea came to me. Not wanting to give myself a chance to question it, I dropped the shield and sprinted for Tanyth. At the last moment, I lunged to the left, using my momentum to carry me halfway up the wall and sweeping my sword in a fast downward arc. Tanyth barely got Fleshrender up in time. Using the prince's hesitation to my advantage, I tightened my grip on the sword hilt and thrust the broadsword straight into Tanyth's stomach.

He dodged at the last possible moment and parried wildly. His sword slid off my armored shoulder guard.

One of the guards rushed past me, his momentum sending me sideways a few steps. I opened my mouth to warn him, but it was too late. Fleshrender arced through the air, slicing through the guard's neck, and he collapsed to the floor, dead.

Tanyth's face was splattered with blood, and his dark green eyes were wild. His lips formed words, though I couldn't hear what he was saying.

"Fight me," I growled. Every step forward I took, Tanyth backed up.

Tanyth glared at me, and to my surprise, he created a star portal and vanished.

"Huh?" I muttered, trying to wrap my mind around what had just happened.

One of the guards moved toward the throne room doors now that the threat of Tanyth was gone. The action reminded me that there were still screams coming from the throne room, which meant Serafina was in danger.

The guard, James, wrapped his hand around the handle and tugged, but the doors didn't budge. He tried again and had the same result.

"They must have it blocked on the other side," I explained.

"We could find something to use as a battering ram," James suggested.

"Magic will be faster," I replied. "Please step back."

James and the other guards retreated a few steps down the hallway. Deciding to use pure force to blast through the doors, I thrust outward with my magic and will. A ball of dark-gray magic collided with the doors, and a loud boom echoed in the hallway. The doors rattled on their hinges but did not give way.

Muffled shouts and more screams came from inside. Fear clawed at my throat. I was trying to hold my dwindling supply of magic in reserve for whatever awaited us inside, but I realized that if we couldn't breach the door, having a magic reserve would be useless.

Tightening my grip on my sword, I stilled my mind and drew all my power into a ball of magic about the size of a plate. Aiming for the center of the doors at the handles, I loosed the magic. It blasted through the doors, sending splinters and pieces of door flying into the throne room.

For a brief moment, I saw Sera on the dais standing near a blood-soaked Fiera. Then, my view of them was obscured as a black-haired and green-robed King Pharaan, in a heated battle with Tanyth, wielding Fleshrender, spun and twisted over the debris in the room. To the left, I spotted another Fae, the blue-haired Onvyr, in a heated swordfight with Bane. I recognized him from my visit to Uaine Palace. Dead bodies littered the floor, humans in dark-gray cloaks mixed with coronation guests in their finery.

Determined to reach Sera, I waded through the fighting, sword spinning through the air, dodging and slicing through enemies. Two humans in dark-gray cloaks rushed me. I blocked the strike to the right and then parried the one to the left, growling low in my throat, as they drew my focus away from my wife. *I could finish them with my magic,* I reminded myself, but when I reached for it, all that was there were wisps, like smoke. I was fully depleted. Throwing myself into dispatching these two, I sped up my attacks, spinning and twisting. A lucky thrust to the left and my sword pierced through the man's side. He fell sideways and dropped his sword.

The other one grinned at me. "Die, Fae filth!" he shouted and ran toward me, frothing at the mouth. I ducked under his attack and thrust my sword under my arm behind me, into his back. He fell with a gurgling hiss.

I could feel the magic in the air as King Pharaan and Tanyth continued to face off. At times, it crackled audibly. Both bore swords and expertly wielded them. I couldn't help shuddering at the malevolence coming off Fleshrender in waves. It would have been a sight to behold were the circumstances different.

A slice across my thigh brought me back to myself. Thankfully, my armor blocked the brunt of the sword, a sharp reminder that enemies were still within the room. High strike, low parry, mid strike, on and on it went. The hood fell back, revealing my attacker. I distinctly remembered him as Sir Bruin from Castle Piore. His bushy brown mustache, messy curls, and mean black eyes had stuck with me. *Is Duke Piore behind this attack? How do Tanyth and Bane fit in?* I was being presented with an opportunity to procure information.

Gulping through a dry throat and hoping my words would sound like more than a croak, I spoke. "Sir Bruin, a surprise to see you here."

Sir Bruin spit in my face and thrust his sword toward my stomach. I blocked just in time, deflecting the knight's sword to the left. Swiping the spit off my face, I leaped forward with a middle strike and a left jab from my fist. The knight blocked my strike but did not pay attention to the punch, and it landed squarely at the bottom of his rib cage, confirming that he was not wearing armor. *Likely too noisy and would draw attention*, I mused.

Duke Piore had not been a fan of me or Lord McCormack during our visit, but this attack was as good as a declaration of war. I heard a twang and an arrow pierced my shoulder, sending me staggering to the side. Growling in pain and annoyance at myself, I spun around, searching for the archer.

Sir Bruin laughed coldly from where he was sitting on the ground, leaning against a column and holding his arm tightly around his chest. I suspected I had cracked or broken a rib or two.

"Help King Pharaan," Serafina whispered through the bond.

Adrenaline and fear surged through my veins, and I sprinted toward her, ignoring the arrow sticking out of my shoulder and her request. Even as I did so, I caught glimpses of King Pharaan's fight and worried he was losing to Tanyth. Desperate to make sure Sera was all right, I prayed the king would hold on until I could reach him.

Sera and Fiera were fighting back-to-back against a cloaked figure. There was a body a few feet away, and I presumed it was the source of the blood covering Fiera. I could sense that Sera still had a deep well of magic within her but likely not the confidence to tap it. Our eyes briefly met, and then she was screaming, "No!" She shot forward, away from Fiera. I spun, looking for whatever had caught her attention.

Tanyth was wiping Fleshrender on King Pharaan's tunic, though the sword seemed to absorb the blood before Tanyth could clean it off. The king's severed head rolled to the side. Tanyth noticed I was looking at him and shot a malicious grin at me.

"Shield yourself!" I warned Sera through the bond. A green-and-gold shield appeared around Sera, like a glowing bubble. Not exactly what I had had in mind, but it would suffice. Tanyth sprinted toward Sera and Fiera. To my shock, he barreled past Sera and plunged Fleshrender into Fiera's stomach. Over his shoulder, I could see the shocked expression on her face as she collapsed in front of him.

"Fiera!" Sera sobbed, but with Tanyth between her and Fiera's body, she wisely stayed where she was. I had no doubts in my mind that Tanyth would kill her too. Sera took a hesitant step toward him, her sword dipping dangerously low.

Bane rushed over, his sword and armor awash in blood, then scooped Fiera's body into his arms and summoned a star portal practically on top of them. When the star portal closed, Tanyth, Bane, and Fiera's body were gone.

With Tanyth and Bane's departure, the guards who had come in with me met little resistance and were rounding up the few remaining gray-cloaked enemies, including Sir Bruin. I peered around the room. Blood, guts, and bodies—so many bodies—strewn about.

Onvyr, King Pharaan's lord commander, limped toward us. His face was drawn, his light-blue hair streaked with blood. Dubhar was directly behind him, his satin black coat covered with a layer of blood. His head was low, as though too heavy for him to carry. I sucked in a breath, recognizing the white-haired Fae Onvyr reverently carried in his arms. My heart sank as I took in how limp Commander Meriel was in his arms. Serafina knelt beside King Pharaan, softly crying.

"Your Majesty," Onvyr said respectfully to Sera.

She tipped her head up to look at him. I could imagine her face was streaked with tears, but I was standing behind her and could not see it for myself. I was not convinced there wasn't another knight or one of Tanyth's assassins lurking in the corner, waiting.

"Onvyr," Sera said in a strangled voice.

"I am saddened to inform you that Commander Meriel did not make it. We were fighting side by side, and she stepped in front of me to block an arrow. It went through her heart. I know the two of you were close," Onvyr said solemnly.

I swallowed hard, my heart breaking for Sera. Commander Meriel had been close to many among the Fae. I imagined, given her familial ties to King Pharaan, that she knew Onvyr well and for many years. Though we had had a shaky introduction a few weeks ago, I felt deep respect for this male who was willing to put Sera's needs and feelings above his own.

The guard James walked over, keeping his eyes on my face and averted from the carnage. "We have cleared the throne room, and the master of the guard has sent multiple squads out to sweep the rest of the palace for enemies who have hidden themselves away. You are welcome to question the two prisoners or allow Declan to interrogate them himself."

My magic was still nonexistent; otherwise, I'd have conducted a magical sweep myself. Through the mating bond, I could feel the well of Sera's magic still bubbling just under the surface of her skin. Her grief was almost overwhelming me through the bond, and I knew it was not the time to teach her another new skill with her magic.

"Your Majesty, who would you like to interrogate the prisoners?" I asked, trying to get her attention. Her subjects were going to need her now more than ever as the kingdom would reel from this attack and significant loss of life on a day that was meant to be a celebration of their new queen.

She rose to her feet and set her hand in mine. "Do you want the honest answer?"

I nodded. *Of course I want the honest answer.*

"I would like to return to our home now and let someone else conduct the interrogation," Sera said, her voice breaking.

I gathered her in my arms, hugging her tightly. Peering over her shoulder at Onvyr, I asked, "Are you staying or returning to Uaine Palace?"

Onvyr sighed. "I need to return with the bodies and make funeral preparations. There is much to be done. King Pharaan does not have living son or grandson to take his place."

Onvyr's words confirmed what I had suspected: that if Serafina wasn't willing to accept her destiny as the Lost Fae Queen, and rightful Queen of the Fae, the four Fae courts would descend into chaos as the three still-living Fae princes fought for the position. It was the last thing we could afford, not with Tanyth out for Sera's blood. *Likely Tanyth's plan.*

I shuddered. Tanyth would profit well if the allies Sera desperately needed were no longer available due to their own conflicts.

"We will send word if anything here changes. Thank you for the assistance today," I said genuinely.

Onvyr nodded. "You and Serafina would have done the same had we needed help at Uaine Palace."

I bobbed my head in acknowledgment, wondering how they would send the call for help, or how they had received one today. *Maybe it was something Meriel had seen.* It didn't matter. They had come, Sera was alive, and Meriel, King Pharaan, and countless others were dead.

"James, make sure that we make a list of all the dead. Set the gray cloaks on the left side of the room and the guests and palace guards on the right," I ordered.

"I will make sure your orders are followed, General," James said, then saluted me.

Keeping Sera tucked into my side, we slowly made our way out of the throne room and into the hallway. I felt Sera's shield around us and was grateful she had taken it upon herself to do that small measure of safety.

Part Two

Twenty

SERAFINA

I woke up with a start. "Fiera!" I gasped, balling my fists up and thrashing around.

"You're safe," Tristan soothed.

The sound of his voice reassured me. Tristan wouldn't lie if I was still in danger. Taking a slow breath, I examined my surroundings. Tristan's arms were wrapped around me. I was lying on top of him on the couch in our residence, and his piercing blue eyes were open and alert. The scratchy gold brocade overlayer of my dress had splatters of blood on it.

"Where is Fiera?" I demanded, struggling against the sleepiness that was clinging to me.

Tristan planted a light kiss on my forehead. "I'm so sorry, my love, but Fiera died. Tanyth killed her right after …" His voice trailed off; his mouth was drawn tight.

Tanyth arched backward, narrowly avoiding King Pharaan's sword, but the King of Fae was off balance from his attack, taking precious moments to recover. With a back-handed strike, Fleshrender severed King Pharaan's head. I felt the blood draining from my face as the memory hit me. The glimpses of the battle that I had seen as I desperately fought against the other attackers back-to-back with Fiera.

Tristan closed his eyes. I could feel his rapid heartbeat against my chest and was certain that he had relived my memory through the mating bond. But his own feelings were still hidden behind a solid wall that even now, with our emotions raw, I could not get through.

Tears spilled down my cheeks. The loss of not only my best friend but also one of my last living family members was a lot to take at once. *They both died protecting me. All I have done lately is get people I care about killed.* "Maybe I should just give Tanyth what he wants—me. Then the killing would end, and the war would never happen."

"Don't say that, Sera. The deaths are not your fault. Fiera, King Pharaan, Commander Meriel, the guards, they all chose to be there to support and protect you. This is what Tanyth wants, to make you feel hopeless. But we have knights, and there are Fae who support you. You are not in this alone," Tristan said. "You don't know him like I do. Turning yourself over to Tanyth would not guarantee anything beyond you being his captive. He has coveted King Pharaan's throne for a very long time. He is not going to relinquish this opportunity to take it without a fight."

My voice cracked as I spoke. "How can I lead the South to fight a war if we can't even protect ourselves within the palace?"

Tristan ran his fingers through my hair and met my gaze. "They're not the same thing, but you're right. It's hard to be confident we can win a war when our vulnerabilities at home are so gaping. I will remind you that Lord John highly recommended allowing the coronation guest list to be open to any who wanted to attend. That choice made the coronation a more likely target."

"Why didn't you say anything when we were discussing it?" I demanded.

"Because it was briefly mentioned before I left with Lord McCormack, and you made the final decision while I was traveling. The only way you're going to learn and gain confidence to make choices without needing me is to do so," Tristan replied.

I shoved his chest hard and rose so I was kneeling. "Is that what the coronation was? A lesson?" *Does he really think I need over one hundred people to die to learn how to be a leader?*

Tristan shook his head. "That's not what I meant. I was just saying that things happen. Sometimes the choices we make don't end the way we intended. That is how you will grow into your role as queen, Sera. You don't honestly believe that I have made the correct decision every single time my entire life?"

I frowned, conceding Tristan did have a point. No one was perfect all the time. It just hurt that my learning curve had to come at such a steep cost. "You seemed to know the one man. Did you meet him on your trip?"

Tristan nodded. "Yes, Sir Bruin. He was at Castle Piore. Too much of a coincidence, and Captain Green warned me about the knights there. Duke Piore was barely hospitable toward us, and the knights were hardly any better."

My eyebrows raised. "Duke *Taylor* Piore?" I asked. Taylor had been one of the first suitors I met and had been quite offended by my time I had spent with the Fae.

"Yes, you know him?" Tristan asked, unsettled.

"Unfortunately, yes. I met him before King Leonard decided to host the competition. He was one of my grandfather's preferred suitors for me," I replied.

"Ah," Tristan said thoughtfully.

"I never got to make my speech," I said softly and swallowed hard as I realized how big of an impact this attack was going to have on the South. It was no longer simply my personal losses but the deaths of many nobles, including the optics of having the King of Fae die in a human kingdom. *I guess it's good that all three human kings already sent their responses declining to aid us against Tanyth because they would be reneging on their proposed alliances with this turn of events.* My stomach plummeted like a rock. *The Fae won't follow us now. They're going to blame me for King Pharaan's death too, saying he'd never have been in danger if he hadn't been here for the coronation. Even if that was twisted version of what happened.*

"We need a full list of the casualties before we can decide what to do. You need to call a war council meeting," Tristan said. "Immediately."

His words tugged me out of my thoughts. It was hard to muster the energy I needed for what was required of me, though I knew Tristan was right—I had to evaluate the extent of the damage before I could decide how to proceed. With the Duke of Piore likely behind the attack, I would have to make my punishment swift but also use caution. My reaction to the duke's treason would set the tone for my reign as Lady of the South. Too harsh and I would anger more nobles; too soft and no one would take me seriously.

"Did anyone come by while I was asleep?" I asked.

"Thomas did for an update and to ensure you weren't severely injured. He agreed that letting you rest was the best option," Tristan replied. "Valerie also stopped by to let you know that Ghilanna and Violet were injured but are resting. Valerie hit her head, but aside from a bad headache claimed she was fine."

"Do you know …" My voice started to crack, and I cleared my throat. I wanted to voice the words aloud. "Do you know who else died?"

He gave my hand a squeeze. "The dead include the high priest and Lord John, Duke Herman, and his granddaughter Lady Francesca." Tristan paused a moment, swallowing hard. "Josiah and Lord McCormack's status is unknown. Lord McCormack and I split up when we arrived, but I did not see him after that. There is one more thing I haven't told you yet."

Bleary-eyed, I met his gaze, wondering what else there was to know.

"Tanyth was outside of the throne room when I arrived. He had Fleshrender, Dragonfang, and the *Bloodsong Grimoire* with him," Tristan said harshly. "He tried blasting me with his magic and failed to penetrate my shield. I have no idea what was going on, but I'm pretty certain the magic artifacts, even though they were united, were not behaving as he had expected."

"That doesn't make sense," I muttered.

Tristan pushed a strand of hair out of my eyes and replied, "I know. I thought he was going to come after you. We fought, but he was not fully invested and then he disappeared. Now the Fae we could have asked are dead. I don't know where that leaves us."

The breath hitched in my throat. Meriel, who had been there for me in her own way the past twelve years, and my only real connection to my mother, was gone too. Just yesterday, Meriel had told me I should seek out King Pharaan's advice and that he was sure to stand behind me as an ally in the war against the Court of Dusk. *Without him, will Prince Almar or Prince Rhangil offer me aid?*

"I am sure there are others in the Court of Dawn who would be willing to help you find the information you seek. Onvyr was here at the coronation too. A good resource if you are willing to ask him for help," Tristan said soothingly.

There was a knock on the door. I reluctantly pulled out of Tristan's arms and swung my legs over the end of the couch. *I can do this.*

The door scraped across the hardwood as it opened. "Your Majesty," came Thomas's voice. My shoulders sagged in relief.

"You may come in, Thomas," I replied.

Through the mating bond, I felt a tingle of magic as Tristan pushed open the curtains, letting streams of sunlight into the room. I blinked rapidly, trying to adjust to the much brighter space.

Thomas walked over to us and stood with his hands behind his back. He bore a bandage on his left bicep and over his right ear. Valerie was just behind him with a large purple bruise on her forehead. "I apologize for the intrusion; however, since Lord John's passing last night, the palace is in turmoil. He oversaw much of the day-to-day operations. I was volunteered by Declan to come here and get things moving this morning. Valerie offered to help too."

"Thank you, Thomas and Valerie, for stepping up. I will do my best to find a replacement for Lord John," I said, adding that task to a growing list.

"Because of the attack, there was no reception; therefore, the speech you intended to deliver was never given. Small groups of protesters are grouping together in the streets. Currently, the number of guards is sufficient to break up the groups. It is critical that you still give your speech and include minor details about the attack and your stance on what punishment traitors will receive, to help settle everyone," Thomas explained.

"What about the dead?" I asked.

Thomas exhaled slowly, taking a moment before replying. "Yes, that is a task for you today as well. Reviewing the list of the dead and deciding how we will handle it. Traditionally, the noble families would claim their family members' bodies and make funeral arrangements themselves."

"The war council must meet," interjected Tristan.

I nodded at his reminder. The attack was treason and a declaration of war, if it had indeed been ordered by Duke Taylor Piore. "Has the prisoner been interrogated?"

Thomas frowned. "Yes and no. Declan is not making any progress."

I knew nothing about interrogation techniques, and I doubted I would be helpful in encouraging the man to provide any information. "Tristan, can you interrogate the prisoner?"

Tristan's eyes brightened, and I could feel his eagerness through the mating bond. "Of course."

"Then it's settled. Tristan will perform the interrogation, and I would like to check on Ghilanna and Violet. If they are fit to return to duty, I will discuss their roles today. Then I will review the list of the dead. We should have the war council meeting after lunch," I said decisively, shoving my sadness and worry away so I could focus on what I could control, the next steps I needed to take.

"As you wish," Thomas said and bowed, then returned to the hallway.

Tristan patted my hand reassuringly. "We'll get through this."

"I hope so," I murmured, then leaned forward and gave him a light kiss. Before he could trap me there, I stood up and moved out of reach. "You have an interrogation."

Tristan sighed. "Yes. I will see you at lunch," he replied, then stood, gathering me into his arms and kissing me passionately. I melted against him, wishing that we could go into the bedroom and forget about the horrible attack from the coronation and ignore all these difficult emotions warring within us. *But we can't,* I reminded myself. *I'm queen. My people are looking to me for guidance. Now of all times, it is critical that I take up the mantle of ruler and not hide in my chambers.*

Tristan reluctantly released me and departed. Before the door to the hallway snicked shut, it swung open again, revealing Ghilanna and Violet, who came in and stood next to Valerie. I sighed in relief.

Moving farther into the room, I took the moment to study the three of them. *My ladies-in-waiting.* My hands shook at the knowledge that Fiera was dead and would no longer be part of this group. Her death was final. She was gone forever. Anything that hadn't been said between us was never going to be said. Blinking, I focused again on the women in front of me. They wore the outfits the seamstress had made for them—matching long-sleeved cream silk tunics, cream-and-gold jacquard vests, and cream silk pants that flared out in such a way they could almost be mistaken for a skirt. I could see the barest outline of a dagger as the fabric on Ghilanna's sleeve tightened around her forearm. Each wore black boots that were mostly obscured by the long pants. I assumed they each had daggers in those as well.

Ghilanna's hair was tightly braided against her head in two plaits. Violet's was coiled into a bun at the nape of her neck with pearl pins, and Valerie's was in a single braid. When Violet moved, she had a slight limp.

I stepped forward and hugged each one of them, catching Violet off guard. She stiffened and then relaxed. "I want to thank each of you for what you did yesterday. I know I would not be standing here if you had not been willing to defend me against the traitors. I sincerely hope that we will not have a situation like that again. However, as the tension grows in the South and between us and the Court of the Dusk, I think the odds of coming under attack again are only going to increase. Your courage is exactly why I selected you to be my ladies-in-waiting. Today, our first task is to review and confirm who died yesterday and to send condolences to their families."

Ghilanna, Violet, Valerie, and I reviewed the list of the dead and made rounds to talk to the injured palace guards. Thankfully, we found Lord McCormack wounded but resting in one of the rooms set aside to care for the injured, and Josiah was escorting those who could return home out to the palace gates. It took about an hour, and by the end, I was ready to go outside for fresh air and a change of scenery.

"I want to go for a ride," I announced as we departed the makeshift infirmary.

Thomas must have heard the comment, for he replied, "The knights that Tristan and Lord McCormack met with on their trip have begun arriving. Declan has them setting up tents in the meadow. It would be good for morale if you were to go out there and greet them."

Violet fidgeted with the hem of her sleeve. "Is it safe?"

I couldn't blame her for her concern, but at this point I wasn't sure there was anywhere "safe." Unless I figured out how to cast magic to prevent anyone without express permission from entering or exiting the palace and its grounds, there would always be a chance that an enemy could slip through. Increasing the number of guards had not been enough to prevent the attack yesterday. "I have you three, my own magic, plus Dubhar and a full squad of guards. It will have to be enough."

Violet lowered her eyes, accepting my response.

"Let's go to the stables," Ghilanna said. When no one else spoke, she led the way.

A groom pushed open the stable doors, and I heard an excited whinny. *Dubhar.* A shiver of anticipation went through me at the thought of galloping around the meadow. *Except the meadow is full of knights and tents,* I reminded myself. I rushed ahead of the group, intent on going to Dubhar. Even though I knew that Dubhar was a Fae Watcher, not *just* a unicorn, it did not eliminate the feelings I had for him and the bond that we had formed. For whatever reason, Dubhar understood me in ways that I doubted Tristan ever would.

After snagging a basket of brushes, I unlatched Dubhar's stall door and shimmied through it. He shoved his muzzle into my chest, breathing softly. Staring into his swirling silver eyes, all my worries and anger felt like they were muted.

"Inspecting the knights?" Dubhar asked.

"Maybe a gallop?" I whispered, praying no one else heard me. Thomas and Tristan would both accuse me of being reckless.

Dubhar bumped the brush basket with his nose. I giggled. "Okay, okay. Brushing first."

I was more relaxed than I'd been all morning when I climbed onto Dubhar's back. *I guess brushing is soothing for both of us.* Valerie cast me a concerned look when I rode out of the stable completely tackless. Unlike her brother, Valerie seemed ill at ease around horses; she sat stiffly in the saddle and her hands were tight around the reins. Violet, who sat next to her atop a piebald white-and-red gelding, reached over to pat Valerie's hand as though consoling her.

"Don't worry. The queen is an excellent rider."

Valerie looked doubtful but stayed silent. I smiled at her, and the guards fell into place around us.

We made our way out of the side gate that took us directly to the meadow. Once we cleared the gate, we picked up a brisk trot. Tents in various shades of gray, brown, and green sprawled across the meadow as Thomas had said, except only one third of the meadow was being used *and* there was still a wide swath around the whole perimeter.

I glanced at Ghilanna. She was the closest to me. "Are you ready?" I asked with a smirk.

Ghilanna threw her fist into the air and whooped, startling the guard's horse closest to her and sending it bucking. Dubhar dug his hind feet into the ground and launched us forward. The other horses scrambled to get out of our way. Clumps of grass and dirt flew into the air as we galloped away.

A quick glance over my shoulder and I saw Ghilanna and Violet were hot on our heels with Valerie and the guards farther behind. Leaning low over Dubhar's neck, I relished the feel of his velvety fur against my cheek and the smoothness of his stride. The wind created by our speed tugged my hair out of its pins, sending it flowing behind me like a russet flag. By the time we started our second lap around the meadow, an audience had gathered. A loose line of knights had formed. A couple had standards and were raising them and cheering.

Adrenaline surged through me and to my wonder Dubhar sped up again. Curious what the unicorn was up to, I adjusted my seat and wrapped my fingers in his mane, knowing that we would soon have to slow down. We were out here to talk to the knights, not just to show how fast I could ride without tack.

As we drew near to the line of knights, Dubhar slowed dramatically. When we were at about the middle of the line, he reared. I heard gasps of surprise and awe from the knights and a loud comment of someone speculating I was going to fall off. Dubhar stayed on his hind legs far longer than a real horse would have been able to. Finally, he returned his front feet to the ground. I sat there gazing at the knights, hoping when I dismounted that my legs would support me. Cautiously, I swung my leg over Dubhar's back and jumped to the ground.

Landing on my feet, I was pleased that I had not made a fool out of myself. I walked toward the knights, bewildered when I felt a crown on my head. *What did he do?* I mused. Knowing it would look bad if I reached up to feel what was on my head, I suspected it was the crown the gold mine had given me.

One of the knights stepped forward. He was wearing a chain mail tunic and plate leg guards. He had light-gray eyes, a trimmed salt-and-pepper beard, and dark-brown hair with streaks of gray.

"Your Majesty," the knight said with a deep bow. "I am Captain Hershel Green. I lead the knights of Hunter's Hollow."

I inclined my head, acknowledging him. "It's good to meet you, Captain Green. Are you in charge here?" Tristan hadn't told me what his plan was for organizing the knights when they showed up. As my general, they fell under his purview, unless he had another plan in mind.

Captain Green replied, "Currently, I am the only officer-ranked knight. Though a scout said the knights from Fort Salmon are due within the hour, and there should be a major with them."

Making a quick decision, I set my hand on my sword. "Kneel, Captain Green."

The knight looked at me uncertainly but obeyed my orders.

"Captain Green, from today onward you are promoted to major." I unsheathed my sword and tapped it on each of his shoulders. "Rise, Major Green."

Major Green slowly rose and then bowed deeply. "I am honored by this promotion, Your Majesty, and promise I will do everything within my abilities to live up to your expectations."

"Thank you. Now, Major, how many knights do we have?" I asked.

"As of this exact moment, five hundred. Fort Salmon will put us at fifteen hundred," Major Green replied.

"It's a start," I murmured.

Major Green coughed. "Pardon me, Your Majesty, but what is the objective of bringing all the knights here?"

"The Fae Court of Dusk has declared war on us, and even now Prince Tanyth is gathering his Fae warriors and preparing to make a move for our border," I replied candidly.

The knight looked thoughtful as he scratched his chin, then his gray eyes met mine. "The last time the South fought the Court of Dusk, each side had about two thousand knights. It would be reasonable to expect we will be close to those numbers when the remainder of the Southern knights show up."

Blowing out my breath, I debated how much to tell him. We were standing in the open. With the other knights milling around, the conversation was far from confidential, but if he was familiar with the last war against the Court of Dusk, then Major Green likely knew most of what I would say.

"The Fae have magic," I started.

Major Green chuckled. "I am well aware. I also know *you*, my queen, possess magic too. You're the first Lady of the South who has ever ruled our kingdom. It is not a surprise that you also have unicorns and griffin riders as allies."

I stared at him, wide-eyed. For a knight who had arrived less than a day ago from Hunter's Hollow, Major Green certainly had obtained a lot of information in a short period of time. "Where did you get your information from?" I demanded.

Unfazed by my tone, Major Green replied calmly, "Word travels. Though Gaskal is the only large city in the South, that doesn't mean information doesn't reach the rest of the kingdom. Besides, I am friends with Josiah."

Josiah, who is my spymaster. I let that information sink in. *I have so much to learn about being a ruler.* Uncertainty filled me; perhaps I should have waited for Tristan to come out here. I was out of my element, and it was becoming more obvious by the minute. I took a step backward and pivoted so I could see Dubhar.

"You haven't had a chance to see the camp," Major Green said conversationally. "It would mean a lot to the men to see you."

Swallowing hard, I knew he was right, and it was why I had come out here—to make sure they knew they weren't just a number, that I valued each and every one of them and the contribution they would make in the war against Tanyth.

"Very well. Please lead the way." I gestured.

Major Green nodded and started walking, keeping his pace slow so I could walk beside him. Ghilanna, Valerie, and Violet were right behind us. Once my guards figured out where we were going, they boxed us in. I wanted to protest, saying that it was almost impossible to see any of the knights with the guards blocking my view, but I knew it was not a discussion I would win. Not with yesterday's attack at the forefront of their minds.

I had to admit that by the time we concluded walking through the encampment, I had a better understanding of why Major Green was not overly concerned about meeting the Court of Dusk on a battlefield without the support of the other human kingdoms. The knights here were veterans. Some, like Major Green, had been on the battlefield last time. Major Green, I discovered, had been only six at the time and was a water boy for the officers. Others had fought against the East or the West over trade and boundary disputes. *War is inevitable*—whether against the Fae or humans. There had been very few Lords of the South in the history of the kingdom who had ruled exclusively during peacetime.

We halted near where Dubhar and the other horses had been tied. "Thank you for your time today, Major Green."

"Anytime, Your Majesty," Major Green responded with a formal bow.

Not sure what else to say, I retreated to Dubhar and mounted. The others followed my example, and soon we were trotting back toward the palace.

Twenty-One

RETHYS

I was fortunate that when King Pharaan died I was in my cave and not flying. The ripple of magic through the world had paralyzed me for over an hour. Eventually, it wore off, and I could move from my position lying atop my hoard of gold coins, but by then I wasn't sure I wanted to. A pulsating darkness was trickling into the gaping void left by the King of Fae's death. *The end of time.*

Knowing it was coming and having the end of time present were two entirely different matters. Unfortunately, I doubted there were any Fae who could feel the end of time. As tension spread between the four courts, the Fae had become less attuned to the nuances of the world and the threads of magic woven through it. The potential existed in Serafina, but there were steps she still had to go through, and time was rapidly disappearing.

I shot forward at the sound of wings approaching the cave. Taking a deep breath, I let the fire rise from my belly into the back of my throat. Smoke escaped from my mouth, obscuring the inside of the cave from whoever was approaching. Jaws open just enough, I waited. A bronze-feathered griffin landed at the mouth of the cave. Without warning, I released a blast of red-hot fire.

A dark gold shield arced around the griffin, blocking my dragonfire. Hissing, I prepared to release more.

"Rethys! Forgive the intrusion. I did not realize you had been released from the Court of Dusk," Marek Fenmyar called.

I swallowed, quenching the fire at the back of my throat as I recognized him with his brown sun-streaked hair and bronzed skin. *"Marek, why are you here?"* I asked harshly. The heir to the Court of the Sun had no business in my cave whether I was here or not. The fact that he was here and had no idea I escaped made me highly suspicious of his motives.

Marek sighed, letting his arms hang loosely at his sides. His griffin—*Asteria*, if I remembered correctly—wisely stayed behind him. I'd eaten a few griffins over the years, and they made quite a tasty meal.

Marek spoke, his voice even and calm. "Dubhar has told me about your extensive library and thought I might find new-to-us information if I came here and perused it."

I snorted, smoke billowing out of my nostrils. I'd heard a lot of reasons for people to seek out my hoard, but looking for information had never been one of them. *"Unfortunately, the information you want is not in my possession. Besides, it's too late. The end of time is already here."*

Marek gave me a sharp look, the vein in his throat bulging. "What do you mean the end of time is here?"

"I can feel the darkness. Can't you?" I snapped, starting to lose patience with him and wondering why Dubhar would have told Marek to come here. Dubhar was one of the few Fae ever honored with the privilege of seeing my library firsthand and knew exactly what was in it.

Asteria bristled and moved between us, though she remained silent. Marek absently ran his fingers through the feathers on her head. "King Pharaan is dead," Marek replied.

Either Dubhar thought Marek was more knowledgeable than he actually was or he had gambled that I'd play nice. Flaring my wings, I resisted the temptation to shake him. Did the male really have no idea how powerful I was or how much more I was attuned to the world?

"*I'm aware,*" I responded drily.

Marek's eyes darkened. "Is this a game to you?"

I blew out a calculated amount of dragonfire. It stopped just short of burning Asteria. "*No. I am not playing games, but you're wasting time that neither of us has. The greatest tool at your disposal is Serafina. You must teach her how to tap into all of her magic abilities so she will be ready when the time comes.*"

"And what about you? Are you going to hide in your cave while we battle darkness for a world you live in?" Marek growled.

Slapping my tail against the cave floor, I sent a wave of tiny pebbles toward Marek. My frustration was growing. "*I have my own role to play, just as you have yours. Now leave!*" I charged him, fire billowing forth from my mouth. Wisely, Marek leapt onto Asteria's back and they flew away. Only time would tell if Marek had heeded my words.

Twenty-Two

TRISTAN

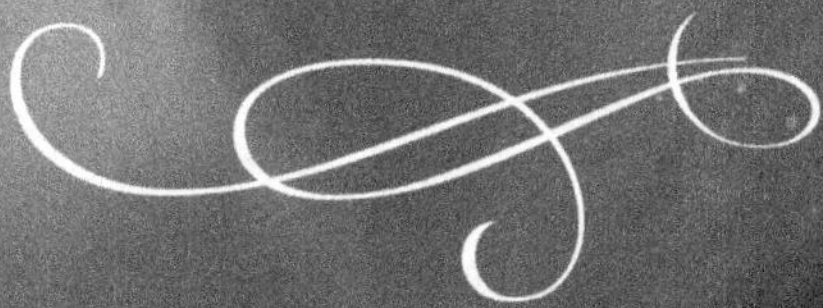

Following the instructions Thomas had given me, I headed down to the dungeon with Nolan and my three other guards. I shivered. The last time I came down here, it was in shackles to await my execution for beheading King Lionel. *How quickly things have changed.* As much as I wanted to get to the bottom of the coronation attack, I was nervous about performing the interrogation. Ever since I had gotten free of the blood contract with Prince Tanyth, I had been trying to put my past as lord commander of the Court of Dusk behind me. Yet every step closer I took to Sir Bruin was one closer to the dark past I had been fighting to forget. Now the memories bubbled at the surface.

Damp stone walls in a windowless chamber. On one side was a small cart with an assortment of tools. I shoved the prisoner hard into the chair without a seat, and it rocked precariously on its spindle legs before stilling.

I swallowed hard and stared at Nolan's back, glad I had someone to follow.

Tanyth handed me a weapon, an iron ball on the end of a chain attached to a stick. Clenching my jaw, I kept my face a cold mask. It was dangerous to show my true feelings here. Tanyth asked the questions, and if the answer was not satisfactory, then I was required to hit the prisoner.

Hissing through my teeth, I remembered the feel of the wood handle, the way the chain moved through the air, and the sound of the iron ball arcing through the air and up under the chair with a soft thud into the prisoner's tender bottom.

Blood dripped from the iron ball, and a puddle formed under the chair. The prisoner sobbed and muttered incoherent words.

Ice gripped my spine, and I stumbled down a step and bumped Nolan's back. Nolan glanced over his shoulder at me, eyebrows drawn together. "Are you okay?" he asked, concerned.

A ball of emotion clogged my throat. I nodded. "Sorry. I'll watch where my feet are." *Focus.*

"If this is too difficult for you, I'm sure Declan will eventually get something out of the prisoner," Nolan said.

I blinked at the kindness Nolan was showing me. *If he knew the things I had done, would he be kind, or would he execute me himself?* A tremor ran through my hands, and I clenched my fists, trying to hide it. *Pull yourself together,* I ordered. *You can do this.* Serafina was counting on me to get the answers we needed.

Squaring my shoulders, I motioned for Nolan to keep going. "I'm fine. Promise."

At the end of the stairs was the door to the dungeon. The guard on duty unlocked it, and Nolan continued leading the way. The hallway was exactly as it had been the last time I was here. A steady *drip-drip* of water and a vague smell of rotting meat. I closed my eyes and opened them. *This is not Dorcha Palace. I am in the palace in Gaskal, married to Serafina.* I repeated these words over and over as we made our way to the prisoner's cell.

He was leaning against the wall, staring at us as we approached, a cocky grin on his face. I knew instantly that I would have to draw on techniques that Tanyth favored to get any information from this man. I could go to the cold part of my mind, the part that had been calling to me on our trek here. *Become the lord commander*. The only consolation was that Serafina had driven me to want to leave my past behind and the knowledge that she could do it again.

Drawing back around the corner away from Sir Bruin, I closed my eyes and sank into myself, embracing who I had been and must become. *Lord commander of the Court of Dusk.*

I opened my eyes, muscles taut, shoulders back, and a steely mask on my face. Nolan met my gaze.

"Open the door," I barked, earning me a confused look from Nolan. Thankfully, he did not question my sudden change of demeanor. Cold detachment flowed through me as I waited impatiently for him to unlock the cell.

I walked inside, lip curling in distaste as I eyed the prisoner, revealing my elongated canines. "Who ordered the attack?" I demanded coldly, my steps more like a leopard stalking its prey.

The prisoner's eyes widened momentarily, then his shock was gone. "I'm not answering your question," he replied smugly.

Without a second thought, I leaped forward and punched him in the stomach, hard. The prisoner doubled over, wheezing. Tipping his head up, he smirked at me but stayed silent.

"Who ordered the attack?" I snarled. The prisoner pressed his lips together and glared at me.

I called a knife into my hand. A series of lightning-quick slices left him peppered with cuts across his arms and torso. None of them were deep enough to be fatal, but they were precisely placed to hurt like hell.

"Fuck!" shouted the prisoner as he clutched his bleeding hand to a wound under his ribs that had been particularly deep.

"Answer my questions, and I will stop." My voice dripped with malice.

I took a step back and then threw the dagger at his head. He ducked as I expected, and the dagger hit the wall and bounced off. The prisoner reached for it, but I vanished it before his fingers could wrap around the hilt.

"I am not answering your questions. You think you're a big bad Fae with your magic, but you're nothing. I trained for years to withstand an interrogation from the likes of you." He made a nasty sound in his throat and then spit at me.

I easily ducked out of the way and retreated closer to the gate, considering what he had revealed. *He's trained for years to resist Fae interrogation techniques? How the hell did he learn what those even are? He must be bluffing—at least about the Fae part,* I mused. Though knowing he had been training meant my list of tactics was not going to work. I was going to have to get creative.

Exhaling sharply, I let the old memories surface, searching for tactics that had yielded results even on the most stubborn of prisoners. A bottomless chair with the iron ball on a stick was an option, but not the only one by a long shot. Scanning the cell, I noted the wall the prisoner was leaning against had a ring bolted into the wall with a chain and shackles threaded through it.

"Guard Nolan, shackle the prisoner, and remove his clothes," I ordered. The door creaked open, and Nolan shuffled past me with another guard. Together, they stripped the prisoner and strong-armed him into the shackles, then retreated into the hallway. As the chain currently was, the prisoner was able to stand on his feet, though his arms were above his head, without any room to maneuver.

Swirls of my gray magic wove around the chain and shortened it. The prisoner's arms were pulled taut, and he had to stand on his tiptoes, or his wrists would take all his weight.

My jaw tightened in distaste as I gazed at Sir Bruin. His body was smeared with blood from the small cuts, a few of which were still dripping. Stepping close, I held the dagger to his left testicle. The prisoner sucked in a shaky breath as I pressed the edge into the tender skin and made the tiniest of slices.

"Who are you working for?" I breathed into his ear, keeping the blade pressed into his testicle.

The prisoner's teeth ground together, and he shook his head. "No."

With the barest of movements, the blade sliced clean through the flesh, and the testicle plopped onto the ground with a sickening *sploosh* sound. Blood flowed freely out of the wound. I kept my eyes on the prisoner's. Tears were trickling down his cheeks.

"You seem to be of the age where your wife"—I noted the flinch. *He has a wife*—"likely still wants more children. I'd hate to see you disappoint her when she learns that you can't sire her children or give her pleasure," I said icily.

"You ... you ... wouldn't," stuttered the prisoner.

I placed my dagger along the side of his cock and lightly caressed it with the blade—not enough to cut, but I was certain it was unpleasant. "Oh, I would."

The prisoner seemed indecisive. As the minutes trickled by and the silence stretched on, I became impatient. Without warning, I cut across the sensitive tip of his cock. Blood sprayed the front of my tunic and the prisoner screamed.

I backed up, not wanting to get kicked as he flailed about on the chain. The cut had been deliberate. It would heal, and he would have full use of his cock, but it would hopefully serve as a warning. *He may not know that there won't be permanent damage.*

Head hanging, the prisoner finally stopped screaming and flailing. "I'll tell you," he whispered. I could only catch the words because of my Fae hearing. I was certain none of the guards had, or they would have reacted.

"What did you say?" I spoke loudly, wanting to ensure Nolan knew we could be close to getting the information we so dearly needed.

"The Duke of Piore gave the orders," the prisoner said clearly, though his voice was rough from crying and pain.

"Who else was involved?" I demanded.

"A Fae woman with pale skin. Her hair was always covered by a black scarf. She met secretly with the duke, and when she left, he gave us the orders," the prisoner explained.

"How did you know she was Fae?" I demanded.

"Her devil ears," he replied.

There were many Fae who had pale skin, and all of us had pointy ears. So far the information he'd provided was almost entirely useless since it implicated over one third of living Fae. Determined to get more information, I growled. "The duke hates Fae. Why would he agree to follow plans proposed to him by one?"

"Money and jewels. He was promised he could rule the South and would also be paid his weight in emeralds," the prisoner replied.

Concern flooded me. The money was something Prince Tanyth did have, but the emeralds were not. Which meant he was confident that he would get them from the emerald mine run by the Court of Dawn.

Not wanting to risk the prisoner clamming up again, I asked, "Do you remember your exact orders?"

"Slaughter everyone in the palace during the coronation. Leave no one alive, except for my men," he replied.

Racking my mind for other pertinent questions, I came up with, "Are you all veteran knights?"

The prisoner shook his head. "No. Most of the veteran knights are dead. They refused the duke's orders, and he had them hanged for treason."

"Then who are the others?" I demanded.

"I don't know. They just showed up. I've never seen them before," the prisoner admitted, then he started sobbing again.

I turned away. Nolan gave me a quizzical glance.

"Not here," I replied. The gate opened, and I stepped out. Remembering that I was not the lord commander and needed to show the prisoner at least a tiny bit of decency, I gave orders to the guard at the gate. "See to it that he is unshackled and given some fresh clothes." The guard nodded and hurried to do as I bid.

Clenching my fists, my nails digging into my palms enough to draw blood, I spoke tersely to Nolan. "We need to go somewhere private." He nodded and motioned for me to follow him, leaving the rest of my guards to take care of the prisoner. With each step, I tried to separate myself from who I had been with mixed results.

I was standing on a platform that was lifting into the sand-filled arena. Longsword in my right hand and a dagger in the left. My torso was bare and oiled, but my black leather pants had metal plates sewn into them and were an effective form of armor, especially when going against an opponent who was inexperienced.

A human woman with long russet hair and a thin shift on faced me.

My toe hit the next stone step. I blinked, remembering where I was, and continued making my way up the stairs.

A whistle sounded, and I leaped toward the woman, sword and dagger slashing. To my surprise, the woman ducked and rolled to the side; my sword whizzed over her back. I realized she was completely unarmed. This is ridiculous. Except I could feel Tanyth's gaze boring into me from above, and I knew I had to put on a show. Sinking deeply into the icy abyss, I walled off my emotions and relentlessly attacked the woman.

My hand gripped my sword, and my shoulder slammed into the wall as I lost track of where I was again.

Nolan cast a glance down at me. "Should we stop?"

"No, I'm fine," I said, waving him off. He didn't look convinced but returned to trekking up the stairs.

The woman had stopped fighting and was on her back in the sand. An easy target. Leaping toward her prone body, I swung my leg and kicked her squarely in the ribs. I felt one crack under the first kick and a loud, satisfying crunch when the second rib broke. My boot was bloody when the guards dragged me away from her.

When we were back in the staircase on the other side of the dungeon door, I leaned against the wall, scrubbing my face with my shaking hands.

"Are you okay?" Nolan asked.

"No," I replied through my gritted teeth. Cold indifference filled me. It felt good to not care what others thought. Or to be worried about the consequences of my actions. Tanyth relished the tactics that I used. *The more blood the better.*

"Did you really cut his testicle off?" Nolan asked, his voice shaky.

My gaze flicked to Nolan, and I shrugged. "I did what I had to to get the answers we needed."

"How do you know he didn't make everything up just to get you to stop?" Nolan responded.

"Many years of using these techniques," I replied in a monotone, before adding, "There are details he provided that I doubt he could have made up, such as the duke meeting with a pale-skinned Fae female." *Maybe I should go back in there and finish the job, just to be sure Sir Bruin isn't hiding anything else.* A small knife appeared within my hand. My fingers gripped it lightly, and I fought the urge to return to the cell.

"Any idea who the Fae was?" Nolan inquired.

Thankfully, Nolan's conversation was distracting enough to keep me from returning to the prisoner. "No. Many Fae have pale skin, though it would not be too far-fetched to assume it was a Fae from the Court of Dusk, especially since Tanyth himself showed up here during the attack. Not that the duke is innocent by any means, but it wasn't his original idea," I replied.

Nolan stopped asking questions and continued the trek upstairs. I leaned against the stone wall until he was almost out of sight, breaths coming in short gasps, as I fought the need to kill Sir Bruin. That was how I did things for Tanyth. When we had wrung all there was out of a prisoner, we promised they would return to their loved ones, and then I killed them. I had learned the hard way in my first interrogation what happened if I refused to kill the prisoner. Tanyth would torture me, the same way I had tortured the prisoner, and then he would force me to make the kill. I cooperated after that, keeping my opinion buried deep within myself.

Tanyth is not here. Serafina would not want me to kill for no reason. Squeezing my eyes shut, I fought to separate General Gilvrye, husband of Queen Serafina, from the former me that was no longer required or necessary. With a shaky breath, I cracked open my eyes and, feeling slightly better, I followed Nolan up the stairs. *At least I no longer feel like sprinting back to the cell and murdering Sir Bruin.*

We emerged from the dark stairwell near the small armory by Declan's office. A patrolling pair of guards saluted me as they went past.

I started to turn to the right, toward my residence, when a throat cleared behind me. I turned slowly, hand subtly dropping closer to the hilt of my sword. Declan was standing in the doorway of his office, holding a sheaf of papers under his left arm, which was tight against his chest in a sling. A bandage was wrapped around his forehead. "Are you going to the war council meeting? It's about to start."

My stomach dropped. I had forgotten. Cold threatened to fill me again. The last thing I needed was to be in a meeting when I was this out of sorts, but it was not my decision. It was Serafina's. "Yes," I said woodenly.

"Excellent," replied Declan. "Let us walk together, and you can tell me how the interrogation went."

Hand sliding to the hilt of my sword, I bristled at his tone, as though I was one of the guards under his command and not above him in rank, as general. "I don't want to repeat it. I'll wait till we have the meeting."

Declan shrugged and stayed silent the remainder of our walk to the meeting room.

Twenty-Three

SERAFINA

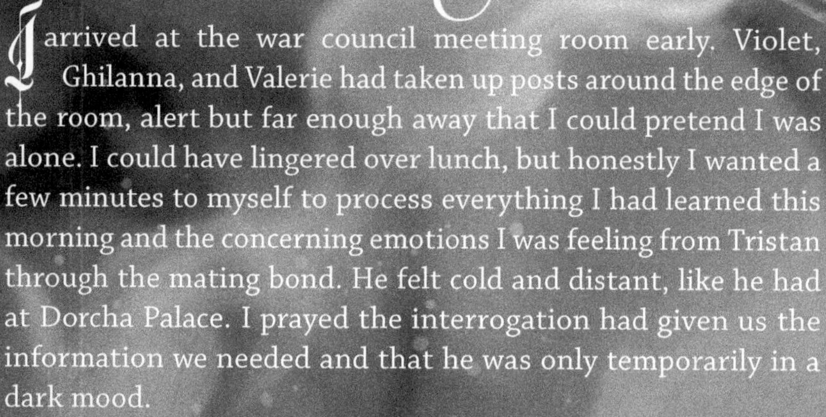

I arrived at the war council meeting room early. Violet, Ghilanna, and Valerie had taken up posts around the edge of the room, alert but far enough away that I could pretend I was alone. I could have lingered over lunch, but honestly I wanted a few minutes to myself to process everything I had learned this morning and the concerning emotions I was feeling from Tristan through the mating bond. He felt cold and distant, like he had at Dorcha Palace. I prayed the interrogation had given us the information we needed and that he was only temporarily in a dark mood.

Lunch after our tour of the encampment had been casual, and Violet spent most of it regaling us with various horse training mishaps she'd had over the years. A welcome distraction from the very real impending war.

Leaning back in my chair at the round table, I ran my fingers over the carved wood. Meriel had once told me I had the makings of a leader, if I wanted to be one. At the time, I had thought she was joking, because other than Ghilanna and Fiera, none of the other Fae would have followed my lead. But now, looking back, I realized she had been right. *Perhaps the adversity I faced with the*

Fae for twelve years has made me a better leader and more suited to be queen than I believed.

Did the citizens of the South truly believe that I should not rule them when the two rituals that required me to be an heir of blood occurred and bound me to the kingdom, the same way that all rulers of the South have been bound for centuries? Whether or not I wanted to be their queen and the first ever Lady of the South was out of my hands. Yet Major Green and his knights had practically welcomed me with open arms. *Perhaps veteran knights know the reality, whereas those who live in the city and the nobles are merely looking for a scapegoat to blame everything on.*

Raising my hands to my head, I carefully removed the crown, which was far lighter to wear than it was to hold. The four points of the crown were sharp. I had already pricked my finger on it once and was careful not to do so again. The largest point had a massive emerald in the middle of it, and the other three were fashioned in the shapes of a unicorn, griffin, and dragon. In many ways, it reminded me of the four Fae courts and their emblems. I still couldn't fathom why this crown had come out the gold mine's table during the binding ritual. It had been one of the questions I was going to ask King Pharaan on our visit to Uaine Palace.

My breathing hitched as reality sank in. That was no longer possible. King Pharaan was dead. He had perished along with Commander Meriel in my throne room. Their wisdom was no longer available to me. Deep down, I knew there had to be others at Uaine Palace and within the Court of Dawn who knew many of the things King Pharaan had. *But will they talk to me?* Among the Fae, I was a bit of an enigma. Many had called for my execution upon discovering my status as a half-blood, though my grandfather would not permit it. I spent twelve years at Jade Wilds and a few weeks at Dorcha Palace as a prisoner, hardly enough exposure to know what most Fae thought of me. *As if their view would have improved from my new status as a queen!* I laughed harshly at the irony. Animosity between the human and Fae kingdoms had existed for centuries. *I doubt having a human title will make them like me any better.*

The door squeaked as it swung open. I smiled in anticipation and was dismayed when Declan, not Tristan, walked through. I pressed my lips together and folded my hands on the table, wondering where Tristan was. A few moments later, Tristan walked through the door, grimacing and avoiding eye contact. He quickly brushed past Declan and took the chair next to me. I leaned in and gave him a kiss. His lips were hard, like marble. Shifting backward in my chair, I stared at him, trying to make sense of what was going on. Even through the mating bond, he still felt distant and not himself.

"Hi," I said softly, hoping if I got him talking his mood would lighten.

"Hi," he replied woodenly.

A light tap on the door pulled my attention away from Tristan. I heard an odd squeaking sound, and then Lord McCormack appeared in a rolling chair that was being pushed by a servant. A lump formed in the back of my throat as I took in his appearance. When we'd seen him in the healing room, blankets had been pulled up over him, hiding everything except his face. His right leg was heavily bandaged from the knee down and his left arm was gone, the sleeve empty. My throat went dry at his injuries. I was at a loss for words.

Lord McCormack gazed at me fiercely. "Do not worry, Your Majesty, I am still here and functioning. No one needs two arms anyhow, right?" he said with a harsh laugh. I cringed at his attempt to make light of the situation.

"Is there anything I can do for you?" My voice wavered as sadness for his loss gripped me.

"Get those bastards!" Lord McCormack shouted and raised his fist in the air for emphasis.

My jaw dropped open in astonishment at his response. Tristan saved me by replying, "You're in luck. I was able to determine who is responsible, so we're a step closer to making your wish come true, Lord McCormack."

"Why didn't you tell me?" I asked testily through the bond.

"I didn't want to repeat it, especially since we weren't alone," Tristan said unapologetically.

I let the matter drop, not wanting to get into a private argument through the bond with an audience. I had called the meeting of the war council. Callyn was the only one left to arrive. Declan took a seat across from me, and Ghilanna moved a chair away from the table and wheeled Lord McCormack into the open spot. As I debated if I should inquire where Callyn was, she walked through the door.

"Sorry for being late. I got detained at the gate again," Callyn explained.

So now the guards are being selective about who they let in. I almost rolled my eyes and barely caught myself in time. Squaring my shoulders, I sat up straight in my chair and began speaking. "Thank you for coming. This morning, I performed an inspection of the knights who have started arriving. There is an encampment set up in the meadow with fifteen hundred knights. I was notified during lunch that the trainees from Fort Salmon have arrived. Overall morale is positive, and Major Hershel Green has assured me they are ready to act upon orders as soon as we decide where they need to march to."

I felt Tristan's curiosity through the bond and a brief crack in the darkness surrounding him.

Lord McCormack smiled. "This is excellent news. Hershel Green is trustworthy. If he says they are ready, then they are ready."

Declan's expression was thoughtful. "He's my cousin, you know. Lord McCormack is right. Major Green is solid. I'm glad you were able to find him on your trip."

I cleared my throat, and all eyes fell on me as I spoke. "I want to discuss the attack at the coronation. Many citizens of the South and guests were murdered in cold blood yesterday, and others came close to losing their lives. We know now that it is not just Prince Tanyth who is gunning for the South. Tristan, if you would please share your findings with us."

Tristan inclined his head respectfully to me, then gazed at each of the war council members in turn. In a clipped voice, he said, "As we suspected, the prisoner revealed Duke Taylor Piore was behind the attack, and the intention was to kill all inhabitants of the palace, not just those present within the throne room. I believe our resistance was successful in preventing the full mission from being fulfilled. However, there was another revelation that is deeply concerning to me. A Fae female with pale skin was observed meeting secretly with the duke, and it was from her whence the instructions came."

I stiffened and saw the glances Lord McCormack and Declan shot at Ghilanna. Thankfully, Ghilanna's skin was dark brown, as far from pale as one could be.

"We have no way of knowing who the Fae female is, only that it's highly likely she belongs to the Court of Dusk. It would not be a stretch to assume Tanyth had a hand in this, especially since he showed up during the attack. Removing Serafina and potentially King Pharaan in one fell swoop would leave the Court of Dawn free for his own taking, and he could put whoever he wants in charge of the South," Tristan explained.

Declan nodded. "It makes sense as a strategy for Tanyth. Tristan, did you learn anything else during the interrogation?"

"Yes. Apparently, most of the veteran knights residing at Castle Piore refused to follow the duke's orders, and they were hanged for their so-called treason. The other attackers came from an unnamed source but were definitely not knights. Perhaps you or Lord McCormack would have ideas for who they might be. Are there any other groups who are being openly aggressive toward Serafina?"

Declan shook his head. "No, not that I'm aware of. There are disorganized groups in Gaskal who have been protesting her since her arrival, but they do not seem to have a leader yet."

I was half expecting Valerie to interrupt since she was part of the Copper Wolves. *Maybe she knows something.* Unfortunately, Valerie remained statue-like in her position. She was either unwilling to participate or lacking information, and I didn't feel it was necessary to put her on the spot to find out.

Tristan turned to me. "This would be a good task to put your spymaster, Josiah, on."

"Josiah is already aware of the dissent in Gaskal. But I will put a bug in his ear about the possibility of a hidden group existing. Now, how did your trip go?" I asked.

Lord McCormack thumped his hand on the table, making me jump. "Sorry," he said with a chuckle. "Overall, our trip went well. If everyone shows up, we should have at least one thousand veteran knights, in addition to the trainees. Which means we're expecting about five hundred more veterans. Word could continue to spread to others we were not able to reach as well. Only time will tell. Other than the Duke of Piore's reception, no one else gave us much trouble, or at least not once we explained why we were there. Two of the lords thought we were coming to collect their overdue taxes."

My pulse returned to its normal rhythm as I relaxed. Half of the veteran knights were coming; it was better than I had dared hope. "Thank you," I said gratefully. Lord McCormack bowed from his seat.

"The opportunity I sought at the coronation reception to address my expectations and my intentions toward the Fae was taken from me. In light of that, I still want to make a public address, even more so now that there is treachery within our own kingdom. Though I dare not wait too long. I am worried that if I do not travel to Uaine Palace and seek an alliance with the Fae now, on the heels of King Pharaan's death, that the window of opportunity will rapidly close. Tanyth has already shown what lengths he will go to to manipulate others into doing his dirty work. It's possible even now that he is whispering lies in the ears of the members of the Court of Dawn," I said.

"Will they still form an alliance with us now that King Pharaan is dead at the hand of a human?" asked Lord McCormack, catching me off guard.

It was a question I expected from Declan, who seemed to dislike Fae even though he had agreed he would work with them. I responded confidently, "King Pharaan did not die at the hand of a human. He was killed by Prince Tanyth, the ruler of the Court of Dusk. Your concern is valid, and had he died at the hand of a human, you're right—it would be difficult to convince any Fae to side with me. I am hopeful we can gain the support of the Court of Dawn and that the Courts of the Moon and Sun will then fall in line." I carefully omitted that upon King Pharaan's death there was no ruler of the Court of Dawn, and he had no living male heir to take his place. Unfamiliar with Fae traditions, I didn't know what the ramifications were, only that it was not good.

"How soon are you going to go to Uaine Palace?" asked Declan.

I exchanged a glance with Tristan. "Immediately after the meeting, if we can. The quicker I can get an answer, the faster we can proceed with planning our move against Tanyth."

Callyn finally spoke after being silent most of the meeting. "Is it wise for both of you to go?"

I knew she meant well and likely was right that Tristan should stay behind, but selfishly I wanted him at my side. I had no experience with a Fae court, at least not one like Uaine Palace. Without my grandfather alive, I had no idea what kind of reception I would receive or if they would even give me an audience. I was half-Fae and *looked* like a human, the perfect reason to bar me from entering entirely.

Taking a deep breath, I replied calmly, "Tristan will come with me, and if it seems like I will have to stay longer than tomorrow morning, Tristan will return to manage things here in my stead."

Declan's brow creased and he popped his knuckles, clearly unhappy at my decision. *I'm queen,* I reminded myself. I did not have to defend my choices to anyone but myself. The others looked at me in resignation.

"While I'm gone, I would like one of you to make a list of the knights who have arrived and perform a gear check. Use the resources in the armory to supply anyone who does not have plate armor or a silver-iron weapon. Upon my return, we shall have a public address just outside the gates of the palace. I want everyone who is able to attend. I also expect scouts to be sent out to our border to keep an eye out for any movement from the Court of Dusk."

I stood, shoving the chair back. "I will see you tomorrow," I announced and then swept out of the room. My ladies-in-waiting hastily followed, with Thomas taking the front position and the rest of the guards boxing us in. I knew Tristan would follow as soon as he could.

I was packing for our trip to Uaine Palace and trying to determine how to approach Tristan about whatever was making him distant when he walked into the bedroom and wrapped his arms around me.

"I'm proud of you," he whispered in my ear, the dark mood from earlier seemingly gone. He nuzzled my neck, sending shivers down my spine.

"Did I do the right thing?" I whispered, trying to focus as Tristan took my earlobe into his mouth and gently sucked on it.

"That depends. If you're asking if you made the right decision to send us both to Uaine Palace, yes. In this circumstance, I think it would be better if we both make an appearance, at the very least to pay respects to the Court of Dawn," Tristan replied, then kissed me. "But if you're asking if you were wrong to tell everyone we would be leaving immediately ..." Tristan slid his hands up to cup my breasts, gently stroking. Hot desire roared through me, leaving me breathless.

"We ... have ..." I gasped as he slid his fingers down the waist of my skirt and plunged them into my soaked folds. "... time."

I arched against him as his fingers tugged and swirled. My core throbbed. His lips were featherlight against my neck, blood thrumming in my veins. There was only one thought in the forefront of my mind.

"I need you in me," I whispered, desperate to feel the fullness of his cock.

Tristan chuckled against my ear. "Needy vixen."

After that comment, I expected him to turn me around or carry me to the bed, but he did neither, though our clothes did vanish. His cock bumped against my butt. I ground against him, wanting, but not sure what to do. Or what I could do with my back to him.

"Put your hands on the wall," he murmured.

I was astonished to see the wall was indeed only a few steps away. I set my hands on the smooth surface, and I felt him come up behind me. He nudged my legs open with his knee. My hands were shaking, whether in anticipation or from the release I was so close to getting, I had no idea.

With one hand on my hip, Tristan, gently guided his cock into my folds. "Is that okay, my love?"

"Mmmhmm," I mumbled. Tristan's warm fingers, still damp with my fluids, lightly massaged my breasts, while he picked up a steady in-and-out rhythm. Muscles tightening as tension built within me, I wasn't sure how long I'd be able to hold myself up against the wall. He must have sensed my concern because his left hand settled on my hip, and he sped up his thrusts to send me spiraling over the edge. My arms dropped to my sides as my whole body relaxed against him. Tristan nuzzled my neck and thrust one more time and then sagged against me, wrapping his arms possessively around me.

I had no idea how long we were there in the dark. I became aware of the fact that Tristan was holding all my weight. I was sure he could hold two of me without any significant effort. "I suppose we should go to Uaine Palace," I said reluctantly.

"Yes, if you want to keep your word to the war council," Tristan agreed.

I sighed. At least for a few moments, it had felt like it was just the two of us with no other worries.

Tristan and I had gotten into a heated debate about who should come with us. In the end, I had to bow to his and Ghilanna's experience with Fae. I had wanted to take Thomas, Violet, Valerie, and Ghilanna with us to the Court of Dawn. Tristan argued that taking humans from the South would put us in a more precarious position, particularly if anyone at the Court of Dawn was determined to blame the South for King Pharaan's death. If we kept the visit to just the two of us, we would hopefully not be perceived as a threat.

We took a star portal from inside the stables, and at the very last moment Dubhar insisted that we bring him with us to Uaine Palace. My best guess was it had to do with being a Fae Watcher, though he had not given me any indication one way or the other.

The star portal took us to the bottom of a hill covered in lush green grass. From what I gathered, Uaine Palace, the seat of the Court of Dawn, was on the other side of the hill.

We emerged from the star portal and took off at a brisk trot. Dubhar was not wasting any time heading to our destination. Dressed in cloaks with hoods drawn up, our intention was to minimize any alarm our presence might create. Tristan ran alongside us. Dubhar slowed when we crested the hill. I was not prepared for the sight of Uaine Palace and its city. A short stone wall marked the city's perimeter. Even from here, I could see how carefully it had been planned out, with streets in precise lines intersecting at ninety-degree angles. A high wall of green granite with spires soaring toward the sky surrounded the palace, which was itself made of light-gray stone, though several of the towers had green windows. I wondered if they were colored glass or something else.

After a brief pause, we continued our way toward the palace at a stately pace. No gate barred entry to the city, so we walked through the archway and down the wide main boulevard. As we worked our way up to the palace, Fae watched us curiously, but none made a move to approach us. *I wonder how often they see unicorns.*

The ornate wrought iron gates were shut, as expected. We had not sent word of our intent to visit, and I knew the guards would only open them for us if they were granted permission by whomever was currently in charge. I pulled my hood down, revealing the gold crown with the three magical creatures and large emeralds atop my head, earning us bewildered looks.

It was a lucky coincidence that Onvyr was in the courtyard and noticed us. He motioned for the guards to open the gates and allow us entrance. "Queen Serafina Wyantha Helias, Lady of the South," Onvyr said with a slight bow.

Whispers spread among the Fae guards, I presumed because they recognized the Fae surname listed with my human one. "Nice to see you again, Lord Commander Onvyr," I replied formally. "I believe you remember my consort and general, Tristan Gilvrye?"

Onvyr nodded. "Yes, it is good to see you again, Tristan Gilvrye."

I was dismayed that Onvyr's tone was less formal and more conversational. The whispering among the guards intensified. *It must not have reached Uaine Palace that Rhys Mongan was actually*

Tristan Gilvrye in disguise. Onvyr glared at the guards and spoke to them rapidly in Fae. I wasn't able to catch the words, but I could tell from Tristan's expression that he could, though he did not inform me privately what they were.

"I seek an audience with whoever is now in charge," I said, choosing to ignore the whispers and Tristan's aloofness.

Onvyr frowned at me as though I had said the wrong thing. "I had your rooms prepared as soon as I returned. Now if you'll dismount and follow me. One of the guards will see that your unicorn is taken care of."

I pressed my lips together at the casual dismissal of the unicorn. *Apparently not all Fae know who the Watchers are.* "Dubhar will decide where he wants to be."

Onvyr shot me a cold look. Confusion flooded me. *Why is he angry that I'm letting the unicorn have a say?*

A groom came forward and tried to reach for Dubhar's reins. The unicorn snaked his head around and snapped his teeth in warning. The groom hastily retreated a safe distance. Onvyr led the way into the palace. I was intrigued by how open and airy it was. There were no huge doors barring the way inside, just a large open archway. Smaller arches dotting the wall allowed for air to flow freely into the building. A delicate staircase spiraled up to the domed ceiling high above us, though I wasn't sure how anyone was expected to climb it. It looked like it couldn't even hold a toddler.

Tristan stayed close by my side, and for that I was grateful. As I stood below the dome, mesmerized by the green glass, I saw that the construction was similar yet different to the ceiling in the Golden Rose ballroom in my palace. A gentle squeeze on my hand brought my attention back to Onvyr. A Fae female with straight russet hair streaked with gray and pale green eyes hovered in the the archway. She wore a black robe with wide sleeves. Her hands were clasped in front of her, and I could see her long, slender fingers. She was hauntingly familiar, though it took me a moment to realize that she reminded me of my mother with subtle differences.

"Who is she?" I asked Tristan through the bond, but he merely shrugged.

Onvyr bowed to the female Fae, piquing my interest even more. "Queen Serafina, may I introduce you to Lady Shelara Wyantha, your grandmother."

A gasp escaped my lips; I had no idea I had more living family. *A grandmother?* Questions whirled through my mind, including why I was just now learning of her existence.

"It's nice to meet you, grandaughter," Shelara said. Her voice was almost identical to my mother's. I felt tears forming in my eyes and willed them to not spill. I didn't want to show any sign of weakness to this female who had waited my entire life to make herself known to me.

"It's nice to meet you, Shelara," I replied with a curtsey. I was not willing to acknowledge her as my grandmother, not with a reception like this.

Beside me, I could feel Tristan bow, his elbow lightly brushing my arm. "Tristan Gilvrye," Shelara said with a nod of acknowledgment.

Trying to regain my composure, I spoke. "We have come here to discuss an alliance." I didn't have time to waste with pleasantries when hours could make the difference for my people, especially on the heels of the attack.

Shelara nodded. "Yes, I know. I have had a room prepared for us to be more comfortable while we talk."

I could hear a patter of feet and a giggle. Then, a young Fae girl in a bright-pink dress threw herself at Shelara, oblivious to the bristling guards. Shelara's face softened, and she picked her up, swinging her in the air before planting a huge kiss on her cheek. Her smiled faded as she glanced over at me. "Serafina, this is Amara, my granddaughter...your cousin."

Not wanting to blame the young girl for any tension between myself and our grandmother, I waved to Amara and she waved back.

A moment later, a gorgeous Fae female with black hair and light green eyes, wearing a dark-brown gown, came in looking worn out. "Amara, you can't just take off like that," she said sternly.

"M..." The female must have noticed the company and changed her words. "Lady Shelara," she said with a curtsey before approaching.

Shelara stood stiffly, and after a few moments, Onvyr stepped in. "Amarille, I'd like you to meet Serafina. Serafina, Amarille is your aunt."

I was surprised he had dropped my title since this was more of a formal meeting. *Unless Shelara instructed him to treat me this way.*

I offered Amarille a tentative smile and was met with a cold stare.

"Nice to meet you, Serafina," she said.

"Nice to meet you too," I replied, keeping my voice calm. It hadn't occured to me that coming here would mean being around a lot of my own family.

Shelara set Amara down. "Off you go, little one. Amarille, I will see you at dinner." I could tell from how she said it that it was more of an order than a request. Amarille nodded and picked up Amara, then disappeared in the direction they had come from. I was intrigued that everyone had completely ignored Dubhar and wondered if by insisting the unicorn join us in the palace I had broken a rule. *I'm not going to learn the rules if no one tells me,* I mused.

Shelara settled her gaze on Onvyr. "Please escort us to the prepared conference room."

Onvyr nodded and motioned for us to follow. He led the way, and we followed a close distance behind. Dubhar's hooves were oddly silent on the marble floor. *He must be using his magic to silence them.* I glanced back at the unicorn and realized he was actually floating just far enough off the floor to prevent his hooves from making any sound.

I examined our surroundings as we walked down the hallway. To the left was the courtyard we had entered. To the right was a large, open, square-shaped room with a massive table inside and a map pinned to one wall. Onvyr led us into the square room, gesturing for us to take seats at the table. Then, he took a post in one corner with the remainder of the guards staying in the hallway.

I waited until Shelara sat down before I chose my own chair. Tristan plopped into the seat beside me and Dubhar moved two chairs out of the way with his magic before taking his spot next to me. When everyone was settled across from us, I dove into my explanation. "I don't know how much you know about what happened leading up to and at the coronation, so I appologize if I'm being repetitive. Several days ago, Prince Tanyth murdered King Leonard and took the Helias family heirloom, the *Bloodsong Grimoire*. He has declared war against me personally and ordered a group of humans to attack me and everyone residing within my palace during my coronation. Tanyth even briefly showed up with the three magic artifacts—*Bloodsong Grimoire*, Fleshrender, and Dragonfang—and attempted to use them on Tristan. Fortunately, the primary attack failed—or at least failed to kill me, though many others were lost—as did his attempt to use the artifacts. I will be forever grateful for the aid King Pharaan offered, and I am sorry for your loss."

Shelara cut in. "You cannot begin to imagine what I have lost, what the Fae have lost, because of *you*."

I shoved myself backward in my chair, hitting the seat back with a thump. "I am sorry. King Pharaan chose to be at my coronation. I did not order his murder or demand that he provide aid."

Onvyr coughed. "Please forgive Lady Shelara."

I glanced at him uncertainly and continued, though my confidence that Shelara would help was diminishing by the moment. "I am at war with the Court of Dusk and was hoping you would offer your support. The knights at my disposal are not going to be enough to face him, not alone."

Shelara stared blankly at me, her fist clenching and unclenching on the table, her bangle clanking with each movement. "If I hadn't promised Pharaan to aid you, then I would refuse your request. But it was the last thing we spoke of before he left for the coronation." Her gaze drifted away from me to the wall, though she kept speaking. "'The dome will shatter, and the end of time is near. Fear not. The wait is over. The blessing has come. The heir of blood is found. The compass will unite.'"

I exchanged a look with Tristan, wondering what Shelara was talking about. It almost sounded like another prophecy, but the words were much different than anything I'd heard before. "I don't understand," I said softly, hoping to draw Shelara out of her trance.

Shelara turned sharply toward me. "He is dead because of you." Tears streamed freely down her pale cheeks. "But *you* will lead us, blessed one, Queen of the Fae."

"What?" I gasped, wondering what she was talking about. Going from being angry and blaming me to calling me *Queen of the Fae*? I felt a tingling on my head and quickly reached up and snatched the crown from where it was sitting. It was hot to the touch, and I could barely hold it. I practically dropped it on the table. Green laced with gold magic was streaming from my hands into the crown. I couldn't tell if the magic was flowing into or out of me.

A flash of movement out of the corner of my eye and I saw Onvyr drop to his knees. "Hail, Queen of the Fae."

Scooting my chair backward, I stood, moving toward Onvyr, intending to tell him to rise and stop this nonsense. I was no Queen of the Fae. Hell, I wasn't even fully Fae. I wasn't qualified.

A light thud had me swiveling around to Tristan, who was kneeling and gazing at me reverently, his voice strong as he said, "Hail, Queen of the Fae." One by one the guards walked into the room and knelt, hands to their hearts, all murmuring the same thing over and over.

I watched in stunned silence. As the magic around me and the crown expanded, objects appeared on the table. The first was the sword that I had been given during the coronation ceremony that I had deliberately left in the weapons cabinet back in my palace. Next was a thick necklace that reminded me of the collars that had been placed on the shapeshifters at Dorcha Palace, except it was made up of five rows of thumb-sized emeralds. Then a pair of arm bands that matched the necklace, and last but not least a robe of shimmering green fabric that had griffins, dragons, unicorns, and emeralds embroidered on it in gold.

Dubhar backed away from the table and gave a half rear. *"All hail Serafina Wyantha Helias, the Lost Fae Queen!"*

There was a loud rumbling sound, and then the room began to shake. I heard Tristan growling under his breath beside me. I formed a magic shield around myself and braced my feet against the floor as it rolled and vibrated. In the distance, I swore I could hear a dragon roaring. Tristan hissed in pain and clutched his back, where I knew the tattoo was.

"What's happening?" I asked, my voice high as fear gripped me.

The shaking stopped as abruptly as it had begun.

"The end of time is near," Dubhar replied, though it was an odd response to my question.

Shelara stood up shakily, her gaze upon the unicorn. "Forgive me," she pleaded.

Dubhar snorted and tossed his head, and for the briefest of moments I swore I saw not the black unicorn, but a Fae male with skin black as midnight, silver hair, and swirling eyes. His facial features were identical to Shelara's, and they were the same height.

"Sister, I forgave you centuries ago. It is you who has to forgive yourself."

Shelara bowed her head, her hair cascading over her face, obscuring it from us. I turned to Onvyr, hoping he could help make sense of all this. Onvyr rose and stepped forward, taking my hands in his. "My queen, all the resources of the Court of Dawn are now yours to call on. Merely give the order, and I will ensure that the warriors go where you wish."

"How many?" I asked, unsettled by the events that had just transpired.

"Two thousand warriors within the Court of Dawn. The Court of the Moon and Court of the Sun have the same. Six thousand all told," Onvyr replied.

Six thousand? With that many Fae at my back, defeating Tanyth would not just be a shot in the dark—we would have a fighting chance.

My legs trembled, the implications hitting me like a sledge-hammer. I wasn't sure how long I would be able to stand without falling over. I had come to the Court of Dawn seeking an alliance, and now I had been declared Queen of the Fae.

Tristan must have sensed my state through the bond. He drew me close, wrapping his arms around me. I leaned against his chest; it vibrated as he spoke. "Two questions, then I would like to request we retire to a room for a few hours." Onvyr nod-ded, and Tristan continued. "The first is, how long will it take to gather the Fae warriors? As for the second, I know that there are Fae traditions surrounding anyone taking up the mantle as ruler of all Fae. Are there additional steps that will be required of Serafina prior to our departure?"

"I can have five hundred warriors ready to depart tomor-row morning if necessary. The rest will take a day or two to get the messages out. As for summoning the warriors of the other courts, that will depend on Prince Almar and Prince Rhangil and is not in my control. The official confirmation of Queen Serafina as the Queen of Fae is simpler than many of the human rituals you had to go through. Put on the items that are on this table, and go to the chamber in the emerald mine. She must go into the chamber alone," Onvyr said. The last was a warning.

"Do we have to send notice?" I asked.

Shelara pushed her hair out of her face. Her eyes were red from crying. "No. What will take place in the chamber at the mine will be felt by all Fae. They will know immediately."

Silence filled the room; exhaustion tugged at me. A nap or at least a chance to get off my feet and away from prying eyes would be welcome. "Can someone escort me to the rooms you had prepared, Onvyr?"

Onvyr snapped to attention. It seemed I wasn't the only one who was trying to figure out the ramifications of everything that had changed in the past few minutes. "Yes, of course. Follow me."

The guards who had come in were now milling around, as though they had no purpose anymore. Onvyr gave them orders in Fae, and the guards filed out into the hallway, then converged around Tristan and me. Dubhar stayed behind.

Onvyr led the way past the end of the square room and then turned down another hallway. Instead of open archways to the outside, this one had doors. "These are family suites," he explained. "This whole wing is for family."

We passed a few more doors, and then he opened one and stepped inside. The room was draped in lots and lots of sheer green fabric. My eyes opened wide as I took it all in. *Frilly*, I thought as I gazed at it. *It's only for a few hours.*

"Food will be here shortly. I'll leave you two for now," Onvyr said and departed before I could thank him.

Tristan sat on the green velvet couch while I walked farther into the room. Besides the sitting area, there was a dining table with space for six. On either side were two doors. I walked toward the one on the left. It was a room with a four-poster bed and a wardrobe. The room on the right was almost double the size of the first one and had a huge bed, and through another door I could see what I thought was a bathroom.

I let out my breath, shoulders sagging, as the enormity of what I was doing sank in and threatened to overwhelm me. Suddenly, Tristan was there, his gray arms wrapped around me, pulling me to his chest.

"I didn't realize you had so much family," Tristan said softly.

I shook my head against his chest and replied, my words muffled, "Neither did I." I had not had much time for detailed conversations with King Pharaan while he was alive, and living family members had been far from my thoughts. Likely because I had spent most of my life without them and had gotten used to the idea of being alone. There was also the fact that Amarille and Shelara had been less than welcoming. *Are all the family members I meet going to be that way?*

Light tapping on the door brought me out of my thoughts.

"Come in!" Tristan shouted, saving me the trouble.

The door opened, and a Fae female with a bright-green apron tied around her waist and a cart of food came bustling in. The female had warm brown eyes, mousy brown hair braided tightly and wound into a bun to stay out of the way, and tan skin. She was shorter than most Fae, possibly even shorter than me, which was a surprise, though I wasn't going to ask her to stand back-to-back to be measured.

The Fae female smiled. "Sorry, Your Majesty. I have been assigned to see to your needs while you are here visiting Uaine Palace."

When the maid departed, I walked over to inspect the food, an assortment of fruits and pastries. Not quite what I'd call a proper meal, but it was enough for a good-sized snack. Tristan's mood had been bothering me. We were alone with at least an hour to ourselves, plenty of time to tackle a sensitive topic.

"You have been distant since the interrogation of Sir Bruin. What is going on with you?" I asked conversationally. I could feel him bristling through the mating bond.

Tristan shuddered and looked away, picking up an apple, tossing it in the air, and catching it. "I had to embrace the dark side of myself—the side that Tanyth created—in order to get any information out of Sir Bruin, and ever since, it has been a struggle to find myself. To break down the wall I built that prevents me from feeling anything."

"Except you *can* feel; otherwise, you'd never have been able to pleasure me the way you did a few hours ago," I replied, blushing.

Tristan growled and briefly met my gaze before breaking eye contact again. "Sex is different. It was a refuge while I was at Dorcha Palace, one of the only things Tanyth never successfully took away from me."

"You have agreed there is a problem, that you embraced your dark side, so my question to you is—how do I reverse it? I *need* you, Tristan Gilvrye, soulmate and husband," I responded firmly.

I watched as Tristan's throat bobbed when he swallowed and the tension started to ebb away. "This ... this conversation, you telling me you care, is helping break the wall down. Knowing you need me." He reached out to me, and I rushed into his arms as he crushed me to him. It hurt, but I didn't want him to ever let go.

Eventually, his hold on me relaxed. I felt him exhale and through the mating bond was aware the moment the wall he had spoken of was gone. Instead of cold and darkness, I felt overwhelming love and passion.

"I love you," I whispered against his lips and kissed him.

"*I love you too,*" he replied into my mind, our tongues busy.

Confident that I had broken through his wall and it wasn't going to get rebuilt—at least not quickly—I leaned back in his arms and gazed into his eyes. "You were not surprised when Dubhar declared I was the Lost Fae Queen. Why?"

Tristan removed the apple from his pocket and took a bite out of it. "The prophecies and things I have witnessed led me to suspect that you are the Lost Fae Queen, but it wasn't until you touched the *Bloodsong Grimoire* in its chamber and released your magic that I knew for certain. However, I didn't want to push you into something you weren't ready to believe or accept. Now, with King Pharaan's death, it makes even more sense why it must be you and why it's now. The Fae courts will rip themselves apart—or at least Tanyth will—with King Pharaan's death. He held Tanyth's ambition at bay for centuries. King Pharaan had no living male heirs. Perhaps that is why he did what he did; because he believed you would take his place."

Narrowing my eyes at Tristan, I scoffed. "You think he waited for centuries for me to come and take his place?"

Tristan ignored my tone. "Fae are a long-lived species. You have said it yourself that Marek and Dubhar told you they have been waiting for you. Is it that hard to believe King Pharaan was also waiting?"

He set his hand on mine and gave it a gentle squeeze. "We came here hoping to decipher your mother's prophecies, but now we don't need to. The answer is you. You are the Lost Fae Queen, queen of all Fae. Destined to face the end of time."

I squeezed my eyes shut. There were so many things pointing to me being the Lost Fae Queen that I could no longer deny it. Just like becoming Lady of the South, I had no say in this matter, and I was learning quickly the cost of refusing would be high for everyone I held dear to me.

I lost track of time as we snuggled on the couch. Tristan held me, and we merely enjoyed each other's company and a brief respite from the duties I knew would be coming my way. Finally there was a light tap on the door. Tristan unwrapped his arms from me and cautiously opened it.

"Yes?" Instead of inviting whoever it was inside, Tristan stepped into the hallway and shut the door.

I sighed and ran my fingers absently over my clothes, hoping the conversation had to do with food. Shortly, Tristan came back into the room. "We have been invited to a family dinner, if you are up to it."

"Family dinner?" I asked curiously.

Tristan nodded. "Yes. It's Shelara's idea for you to get to know your family. Then, after dinner, we will go to the mine."

Swallowing, I couldn't think of a reason to refuse, and I also worried that if I did refuse I would lose the only opportunity I had to get to know them. "Yes, I would like to go."

"Guards are waiting for us in the hallway," Tristan said. I nodded and passed through the door he held open for me.

When we arrived at the dining room, escorted by a squad of guards, a boisterous conversation was going on. As I stepped into the room, it immediately became silent. Ten pairs of eyes stared at me as I approached the table. I made myself keep moving forward, aiming for the empty chairs in the middle.

Shelara cleared her throat. "Everyone, this is Serafina. She is Solana's daughter." The reactions were mixed. The expressions I could see of some of the Fae at the table showed shock, anger, and excitement, indicating that not everyone had been informed I was coming to dinner.

I pulled the chair out and sat down, and Tristan settled next to me. Greetings were mumbled. I was curious about the shape of the table; it was a massive circle, similar to the one we had in the war council room. To my right was a Fae male who by appearance I thought might be about the age of Fiera and Ghilanna, but I wasn't entirely sure. On his other side was a Fae female with dark-brown hair and gray eyes who offered a nod in greeting. I bent my head in acknowledgment before gazing to my left, where an older Fae female sat. She had dark-brown, almost black hair and pale-gray eyes. She gave me a look I could not decipher, although it was not friendly.

Shelara spoke, her voice stiff. "I'm so glad you were able to join us for dinner tonight, Serafina. Let me introduce you to everyone."

She started with the Fae male on my right. "Goras is betrothed to Ariawyn. She is Amarielle's oldest daughter." She then moved to the young Fae girl next to Ariawyn. I recognized her as Amara, and beside her was her mother, my aunt, Amarielle. Then, she gestured to Onvyr with his long pale-blue hair and golden eyes. Onvyr dipped his head in acknowledgment and I smiled at him, glad to see a friendly face. But he looked away to the female next to him with black hair and gray eyes. "I know you have met Onvyr. He is my daughter Pilar's mate." She gestured at the Fae female. Pilar met my gaze with a cold stare.

Shelara continued. I was only loosely paying attention to the other names until she reached the female next to Tristan, with the dark-brown hair. "Sorisana. She is Solana's twin."

I gasped, unable to contain my shock. *My mother has a twin!*

Sorisana spoke. "Perhaps sometime in the future, you and I can talk."

Eyes wide, I blinked a few times. trying to make my mouth work properly. "That would be nice," I finally managed to squeak.

Food was served, and an awkward silence fell across the table, with only the sound of utensils clicking against the plates permeating the room. Although Sorisana's initial introduction had felt mostly welcoming, she did not do anything to encourage me to talk to her throughout the meal.

"Goras, what new training techniques have you been working on?" Shelara asked, giving me a smile.

Goras frowned, his gaze sliding from me to Shelara. "I finished spear throwing from horseback a week ago," Goras replied in a clipped voice. Before I could ask any questions, he turned his back to me and fell into a quiet conversation with Ariawyn, speaking too softly for me to catch any of the words.

Tristan gave my hand a light squeeze and faced Sorisana. "I've heard that twins can share a bond similar to a mating bond. Is it true?" I held my breath, wondering if Sorisana would answer such a personal question from a male she didn't know.

Sorisana frowned, then replied, "I could sense Solana's thoughts if we were within range of each other. Once she went to the South, though, the connection disappeared. This is a private matter I don't want to discuss further."

Tristan murmured an apology. No one else was willing to say more than a few words before returning to a discussion with their dinner partners. Onvyr kept shooting me apologetic glances but took no further action to include Tristan or me in his own conversation—though even if he had, it would have been awkward to shout across the table. The tension at the table was palpable. When Shelara declared the meal over, relief filled me. I slid out of my seat as soon as was polite and quickly headed in the direction of my room, Tristan following hot on my heels.

When we reached the room, he pulled me into a hug. "I'm sorry your family was not more welcoming."

"Me too," I replied and tightened my grip around him. The only consolation about the dinner was that my family knew I was the Queen of the Fae, and yet they had not tried to win my affection or favor. My new title was not an influencing factor. *Unless they didn't believe I deserved the title. Can the binding ceremony at the emerald mine reject me if I am not meant to be the Queen of the Fae?*

"Onvyr said we must go to the mine after dinner. You were also told that you'd have to wear everything that had appeared on the table during our meeting," Tristan reminded me, his words breaking through my thoughts.

Reluctantly disentangling myself from his arms, I caught sight of the robe draped over a chair and the necklace, arm cuffs, and sword on the table with the crown. I had discarded it earlier, not wanting to taint my family's first impression of me by throwing the fact that I was now their queen in their faces. I had hoped that we could find some common ground.

"Do I wear anything under the robe?" I asked, lifting it up off the table and inspecting it.

Tristan came over and rubbed the fabric between his two fingers. "It's thick enough to be a standalone garment, and there is a cord to belt it around your waist. Remember, Fae are not shy about their bodies. I expect if Onvyr did not instruct you to wear any additional garments that you will not be permitted to do so."

"I suppose I should count myself lucky I don't have to do this naked, then," I muttered.

Tristan chuckled. "But you do have to get naked to put it on. We could ..." He pulled me close and planted a passionate kiss on my lips.

I squirmed in his hold. "What if Onvyr walks in on us?"

Tristan shrugged. "I doubt it would bother Onvyr. We could likely go have sex in the hallway, and he wouldn't bat an eye."

I stuck my tongue out at him. "Well, you definitely won't be having sex with me in the hallway, sir."

There was a loud knock on the door. "We're preparing to leave for the mine. Are you ready?" came Onvyr's voice through the door.

Using my magic, I vanished the clothing I was wearing and quickly slid the robe on. It didn't have sleeves, though the arm holes were small enough it wasn't going to reveal my breasts if I moved wrong. Tugging it into place and tying the gold cord around my waist, I realized Tristan was right—it did cover me enough to not need any clothes underneath. I slid the arm cuffs onto my wrists and up until they stopped at my biceps. The gold was icy to the touch. Reluctantly, I picked up the heavy necklace with its five rows of emeralds. Raising it up to my neck, I held it in place. "Tristan, can you clasp it for me?" With the weight, I was afraid I would drop it if I tried to clasp it one-handed.

Tristan's fingers were featherlight on my neck as he brushed my hair out of the way to see the clasp. "All done," he announced and stepped back. I released the necklace, and it settled in place. Thankfully, it did not feel as collar-like as I thought it would. Tristan picked up the crown and reverently placed it on my head, then offered me the sword. I took it, wondering if I was supposed to just carry it in my hand. The cord around my waist did not seem heavy enough to be able to serve as a makeshift belt to tuck it into.

Placing a kiss on my forehead, Tristan opened the door. Onvyr stepped halfway in, gazing at me, presumably to confirm I was indeed wearing everything. Then, he motioned for us to follow. "Come."

Holding hands, we walked through a pair of emerald columns in one of the palace courtyards, and the surroundings changed from the Uaine Palace courtyard to the hint of a steep hill covered in thick green foliage. I sucked in a breath, remembering the first time I had come here with King Pharaan. I shuddered, remembering that upon our departure I had been captured by Travaran Neriwraek and had nearly lost my life.

Dubhar was waiting on the other side of the portal. Onvyr and the others had come through ahead of us.

Onvyr bowed. "You need to ride Dubhar," he informed me. I raised my eyebrows but did as I was told.

Stomach jittering, I shoved away the memory of my capture, focusing on what awaited me. The ritual or ceremony that would confirm me as the Queen of Fae and pass this knowledge to all living Fae throughout the world. The closer we got to the mine, the more details we could make out. At the base of the hill, layers had been cut away from the bottom to about one-third of the way up, as well as layers into the ground as well. The air shimmered with the magic shield. Last time, an opening had appeared.

To my dismay, Dubhar kept walking. "You're going to hit the shield," I hissed under my breath. Dubhar snorted and sped up. We passed through the shield. I felt the crackle of magic along my skin and nothing else. Twisting in the saddle, I realized that Tristan, Onvyr, and the guards were stuck on the other side.

"Now what?" I asked. The mine was large, and I did not think that the short trip I had made months ago qualified as giving me familiarity to find my own way.

"*Hush. I will not let you get lost,*" Dubhar said into my mind.

Pressing my lips together at the rebuke, I kept my thoughts to myself. Dubhar trotted along the road through the middle of the area dedicated to the emerald mine operation. I recognized the path. We had walked down to the bottom of the mine where there were bins full of emeralds in orderly rows. Today, the mine was empty. *Where did they all go?* Certain Dubhar would be annoyed if I asked another question, I filed it away to ask when we were done with this task.

I became aware as the road became steeper, the hill rose above us until we were completely under its shadow, blocking out all the remaining sunlight. Dubhar halted in front of an elaborate obsidian archway.

I stared at the archway and swore I could hear King Pharaan's voice and the conversation we had in the room within the mine. *"This is where the Court of Dawn creates magical objects. We primarily craft jewelry, though over the lengthy Fae history, a few times we have made non-jewelry objects," King Pharaan said.*

Dubhar shook himself, pulling my thoughts back to the present. *"You must dismount and go inside. I cannot follow."*

"How will I know what to do?" I demanded as I slid off his back and onto my feet, straightening the robe.

"You will know," Dubhar said. He nibbled lightly on my fingertips, then trotted back down the road and through the shield.

I sighed, wishing everyone didn't have to be cryptic. Squaring my shoulders, I marched through the archway and into the room whose walls were carved from obsidian. Unlike the room the *Bloodsong Grimoire* had been in, the walls were neither smooth nor egg-shaped. Here and there, glowing emeralds were embedded in the walls. In the middle of the chamber were two giant natural emeralds glowing softly, just bright enough that I could see the different colors of green and crystal throughout them. Between the two emeralds was a third emerald in the shape of a rectangular table that came about to my waist. Unlike the table at the gold mine, which was mostly a giant block of gold, this emerald had been exquisitely carved. Running my hands along the edge, my breath caught as I recognized the pattern. *The same as the case that had held my sword.* There was no way it was a coincidence that this pattern was here and on the case, or that the same Fae creatures were on the crown I wore on my head.

The table started to glow. I snatched my hand back, and it stopped. During my previous visit to the emerald mine, the table had shown an image of Dragonfang, the dagger that Prince Tanyth possessed, and the vision had scared King Pharaan. I realized now that had likely been the event that made my grandfather suspect the Lost Fae Queen prophecy had to do with me.

Cautiously, I held my right hand out again over the table. In my bones, I knew that the ritual I was supposed to perform required me to touch the table. Gritting my teeth in determination, I placed my hand on the table and waited. Nothing happened. Frowning, I gazed around the room, wondering if I had missed a critical step that no one had informed me of. *Maybe it's both hands?* Slowly, I placed my left hand next to my right. The change was instantaneous. Every emerald in the room flared with bright light. I squeezed my eyes shut against the overwhelming brightness. A low whistle emanated from the tall emeralds on either side of me. I cracked an eye open, hoping I wouldn't have to run if the mine started to collapse.

There was an image on the table before me: a midnight-black unicorn with an iridescent black horn and silver mane and tail. *Dubhar.* A bronze-colored griffin. *Asteria.* A dark-green, almost-black dragon. My hands shook as I recognized Rethys, the dragon Tristan had faced in the Dorcha Palace arena. Prowling around the three creatures was a blue-eyed snow leopard that I would recognize anywhere. *Tristan.*

As Dubhar, Asteria, Rethys, and Tristan faded, they were replaced with an image of my mother. A strangled sob escaped my lips. Solana smiled, her russet hair in twin braids at her temples with the rest flowing down her back. She raised her hand as though she could touch me.

"Dearest daughter, your time has come. If I could have spared you the heartache and taken your place, I would have. Alas, the gods did not give me this task. It fell on your shoulders. Do not fear, Sera. You are loved by many. Do not be afraid to lean on them if you falter. While it is your burden to lead Fae and humans, it doesn't say anywhere that you must do so alone." Solana's musical voice caressed me, and it felt so real—like she was there in the room. Tears trickled down my cheeks and splattered my hands and the table. Afraid to remove my hands too early, I stood there in stunned silence as my mother's image faded away.

My father, Gareth, was next. "Papa," I gasped.

His eyes met mine and then slid away, as though he couldn't see me or hear me. Gareth's mouth opened, but unlike Solana's words that were uniquely her own, he was reciting a familiar prophecy.

"When tension rises and war with the humans has come, the

Lost Fae Queen will return.
First, she will prove her battle prowess.
Look closely or you might be blinded, for when the Fae Queen
returns,
Not all will know her, yet everyone will follow her.
Be warned, the Fae Queen must stay pure until the Great Cat
finds her, and their souls unite.
With their souls bound, the heir will be found.
The Fae Queen's magic will return, and together they will
defend the Fae from the end of time.
Time is of the essence, or the Fae will fall to the darkness.
When Fleshrender, Dragonfang, and Bloodsong Grimoire are
united
The dome will shatter, and the end of time is near.
Fear not,
The wait is over, the blessing has come,
The heir of blood is found.
The compass will unite
Griffin, dragon, unicorn,
Fae and human.
Together they will battle darkness."

I yanked my hands back, but they were stuck to the table. The beginning of the prophecy had been the one I'd known about for years as a story in *Bedtime Tails*. The second half was new to me, and yet I would've sworn I'd heard bits of it somewhere. Then I remembered. *Shelara spoke it during our meeting earlier.*

Gareth's image faded away, and the table's glow dimmed. My fingers tingled, and I noticed tendrils of magic swirling around them. In fact, I realized I could feel the magic within me stirring. Closing my eyes, I dropped into the core of my magic, and that was when I felt it: the magic within the emerald mine, and the land beyond. In the far distance, I could even identify the South's gold mine.

A bell chimed. I stumbled backward, and my hands released from the table. Windmilling my arms to keep from toppling over, I caught myself hard on the table's carved edge. Panting heavily, I tried to settle and found the magic surrounding me was at the periphery of my awareness. *Is this what it means to be Queen of the Fae?*

Taking a deep breath, I calmly walked out of the room, through the carved archway, and halted at the top of the road. It was a dark, moonless night, but I could see flickers of magic in the Fae waiting for me. Tristan's dark gray, Onvyr's light blue, Dubhar a black iridescent sparkle, the guards a mix of silver, gold, and blue. The trees beyond them were also filled with twinkles of green-and-brown magic. I glanced down at my hands and saw threads of green-and-gold magic running through them, as though they were my veins filled not with blood, but magic. With every step I took toward the group, my awareness deepened—not just of their magic, but hints of their emotions, fears, concerns ... and underneath it all, hope.

Twenty-Four

TRISTAN

Unable to stand and wait patiently at the shield preventing our entrance to the mine, I excused myself from the group, shifted, and headed for the edge of the forest. The grass was soft beneath my paws and gave me something to focus on other than worrying over what Sera would encounter within the mine.

Abruptly, I sat down as fear for what we would soon be facing and the uncertain outcome welled up in my chest. Those feelings likely had contributed to how easy it had been to get lost in my dark side. Walling off my emotions was far easier than facing them, except Sera had been right; I was useless to her in that state.

When she crossed through the barrier to the emerald mine, the mating bond had become only the barest of whispers. I speculated whoever had designed this ceremony had wanted the male or female's attention fully on the task at hand and not distracted. It was a momentous event, and my wife was about to become one of the only females in the history of Fae to wear the mantle of Queen of Fae.

I rose to my feet, then took off at a sprint. Crossing the threshold into the forest, I noticed a visible difference in the way the air looked and felt; subtly foggy, heavier. I could see the moisture beading on the leaves of the bushes and tree trunks as I passed by.

Following the sound of dripping water, I eventually reached a small pool with a tiny waterfall, barely more than a hand wide, trickling from the creek I had crossed moments ago. Dipping my tongue into the water for a drink, I stared at my reflection. Light-gray fur with white fringe and black spots, bright blue eyes. The water rippled as a frog jumped in. It was tempting to swat the frog as it arched within my reach, but I kept my paws still. There was no reason to kill the frog.

A shape was forming on the surface of the water. A low warning growl rumbled through my body. Teal skin and dark braided hair appeared. I took an involuntary step backward.

"Betrayer, your time is coming," Travaran said coldly, as he sharpened a dagger on a whetstone. It took me a moment to recognize the dagger, mostly hidden in the shadows of the water—the silver-dragon-headed handle with the emerald eyes.

"*No,*" I replied, projecting my thoughts to him, knowing it was futile. Travaran was dead, and this was a hallucination.

A pair of bright gold eyes was rising over Travaran's shoulder. I could barely make out anything other than the eyes. As the water rippled, I caught sight of reptilian nostrils with tiny tendrils of smoke curling out of them. Worried and tired of this hallucination, I jumped into the water, and the image disappeared with a splash. I paddled across to the other side, then bounded out of the pool and shook water out of my fur. *The stress of everything must be really getting to me if I am imagining Travaran and a dragon.* My relationship with Travaran had been complicated. The deep friendship during our time together at Ember Mountain had started to unravel at Dorcha Palace once Travaran no longer had to follow the strict orders of our commanding officers. Tanyth had often looked the other way as long as Travaran did not disobey direct orders—orders his father expressly gave him. That was not true if Travaran disobeyed orders that had been given to me.

He's dead, I reminded myself, *killed by Fiera*. It no longer mattered what he did, or how frequently I had felt taken advantage of by someone who was supposed to be my friend yet seemed to only look out for his own best interests. Growing up, I had had friends until I discovered I was a snow leopard shifter. Then, no one wanted to be my friend anymore; even my father had treated me differently. *Maybe that's why I jumped at the chance to be Travaran's friend—because he was the first person in a decade who had genuinely wanted to talk to me.* I snorted as I realized that with what I had learned about Travaran over the years, the odds of him having accepted me for all of me, if he'd ever found out about the snow leopard shifting, was zero. Tanyth's hatred for shifters had been instilled in his son. Thankfully, Callyn and Sera were not afraid of me, nor did they feel I should be punished for the type of animal I was able to turn into. *Not that I had had a say in the matter.* From what I knew, the animal or creature a Fae could shift into was random.

Losing track of time, I wandered through the forest, following deer trails that led seemingly nowhere. The moment Sera was bound to all Fae as our queen, I became aware of her magic spreading throughout the land, and then it vanished, as though our mating bond had shown me something I shouldn't have seen. Using our mating bond as a beacon, I wove my way through the forest back to the path where Onvyr and the guards were waiting.

I shifted a hundred paces from the others and jogged the rest of the way, taking my place next to Dubhar as Sera stepped through the magic shield. Her hair was disheveled, and the robe was sliding off her shoulder. My fingers itched to help her remove it. I closed my fist to prevent myself from doing something I'd regret in front of an audience. She had a faint aura around her, as though she had so much magic, her body was not enough to completely contain it. I glanced at Onvyr, but he was focused on Sera.

Sera's blue-green eyes met mine, a smile playing at the corner of her lips. I wondered if she had caught my thoughts through the bond. "My love," I said and took a step forward.

Onvyr threw his arm out, blocking me. I growled low in my throat, bristling. "Be patient," Onvyr said, his voice clipped.

Onvyr, hand in a fist over his heart, bowed deeply. "Your Majesty. The ceremony is complete. You have been accepted as Queen of Fae and are now bound to all four courts. Let us return to Uaine Palace."

Sera rubbed her palm over her heart, and I dug my nails into my palm, trying to quell my rising desire. She replied, "Very well. Are there any additional matters I must attend to tonight?"

Dubhar nuzzled her shoulder affectionately. *"No."* The unicorn paused, and his silver eyes met mine. *"Though I would recommend some alone time with your mate."* I was positive those words had only been sent to Sera and myself. Otherwise, Onvyr would have reacted.

Sera gave my hand a light squeeze, then focused on Dubhar. "May I ride you? My feet are not as swift as those of a full Fae."

"I would gladly carry you to the palace, my queen," Dubhar replied. Wrapping her hands in Dubhar's silver mane, Sera gracefully pulled herself onto Dubhar's back. Without warning, the unicorn reared and whinnied. I felt his call in my bones and wondered if we should expect more guests tomorrow.

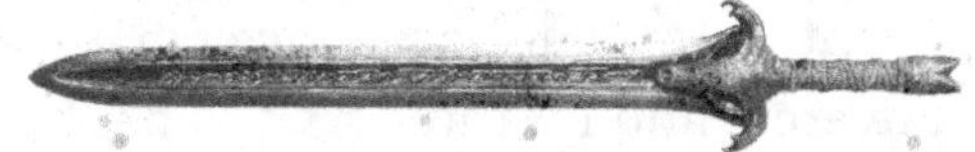

Sera led me through the door. Instead of turning to shut it, I sent a small burst of magic, and the door shut and locked firmly behind us. The robe was slipping off her shoulder again. I reached out and helped it slide all the way down her arms. Pulling her close, I trailed kisses down her shoulder, lingering on the delicate column of her throat. My cock was hard with need, but I didn't want to rush. I wanted to savor tonight with my love, my queen. Sera melted under my lips, but was not touching me at all. Straightening, I lightly clasped her shoulders and met her gaze. "What's wrong?"

She pressed her lips together, brow furrowing. I waited while she found the words she wanted. "Why me?"

My eyebrows shot straight up, and my stomach hardened in confusion. "What do you mean?"

Sera twisted a stray piece of hair between her fingers, averting her gaze from mine. Her voice was tentative. "Why do you love me?"

I swallowed, my throat suddenly dry. "You're stubborn, fight for what you believe in even against the odds, and you make me want to be a better male, the male I was never able to be when I served Tanyth. Instead of hating or punishing me for being a snow leopard shifter, you have embraced it. Even though I have made mistakes, you have found it in yourself to forgive me, for which I will be forever in your debt. You are my mate, Serafina. I feel as though I've been waiting my whole life for you, and now that you're here you're a part of me that I didn't know I was missing." I gazed at her fiercely, waiting for her to say I was wrong, that I wasn't allowed to have these feelings or that she no longer wanted me.

Tears trickled down Sera's cheeks. She entwined her fingers with mine and peered at me. "Good. I love you, Tristan. You believe in me, even when I have doubts, and you are the only man or male I want at my side as we face whatever awaits us." Her lower lip quivered, and I wanted to kiss her but held myself still, not sure if she was done speaking. "I want you to know that no matter what happens in these coming days, it will only ever be you."

My lips parted to respond, but Sera's velvety mouth captured mine, her tongue demanding entrance. Chuckling, I obliged and let her take control. My back was pressed against the door, the handle digging painfully into the dragon tattoo. I inhaled sharply as Sera slid her hand down my abdomen and unlaced the tie on my pants. Her fingers blazed a trail of desire in their wake, till she gently cupped me. I fleetingly wondered if I should suggest moving away from the door—and the guards who were stationed on the other side.

Sera took a breath, a smile flitting across her face. "Worried about the guards?" she teased.

"Only if you are," I replied and kissed her, pulling her into me hard enough that my back thudded into the door, making it rattle on the hinges.

"Is everything okay in there?" called a guard.

Sera burst out laughing. "Yes!" Then, she stuck out her tongue at me and twirled away. She didn't make it far since the robe was dragging on the ground behind her, and she got tangled in it and tripped, skidding to a halt on her back. I dashed after her, eyes on her face, concerned that she was hurt. My foot hit something, and I stumbled. Years of training had me tucking into a roll. A fist in my gut stopped my momentum, and I sprawled on the floor. *What the hell?* Serafina was next to me, giggling.

I rolled my eyes, wondering what she was up to, when faster than I thought possible, she was straddling me. With my back on the floor, I had the perfect view of her glistening folds. I licked my lips, wondering if she would be open to a new position. *Ride my face?*

She must have felt my thoughts through the bond, because Sera clicked her tongue in disapproval. Her hand released my shaft from my pants; it sprang free and stood like a sentry between us. I moaned as she dragged her fingernails along my length. Need shot through me.

"Now you know how it feels to have to wait," she murmured.

I bit the inside of my cheek, drawing blood. Sera was right, and I knew it. There had been several times she had wanted my cock inside of her, but I had insisted on drawing out the foreplay.

I lifted my hand, and she shook her head. "No touching. Or ... I will leave you alone to pleasure yourself."

I smirked and raised my hand, wrapping it around the base of my shaft below hers. "Would you like to watch?" Sera gasped, and I chuckled.

She didn't reply, but she did dip her head down, her breasts swinging deliciously until her hair blocked them from view. Her tongue swirled over the tip of my cock, and then she sucked, and a spasm rolled through me. Opening her mouth wider, she consumed my cock. I bumped the back of her throat, and she found her rhythm.

"Sera," I whispered, barely able to form words as pleasure rippled through me. My cock jerked in her mouth and still she kept going, not deterred by the flood of my seed in her mouth. When she had wrung everything out of me, she sat up, moistening her lips and deliberately swallowing.

She scooted along my body, her breasts pressed against my chest. I gasped when her damp thighs brushed my spent cock. Then, her lips met mine. The taste of my seed mingled with her own sweet flavor had me craving more.

Reaching between us, I plunged my fingers in her folds. When they were dripping, I brought them up to my lips, met her gaze, and gently sucked one, then the other. Her eyes widened, and I could feel her heart rate speeding up. "You are delicious," I said softly.

Raising my hips, I thrust upward, plunging my cock into her folds. I took up a slow in-and-out rhythm, trying to make my exhausted body work. My libido might be demanding round two, but one or both of us was going to have to do the work to make it happen.

"Oh," whispered Sera as I thrust deep inside of her. I could feel our fluids mingling and dribbling between us. With a little coaxing, Sera matched my rhythm, up and down. I could feel her muscles bunching as she used them, strengthened from years of training. As she rode me, I could feel the tension building in her core, and her movements became more frantic. Taking a wild guess, I lightly pinched her nipple between my thumb and forefinger and gave a light tug.

Pleasure exploded through me, Sera sagged against me, and I sat up, holding her, as our bodies spasmed together. When our breathing returned to normal, Sera brushed a strand of my hair out of my face.

"I didn't think that was going to work," she admitted.

"That I could perform twice?" I asked.

Sera giggled and shook her head. "No. You've done it before. I figured with the right encouragement that wouldn't be an issue. I meant … tripping you."

I laughed and gave her nose a light flick. "You did a pretty good job of distracting me before you tripped me."

"Note to self, distract Tristan with my body before I try to attack him. Got it," Sera teased.

I kissed her. "I love you."

Sera replied, "I love you too."

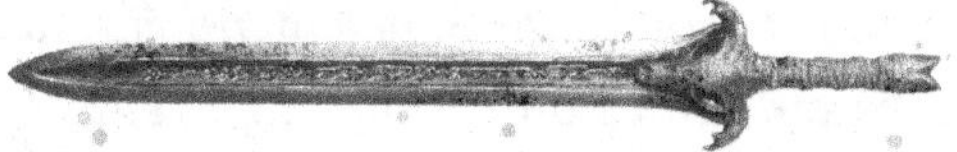

Rigidly, I sat in a solid wood chair on the ledge of the arena, barely enough space to maneuver in and out of the chair without falling into the sand fifty feet below. Tanyth was sitting next to me, his crown of antlers perched atop his head, the black cloak with snow leopard paws on its shoulders a harsh reminder of my fate if he discovered my secret.

The fight unfolded below us and as much as I wished to look away, I could not avert my eyes or, I discovered, move from the position I was in. Rethys, a small dark-green dragon with a chain around his leg, was stalking a group of five Fae, who were seemingly unaware of the predicament they were in. Recognition shot through me as I identified Callyn with her white hair and pale skin, a stark contrast to Ghilanna's dark-brown skin and unruly black curls. Focusing intently on the Fae below, I realized that I knew all of them. Marek, with his bronze skin and reddish-brown hair, was not as identifiable without Asteria present. Chained to Marek was the blue-haired unicorn shifter Onvyr, a heavy silver collar clamped around his neck preventing him from shifting. Rounding out the group was Sera's grandmother Shelara. Of the five, her presence confused me the most, given I'd only just met her.

Watching Onvyr's lips moving, I realized he was reciting words, the same words Travaran had once spoken by my side when faced with Rethys: "Breathe fire, thick skin, poor eyesight."

A flurry of movement and together Onvyr and Marek charged toward Rethys, swords drawn. I gripped the chair hard, afraid of what would happen to the Fae in the arena and of what might befall me should I topple below.

Rethys shuffled side to side with wisps of smoke curling out of the corners of his mouth, waiting for the opportune moment to strike. I sniffed the air and immediately regretted doing so. It smelled strongly of rotten eggs. When Marek was a few strides away, Rethys struck, snaking his head toward him, pearly white teeth dangerously close to snapping his sword arm in half. The glowing arena light reflected off Rethys's iridescent scales on his top ridge, similar, I realized, to Dubhar's horn. Drawing back slightly, Rethys opened his mouth and blasted a jet of fire. Onvyr rolled to the right, and Marek sprinted to the left, ducking under Rethys's wing at the last moment.

While Rethys spun in a circle, snapping at Marek, Ghilanna and Callyn sprinted for his tail. I admired their courage. As Callyn raised her sword, the tail whipped side to side, slapping her across the face and sending her flying through the air. Ghilanna shrieked in rage and started hacking at Rethys's side. The dragon whirled, spraying fire across the whole arena and burning all five of them. Their screams of pain and anger rose up to my ears. Biting my tongue, I relished the coppery tang of blood that flooded my mouth and prayed whatever was holding me here would let me go, so I could drop into the arena and fight Rethys to punish him for killing our friends.

Rethys reared up on his hind legs, wings flared, and roared. His eyes caught mine. A dark voice echoed in my head. "I've been waiting for you."

I woke up with a start, my back slick with a cold sweat. Serafina had rolled away from me, for which I was grateful. I slipped out of the bed and padded over to the couch. Running my hands over my face, I tried to make sense of the dream. I thought I had been reliving the moment Rethys had spoken into my mind, saying, "I see you," but now that I was awake, there were many things that had happened in my dream that were different. *Did Rethys send me the dream?* Yesterday, I would have scoffed at the idea that there was a connection between me and Rethys. Now, after everything that had happened and the second half of the Lost Fae Queen prophecy being revealed, I no longer knew what I should believe.

Instead, I focused on what I knew: that Rethys was one of the only living dragons, I had a dragon tattoo on my back from being stabbed by the very dagger that could control Rethys, and now he was talking to me in dreams. Tendrils of fear gripped me at the possibility that Rethys was not on Sera's side but was working for Tanyth and trying to drive a wedge between us to weaken her position as Queen of Fae. *Nothing better than turmoil within the royal house. Though he doesn't need to split us up for that. Sera's family has been less than welcoming.*

The room was dark, but I could see a hint of daylight at the edge of the curtains. Something sitting on the edge of the table caught my attention. Stretching my arm out without shifting positions, I was able to just barely snag the edge of the book. Calling a bit of Fae light so I could see what the book was, I was disconcerted to see it was *Bedtime Tails*, with a snow leopard tail forming the *S. Where did it come from?* I mused. There hadn't been a book on this table before we went to sleep. My lips twitched, and I admitted I had not been paying much attention to anything other than Sera after we entered the room. *Someone wanted us to find it.*

Shrugging, I leaned back against the couch and thumbed through the pages, pausing when I reached the one about Rethys. The illustration depicted the dark-green dragon with black belly scales standing over a treasure hoard of gold and jewels. I shivered at how accurate the drawing was; even the iridescence of Rethys's crest was captured. The story was longer than I remembered. Intrigued, I started reading.

The treasure of Rethys is hunted far and wide by seekers of fame and fortune. Hundreds have perished in their quest, intent only on their personal gain.

One day, a Fae accidentally stumbled upon Rethys's cave, seeking shelter from the storm. He saw the sleeping dragon and could feel the warmth radiating off the creature. The Fae curled up in a ball against Rethys's side and fell asleep.

When he awoke, the first thing he noticed was a mark on his arm. The light in the cave was dim, so he stepped outside to inspect it. In the sunlight, the mark became clear: It was a tattoo of a dragon.

"You are the first to come here, not to steal, but because you needed shelter. If you are ever in need, you can summon me through the mark. If your heirs are worthy, they too will be able to summon me through the mark, if they can earn it," Rethys spoke into the Fae's mind.

"Thank you," the Fae said.

"Fuck," I growled and dropped the book on the cushion, then leaped up off the couch and paced. *Marek said something about Rethys,* I reminded myself. *So did Callyn and Dubhar.*

I recalled fragments of Callyn's words first: "A magical object can mark someone … Tanyth could be using it to track you." Groaning, I realized that we had already figured this out, that

Tanyth was tracking me through it, which meant he knew precisely where we were now. Especially with the magic Sera released last night connecting her to all Fae, a beacon that, at least temporarily, broadcast her precise location too. *He knows the South is vulnerable without us.*

I took a few steps toward the bed, thinking I should wake Sera up and encourage her to leave immediately and return home. I stopped in my tracks as the conversation with Marek entered my thoughts. Marek's opinion that being marked by Dragonfang was terrible had been tempered when I revealed that Rethys is alive: "The prophecy is true."

Scrubbing my hands over my face, I sorted through the prophecies I was aware of. None of them had to do with Rethys directly. *Unless ...* I dashed back to the couch and flipped open the book to Rethys's story, whispering the words, "'If you are ever in need, you can summon me through the mark.'" My hands trembled as I clutched the book to my chest, afraid to consider the impossible: that I could summon Rethys because of my ancestor's pure heart.

I heard Sera's light footsteps and immediately felt sorry for waking her up. "What's wrong?" Sera asked, concerned.

Setting the book down, I faced her, brushing a strand of hair off her cheek. "A dream woke me up, and then I found a copy of *Bedtime Tails* out here. I'm sorry if I disturbed you."

She leaned into my hand on her cheek before meeting my gaze. "You didn't. Besides, its past dawn, and Onvyr said there are matters I need to attend to today. We were hoping to go back this morning."

"I can return to the South. If we have any actionable reports of Tanyth's movements, I can give the orders for the knights to begin their march while you wrap up your responsibilities here. It would be a simple matter to use star portals for the Fae warriors to reach us in time," I offered. Though it pained me to consider leaving, it was one of the few tasks I could do without her.

Sera frowned, then placed her head on my chest with her arms around me. "You're right. I don't want you to go, but I don't have time to spare, especially if Tanyth is on the move."

I kissed the top of her head, considering if I should tell her about Rethys. *Secrets have already driven us apart.* "From what I have gathered in *Bedtime Tails* and conversations with Callyn and Marek, there is a prophecy that directly links me to Rethys. If I am correct in my interpretation, the dragon tattoo on my back will allow me to summon Rethys."

Sera pulled out of my embrace and crossed her arms over her chest. "Summon Rethys to do what?" she said warily.

"To help us," I said solemnly.

Her eyes narrowed, and I could see the tension in her shoulders. "Why would Rethys, who you fought and injured in Tanyth's arena, have any reason to aid us?"

"I know, I know. It sounds far-fetched. But the story in this book says that he marked a Fae with a dragon tattoo and promised to come if he should ever need help." I plunged onward. "He was in my dream, Sera. And the last time I saw him he spoke in my mind. As difficult as it is to believe, everything is pointing at the same thing: Rethys and I are connected."

"Tanyth is the one who marked you, not Rethys. How do we know this isn't just another trick he's playing to drive us apart? Or give us false hope?" Sera demanded.

I knew she had a point. "We don't. But what I do know is that dragons are like unicorns and griffins. They are sentient beings, with thoughts and feelings, and often their own kind of magic. Tanyth held Rethys captive for longer than I was there. Do you really believe that Rethys feels any loyalty to him?"

Sera's eyes flashed angrily. "You swore an oath and a blood contract to Tanyth and did unspeakable things for thirty years.

I still don't understand why you made those choices. Who are we to understand the motives of an ancient dragon?"

Taking a deep breath, I walked away, wanting space. Everything Sera had said was right. We knew absolutely nothing about Rethys. Fae prophecies were confusing and often, as we were finding, only provided minimal information. Relying on one as a basis for which to trust a dangerous creature like a dragon was not smart. With the additional Fae warriors now accessible to us with Sera's new position, likely having Rethys on our side would not make a difference in how we fared when we finally met Tanyth on the battlefield. The risks were high that summoning Rethys would force us to fight the dragon and unnecessarily waste our precious resources.

Mind made up, I wandered back to Sera. She was rooted to the same spot, her face unreadable. Wanting to offer reassurance, I said calmly, "I will refrain from summoning Rethys for the time being. I felt that it was critical you knew of this new development before we parted ways."

Sera nodded tensely. "Thank you. You should get ready to go." Her tone was formal. The last thing I wanted to do was leave when there were unresolved matters between us. But I wasn't sure how to mend things. We were entitled to our own opinions.

Twenty-Five

SERAFINA

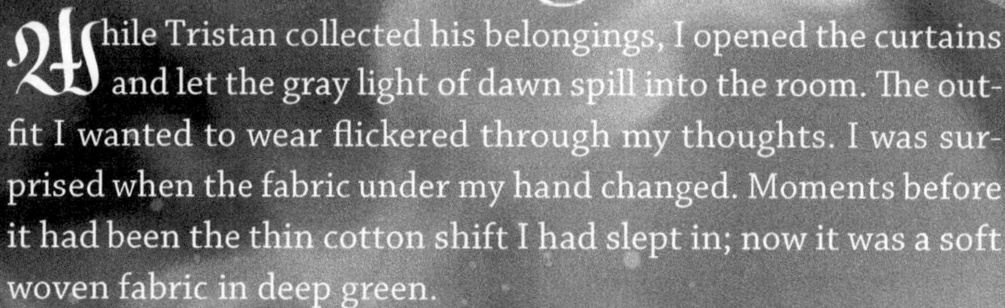

While Tristan collected his belongings, I opened the curtains and let the gray light of dawn spill into the room. The out-fit I wanted to wear flickered through my thoughts. I was surprised when the fabric under my hand changed. Moments before it had been the thin cotton shift I had slept in; now it was a soft woven fabric in deep green.

I strode over to the mirror to inspect myself and noticed a soft green glow shimmering around me. The deep-green fabric made up a waist-length jacket and matching wide-leg pants. I wore a white silk tunic and had a black scabbard at my waist with the sword. My russet hair was braided like a crown around my head. *What changed?* I considered how quickly I had crafted the clothing, without much thought at all, unlike previously when I had to think about all the minute details.

Wanting to test myself, I thought, *Shield.* A pale-green transparent bubble formed around me. Not very subtle, but it was a start. Willing the shield to be invisible and fitted to me like a glove, I thought about other skills Ghilanna and Tristan had shown me. *Balls of magic.* Three floated in the air in front of me.

I flicked one lightly and my finger passed through it, though the ball did not disappear as I had expected it to.

A light tap sounded on the door. Glancing over my shoulder, I debated opening it, when I saw the doorknob turn, and the door sprang open. Onvyr emerged through the doorway, his surprise mirroring my own. *How did the door open?* I wondered.

The balls of magic caught Onvyr's attention. They were still floating in front of me. "Did you open the door?" he asked.

"Maybe?" I replied hesitantly. Honestly, I had no idea if I had opened it or not. My magic was being far more responsive than anyone had told me it would be.

"King Pharaan said once that his magic had changed when he went through the ceremony binding him to the four courts and all Fae. Unfortunately, he did not elaborate on *how* it changed, and I was not alive at the time, so I cannot tell you what the differences were with a firsthand account. Considering you are racing toward a battle that has been foretold since Fae themselves came into existence, I would not be surprised if the ceremony you went through last night connected you far deeper to the world around you. Where it will take little more than a thought to make something happen, because your magic is that in-tune to your needs and those of our land," Onvyr explained.

I wanted the magic balls to disappear, and they did. "You're saying that I don't even need to formulate a complete thought, and something magical will happen?" The idea was concerning. *What if I was weighing two bad options? Will my magic remove the choice from me?*

Onvyr frowned. "Yes and no. Think of your magic as an extension of yourself. I knocked on the door. You were not under any threat, so there was no perceivable reason not to open the door. Therefore, your magic opened it. Just like getting dressed. Another way of thinking of it is that you can essentially bypass learning to use your magic like the rest of us had to do. Because of your attunement, you should be able to decide how to use your magic and it will immediately happen. We can test it later if you would like."

I nodded. The idea of experimenting here, in a palace full of Fae who were trained in their magic, was far more appealing than waiting until I was on the battlefield and hoping Onvyr's theory was correct. "Yes, I would like to experiment with my magic. Tristan is returning to the South. I will stay here to wrap up whatever else you wanted me to attend to."

"Good. I will give you a few minutes to say your goodbyes and then I'll return to escort you to meet with my second-in-command—your aunt Sorisana," Onvyr announced.

Our plans for the day caught me off guard. Inhaling sharply, I considered how dinner had gone. Sorisana had said she wanted to talk to me again, yet our interactions had been distant during the meal. If I was being honest, it felt like none of my relatives wanted me to be part of their family. *Perhaps they blame me for King Pharaan's death.* Shoving the thought away, I considered what I was hoping to gain by talking to Sorisana. I wanted to talk to her about my mother, to learn more about the female whom I'd only had eleven short years with. I suspected that our meeting was not for that purpose but to give me additional information about my role as queen. *I haven't even figured out how to be Lady of the South, and now I have to learn even more protocol.* A dark thought crossed my mind. *If I die in the war, I won't have to worry about learning protocol for a Fae court and a human kingdom. It will no longer be my problem.*

"Is everything okay?" Tristan asked, coming up beside me.

His formfitting black leather pants were distracting. "Fine. Are you ready?" I asked, dragging my mind away from dirty thoughts.

"Yes," Tristan said, his eyes bright with mischief.

"I will be back shortly. Safe travels, Tristan," Onvyr said politely and then departed.

Tristan pulled me into his arms. I squeaked as his lips met mine, eager and demanding. *He needs to leave,* I chided myself, even as my mouth parted and our tongues danced together. Tristan's hands caressed my back, then dropped lower, gently lifting my hips. Taking the hint, I did a little hop, and he picked me up. I wrapped my legs around his waist, gasping as his cock bumped against the apex of my thighs. My blood heated as desire blazed through me.

"Do we have time?" I mumbled against his lips, then he bumped me again. This time, the barrier of fabric that had been between us was gone.

"I doubt anyone is going to tell the Queen of Fae she can't have sex with her husband," Tristan whispered in my ear. His next thrust drove his shaft all the way into my canal. My legs tightened around his waist, sending him deeper. To my amusement, he proceeded to carry me over to the bed without disengaging. The lack of friction was driving me wild with need, and I squirmed, wanting to take matters into my own hands, but I was in an awkward position.

"So impatient," he teased.

I nipped his lower lip hard enough to draw blood. "You're the one who stopped," I muttered.

Tristan set me down on the bed and adjusted my legs, so instead of being wrapped around his waist, they were draped over his shoulders. Then, he withdrew from me. A complaint was on the tip of my tongue when he rose to his knees and guided himself into my entrance. Sighing in relief, I let myself sink into the mattress. His strokes quickened, and my muscles tensed as he drove me closer to the edge. From the tightness in Tristan's jaw and shoulders, I could tell he was close too. Closing my eyes, I savored the feel of his thickness inside of me and how he glided in and out. Suddenly, Tristan's fingers were there, one alongside his cock, while the other lightly flicked my clitoris. Intense pleasure flooded my senses, and I felt as though I was going to black out. Tremors rolled through me as Tristan wrung every last drop from both of us. I could feel his arms shaking against my legs, and then he bellowed, "Serafina!" as his body spasmed with his release.

Slowly, I lowered my legs from around his shoulders, letting them flop onto the coverlet. Tristan rolled to the side, curving around my body. We fit together, like we'd been made for each other and no one else. *But we were ...* I snorted as that realization came to me. The Lost Fae Queen prophecy had existed for centuries and spoke of the female and her mate, the Great Cat. Which begged the question: Had the gods created us for each other? Or had a series of events pushed Tristan and me into those roles, and it was happenstance that it felt as though we had been made for each other?

"You need to go," I informed him, scooting out of his arms. I needed space between us if I was going to convince Tristan he still needed to return to Gaskal. Taunting him with my nakedness was a guaranteed way of him *not* leaving.

Clothes, I thought, recalling the outfit I had worn this morning. My skin warmed, and then I felt the soft woven fabric between me and the sheets.

Glancing over at Tristan, I saw his lower lip stuck out in a pout. "You just ruined my plans for round two."

I smacked him on the arm. "We're lucky Onvyr hasn't returned yet."

"I told you earlier, he's not going to interrupt. Sex is natural, accepted, even encouraged among Fae. Besides, we're not exactly quiet ..." Tristan said with a grin.

I smacked him again. "You're saying that everyone in the palace heard us just now? And last night?"

Tristan chuckled. "Not everyone, but probably those in the hallway and any rooms sharing this courtyard."

"You should have told me. I don't want them to know how often ..." I started to say.

Tristan captured my hand in his and kissed the inside of my wrist, sending my pulse racing. "I promise no one cares. You spent twelve years at Jade Wilds and were also at the battle at Emerald Valley. Certainly the Fae in those places did not hide in the shadows to fuck."

I grimaced at his words, yet I had to acknowledge he was right. Over the years, Fiera and Ghilanna had had their share of partners, and there was certainly plenty of fucking happening in Emerald Valley. I blushed remembering walking in on Ghilanna and a male in our shared tent.

"It is going to take some adjustment for me to not care about things like this. However, if we are spending time here and in the South, it would be prudent to make a habit of more conservative practices. The humans most definitely will have a problem if they think all we're doing is having sex round the clock."

Tristan tugged me into his arms and kissed me, then stepped back. "I love you, and I will see you soon." With no need for secrecy, Tristan made a star portal in the room and stepped through. The dark-gray magic vanished with my husband.

I found myself in the same square room that Tristan and I had spoken to Shelara in yesterday, except this time my aunt Sorisana was facing me. I itched to ask her questions about my mother but was wise enough to know this was not an appropriate time for that discussion. Spread on the table between us was a map of the four Fae courts and the four human kingdoms.

Sorisana's hair was braided severely against her head, making the angles of her cheeks even sharper. She was wearing thick leather armor with the Court of Dawn's emblem on the chest plate and looked far more like a real second-in-command than she had at dinner last night. "How many knights did you say had answered your call?"

Her question caught me off guard. I was expecting a greeting, not plunging straight into whatever this meeting was about. "I have about fifteen hundred as of yesterday morning."

Sorisana moved two gold rocks onto the map where my palace in Gaskal was depicted. Two green ones were at the Court of Dawn. She picked them up and moved them over to Gaskal as well. "Each of these represents one thousand," she explained. Two dark blue rocks sat at Dorcha Palace, two silver at the Court of the Moon, and two orange at the Court of the Sun. They represented the number of Fae warriors Onvyr had listed last night.

"Why have you not also moved the Court of the Moon and Sun warriors into the South?" I questioned. *Those four rocks could make the difference in this war.*

Sorisana rubbed the bridge of her nose, then responded, "I'm sure Onvyr told you it will take time to get their responses. You have said it yourself—all you know is war is coming. We don't know when. If Tristan were to send you notice that Tanyth was marching on the South at this very moment, you would have almost four thousand at your disposal. When you receive confirmation that Prince Almar and Prince Rhangil will send their warriors wherever you need them, I will move their pieces into place."

My aunt's words gave me far less confidence than Onvyr's had that Prince Almar and Prince Rhangil would heed my call to arms. *Four thousand is better than two thousand,* I reminded myself. *It should be almost double what Tanyth will have.*

"I want to ensure all preparations are being made for the two thousand warriors to use star portals to go to the battlefield as soon as we know where it will be," I ordered.

Sorisana gave me a look I couldn't decipher, then responded, "They are ready. Star portals will simplify matters. All I need now is their intended destination."

Onvyr clapped his hands together. "Great. Now, Serafina, let's go work on the training I promised."

Onvyr halted in the middle of a hard-packed dirt practice ring. To the left was a set of three dummies with canvas padding. To the right were three in full plate armor. I felt the shield he put around the ring instantly. "We're going to test your abilities. I don't want to destroy Uaine Palace or injure anyone unnecessarily."

I gave him an amused smile. "You have more confidence than I that I possess the magic to do so."

Onvyr shrugged and replied nonchalantly, "I served King Pharaan for three hundred years. I've seen many things."

"Where do we start?" I asked, rubbing my tingling hands together.

Onvyr dragged one of the plate-armored dummies to the center of the ring. It had a bright blue circle painted on the middle of the chest. "You will throw balls of magic, three in quick succession, at this dummy. Your target is to hit anywhere within the circle. In the heat of a battle, you will not have time to send one at a time, so we will not waste our time practicing that way."

He motioned for me to stand on a white line I hadn't noticed before. It was near the edge of the circle, putting me about twenty strides from the dummy. "You may begin when you're ready."

I focused on the task, three balls of magic in quick succession. My hands barely lifted when three balls of green magic shot forth and struck the dummy hard enough that it almost toppled over. I could've sworn I heard Onvyr gasp in awe, but when I cast a glance over at him, his expression was neutral.

When the dummy stilled, Onvyr said calmly, "Again."

We repeated the exercise five times, each with the same result. Though by the fifth set, I found I didn't even need to move my hands at all. The magic was just there, ready to do my bidding.

"Now what?" I asked. There was no way we'd just come out here to watch me throw three balls of magic at a plate-armored dummy. There had to be more to it.

"I want you to aim for the head," Onvyr replied.

I understood immediately. The head was a smaller target than the chest and would give me a chance to fine-tune my accuracy.

My breath fluttered in my nostrils as I exhaled, then released the balls of magic. Green blurs hurtled toward the dummy. The first one missed its mark and sailed over the shoulder. The second hit the chest, and the third hit the mark, blasting a hole the size of my fist through the dummy's head.

Onvyr chuckled. "That's one way to do it. Now you have an even smaller target. Aim for the hole. Go."

Rolling my shoulders back and letting my arms hang loosely at my side, I sent three more balls toward the dummy. They went through the hole and out the other side, disappearing into wisps when they encountered the shield.

"Good. Now, we will move the target," Onvyr explained and dragged the dummy so it was almost against the shield, doubling the distance. "I'm going to skip the chest target and have you aim for the hole in the head again."

I nodded and pressed my lips together into a thin line, concentrating. With the longer distance, I'd have to put more power into the balls to ensure they wouldn't fizzle out before going through the hole. The air thrummed with magic, and the shield flickered with the impact. My eyes widened in surprise that it had happened so quickly, and I had made the target.

Onvyr clapped me on the shoulder. "Maybe I started too easy."

"Two days ago, I wouldn't have been able to do this at all," I admitted. "I could control one ball of magic as a weapon and hit a nearby target, but definitely not like this."

"I told you earlier, your magic has changed now that you're queen. These tests we're doing today will let us explore your limits but should also help give you confidence in what skills you have. For example, now we know you can be accurate for this distance even with a target the size of your fist. I suspect increasing the distance will have the same result. The next step is to add a distraction. Give me a moment to set up, and then we can begin," Onvyr said.

Nodding in agreement, not that I had any choice in the matter, I observed as he moved the other two plate-armored dummies so they were at points of a triangle at the edge of the circle. He then unsheathed his sword and moved to the middle of practice ring. I unsheathed my sword and met him.

"We'll start simple. A basic high, low, middle drill. I will start with strikes. We'll do two sets, then swap. While we are doing the drill, every time you block or strike, I want you to also send a ball of magic at one of the dummies. I don't care which one, but you need to hit them in the chest or head," Onvyr explained.

I had been anticipating him telling me to shield myself, not run a drill. *This will work as a distraction just as well as trying to maintain a shield.*

We crossed our swords, and then Onvyr started a high strike. I blocked and sent a ball of magic at the dummy to my left. It went wide of my mark and sent ripples through the shield. Distracted by my failure, I barely got my sword up in time to block the middle strike and entirely missed my chance to send the second ball of magic.

My palms were sweaty. *Calm down*, I ordered. This was practice. We were doing things I knew how to do, nothing out of the ordinary. I took a deep breath, held it, then slowly exhaled. The next set of blocks was smoother, and all three balls of magic hit the dummies, though not in the target circle. It was a marked improvement. As I swept my sword in a high strike, I imagined the ball of magic hitting the dummy in the head. There was a loud clatter as the dummy toppled over, but I forced myself to continue the drill: middle strike, then low.

Over and over we went. As I became more comfortable with the exercise, my accuracy improved. Sweat trickled down my back, and I realized that Onvyr had subtly shifted out of the drill into a sparring match. He feinted a high strike and then thrust toward my stomach with a middle strike. I hopped backward, throwing a ball of magic at the closest dummy, and then pivoted, slashing at his exposed left side.

A loud cough sounded to my left and I hesitated for a split second. Onvyr's sword caressed my throat. He had a smirk on his face. If he were the enemy, I was out of options to maneuver out of my throat getting slit. *Unless* ... Keeping my face a careful mask, I sent a ball of magic hurtling toward his chest. He was close, an arm's length away, and the green magic sent him flying through the air, shock clear on his face, his arms windmilling.

Onvyr landed flat on his back, making odd sounds. I dashed over to him, fear flooding me. *Did I kill him?* I pulled up short when I realized he was laughing. Onvyr clutched his sides as laughter bubbled out of him.

"Why is this funny?" I demanded sharply. It was tempting to throw more magic at him and see if he still found it amusing.

When his laughter subsided, Onvyr sat up, wincing, though he quickly hid the pain. "You're astute. The whole point of the drill and then sparring was to get you in the habit of using your warrior training and mixing it with magic. Instead of giving up with the sword at your throat, you came up with an alternative, and it worked. Even if you feel that this is not working, it is. You just proved it."

I turned away and caught sight of Sorisana hovering on the other side of the shield, looking annoyed. "Let me in," my aunt called harshly.

Onvyr had made the shield, and to my knowledge it would have to be released by him. I wasn't sure he'd noticed Sorisana yet though. Letting my eyes flutter shut, I could feel Onvyr's shield through my connection to the land. Using my magic like shears, I cut through it. When I opened my eyes, the shield had vanished and Sorisana was walking briskly toward a now-standing Onvyr.

"I'm fine," Onvyr snapped, shoving Sorisana's hands away from him.

"This is dangerous," Sorisana replied.

I stepped forward, not wanting to waste time with their quarrel. "Enough. Onvyr knows the risks. It is not your concern." Sorisana glared at me but stayed silent. "Now, what is it you came out here to say?"

"Captains Revalor and Goras have arrived," Sorisana said roughly. I recognized Goras's name from dinner last night; he was married to Pilar. I was intrigued that he had also married into the Wyantha family and had an officer position within my court.

Onvyr shrugged. "They can wait till we're done."

Sorisana's cheeks reddened, making me wonder how long they had worked together and if they were always at odds. "Marek Fenmyar is also here," Sorisana said, keeping her gaze on Onvyr's.

"What does Marek want?" I demanded.

Sorisana's gaze flicked to mine, then back to Onvyr. "You've met Marek?"

"Yes," I replied. Sorisana was my aunt, but she was also required to accept my authority as her queen. The last thing I wanted to do was dive into my history with Marek.

Onvyr sighed. "I guess we will have to finish this later. I was hoping to get further before you depart."

A flicker of magic caught my attention. It was bronze in color and familiar. It took me a moment to realize I was aware of it only because of my new heightened magic from completing the ritual at the mine. The others were not yet aware Marek was heading this way. Brushing stray hairs out of my face, I sheathed my sword and straightened my tunic. Onvyr and Sorisana were still having a heated discussion and not paying attention to me.

I moved over to the edge of the practice circle. Marek rounded the corner, his expression serious as he made a beeline for me. "Queen Serafina," he said formally, bowing with his hand over his heart.

"Marek, to what do I owe this meeting?" I asked.

Marek gazed warily around the practice ring, his eyes lingering on the dummies missing their heads, before returning his attention to me. "Tanyth is on the move. He'll be at your border in a day, maybe less."

Sucking in a shaky breath, I considered the news. *We're not ready ... I'm not ready.* The responses hadn't arrived yet from Prince Almar or Prince Rhangil. "I should return to Gaskal at once," I said firmly. Reaching out to Tristan through the mating bond and hoping he could hear me, I passed on Marek's information. *"Tanyth will be at the border in less than a day. The knights need to move now."*

Tristan's voice came calmly through the bond. *"I will ensure the knights are there in time. See you soon."*

"I'll inform Sorisana and Onvyr. I'll return to Gaskal in a few hours," I replied.

Marek set his hand on my arm, and I jumped slightly. He gave me knowing look, then spoke. "Yes, you should. But there are two things. The first is, do not take a star portal directly into the palace. Tanyth has spies in place. It would be better if you entered on foot through one of the less well-known entrances." I questioned his advice since the knights were moving and there was not entirely a need for me to even go to the palace. *He's never steered me wrong before,* I consoled myself.

"And the second?" I demanded.

"There are a few things I want to show you with your magic. It won't take long. Then you can go," Marek said.

"Very well. I'm willing to learn," I replied.

A quick lesson with Marek and a brief chat with the Court of Dawn Captains Revalor and Goras, then I was in one of the courtyard gardens, preparing to summon a star portal. There was a large bird bath that had several brightly colored birds perched on it. I watched the birds while they drank water and chirped. A delaying tactic, I knew. One I allowed myself, because once I left, I had no idea when I would be in such a peaceful spot again. *Maybe never.* Determination filled me. *I can do this.*

As a precaution, I was wearing full plate armor, my sword on my left hip, a dagger on my right, and two more daggers within the tops of my boots. A skintight shield was formed around me as well. Onvyr and Sorisana stood in the archway into the garden, waiting for me to depart.

I had looked for Dubhar, thinking we'd return to Gaskal together, but he had disappeared after bringing me back from the emerald mine, and no one in the palace knew where he'd gone. A small part of me felt hurt that he would abandon me on the eve of such an important battle, but a larger part of me knew that he traveled where he wished, and he would return when I needed him.

With the slightest of thoughts, a star portal, shimmering green laced with gold, appeared in front of me. Back straight, wearing my confidence like a cloak, I stepped through.

The portal vanished behind me, and I gazed around my surroundings. I was at the edge of the forest looking out over Emerald Valley. I imagined the rows of tents. Fae warriors, preparing for battle, were still here. I shook my head. *No one is here but me.* Marek had told me not to go directly to the palace, but to portal nearby. Deciding to opt for extreme caution, I chose to make my way to the South in multiple steps. It was also a good opportunity to practice my control over star portals with my newly enhanced magic.

Summoning the next star portal, I stepped through and into the jungle surrounding Jade Wilds. A heavy net of woven metal and rope landed on top of me. I thrashed, and it tightened further. I lost my footing and fell over, catching a glimpse of what looked like antlers before hitting my head on a rock and losing consciousness.

"Well, well, well, what do we have here?" came an ice-cold voice that sent a shiver of fear down my spine. Twisting in the net, I reached an angle where I could see the owner of the voice, a male who was taller than any I had seen before. He had teal skin. His blue-black hair was in hundreds of tiny braids with small beads at the ends. On top of his head was a large crown that had been formed from antlers. On his shoulders, holding his white cape in place, were large pale gray paws with huge claws, almost as though a cat were resting his paws there. A chain connected the two paws and had large teeth strung along it. My eyes widened in recognition. Prince Tanyth.

My head was throbbing, and I could feel sticky blood covering half my face. Opening my eyes the barest of cracks, my blood ran cold when I saw Tanyth leaning against the wall of the cave, deep in conversation with Fiera. Blinking rapidly in confusion, I determined I must be hallucinating. Fiera had died in front of me. Bane's sword had gone clean through her, spilling excessive amounts of blood. *He took her away,* the darker part of my mind whispered. *You never saw the body to confirm she was dead.* Tremors ran through me as fear and despair flooded my thoughts, unwilling to believe that Fiera was anything more than an illusion.

Even in the dim light, I would recognize Tanyth anywhere. Gone was the antler crown and cape from my dream. He was wearing a black sleeveless tunic and leather pants. The air shimmered with his teal magic, making me wonder what was going on. I couldn't recall him ever not having his magic under control. *I shimmer like that now ... perhaps this is a change since he united* Bloodsong Grimoire, *Dragonfang, and Fleshrender.*

My magic. Since the Queen of Fae ceremony, I'd been brimming with it. Gasping, I realized it was gone. Shivering, I heard a faint metallic sound near my ear. My hands were bound together, but I discovered I could move my arms. Carefully running my hands over my body as much as I could, hunting for anything that would be useful, I froze when I came in contact with the collar. *No!*

Curling into a ball, I rocked myself as helplessness filled me. Of all the scenarios I had considered, it had never once crossed my mind that Tanyth would capture me again. That I would ever be in a situation where he *could* capture me. I had taken precautions, shielded myself, followed Marek's instructions, and yet here I was—a prisoner, with no magic, *again.*

Twenty-Six

RETHYS

Stretching my wings, I stood at the mouth of my cave, watching the sunrise over the hill, the fingers of dawn creeping across the spruce forest. Thankfully once I was free of Dorcha Palace, my magic had quickly returned till I was brimming with it. I took a deep breath; smoke wisps filled the air as I exhaled.

Marek would see to it that Serafina received the rest of the training she needed, which meant there was one more task I needed to see to. With Meriel Leoydark dead, no one else knew where Fallon was—or his heritage—except me. As much as I despised the idea of returning to the Court of Dusk, I owed it to both him and Meriel to ensure Fallon knew the truth.

Dragons had long been tied to the Court of Dusk, which made it a simple matter to read the magic signatures of who was in the court's territory and the palace at any given time. Prince Tanyth was a few hours from the shared border between the Court of Dusk and the South. With my magic restored, unless I was within one hundred yards of Dragonfang, I could prevent its magic from having control over me.

I leapt into the air, wings beating, and steadily gained altitude until I soared in the clouds, heading west toward the Court of

Dusk with the sunrise at my back. Within an hour I could see the snowy peak of Ember Mountain rising above the clouds.

Lazily circling the mountain, I reached out with my magic to Fallon. His surprise was palpable but he was swift to answer my summons. I was certain Tanyth's absence simplified Fallon's ability to discreetly go to the dungeon and stand on the stone I had used to leave.

A buzzing sensation filled me when he was standing on the stone. Drawing on my magic, I transported Fallon from the dungeon in Dorcha Palace to a small cave at the summit of Ember Mountain. Tipping my head down and pulling my wings back, I dove toward the cave. The sheer mountainside rushed up toward me, and at the last moment I flared my wings and glided to a stop at the entrance of the cave.

Fallon had his long brown hair braided back from his face and wore a blue robe and a longsword in a blue scabbard. He was watching me, hands on his hips, with a droll stare. "You're reckless," he commented.

I huffed out a breath and smiled at him. "No one but you can see me or is aware I am here."

"How can you be sure?" Fallon demanded.

I blew a small puff of fire at him. "Because Tanyth is on the other side of the territory and so is Dragonfang. Nothing else is powerful enough to allow Fae to see through my magic unless I want them to. Now if you're done questioning me, can we get down to business?"

Fallon shrugged. "Sure. I have no idea why you summoned me anyhow."

I shifted side to side, my claws scraping on the cave. "Your birth mother, Meriel Leoydark, is dead."

Fallon frowned. "You returned to the Court of Dusk, risking your life—and mine, if I'm caught—to tell me that my birth mother is dead? Are you serious?"

I hissed at him. "No, that is not all I am here to tell you. You are being impatient."

"I'm only impatient because if someone learns of my absence it'll be my head, not yours," Fallon snapped.

"Come with me," I said and walked past him, deeper into the cave. When we reached the back there was a flattened area, and I turned so I was facing it. A dark-green, almost-black magic swirled out of my front feet and rose until it created a circle. The magic faded and was replaced by an image of Meriel Leoydark. Her skin was smooth and free of worry lines and wrinkles, her hair was white, and her gray eyes shone with emotion. She was wearing a formfitting dress and her hands rested lightly on her very round stomach.

"Fallon Leoydark Darelei, my son—and if you are watching this, then it means that you are also the heir of the Court of Dusk. I was foolish and fell in love with Tanyth Neriwraek. I didn't know I was pregnant until months after I had broken things off with him. I am sorry I could not tell you myself. But you, my love, are pure light, and I believe that no matter what you have endured, you will persevere. And should the Lost Fae Queen be victorious, one day you will be able to take your place and right the wrongs that the last five Court of Dusk princes have committed," Meriel's image said.

Meriel had given me this bit of magic to keep safe should she die without talking to Fallon herself. Her seer abilities had let her see bits and pieces of what her son's life would be like before he was born, but she had not known everything. Fallon stared blankly at the wall long after the image disappeared. Finally, he turned to me, and I could see tear tracks smudging his face.

"It's true, then, that Serafina *is* the Lost Fae Queen?" Fallon asked, his voice rough.

"Yes," I confirmed. He should have felt when Serafina completed the ritual to become Queen of Fae.

"Then Tristan is the Great Cat," Fallon stated.

I nodded. *Maybe he paid more attention than I thought.*

"Too many Fae at the Court of Dusk are terrified of Bane and Tanyth. I would not be able to get them to turn against them. Many signed blood contracts and are bound like me ... unless Queen Serafina's new magic will allow her to break a blood contract," Fallon responded.

I was intrigued by the idea and thought it could be worth trying at least. "I anticipate the Fae warriors from the Court of Dusk will be moving into position soon. Tanyth is not patient, and he would know that if he gives Queen Serafina too much time to prepare, he will lose the advantage he believes he has. Perhaps she can attempt something on the battlefield to break the blood contracts," I offered. I was not entirely sure how Serafina's magic worked, especially with her ties to the human kingdoms and therefore their mines, as well as the Fae magic. What I did know was that her magic was distinctly different from mine *and* from all the other Fae.

Fallon rubbed his arms with his hands as though trying to warm up. "I need to go."

I knew he was right and there wasn't any more information I had to share with him that would be helpful. Only a few words of encouragement. "Remember you have allies outside of the Court of Dusk."

We made our way back to the mouth of the cave. Fallon positioned himself over the dragon etching. The air filled with my dark-green magic and then Fallon disappeared. I blew a stream of dragonfire into the cave, wishing I could use it to burn Tanyth instead of nothing.

Leaping out of the cave mouth, I spiraled up, using the thermals rising off the mountain to fly high above the clouds. Dipping my wing down, I banked until I was facing east.

Soon it will all be over, I reminded myself and headed back to my cave.

Twenty-Seven

TRISTAN

Leaving Sera behind at Uaine Palace was excruciating. No matter how many times I told myself that it was necessary for us to split up, I couldn't fight the feeling that we needed to stay together. *Yet if I insist on being by her side, will she ever come into her own as the Queen of Fae?* Swallowing hard, I shoved these thoughts to the back of my mind. I couldn't afford to doubt myself or the decisions we had made.

When Sera's message reached me through the bond, I had just completed doing inventory of the knights in the meadow. Servants were wheeling carts laden with silver-iron swords out to the encampment, and Major Green was overseeing their distribution.

I expected to hear the news that Tanyth was on the move. Likely he had felt, as did all Fae, the Queen of Fae ritual and the binding between Serafina and the land. Though Marek's information had not confirmed whether or not Tanyth was with his Fae warriors, it made no difference.

I was reviewing a list of captains and squads, trying to come up with a battle plan, when I heard a loud knock on the door. "Come in!" I called, pushing the list to the side.

Nolan rushed over to the desk. His face was ruddy, and his chest heaved as he took raspy breaths. "A fight has broken out at the palace gates!"

Leaping out of my chair, I grabbed my broadsword from the weapons cabinet and strapped it on my back, then checked the dagger that was already in my belt. "Lead the way," I ordered.

Even though he was winded, Nolan ran, leading the way to the palace gates. Breathlessly he explained that he had sent a message to Declan, and Thomas had promised to meet him at the gate with more guards. I could have gotten there faster if Nolan and my other guards had allowed me to run alone, but I admired their commitment to keeping me safe. Nolan skidded to a halt. I leaped over his head, startling him but preventing myself from knocking him over, as I threw myself into the fray unfolding at the palace gates.

Drawing my sword in a smooth movement, I easily blocked the heavy-handed chop aiming for my stomach and threw a kick at the assailant's knee. Howling in pain, he slumped to the ground, and I moved on. I thought I saw Valerie fighting alongside the assailants against the palace guards, though I must have been mistaken, because that made no sense whatsoever. *Valerie is on Sera's side.* Over the heads of the guards, I could see a familiar pale head of hair as Callyn sprinted toward us from the road to the palace, leaving a swath of bodies in her wake.

"Tristan!" Ghilanna's shout reached me from my left. Sparing a glance in her direction, I noticed she was flanked by two unfamiliar Fae. *Unfamiliar to me,* I amended, noting the ease at which they fought together, coordinating their movements, and picking off more of the humans. *Warriors from the Court of Dawn have already arrived. I see Sera moved quickly.*

My hands were covered in blood as I cut my way through till I reached the remaining palace guard and the woman who looked like Valerie. Then I realized it *was* Valerie.

"What are you doing?" I shouted.

Valerie hesitated for a second and then brought her sword across the guard's throat in a two-handed sweep. Blood sprayed as she hit the guard's jugular vein, and he toppled over. Time slowed as the ramifications of Valerie's actions hit me. *Traitor!*

Sword held ready, I focused intently on Valerie, looking for any tells as she whirled to face me. "Fae filth. I should have killed you in your sleep." She was wearing chain mail armor and over the top was a tunic blazoned with a wolf in rust orange. *Copper Wolves.*

Valerie swung her broadsword effortlessly with a single hand. *She's been holding back in their practices,* I realized. It dawned on me that she was married to a blacksmith, and clearly far stronger than she had let on. Our swords clanged together, sending sparks and drops of blood flying. A deft twist of my wrist separated the blades. Valerie circled. I followed, not wanting to let her get behind me. *I could end her with magic.* I rejected the idea immediately. It wouldn't get us any answers. Answers we desperately needed if we had not seen this coming.

"You supported Solana all those years. What changed?" I asked, blocking her low strike and then starting a high-low combination.

Valerie stumbled over the guard's body, making her block sloppy. "Solana was a means to an end, a way to get close to her daughter when she dared show her face here again. King Leonard hated Fae, and I am only doing what he was afraid to order himself. Taking action where he couldn't because of politics with the Court of Dawn."

I bit my tongue to keep from responding that she was insane. King Leonard would never have condoned this attack. He might not have liked Fae, but trying to eliminate them entirely from the South would push the kingdom into a war against the Fae courts it would never win.

Valerie swayed from side to side, trying to throw me off. I merely waited. She dropped weight onto her left foot and then swung her sword. I parried, throwing my weight behind the much larger broadsword and forcing her to give up ground.

My eyes flicked past her for a split second. Ghilanna was there. I gave her a subtle nod, and she poked her sword into Valerie's back. "There is nowhere for you to go. Surrender."

"Never," Valerie snarled and charged forward, intent on spearing me with her sword. Ghilanna was quicker. Her sword thrust through Valerie's back, the tip protruding before she yanked it out. Valerie's eyes widened; her sword toppled out of her hand, and she clutched her stomach, the blood seeping quickly. Blood dribbled from her lips. "The Fae will burn, and the South will return to the hands of its rightful ruler."

Dropping my sword, I grabbed Valerie by the shoulders and gave her a shake. "What do you mean? What did you do?"

Valerie gave me a bloody smile, then slumped sideways. I released her, letting her lifeless body fall.

Ghilanna's face was full of concern. "Where is Serafina?"

Blinking, it took me a moment to process her question. "I left her at Uaine Palace. She's safe."

Ghilanna toed Valerie's body. "Not if you believe anything Valerie said."

My eyes tightened. "She is safe."

Callyn walked over to us and exchanged an odd look with Ghilanna before focusing on me. "The guards can clean this up. The three of us need to talk."

With no reason to disagree, I led the way back inside, deciding we could use my residence. At least there I could easily shield it from any unwanted observers.

Sitting at the dining table, the three of us gazed at each other. When it was clear I wasn't going to be the first to speak, Callyn took it upon herself. "Serafina is the Queen of Fae. We all felt it, even here." Ghilanna and I murmured our agreement. "Fae from the Court of Dawn are starting to show up, which is good. However, this attack at the palace gates ... Valerie was not the only one wearing the emblem of the Copper Wolves. That changes things."

"We can't afford to have our attention divided. It's what Tanyth wants. We can't fight Tanyth if we're neck-deep in a civil war. He is already on the move and will reach our borders by dawn tomorrow at the latest," I said in a clipped voice.

"You just said it," said Callyn, smacking her hand on the table for emphasis. "This is what Tanyth wants, our focus divided."

"Why does it matter if Tanyth is the one who encouraged an anti-Fae human group to attack us now?" I inquired.

Ghilanna drummed her fingers on the table, then chimed in. "There are two options: Either he didn't give them any specific instructions other than to create a distraction at any time after Serafina took the throne, or it was specifically tied to her becoming Queen of Fae, which leads me to believe he is afraid of what she is capable of in her new role. Consider everything we know."

My heart dropped into my stomach. I whispered, "Sera is also tied to all four of the human mines."

Callyn eyed me with concern. "She is also bound to the four Fae courts. If you combine her two bloodlines and the magic she now has, with some training, she will be unstoppable, even if Tanyth has the fabled power of *Bloodsong Grimoire*, Dragonfang, and Fleshrender at his fingertips."

"No one can be in two places at once," Ghilanna added. "Not us, nor our knights, nor Serafina."

I frowned. She was right. If Sera's attention was divided, then she would leave either the South or the Fae unprotected. I had no way of knowing which she would choose if she were forced to do so. "She is supposed to come this evening. Are there any survivors from the attack?"

Callyn shook her head. "No, they all died."

"Likely also part of Tanyth's plan," Ghilanna said sagely.

Belatedly, I remembered she was a niece to Prince Almar. No matter how much younger Ghilanna was than Callyn and me, she likely had received more training from her uncle than she had led us to believe. The Court of Dawn was indication enough that the Fae families valued their own and ensured they were educated and could hold various positions within a court. "When I left Uaine Palace, we were waiting to hear from Moon and Sun. Has Prince Almar sent word to you directly?"

Ghilanna shook her head. "Unfortunately no. Though I can't imagine he would refuse, regardless of his opinion of Serafina being only half-Fae. He is not one to deny that a Fae ceremony that is impossible to tamper with has accepted and made her Queen of Fae."

"The prisoner I interrogated revealed that the Duke of Piore had hired a group of fighters to attack Serafina during the coronation when the veteran knights refused. I was not able to find out who they are, but it must be the Copper Wolves. Now that the Fae are arriving, it's an ideal time to create more chaos," I said.

"You should interrogate Josiah," Callyn suggested. "Valerie and Josiah ran the Copper Wolves together and helped Solana and Serafina escape all those years ago. If she was working against us, I assume he is doing the same. Or at the very least he knew she was up to something."

I shook my head. "I'm confident Josiah is not part of this. He has been traveling around the South—spying as he was instructed. Besides, we don't have time for another interrogation. If we don't have anyone at our border, then the Court of Dusk will cross, and it will send a message to the South and the other kings that our queen doesn't value her people enough to ensure we're defending our border. Not a message we can afford. Right now I am going to issue orders to the major and lieutenant and get the knights on their way to the border."

Major Green had assured me that the knights were ready to go. All they had left to do was collapse the tents. Even the supply wagons were on standby. Within an hour the steady beat of booted footsteps could be heard as the knights headed down the western road toward the border crossing the Court of Dusk would have to use.

Desperate for a distraction when it was clear that Sera was not responding to my calls through the bond, I took Callyn up on her offer to spar. Ducking under Callyn's punch, I maneuvered behind her and did a quick right-left jab into her lower back. She staggered forward but didn't lose her balance. I lunged forward right at the same moment Callyn threw her leg back in a kick and her heel landed in my groin. Snarling under my breath, I backed up to get some distance.

Callyn chuckled as she pivoted to face me, bouncing back and forth on the balls of her feet. "You're distracted," she claimed.

Instead of answering, I took a step toward her, then lifted my knee and rotated my body and foot in a semicircular motion to the left, finishing the kick with a full extension of my leg. My heel connected with Callyn's forearm block. Landing lightly on my feet, I dodged her uppercut and threw a cross. My fist collided with her collarbone.

Round the practice space we moved, bobbing and weaving as we threw punches and kicks, neither of us really gaining the upper hand. Worry gnawed at me. I had expected Sera to be back by now, but she wasn't. Fae continued to arrive, including Captains Revalor and Goras with two hundred and fifty warriors apiece. I sent Captain Revalor with all five hundred warriors to accompany the group of knights, instructing Captain Goras to stay behind in case more showed up so he could give them their orders.

Declan's failure to prevent the attack at the palace gates grated at me. One attack I could let slide, but two? That was a bit much. With his position as advisor on the war council and master of the guard, I did not want to overstep my authority and place him under arrest without Sera's agreement, but I was reluctant to leave the palace in his hands.

Tension was running high in Gaskal with the increased number of city guard patrols and the additional business from the knights and Fae. The South needed its queen, but she was not here.

"Do you think I should go back to Uaine Palace and bring Sera back?" I finally asked when we paused for a water break.

"That depends on why you want to get her. Is it because you want to fuck her to satisfy the needs of your bond or because you think that what is happening here is important enough to warrant disrupting whatever she is in the middle of there? If she's not responding, it's because she's busy," Callyn said gruffly.

"It has nothing to do with fucking her," I growled, my lip curling in annoyance.

Callyn lightly punched my arm. "Uh-huh ... especially since that seems to be primarily what you're doing behind closed doors these days."

I slapped her hand away. "Be serious, Callyn. She told me she'd be back by now, but I haven't heard from her in hours, and she isn't responding through the mating bond. Does it not concern you she hasn't shown up or reached out again, especially after Marek's warning? I understand that this is a monumental event both for her and for Fae and there are matters she must attend to, but we are on the eve of war with Tanyth, and now there is civil unrest in Gaskal. If she doesn't show up soon, things here are going to get out of hand, and her presence won't be enough to stop it."

Twenty-Eight

SERAFINA

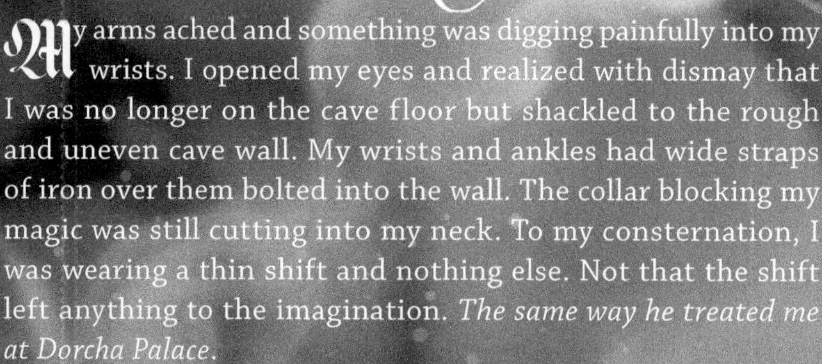

My arms ached and something was digging painfully into my wrists. I opened my eyes and realized with dismay that I was no longer on the cave floor but shackled to the rough and uneven cave wall. My wrists and ankles had wide straps of iron over them bolted into the wall. The collar blocking my magic was still cutting into my neck. To my consternation, I was wearing a thin shift and nothing else. Not that the shift left anything to the imagination. *The same way he treated me at Dorcha Palace.*

A moan caught my attention. Painfully, I focused on where it had come from. A bed was on the other side of the cave directly across from me. In the gloom, it took me a moment to make sense of what I was seeing—Tanyth and Fiera, fucking. I gasped, certain I was wrong. *Fiera is an illusion.* Widening my eyes, trying to make them focus better, I could not deny the proof in front of me. Fiera's familiar chin-length red hair stood straight out as she rode Tanyth's cock. I squeezed my eyes shut and wished I could block out the sounds too. Bile rose in my throat listening to them. *I am a fool to have believed her story. She duped all of us into believing her.* Swallowing, I wished for a drink of water to get the bitter taste out of my mouth but knew asking would be futile, especially while they were occupied.

Sharp fingernails gripped my chin. "Open your eyes," Tanyth ordered. Grinding my teeth together, I ignored him. I felt a tingling sensation, and my eyes opened of their own accord. His fingers blazed a trail down my arms, tracing the words that appeared tattooed on them.

"Why do you have words from the *Bloodsong Grimoire* on your skin?" Tanyth hissed.

Defiantly, I spit in his face. Tanyth's eyes darkened, then he stepped close, pressing into me. I shivered in revulsion at his nakedness and the feeling of his hard cock, dripping with fluids, on my thigh. Then, he mashed his lips onto mine, forcing his tongue into my mouth. I wanted to bite him, but I was immobile. My body would not obey any of my commands.

Fiera, with a robe of gold draped over her shoulders left brazenly open, walked up behind Tanyth, wrapping her hands around his waist and pressing her breasts into his back. She tried to entice him away from me. Her voice was whiny. "Come back to bed, my love. She's not worth your time."

Tanyth whirled and slapped Fiera hard enough to send her stumbling backward, blood flowing freely from her lip. "You *do not* get to order me to do anything, *wife*."

I became aware that I could indeed feel the mating bond blazing between the two of them. Just as I had felt my mating bond with Tristan last night after I became the Queen of Fae.

Fiera stood up, eyes blazing, fists clenched. "I am not just your wife. I am your soulmate. Even you cannot deny the connection between us." Betrayal and guilt filled me as I listened to their exchange. I was stupid enough to have believed Fiera had escaped Tanyth.

"I killed my first soulmate. What's to prevent me from killing you as well?" Tanyth snarled.

I gasped in shock. From what Tristan had told me, Travaran's mother had died tragically giving birth to him. A Fae killing his or her own soulmate was unthinkable.

"You need me," Fiera shot back. "Your plan to get information from Serafina's war council would've never worked without my help, and you know it."

With a swirl of teal magic, a sword appeared in Tanyth's hand. Color drained from my face as I recognized the dark blade, Fleshrender. *No, no, no.* I was not going to idly watch him kill Fiera. No matter what had changed between us, I did not want her dead.

Fiera backed up till her legs bumped the edge of the bed. Tanyth charged at her, and just a hairsbreadth before the blade caressed her throat, he stilled Fleshrender. I could see a trickle of blood dribbling down Fiera's neck. I was not prepared for what happened next. Tanyth, with his sword at Fiera's throat, pressed her back onto the bed, and then they fucked.

Emotions warred within me as I was forced to watch. First and foremost was my anger at Fiera's betrayal. *How much has he twisted her that she thinks this is a healthy relationship?* I was not certain the Fiera I loved still existed. *Is this what he's going to do to me? Break me so thoroughly that even Tristan won't be able to bring me back?*

Tanyth must have removed the spell keeping my eyes open. When I came to again, I was stiff from being shackled to the wall and unable to move, my throat was dry, and a pang in my stomach made me wonder how long it had been since I was captured. Fiera was nowhere to be seen, but I could hear Tanyth and Bane talking, their voices echoing in the cave.

"The easy solution would be to peel her skin off and put it inside the book. Then, the words would be reunited with the object," declared Bane.

Remove my skin? I gasped at the thought of being alive for that.

I heard what sounded like pages turning in a book, then Tanyth responded, "While I admire your imagination, I'm not ready to kill her just yet. Especially without knowing that your suggestion would work. I'd hate to gamble and be wrong."

"We could test it out. Skin regrows ... eventually," Bane replied eagerly.

"No," Tanyth barked.

I ran over what I knew of the book in my mind. It had originally been blank, but words had appeared when I touched it the first time. My second time with the *Bloodsong Grimoire*, the words transferred onto my body, the dark magic that had been binding my memories released, *and* I got my magic. I had an idea. *The collar prevents magic from being used, and the book is magic.* I choked back the laugh threatening to bubble out of my lips. *What if the very thing he is using to hold me here is why he cannot access the full magic of the three objects?* I knew from what Tristan had said that Tanyth had tried and failed to make the three artifacts work during the coronation battle, but I had also been out of sight of them.

"I can help," I called out, my dry throat, making my voice more of a croak than anything. Tanyth and Bane continued their discussion, not noticing I had made a sound at all.

Sweat beaded on my upper lip and I tried again. "I can help you!"

This time they both turned. Bane's bafflement was unmasked. Tanyth gave me a cold smile and stalked with a predator's grace toward me. "How do you propose to help me, little queen?"

"The words from *Bloodsong Grimoire* are on my skin, but this collar is preventing the magic from working. What you see as tattoos is normally words scrolling continuously across my skin. Never a single frozen set of phrases," I said roughly. If he would give me water, it would help, but I doubted Tanyth would show me even a small kindness.

"Why should I believe you?" Tanyth rumbled.

I shrugged, then remarked, "That's your decision." The only way I was going to get out of this mess was to get the collar off, but if my theory was correct, once the collar was off, Tanyth would also have full control of the magic of the three artifacts. The few hours of testing with Onvyr and then Marek had given me insight into what I was capable of, but I couldn't help but worry that they had been wrong, and I would be going to my death if I went head-to-head with Tanyth.

I could not decipher Tanyth's expression. Tristan might have known the prince for fifty years and been able to offer insight into how to read him, but I was not privy to that information. A prisoner for three weeks with minimal interactions between us hardly made me an expert.

Bane unlocked the cuffs, and I fell unceremoniously at his feet. Instead of offering me a hand, a booted foot connected with my ribs. I heard a loud snapping sound, and I knew at least one had broken. Sucking in a breath, I immediately regretted doing so as sharp stabbing pain hit me. *Definitely broken.* Moving was difficult. My whole body was stiff from being shackled to the cave wall. Bane drew his leg back to kick me again when Fiera called for him.

Taking a deep breath, I opted to start small, wiggling my fingers, then my toes, then moving from the extremities up, until I had confirmed that sitting up and even walking would be possible. *Swinging a sword?* I pondered—not that I had any way of getting my hands on a sword. The only weapon I could see was attached to Bane, and he was the last male I wanted to tussle with.

The skin under the collar was raw, but until it was removed, I could not do anything about it. Keeping my movements slow, both to keep their attention from me and because it was all I could manage presently, I rose onto my feet, bracing against the wall when my legs started shaking uncontrollably. Closing my eyes, I made myself breathe, and the shaking subsided. *I could use Tristan right about now,* I thought, breath hitching at the thought of our bond once again being blocked.

An idea was nagging me. *How strong are the collars really?* The collars were very effective against normal Fae magic. But my magic was not *normal*; I was linked to the human mines and Fae magic. I doubted Tanyth had forged this collar with the intention of blocking magic he was unfamiliar with or didn't know existed.

Hope welled within me. Keeping my eyes shut and breathing shallow to trick anyone looking at me, I sank into my core of magic. It was dull green, and the gold was nearly invisible, but beneath were tiny threads of shimmering white that ran from me down into the ground and away, farther than I could sense. There was gold ore in the depths of this cave, and I could feel it calling to me. Not entirely sure how helpful gold ore would be, I tucked the information away and withdrew from the metal magic, returning my awareness to the Fae in the cave.

Bane was walking back over to me with Fiera at his side. She had a bundle of clothes in her hands. "These are for you," Fiera said testily and tossed them at my face. I raised my arms to catch them, but my reflexes were too slow, and the clothing hit me in the face, then slid into my hands. Heat crept into my cheeks, not that it mattered. It was just clothes.

"Put them on," Fiera ordered.

Shaking out the clothes, I discovered there was a tunic and pants. Grateful for a chance to cover myself and no longer be under Bane's prying gaze, I tugged the tunic on and then turned my attention to the pants. I quickly realized my body was too weak to stand on one leg. Lowering myself onto the ground, I put on the pants, then stood up.

"Tanyth wants you," Bane muttered and grabbed my bicep, his nails digging into my skin through the tunic. He half-dragged, half-led me toward the mouth of the cave. Tanyth was standing in front of a table that had Dragonfang, Fleshrender, and the *Bloodsong Grimoire* sitting on it. My gaze slid over the objects and instead focused on the opening of the cave and what was beyond it. *A rocky hillside.* The view did not provide any insight into where I was, though the presence of the gold ore indicated we were still in the South, potentially in the mountains where the gold mine was and right under Tristan's nose.

A hand in the center of my back propelled me into the table. My hip connected with the corner hard. The table vibrated, and the two weapons clanged together.

"Watch it," growled Tanyth.

Bane smirked at me, then moved away. Fiera hovered on the opposite side of the table. I was afraid to move, lest Tanyth assume I was threatening him. "Tell me what you did that caused the book to put its words on you," Tanyth barked.

I opened my mouth to speak and started coughing. "Water," I choked out.

Eyes blazing in anger, Tanyth shoved a glass of water into my hands. I took it and drank greedily. The cool fluid was soothing against my dry throat. Setting the empty glass down on the table, I tried to speak again. "I set my hand on the cover."

"And ... ?" Tanyth demanded.

"That's all I did," I replied cautiously.

Tanyth's dark green eyes bored into mine. "You expect me to believe that the words went from these pages onto your skin because you merely set your hand on the book."

I shrugged. "I'm telling you the truth." I was floored when Tanyth looked away first. I'd never seen him back down like that.

"Fine. Put your hand on the book," he said harshly. His hand snaked out and latched onto my wrist. He smashed my hand onto the top of the book.

I winced as he ground my fingers into the hard leather cover, as though doing so would make the magic work faster. The two times I had set my hand on the book, it had felt slimy and evil. Now, there was nothing. But I was wearing the collar, designed to block magic just like what the book possessed.

"Is it working?" Tanyth snapped.

I pressed my lips together to keep from reacting to his impatience, like he was a youngling. He could see as well as I could that the words tattooed on my hands weren't doing anything. Nor was the book. "I don't think so," I finally replied calmly.

Tanyth snarled and snatched Dragonfang off the table, brandishing in my face. "Fix it, or I'll cut off your hand."

Patiently, I explained, "I told you earlier, the collar is likely blocking the magic of the three objects." I refrained from asking him to remove it. I would likely give away the advantage I was hoping for if he thought I was planning something.

Fiera, bracing her arms on the table, peered at us. "The solution is obvious. Remove the collar, and the words will return to the book."

Tanyth's muscles bulged as his grip tightened on Dragonfang. He did not take Fiera's desire to be involved well. *Maybe I can use that to drive them apart.* "It's too risky," he ground out.

Bane stepped forward again, sword in his hand. "With my sword at her throat, she wouldn't dare do anything."

I prayed Tanyth would agree. I knew in his boots I'd be wary too, though I was puzzled that he didn't just kill me, since he'd already made several attempts on my life. It was strange that now that I was in his possession, he wouldn't finish the job.

"Fine," Tanyth agreed. "Serafina, do not do anything stupid, or I will kill you and burn the South down till there's nothing worth saving."

A shiver went down my spine at his words. Numbly, I nodded in agreement. Bane raised his sword, so it was under the edge of the collar. Tanyth touched the collar with his fingertip, and it popped open, falling into his hands. I whimpered as the *Bloodsong Grimoire*'s magic wrapped around my hand. The air smelled like old blood and decay. Tanyth's eyes widened as the words on my skin began moving and the air around me glowed.

An invisible shield of magic formed around my skin, impenetrable by an ordinary weapon. I brought my elbow back hard, slamming it into Bane's stomach. The grip on his sword slipped, and it should have sliced my throat open, but my shield held. Gripping the very end of the hilt, I yanked one-handed, trying to pull the sword out of his hands to no avail.

Tanyth slashed at me with Dragonfang. Fleshrender was still on the table, and my hand was stuck to the book. Shuddering in revulsion and refusing to pick up Fleshrender, I tucked into a roll, hugging the book to my chest and hoping it would release me soon.

All three of them sprinted after me as I ran for the cave mouth. Casting a glance over my shoulder, I didn't see the uneven floor, and I fell forward, skidding across the stone until I stopped at the edge of the overhang. Pebbles cascaded off the ledge, and I couldn't hear them hit anything. *Not a way out.* A booted foot slammed into my back, and a dagger caressed my throat.

"I've been waiting for this for a long time," Tanyth said. Using his magic, he flipped me over. Blood smeared my face, my cheek burned, and I thought I might have broken or cracked another rib. The book was lying loosely on my stomach now, having finished whatever its magic needed me for.

My shield dropped when I tripped, but I summoned it into place like a security blanket, hoping it would be enough protection from even a weapon like Dragonfang. Tanyth stabbed down for my throat with the dagger. I raised my hand, and a blast of vibrant green-and-gold magic erupted from me, slamming into Tanyth's chest and launching him into the air.

Seconds before his head smashed into the cave ceiling, Tanyth halted his trajectory with his own teal magic and landed on his feet. I dragged myself into a standing position, tucking the book in the waistband of my pants and raising my fists. Blinking, I realized that I was doing was what came naturally to me—combat training—when my magic was at my fingertips. I only had to dream up what I wanted to do with it.

Keeping it simple, I threw bright-green magic balls at Tanyth in rapid succession. The first one met the mark, singeing a hole in the shoulder of his jacket. He ducked under the other two, and a pulse of teal-and-brown magic released from Dragonfang. Creating a second shield reminiscent of a metal one, I barely blocked the attack in time.

Tanyth's face twisted in rage. Waving Dragonfang in the air like he was brandishing a stick, he sent long tendrils of teal magic at me. Each impact on the shield made it waver, and I knew it wouldn't hold for long. *This isn't working.* Running advice Onvyr and Marek had given me through my mind, I sent wave after wave of balls toward Tanyth. With his shield in place, they were sizzling out. Marek's words echoed in my thoughts: "Precision, speed, then power." I had speed and accuracy on my side, but it was becoming blatantly clear that I was lacking in the power department. Nostrils fluttering, I inhaled and summoned more magic, this time drawing not only on myself but on the land, specifically the gold ore that had been calling to me. The balls of magic changed. Instead of swirling threads of transparent magic, they became more opaque and metallic, as though they were actual balls of gold.

Throwing my arm forward, I sent the balls flying at Tanyth. *Pop. Pop. Pop.* They punched holes in his shield, then thudded to the ground, making way for the next round and hitting a startled Tanyth. He stumbled backward, and his shield momentarily dropped.

Sweeping my hand to the side as though I had a sword, I gasped when a sword appeared in my hand, one of pure golden light. I leaped at Tanyth, and he blocked clumsily with Dragonfang.

Vines of his teal-and-brown magic wrapped around my wrists, burning.

"You can't defeat me," he snarled, his dark green eyes almost black.

Not wanting to give him the satisfaction of a response, I struck again, nicking his blackened shoulder and leaving myself exposed. Tanyth made lightning-quick jabs, and Dragonfang sliced along the edge of my rib cage. I cried out in pain, and the golden sword vanished.

Tanyth advanced, his face contorted in rage. "You. Are. Nothing."

I backed up. A cool breeze hit my arm, and I realized I was at the edge of the cave. One step farther, and I would fall off. "Are you sure you can defeat me in combat? Or is your plan to make me fall off the edge and conveniently die? Absolving you of the need to win a fight."

Tanyth grinned maliciously. "You cannot even win in a fair fight. Your skills are no match for a Fae, half breed—" His words were cut off. Fleshrender was protruding from his chest, the dark metal awash in blood. I could feel the evil blade humming in satisfaction. In the shadows behind him, I saw Fiera, her eyes wild, as she yanked the sword out. Tanyth collapsed and burst into ash. Dragonfang clattered into the space between me and Fiera.

Gathering myself, I took a step forward. Fiera had saved my life. She must have been pretending with Tanyth all along so that she could help me. "Fiera, thank you."

Fiera's gaze met mine. Her eyes were no longer blue. They were solid black. As I watched, armor made of the same dark metal as Fleshrender encased her. "I am the End of Time."

"What!" I gasped in shock. *There was no way.* I gazed at her, heart pounding in my chest. "We've known each other for almost twelve years. You killed Travaran to save me, and I took the blame. I will not accept that you are the End of Time."

Fiera's mouth twisted into a sneer. "Tanyth beheaded King Pharaan, destroying the magic that banished me. His next action—killing the Fae you knew as Fiera with Fleshrender—made her body a vessel to for me to inhabit, a tool for me to use to destroy the humans and Fae standing in my way. Your friend is dead."

A pit formed in my stomach when it was clear the only option Fiera was presenting me with was to fight. The ease at which she had killed Tanyth left no doubt in my mind that it would be a fight to the death. I was exhausted and wounded, not in ideal shape for a fight like this. Gritting my teeth, I started gathering the shreds of my strength.

Wingbeats sounded behind me. *"Jump! I'll catch you!"* Asteria's voice entered my thoughts.

Fiera took a menacing step toward me, raising Fleshrender. Blood dripped onto her hand. The sword glowed black, and the smell of blood and decay threatened to overwhelm me. *I can't give up on her.*

I hesitated, desperate to find a different outcome. "We can fix this," I told Fiera.

Fiera laughed darkly. "There is nothing to fix. I am who I was meant to be. The End of Time. Now, die!"

She charged. Sucking in a breath, I spun one hundred eighty degrees and launched myself off the ledge, praying that Asteria was indeed there to catch me.

The air rushed around me, and the rocks below were precariously close, when suddenly the griffin swooped above me and caught me around the middle. Her claws were sharp, and pain rolled through me at the pressure on my broken ribs. I blacked out.

Part
Three

Twenty-Nine

TRISTAN

I woke up with a start. My low back—*the dragon tattoo*—was throbbing. Growling under my breath, I threw off the covers and started in the direction of the bathroom when I became aware of the rough woven rug under my feet. Giving myself a moment for my eyes to adjust, I remembered that I wasn't in my residence at the South palace. I was in a tent a few scant miles from the border the South shared with the Court of Dusk. Standing up, I stared at myself in the mirror with its washbasin and pitcher of cold water. Worry lines etched my face, and my skin was paler than I'd have liked. Smoke formed in the mirror. I cast a glance over my shoulder, but no one was there with me. Tension rolled through me as I returned my eyes to the mirror. Through the smoke, bright gold eyes stared back. Brief flickers of movement, and the smoke swirled away, revealing a dark-green dragon with an iridescent crest.

"Rethys," I whispered in shock.

"*I will see you soon.*" The voice wrapped around me. I opened my mouth to reply, but the smoke and Rethys were gone. The throbbing in my back remained.

Curiosity piqued with a healthy dose of concern, I got dressed. The throbbing lessened, until I could've sworn it felt like tugging. News from Marek on the search for Sera had been limited. Awake from the tugging with no reason to ignore it, I decided to follow the magic to see where it led, praying it wasn't Tanyth or Bane leading me away from my warriors and knights to leave them vulnerable.

Unwilling to throw all caution to the wind, I donned plate armor and grabbed weapons. Slipping out of my tent, I peered around, relieved that the night patrol was currently on the far side of the encampment and would not question me. *Not that they would question their general, but someone might tell Callyn I was being odd, and she most definitely would stop me.*

I almost made it past the outer edge of camp when a Fae male approached. It took a moment before I recognized Captain Goras, his wavy black hair loose around his shoulders and blue-gray eyes assessing me. "Pardon the intrusion, General Gilvrye," Goras said formally with a bow.

I arched my eyebrows in surprise. "How can I help you, Captain Goras?" I was eager to get on my way to wherever the tugging was leading, but curious about why Goras wanted to talk.

Goras squared his shoulders. "I owe you and our queen an apology. Amarielle told Pilar some horrible things about the queen that I now know are untrue before we had dinner at Uaine Palace. It colored my judgment and I fear I was disrespectful to both of you."

I coughed to keep an amused chuckled from escaping. "I appreciate your apology and understand that family is complicated." I almost offered him my hand to shake when I realized that it was a very human gesture. Instead I bowed the precise amount a general should to a captain. "Please excuse me, but I am running an urgent errand." Goras bowed, turned sharply on his heel, and headed back into the depths of the encampment.

Taking a deep breath, I resumed following the tugging past the outcropping of rocks, and then I took a sharp left into the dense forest. The temptation to shapeshift was strong, but I buried it, knowing a sword gave me far more options than my paws, especially when I had no idea who or what awaited me.

I climbed to the top of the slope that was between me and the camp and halted in a small clearing that was hidden by massive boulders, though I could see the tents sprawling down below. To my astonishment, Dubhar emerged from behind a rock, nibbling on a few sparse weeds. I approached, but Dubhar continued to ignore me, even when I was a few feet away.

The air in front of us shimmered. When the magic dissipated, it revealed Rethys, with no evidence that he had ever been in captivity.

"Good to see you can follow instructions today," Rethys said in my mind.

I arched my eyebrow. "When did I not follow instructions?"

Dubhar snorted beside me, as though he was privy to all the times Rethys had supposedly tried to give me instructions and I'd failed to follow them.

"You could have summoned me yourself once you found the longer prophecy," Rethys replied. I blinked, wondering how I was supposed to know that the prophecy was real and that I was related to the Fae in the story. *"It doesn't matter now."*

"How do I know I can trust you?" I asked.

Rethys stared at me. *"We don't have time for this. Dubhar, tell him,"* the dragon commanded.

Dubhar lifted his muzzle from the scraggly weeds. One was hanging out of his lips as he gazed between the two of us. *"We need a dragon to face the End of Time. Unless you know where another one happens to be who actually likes you ... Rethys is who we've got."*

I swallowed hard and started choking on my own spit. *Rethys likes me?* The two magic creatures waited while I collected myself. "I see. So this has to do with the prophecy."

"*Yes,*" Dubhar replied, stamping his hoof.

"How are you going to help us?" I asked, not sure what else to say.

"*For starters, every aspect of the prophecy that is fulfilled gives Serafina more power. With a griffin, dragon, and unicorn at her back, the odds of being successful increase tenfold. That's one of the reasons Tanyth was so set on killing or capturing magical creatures. To prevent the Lost Fae Queen from becoming more powerful than him,*" Rethys explained.

"What about the fact that Dubhar is not a unicorn but a Fae Watcher?" I asked.

Dubhar snorted and stamped his foot. Sera would know how to interpret the actions, but I had never had a good relationship with a horse, let alone a unicorn. "*I told Serafina that I am a unicorn who can become a Fae, so yes, I count, and you are not held responsible for finding one of my brethren who is a 'normal' unicorn.*"

The unicorn's ears flicked forward as though he could hear something, I strained, but even with my superior Fae hearing, there was nothing to be heard. "*You need to go. Serafina will be back soon,*" Dubhar announced.

"How does this work?" I demanded, feeling as though all they were leaving me with was more questions than answers.

"*I will be there for the battle,*" Rethys said, then he vanished.

My mouth gaped open. I hastily snapped it shut, my teeth clacking together.

"*Dragons ...*" Dubhar said but didn't finish his thought.

"The Court of Dusk is almost here," I responded.

"*Of course they are. You can see them approaching,*" Dubhar replied, swishing his tail. I followed his gaze through the rocks, and sure enough, I could see lines of Fae warriors winding their way down the hillside toward the river crossing which would take them into the valley between the two rivers. It offered the advantage of high ground at the price of being littered with black rock, which was sharp and uneven in places.

"I must warn my men," I growled, itching to leave.

"Let me help you," replied Dubhar.

I opened my mouth to ask for an explanation when the air shimmered around me with black magic and then the rocks disappeared, and I was back inside my tent, staring at my cot.

"Serafina," I called through the bond. It was difficult to take Dubhar's or Rethys's word that she was fine when I could feel nothing myself, except for a brief moment a few hours ago, when I had felt her in the mountains near the gold mine.

"General!" shouted Major Green from outside of my tent.

Instead of inviting him in, I walked out, catching the knight off guard. "If you are about to tell me the Fae warriors are close to crossing the first river, I am aware. Please let the knights know that we are mobilizing in ten minutes."

Major Green nodded and then coughed uncertainly. "Pardon the intrusion, General, but the men have been asking when Queen Serafina is going to speak to them. If battle is eminent, it needs to be soon, or they will lose morale."

Clapping him on the shoulder, I responded, "Yes, Major, I am aware of the circumstances. Unfortunately, I do not know where Queen Serafina currently is. What I do know is that as soon as she shows up, they will be the first to know."

Major Green gave me a salute and marched away. I scrubbed my hands over my face. I needed to figure out what to do about Sera. Rethys had said she would be here soon but had not explained anything else. *Where has she been? Is she injured?* I felt helpless without more information.

A commotion by the blacksmith's tent had me sprinting down the path. Asteria was circling just overhead, preparing to land. Marek and Major Green were attempting to direct the warriors and knights, but they were not following orders well.

"Clear the way!" I barked.

Everyone immediately snapped to attention and backed up, leaving a twenty-by-twenty space for Asteria to land.

Flapping her wings, Asteria hovered a few feet above the ground. Sera's feet were almost touching the packed dirt. I walked forward and placed my arms under Sera. Asteria released her, and I carried Sera out of the way so the griffin could land. Staring at the knight closest to me, I said, "Anything the griffin needs, you get it. Food and water." The warrior nodded.

The blacksmith had a table at the front of his tent. Walking briskly into the tent, I used my magic to clear everything off the table and cover it in a clean cloth.

Sera was starting to wake up as I laid her down on the table. Relief coursed through me when her blue-green eyes opened and met mine.

"Hi," I said softly. Marek came into the tent, hovering near Sera's feet.

"Hi," Sera replied.

I inspected her, making note of the raw wound around her throat and cuts on her arms. I lifted the hem of her shirt and saw the green-and-blue bruising spreading across her ribs. "What happened?" I asked. We needed answers. Except with the knights beginning their march, we did not have any time to spare.

Sera bit her lip in thought. I ran my hands lightly through her messy hair, trying to offer her comfort so she'd tell us. Eventually, she spoke. "They set a trap for me in Jade Wilds. When Marek told me to not use a star portal straight into the palace, I thought splitting the trip would make it more challenging to track me. I was wrong."

"Who set the trap?" I asked. I thought I knew the answer, but I needed her confirmation.

"Tanyth. Can I have some water?" she asked abruptly, sitting up.

I nodded, and Marek came forward with a glass of water. She took it and drank greedily, draining the entire thing before continuing. "I don't want to explain everything that happened because most of it is irrelevant."

I frowned. *It might be irrelevant to the war, but being held prisoner for any amount of time is not to be taken lightly.*

Placing the glass on the table, Sera looked at me and Marek. "Tanyth is dead."

"You killed him?" Marek asked in concern.

At the same time, I replied, "Then who is leading the Court of Dusk warriors?"

Sera's gaze flicked to mine. "Bane disappeared while we were fighting. My assumption is he is leading the Court of Dusk and may or may not be aware of Tanyth's demise."

"Bane wouldn't care if Tanyth is dead or not. He takes pleasure in killing, especially humans. He would have no reason to stop his advance," I replied.

"The End of Time killed Tanyth," Sera replied.

My jaw dropped open. *The End of Time is a who?* I had always assumed it was a when.

Her voice was cracking. "Fiera is the End of Time."

It felt like the ground was tilting underneath me. I closed my eyes, hoping I wouldn't fall over in front of everyone. *How did we miss this?* "Bane killed Fiera. We both witnessed it," I retorted.

"How do you know for sure?" Marek asked.

Tears trickled down her cheeks. "She told me, after she killed Tanyth with Fleshrender." I shuddered at the mention of the sword. "King Pharaan's death destroyed whatever seal or magic had kept the End of Time banished. From my understanding, the use of Fiera's body was merely because it was convenient."

Focusing on my wife's face, I had missed the fact that she was faintly glowing. In fact, she was sitting up straighter, and though she seemed sad, the creases in her face from pain were disappearing.

"Are you healing yourself?" I inquired.

Sera blinked in bewilderment. "No? ... Yes," she said, tugging her shirt up and revealing that her bruising was the faintest hint of yellow. "My magic has been ... I guess you could say, acting of its own accord. If I think about something, then it has been doing it. When you sat me down, I was thinking about how we would need to get a healer."

"King Pharaan's magic would do that occasionally," Onvyr said as he walked into the tent.

"You came," Sera said with a half-smile.

"Of course," Onvyr replied. "I told you I would come. You are my queen. I swore an oath to you and the court. I do not break my oaths."

"Unlike some people," I growled darkly. "Valerie betrayed you. She was working with the Duke of Piore and helped them get into the palace to launch the coronation attack. There was an attack at the palace gates too," I said desperately.

"We're out of time. The civil matters will have to wait until we handle the Court of Dusk and face the End of Time," Sera said firmly.

"What do you mean?" I demanded.

Sera rolled her eyes. "I can feel Fiera's ... the End of Time's magic through my ties with the land and the mines. She's not with this first group, but she isn't too far away."

"How long do we have?" asked Onvyr.

"A few hours. Though the Fae warriors will be in the rocky part of the valley long before then," Sera replied.

Thirty

SERAFINA

It was a few hours before dawn. Mist was rising from the river, obscuring much of the valley. I could feel my magic coiling within me, waiting for me to release it. Despite what everyone had said about magic having limits, mine seemed to be infinite, healing me completely in the amount of time it had taken to maneuver thirty-five hundred knights and Fae warriors into position.

I could feel the magic being drawn from the ground beneath my feet and tasted the metal ores as the ancient magic that bound me to all four mines combined with the Fae magic. I understood now how thousands of years ago, Fae and humans had lived peacefully, and there were a select few marriages. These unions allowed for the creation of the magic that permitted the mines to be tied to a specific human bloodline.

The Fae and humans standing on this battlefield had placed their trust in me to lead them to victory against the End of Time; to do what King Pharaan had tried and failed to do. A tremor ran through my hands, and I hid them by my sides, hoping no one would notice. I was terrified of making a mistake, because the price would be the lives of those I loved. I couldn't bear to see a single one of them die for me. With everything we'd been through, I knew Tristan and I were on the same page—that we would do whatever it took to save the South and the Fae from falling under the power of the End of Time, even if it meant the ultimate sacrifice from one or both of us.

I could feel Tristan's determination and infinite love for me through the bond and prayed that we would have a future together.

Dubhar nudged my shoulder with his velvety nose. I met his silver gaze with mine. *"I will stay with you,"* Dubhar promised.

I had no idea how the unicorn knew what I had been thinking about, but it didn't matter. Under the command of Major Green and Tristan, the knights of the South formed lines on our right flank and marched their way toward battle. Our left flank comprised the Fae warriors from the Court of Dawn under Onvyr's command with the Uaine Palace guard serving as long-range cover for the humans. I would be positioned in the center, in the most visible location, a beacon of hope for us all. Marek would be on Asteria, and Rethys would patrol the skies and eliminate any threats from above.

I remembered how not too long ago I'd been certain we needed alliances of kingdoms and courts to persevere. Yet since then, I had discovered my best tool was myself. I only wished I had accepted this before Tanyth had captured me the second time.

Magic hummed in my ears. "Are you ready?" called Tristan.

I blew out my breath and squared my shoulders. My answer caught in my throat as he rounded the corner and came into view. Tristan's slate-gray hair was braided back out of his face, and his vibrant blue eyes glittered in the torchlight. He wore silver-iron plate armor with a snow leopard etched in gold on the breastplate. His broadsword was strapped onto his back with a more practical longsword at his side.

"As I'll ever be," I finally replied. We had agreed not to say goodbye. Tristan felt strongly that if we said it, then it would likely come true that one of us wouldn't walk off the battlefield. Not wanting to argue over the matter, I had agreed.

Tristan held his hand out, and I set mine in his, using it to give me leverage to mount Dubhar. When I was settled, we trotted toward the center. Tristan easily kept pace with Dubhar's long strides.

I could see the movement ahead as Court of Dusk Fae fanned out across the black rocks on the other side of the valley. Memories resurfaced of the battle at Emerald Valley, where I had my first taste of war. This time, though, it was far more than a mere squabble over a human king getting too greedy over resources. No, this was a fight for freedom. For if the End of Time won, there was no doubt in my mind that the world that we knew would be gone. Wiped from existence and replaced with darkness we've never witnessed before.

Both sides crept forward, closing the gap, gradually becoming more visible as the sky lightened and dawn approached. A loud screech pierced the air—Asteria's signal—and a volley of arrows accompanied by bursts of magic flew toward the Court of Dusk's troops. The arrows and magic hit a shield and fizzled out. For a fleeting moment, though, the shield was visible.

"We're going to have to punch through that before we do any real damage," I commented to Tristan.

He shrugged. "It won't matter."

Instead of retaliating, the Court of Dusk waited. Tristan gave the signal, which was passed down the line for our next phase. The battlefield was silent enough to hear the telltale creak of wooden wheels as the catapults were wheeled into place. Callyn and Ghilanna were overseeing their operation and adding their magic into the carefully crafted ammunition: gold-encased vials of oil that would burst on impact.

Thwack. The twenty catapults loosed their loads. The shiny gold spheres were difficult to track in the morning gloom, so I didn't try. Instead, I focused on the shield. The first sphere slammed into it and exploded, spraying hot oil across a wide swath. The oil burst into flame. Even from here, I could see the tendrils of Callyn and Ghilanna's magic as the oil burned through the shield. Screams as it hit the unprepared Fae below.

I shuddered and looked away. A high-pitched whistle drew my attention back to the field. Thousands of arrows were arcing through the air, heading for us. I took a breath and released my hold on my magic. There was a puff of green laced with gold, and the arrows simply disappeared. Not giving Fiera a moment to regroup, the catapults released their loads a second time. When the gold spheres hit, some fell completely through the shield, exploding into a fiery mess.

A horn call sounded from our right flank and the order to charge was given. Tristan shapeshifted to a snow leopard and we shot forward, sprinting toward the enemy. Sword in my hand and the crown on my head, green magic swirled around me of its own accord. Unfortunately, it was one thing I had not figured out how to control, and it painted quite a visible target for our enemies. *Want to kill Serafina? No problem. Shoot at the bright green thing!* Knights of the South slammed into Fiera's front line, the clash of swords ringing around us.

With Tristan at my side and Dubhar beneath me, none of my enemies got close enough for me to even use my sword. Frustration welled within me that they were denying me a chance to fight. When another wave of arrows darkened the sky, as I focused on blocking the arrows with a shield, I realized that because Dubhar was protecting me, I was able to keep everyone else safe.

The End of Time was a black spot of magic at the edge of the Court of Dusk warriors. I could feel the malevolence permeating her warriors, tinging them with her darkness. I wanted to go after her, but fear for the others held me back. If I went after Fiera I would not be able to keep the shield over my warriors too. They would be exposed to any long-ranged attacks Bane sent their way.

I continued to block wave after wave of arrows, buying the knights and warriors time to drive their way through the enemy. We were gaining ground slowly, slower than I had anticipated given we had the advantage almost two to one. Except it had been years since I'd been to this valley and I had underestimated the terrain, not realizing the black rocks covered the entire valley, not just the side Fiera would be approaching from. None of my advisors had corrected my mistake, and now here we were in the thick of things.

Rethys passed overhead. I could feel his magic, though he was cloaked until he swooped down and breathed fire on the Court of Dusk's trebuchets, causing havoc behind their lines. Occasionally, the dragon would pass information on regarding any changes the End of Time was making to her lines too. Not that we had the ability to adapt now that we'd committed to this particular formation.

Thirty-One

TRISTAN

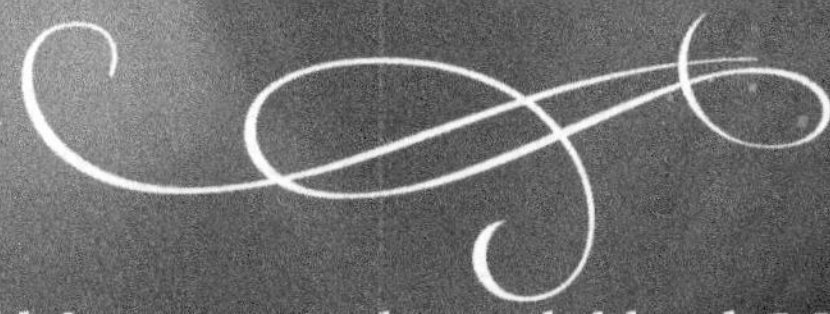

My paws and fur were sticky with blood. When it was clear that Major Green had the knights under control, I shape-shifted and worked my way toward Serafina and Dubhar. Every slash of my claws that eliminated an enemy didn't make much of a difference. Another came forward, filling the gap. On and on the fight went. Peering to the right and the left, I determined this was not isolated to me but was how our side was faring, at least as far as I could see.

A familiar warrior's cry rang out over the heads of the enemy. *Bane.* Without another thought I bounded over the pile of bodies, weaving through the Fae. Though I was large for a snow leopard, they did not pay me much heed, wisely keeping their eyes on the field instead of at their feet.

As I walked toward Bane, I left a trail of destruction in my wake, rending with my claws through the unprotected backs of knees and sending many toppling over, no longer able to bear their own weight.

Bane's blond hair was slicked back with blood and pieces of gore and flesh flecked his armor. He swung his double-headed axes with ease. Leaping at him, I shifted in midair, broadsword in my hand, and chopped down at the exposed area of his neck. He brought the axe up, blocking my maneuver. My feet hit the ground with a thud. I rolled to the side as Bane did a double-handed swing, narrowly missing splitting me in two. We slashed and cleaved, blocked and parried. The war waged around us, but no one dared interfere.

I miscalculated my block, and the knuckles on my right hand burned as the axe grazed the top of them. I retreated a few steps, sucking air through my teeth. Bane's gray eyes flashed in triumph. He twirled the axe in his hand, the blade spinning faster and faster. He swept his axe in a fast arc. With a two-handed grip, I plunged my sword upward at an angle, under Bane's guard. Luck was with me that that sword hit his armor at a weakened spot, and with a burst of magic, I pierced through his armor and into his rib cage.

Bane's eyes widened. "Tristan," he gasped.

I kept my mouth shut. I had nothing to say to Bane. His actions were unforgivable. Yanking my sword out, I turned away, not wanting to waste precious time on Bane when I needed to get back to Sera.

Except I could no longer see her, which meant I was either too far away, or something had happened and she was no longer on Dubhar's back. A black-armored Fae charged at me, screaming curses. I blocked the wild strike and parried, forced to focus on the enemy around me. *Sera can handle herself.*

Thirty-Two

SERAFINA

A brilliant move on Dubhar's part. He had bucked, kicking an enemy squarely in the stomach. I felt his hooves connect just as I lost my seat in the saddle and went sailing through the air. Using my magic to catch myself, I landed on my feet, sword ready. Fae in dark armor from the Court of Dusk swarmed around me eagerly, and soon I was completely blocked off from Dubhar. *Now is my chance.* Tristan and Dubhar were fighting their own battles; I could go after the End of Time.

Alternating using small blasts of magic and striking with my sword, I cut a path through the enemy Fae—*and humans*, I realized with shock. I recognized the emblem belonging to King Hanover, Lord of the West, among the Fae, wondering when Tanyth had made an alliance. Magic hummed in the ground just below the surface, and I resisted the urge to draw on it. I knew I needed to get closer to Fiera, or my attack would be for nothing.

My boot caught on a piece of the smooth black rock, and I stumbled forward. I felt the cold kiss of a sword on my throat, and I froze.

"Well, well, well, what do we have here?"

It took me a moment to realize it was Fiera. The voice was familiar yet different—colder, more metallic. Pressing my palms to the ground, I thrust against the earth, giving me enough momentum to roll out from under the sword and swiftly get to my feet.

Sword gripped tightly in my hand, I faced the End of Time. I knew with certainty that my friend was no longer in there. The blood in my veins turned to ice when I met her eyes, which were pools of blackness. Her teeth were all razor sharp, her bright-red hair had been styled into short spikes, and her armor looked like Fleshrender, dark metal awash in blood. Eerie dark red pulsed from Fiera and the sword.

"Yield," the End of Time ordered.

I huffed. "Or what? You're going to kill me anyway. Why would I yield?"

The End of Time bared her teeth. "To spare your lover and your friends."

I rolled my eyes. "You don't think I'm that stupid, do you?"

The End of Time lunged toward me in a fast upper slash. I blocked and spun, trying to find better footing. "No one is going to save you," the End of Time taunted.

"Who said I need to be saved?" I retorted. I launched into my own high-low combination, and my sword screeched across her armor. The End of Time cackled. Spinning and whirling, a dance of death. One wrong move and I would die, of that I was certain. But the End of Time wasn't perfect; she was making her own mistakes.

I switched my sword to my left hand and went high, slicing across her lower jaw. The End of Time hissed and retreated a few steps. Lifting my sword, I prepared to do a low feint and gasped when black magic slammed into my hand where I was holding the hilt of the sword. I dropped it instantly, sucking in air through my teeth and hugging my hand to my chest.

A quick glance at my sword told me I could not afford to grab it. *Magic it is.* Reinforcing my own shield, I started launching a series of magic balls at the End of Time, except she was wearing her own shield, and all my attempts simply fizzled out. Sweat trickled down my forehead. I was running out of ideas.

A loud screech ripped through the air and a blaze of hot red-and-orange dragonfire sprayed on the End of Time. From my left leaped Dubhar, striking the End of Time with his hooves, making huge indentations on her armor. Asteria swooped down, talons outstretched, and scraped the top of the End of Time's head, then swerved out of reach before she could get scorched by the black fire pulsing out of the End of Time. I made a second shield around me, pushing it farther out, praying it would be enough against the black fire.

A flicker of movement overhead caught my attention, and I stared wide-eyed in horror at Rethys. *Dive down! Pull up!* I cried in my thoughts, wondering what idiocy had entered the dragon's mind. His angle was too steep. Instead of flaring his wings, Rethys barreled into the End of Time, rolling the two of them end over end. Snatching my sword off the ground, I sprinted after them, Dubhar at my side and Asteria just overhead.

Rethys twisted away from the End of Time. His left wing was torn, and I could see his blue blood on the rocks. But the End of Time was also injured; vile black blood seeped out of a wound on her hand, and there were large rends in her armor.

"*On the count of three,*" commanded Rethys.

Sucking a breath through my teeth, I readied myself, drawing on the magic pulsing in the ground. A light brush of fur on my leg was the only indication that Tristan was there by my side.

"*One, two ...*" Rethys bellowed, and his mighty jaws opened.

A huge wave of black-and-brown magic shot through the air toward us. Strengthening my shield, I curled into a tight ball, praying the others would do to the same for themselves. The ground rolled under me, threatening the iron grip I had on my shield.

When the ground stopped moving I slowly let out my breath. Moments ticked by, and the silence became unbearable. Cautiously, I withdrew my arms from around my head and peered around. Rethys and Dubhar had been thrown into one another and were unmoving to my left. I couldn't find any trace of Asteria, as though she had been obliterated, and Tristan was lying in a rapidly expanding pool of blood.

"Tristan!" I shouted through the bond and was greeted with silence. He wasn't dead, but the mating bond was barely flickering. As Queen of Fae, I could heal, but the only way I would be able to do that was if the End of Time was dead.

Lifting my gaze, I found myself staring into the End of Time's black eyes. Blood spattered her face and had flattened her spiky hair, but she was alive. With my palms flat on the ground, I could feel the magic I had been summoning simmering below the surface. I gave it a light tug and continued funneling it into my core.

"Three!" I shouted and threw my hands forward, releasing all the magic I had been drawing in as a massive arrow of power toward the End of Time. When it hit her, a shockwave launched me through the air backward. As I flailed in the air, I saw the End of Time burst into black flames and ashes drifted through the air. Relief coursed through me—and exhaustion. I tried to slow my fall with my magic, but it was gone. I was completely drained.

My head hit a rock with a sickening crunch, and I blacked out.

Thirty-Three

TRISTAN

I watched in horror as Sera sailed through the air and hit the rock. But there was nothing I could do to prevent it. My body would not obey me; I couldn't even stand. I could feel the pool of sticky blood I was lying in and knew unless a healer found us in mere minutes that I was not going to ever see Sera again, if she was even alive. My feet got cold and my eyelids were heavy, as though someone had placed rocks on them, as I slowly lost the battle to stay conscious.

I woke up on a cot, surprised to find myself still a snow leopard, when the memories of the whole battle crashed down on me. Growling in frustration and determined to find someone who could tell me what the hell was going on, I hopped off the bed, and my legs gave out under me. An all too familiar giggle met my ears from nearby. Relief made my legs even shakier, and I sat down hard on my haunches. I cautiously lifted my chin up and saw Sera, her face pale with shadows of bruises on her cheeks and hands, clutching the sheet to herself, but very much alive.

"We're both alive," she said softly.

Yet the way she said it made me wonder who was not alive. Though my body was weak, my magic had replenished, making me wonder how long we had been wherever it was we were. Lying down on the floor, I closed my eyes and focused on my Fae form. The shift was much slower than normal, but eventually I completed it.

Sera was watching me intently. Though she hadn't moved from her cot, she smiled when my gaze caught hers.

"Where are we?" I asked, peering around the room. The only thing I knew for certain was it was a room with four stone walls and not a canvas tent.

Sera rubbed the bridge of her nose before answering. "We're in the South, at the palace. It was the easiest location to transport the wounded to for care."

"How many days has it been?" I asked.

Sera shrugged. "I'm not entirely sure. I also just woke up. Though there were a few times I thought I heard Callyn's voice in the room."

Just then, Callyn walked in. Her white hair hung loosely around her face and needed a good brushing. She rushed over between us. "Thank the gods you're both awake."

"What happened?" I demanded.

"When the End of Time fell, the magic she cast that was binding all of her troops to her broke, and most of them surrendered immediately. They were only fighting for the Court of Dusk banner because they were being blackmailed or forced into it another way," Callyn explained.

"Where does that leave us?" I asked.

Callyn smiled. "Well ... Serafina is still the Queen of the Fae, and the rest will be up to her to decide."

Thirty-Four

The warm wind ruffled my hair, teasing at the spring that was coming but not yet here. I leaned over the balcony, staring at the dormant rose garden, eager for winter to give way to spring and the new beginnings that were just over the horizon.

A flicker of movement caught my attention and I lifted my eyes to the sky. The sun shimmered on Rethys's iridescent crest and belly scales as he barrel-rolled overhead, then swooped up into the clouds. I swallowed a lump in my throat at the stark reminder of Asteria and Marek, who would never fly the skies again, and the many others who had made sacrifices in the battle with the End of Time.

Tristan came up behind me and wrapped his arms around me, his hands lightly resting on my stomach, a welcome distraction with the direction my thoughts had taken. I still hadn't gotten used to the idea that I was pregnant and that in the fall we'd be welcoming a child of our own.

"I thought you might be out here," he murmured in my ear, breath sending shivers down my spine. Chuckling, Tristan gently took my earlobe in his mouth and sucked. I hissed in pleasure, wanting nothing more than to drag Tristan into the bedroom.

A thump behind us told me we had company, and any bedroom plans would have to wait. Twisting out of Tristan's grip, I walked back inside. Ghilanna was sitting at the dining room table, a stack of papers in front of her.

"Now what?" I demanded.

"King Hanover is finally offering reasonable trading terms," Ghilanna replied.

I smiled, pleased that Ghilanna had taken well to her new role as my steward. I had gone the unconventional route to appoint a Fae into a high-ranking position in a human kingdom. After the battle in the valley—now referred to as Death Valley—my tolerance for the political games of the three human kings had become nonexistent. While I was not going to stoop to Tanyth's level and threaten them, I refused to accept any trade agreement or alliance that would not benefit my subjects, Fae or human.

Thankfully, with the deaths of Tanyth and Bane, Fallon, who Rethys revealed was the son of Commander Meriel and Prince Tanyth, had willingly stepped up, declaring his intent to eliminate the darkness that had plagued the Court of Dusk since the time of Thananil Neriwraek. As Queen of Fae, the decision to grant Fallon his request had fallen squarely on my shoulders. I had agreed on one condition—that the arena and dungeons be destroyed and never used again.

Fallon had eagerly agreed and even hosted a demolition party encouraging the other courts to come and celebrate the Court of Dusk turning over a new leaf. Callyn was helping Fallon establish his court over the summer.

"I am glad he is finally seeing eye to eye with us," I replied.

"One king is a start, but we have a long way to go," Ghilanna warned me.

I smiled and caressed my belly, cooing through my magic to the youngling in my womb. "I have nothing but time."

The End

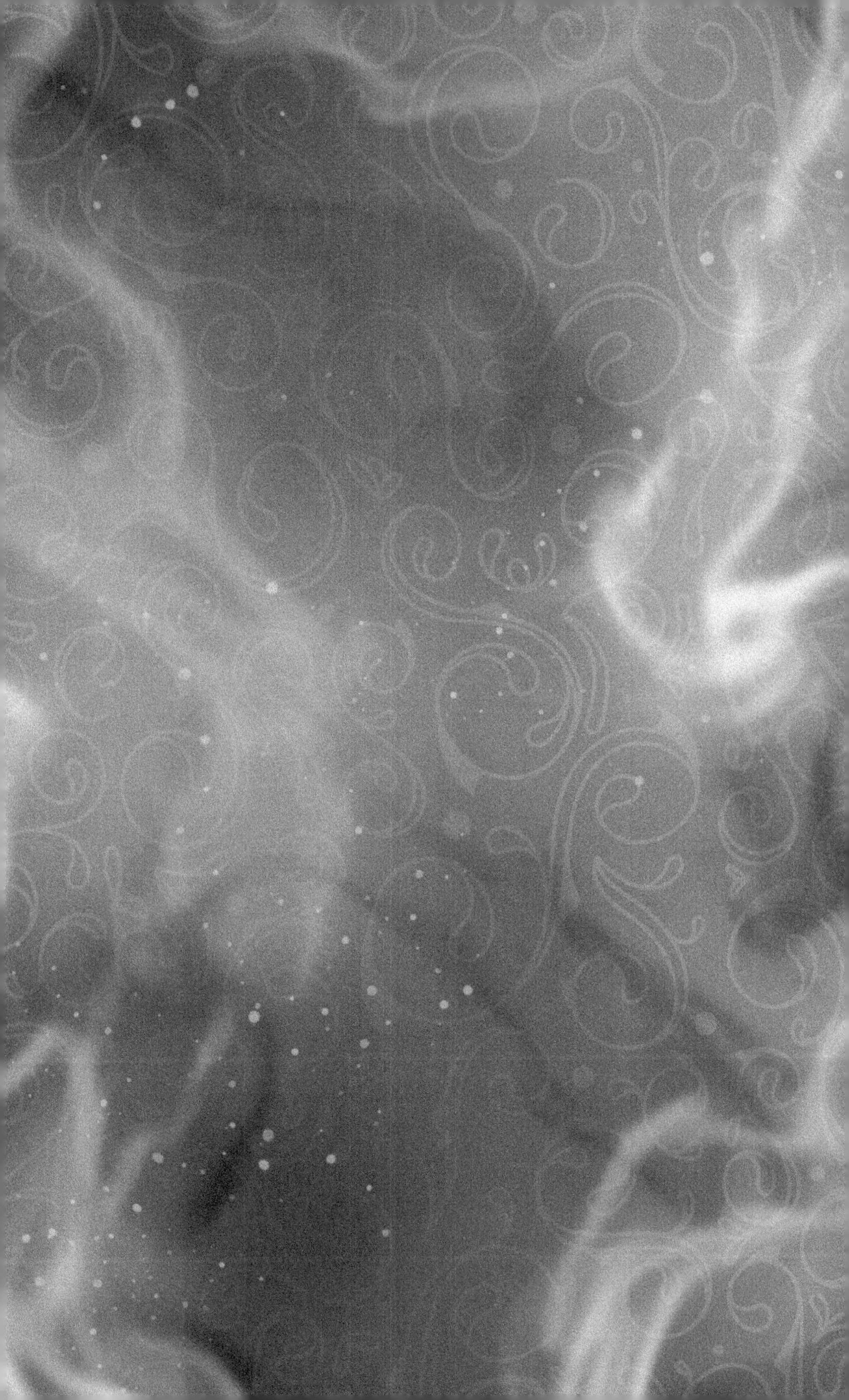

ABOUT THE AUTHOR

E.R. Jensen was born and raised in Los Angeles, California. She has lived in Oregon and Idaho, and currently resides in Atlanta, GA with her husband and three sons.

When not writing E.R. can be found enjoying her horses, traveling, and spending time with her family.

ACKNOWLEDGMENTS

The fantasy genre has been near and dear to my heart since elementary school. Writing the *Lost Fae Queen* trilogy allowed me to weave a few different plots that I thoroughly enjoy reading and watching into a unique story of my own. Thank you to my readers to following me along this journey through the *Lost Fae Queen* trilogy. I have enjoyed it immensely and appreciate all of your feedback.

Thank you to my crew of professionals who help me bring this book to life through many rounds of editing and beautiful artwork. And thank you to my family for putting up with random discussions about all these characters that live in my head.

KICKSTARTER SUPPORTERS

A warm thank you to everyone who supported the November 2025 Kickstarter campaign.

Rethys's Hoard Tier:
Roger Hill

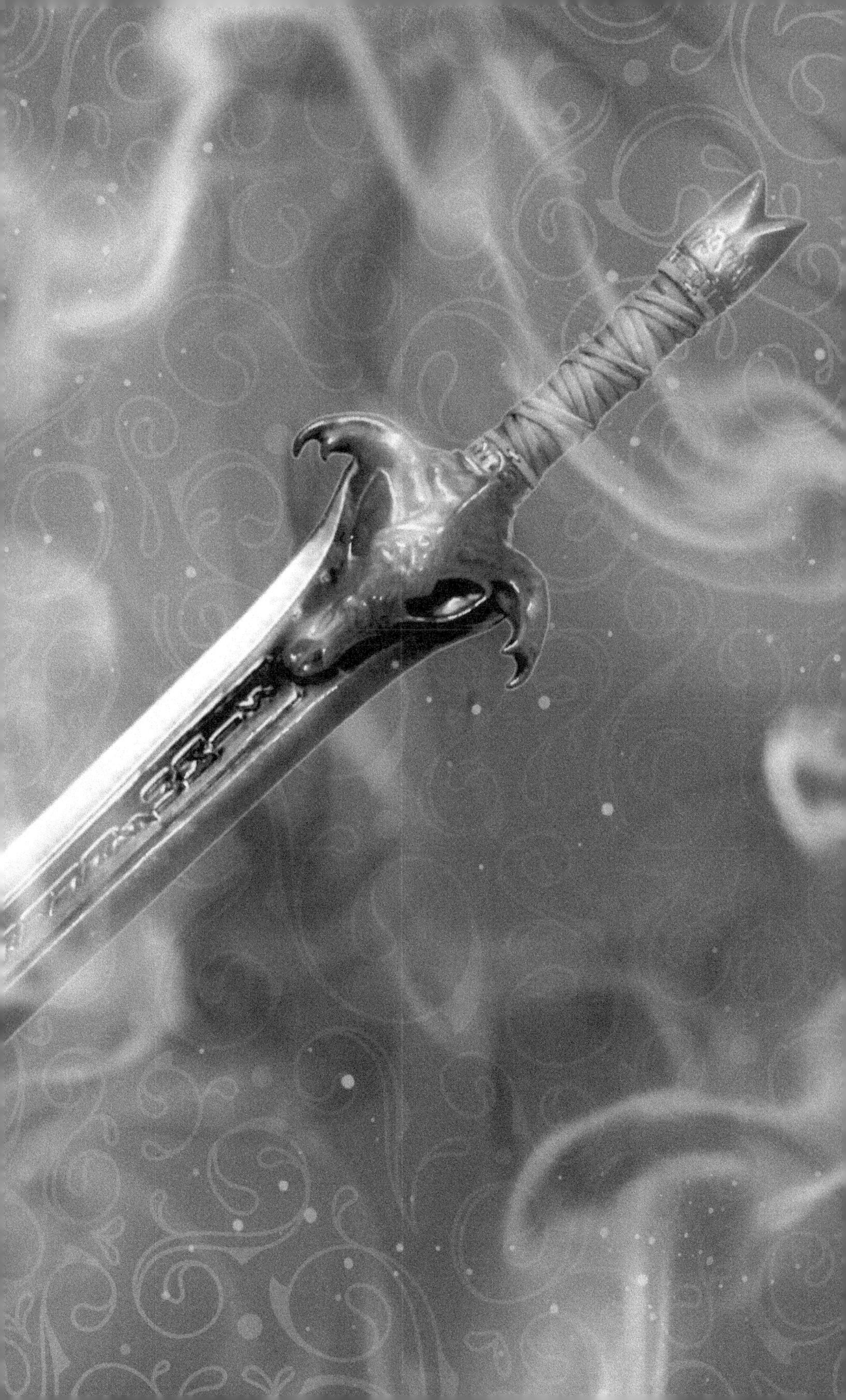